APPALACHIAN HIGH

A Dreamer's Tale

Edward Collins

Fouled Anchor Music

3 CHORDS AND A LIE

A Trilogy

Appalachian High - A Dreamer's Tale

Book One

The Broken Compass

Book Two (coming 2026)

Devil to Pay

Book Three (coming 2026)

Published by Fouled Anchor Music
www.fouledanchormusic.com
All rights reserved.

Edited by Shelly Collins and Kim Wood

Library of Congress Control Number: 2025921074
ISBN-13: 979-8-9930657-0-0 (Paperback)
ISBN-13: 979-8-9930657-2-4 (Hardback)

Cover and Illustrations by Ed Collins

CONTENTS

To the coal miners of Appalachia, whose hands carved both hardship and heritage out of the earth's dark veins. Among them, my grandfather, William Collins of Palmer, Tennessee, a man I never met, yet whose shadow and sacrifice live on in every miner's breath and in every character of this story. He gave his lungs to the coal, and with him, generations carried the weight of survival. To my father, Randy Collins, who broke the chains before the call of the mines lured him to the jagged edges, chasing instead the call of the sea, a dreamer in his own right, charting a course far beyond the horizon. And to the dreamer musicians, singers, and songwriters, those who trade certainty for the chase of one more note, one more stage, one more chance. Some will never be crowned by Nashville's fickle clock, yet their dreams live on, unbreakable and undimmed. This book belongs to both: the miner who endured and the dreamer who believed, two voices of the same spirit, singing through the mountains and beyond.

THE MUSIC OF APPALACHIAN HIGH

Stories and songs are cut from the same cloth. One works in words, the other in melody, but together they become something deeper, an experience you feel as much as you read or hear. *Appalachian High – A Dreamer's Tale* was never meant to stand alone. It walks with music by its side, each illuminating corners the other leaves in shadow.

The characters of White Oak Hollow breathe through Raleigh's voice and keys, and his music echoes the struggles, triumphs, and heartbreaks that shape this tale. Just as a novel unfolds chapter by chapter, this companion soundtrack unfolds track by track, guiding the reader through the hills, hollers, and heart of Appalachia.

The songs listed below are meant to be listened to in order, on your favorite streaming service, as each corresponds to a thread in the story. One song, "New to Nashville," is borrowed from Raleigh's *A Tale of 7 Cities*. Its inclusion is deliberate, a perfect reflection of Danny's descent into the noise, neon, and hard choices waiting on Broadway in Nashville.

The Companion Songs of Appalachian High – A Dreamer's Tale

Read the story. Listen to the songs. Let the two carry you as one.

THE HOLLOW

Suggested Listening: The Farmacy and Appalachian High by Raleigh Keegan. Let the melody introduce you to White Oak Hollow and put you on an Appalachian high.

"Y̲ou sap-sucking coal mine tu̲rd!" bellowed one of the men, his voice slurring as he staggered on unsteady feet. The dimly lit bar echoed with laughter and the clinking of glasses, the air thick with the smell of spilled beer and whiskey. The town drunkards were at it again, their faces flushed, and eyes glazed from an afternoon of heavy drinking.

One of them, a wiry figure with a weathered face and a frayed cap, pointed a shaky finger at his companion, whose shirt was stained with more than just beer. His speech, as tangled as his unkempt hair, punctuated the tension rising in the room. Percy Harlan stood behind the bar with a resigned smile, his gray hair catching the dim light, the epitome of patience as he wiped down the counter.

"Now, now, don't go makin' a mountain from a molehill," Percy said, his voice calm but firm. "You know it just turns to dust."

Earl watched with a mix of amusement and worry from the end of the bar. His piercing blue eyes reflected years of hard-won wisdom, and he leaned back in his stool, shaking his head at the familiar chaos. He was ready to give some McKinney schoolin'.

"Hey, you knuckleheads, how 'bout you save the theatrics for the stage?" Earl called, his voice steady but carrying a hint of mirth. "Ain't nobody here wantin' to deal with your nonsense tonight."

As the argument escalated, voices rose over one another, creating a cacophony of half-hearted insults and drunken bravado. The Gutter Choir, as many of the bar's regulars called them, shared an unshakeable bond forged through daily hardship, their gallows humor masking deeper pain. They finished each other's sentences, weaving a tapestry of words that only they could decipher.

Just then, Danny Wallace entered the bar, his dark hair falling across his eyes as he took in the scene. The chaos felt familiar, the way the bar seemed to pulse with a life of its own. He paused at the entrance, the weight of the world resting on his shoulders, feeling the coal dust of White Oak Hollow settle deep in his bones.

"Percy, what's the good word?" Danny asked, his voice steady despite the turmoil around him.

Percy nodded towards the scuffle. "Just a bit of foolery, Danny. Same old song and dance."

As he moved further in, Danny caught a glimpse of Jimmy "Half Pint" Carter, perched at the bar with a half-empty glass in hand, staying out of the fray as he sometimes did when he hadn't consumed enough liquid courage to contribute to the shit show. Jimmy's jovial spirit was a mask for deeper struggles, but right now, he offered a lopsided grin, as if he were in on a joke that nobody else knew.

"Seems the choir is at it again," Danny muttered,

shaking his head. "What started this time?"

"Something about a missing bottle and a half-hearted apology," Percy replied, pouring a drink for a new patron. "But you know how it is."

Danny watched as the scuffle intensified, the laughter mixed with shouts, their voices blending into a discordant melody. He rubbed the back of his neck, feeling the familiar weight of nostalgia and melancholy washing over him.

Finally, as the tension reached a peak, one of the drunkards shouted, "We ain't got nothin' left, but we still got each other!" The room erupted in a chorus of laughter and cheers, echoing the bittersweet reality of their lives.

Danny stepped back, the scene swirling around him like a tempest. With a hint of resignation, he let out a sigh, his shoulders slumping slightly under the burden of their collective despair.

"The sky's been falling here a long time," he said softly, reflecting the heavy truth that hung over them all.

As the laughter faded into murmurs, Danny wondered how long the town could survive under the weight of its struggles. The bar continued to pulse with life, but for him, it was just another night in White Oak Hollow.

He waited until the overhead bulbs in Percy's Bar began their low moaning to quit, the way sick animals did, losing the fight a slow watt at a time. The last call bell had rung on a curve, gentle as a Sunday knell, and the regulars had unlatched their elbows from the sticky pine counter, leaving behind prints and damp coasters, rings weeping onto the wood like stigmata.

Danny sat at the end as far from Jimmy "Half Pint" as he could, peeling his forearm from the lacquered edge, letting the pulse of the glass in his hand steady out the last of his nerves. The taste was the same as it had been, something sharp that worked its way down with a miner's stubbornness, a reminder that he was alive or something very much like it. Behind the bar, Percy had already begun his nightly subtraction, coaxing the till to come clean, scrubbing away the night with bleach and a lopsided cloth. He was longer and slower than earlier, and his look carried no wisdom, only wear. There was a mutual understanding this shift was less a closing and more a soft lowering on a casket-lid.

Danny scraped back the stool, legs screeching in protest, and stood to full height. He reached for the guitar case that waited on the floor beside him, the old battered black paint coming off on his fingers. It was cheap plywood, bought used at the shop on Main, and if you held it up in the right light, the grain of the pine showed through under the chips and nicks, faint lines that ran like an afterthought, an echo from another time. The strap caught on the door as he turned to leave, and the case swung behind his back like the burden it was.

Outside, the night had gone brittle. Early April, but the freeze clung like regret. He drew in a lungful, expecting only the bite of coal and woodsmoke, but there was more: stale whiskey, charred tobacco, and honeysuckle blown down from the cemetery on the ridge. The mixture caught behind his palate and stung his eyes a little. Streetlights burned only every other bulb to save the city a dime, and what light there was spilled into puddles on the sidewalk, making each step a guessing game. The coal dust was worse here, tracked up from the shaft at the edge of town, drifting in from the cut-backs to settle on every flat surface, every unmoving body. Danny looked at his boots, the dust was already working into the creases.

He set out toward his rented room, case slung tight to his shoulder. It was three blocks, then up a hill, but tonight the walk felt like more. Every footstep flicked up a soft cloud, and in the green glow of The Farmacy sign across the street, the dust looked radioactive. The Farmacy's cross hung over the block like a second moon, the neon buzzing in a high, broken key, flickering as if at any moment it might gutter out and take the whole street with it.

The front windows of The Farmacy were open to the night, and the inside was bright as a gymnasium. Danny could see them in there, bodies lined up at the counter, exchanging slips of paper for small orange bottles, heads drooped in patient, dignified suffering. From where he stood, the place looked less like a drugstore and more like a confession booth, a procession of sin and grace.

He paused under the cross, just out of reach of the light, and listened to the voices tumble out into the night. They were low, almost hymnal, sometimes cresting into laughter or a cough, then dipping again. The air tasted of crushed acetaminophen and blue menthol, and as Danny breathed it in, a line from his own song came back to him. "Whisper in the willow, willow in the sky." He hummed it under his breath, but the melody got lost in the static from the sign.

A girl stepped out of the pharmacy, hoodie pulled up so tight her face was just a shadow. She carried a paper bag to her chest the way folks on TV held newborns, and when she passed him, she didn't look up. Danny could smell the hospital tang of antiseptic on her, could see the white of her knuckles against the bag. Her feet barely touched the ground as she hurried off down the block, shoes leaving no imprint in the coal dust.

He pressed on, but the sign's green reflected off every windowpane, every windshield, every puddle, and he couldn't escape it. There he was, in one window not yet crackled with film, a reflection of a young man with hope. He still had the spirit, or at least the green hue of neon made him look that way. He tried to remember when that light had first gone up, years ago, maybe more. Back then, the old drugstore had a tin sign, hand-painted, and only carried whatever was in the back room, not in the back alley. Folks went there for cough syrup, Band-Aids, and a little conversation. Now the place ran on scripts, 24/7, never shutting the doors, always ready to serve.

He shifted the guitar case, palm sweating on the handle. He could feel his own pulse in his fingertips. A car idled at the curb, radio leaking out a twangy, sad country song. The sound washed up the block, then faded, and Danny let himself drift with it, imagining what it would be like to play in a real venue, somewhere that didn't reek of closing time or sickness. But that was a dream for another life, another boy.

The wind picked up, lifting dust off the stoop and swirling it into eddies. It caught the neon glow and painted the whole street in sickly, phosphorescent green. Danny slowed, letting the dust settle in his lungs. He thought about the hills above, dark shapes humped against the horizon, and how they'd always watched over this place, keeping the secrets of the town buried deep.

He reached up and brushed the back of his hand over his cheek. It was gray and wet, bearing traces of mist and coal. The green light danced across the patch of skin, and he watched it for a long moment. Hope and poison, he couldn't tell where one ended and the other began.

He kept walking, boots barely whispering against the sidewalk, and left the cross flickering behind him, the buzz receding like a bad dream.

He turned the corner at the next block, the street falling away beneath the waxy slice of moon, alley lamps fighting a losing war against the dark. Most of the bulbs had burned out. The ones that hung on did so out of spite, casting their watery light across sidewalks patched with frost-heave and dead leaves. The houses on this stretch had once been painted in hopeful colors, turquoise, lilac, lemon yellow, but now the wood was a dull, chalky gray, each porch stripped bare by the freeze and the sun. The porches sagged forward, railings bowing under the weight of years and too many bodies. Every stoop had a different pattern of creak. Danny knew them by heart.

He slowed his pace, letting his fingertips ghost along the splintered rails, picking off flecks of paint with his thumb. The paint came off in brittle curls, pale and thin as fingernails, and drifted to the ground. He looked at the chips on his palm, remembered the hands that had layered them on, old men and wives, children grown and gone. He thought of the song again, the one about the family pharm, farming in the dark. The words scuffed around in his head, half melody, half curse.

Every other window on Main was shattered or

boarded up. Some were painted with spray-can warnings - NOTHING HERE, STAY OUT, GO HOME - while others just stared, blank and toothless. On a good day, you could see the sun catch on broken glass and throw rainbows onto the street, but tonight there was only the hard blue of the moon, rimmed in frost.

Danny glanced into one of the open windows, saw the gutted remains of a sofa and a stack of yellowed magazines fanned out on the floor. He could just make out the shape of a figure slumped in the far corner, motionless but not asleep. He watched for a second, expecting movement, but there was none. Just another ghost riding out the night.

Up ahead, an old bank building squatted on the corner, its sign long since stripped but the pillars still holding up the sky. The front steps had cracked in two places, forming a perfect cradle for rainwater and trash, and Danny hopped over the puddle, landing light. His boots made no sound, the ground softened by lightly packed coal dust.

He cut across to the opposite sidewalk, the guitar case thumping against his spine. The instrument inside was old, the strings worn soft and freckled with rust. He hadn't played it for anyone in months, not since the last bar gig, the one that ended in a fight and a blood trail through the parking lot. He flexed his fingers on the case, remembering the way the crowd had gone from rowdy to hungry in a single chorus, how they'd wanted him to play the old songs, the ones that everyone knew but no one wanted to claim as their own. They sucked his soul away, but he'd obliged, then left in a hurry.

On the far side of Main, a row of storefronts lined up like a jury. Hollow Hardware, Percy's Pawn, Mountain Mended Thrifts, and a payday lender. All shut tight, metal grates drawn over the glass. The signs were ghosts of their own, the letters mostly peeled away, so that all that remained was a negative, the absence of meaning, an alphabet of nothing.

He stopped in front of Percy's Pawn, pressed his hand to the plate glass. Inside, the lights were off, but a faint green glow drifted from the back, bleeding through the shelves of used electronics, hunting knives, and cases of bad reminders of worse relationships. The air through the crack in the doorframe smelled of burnt wire and old pennies. Danny closed his eyes and tried to imagine the place open, bustling with the sounds of barter and half-meant jokes, but the memory slipped through his fingers.

A truck rolled down the street, headlights sweeping over him. He flinched, stepping back into the shadow of the awning, and watched as the truck slowed, engine coughing, then eased past and out of sight. The silence that followed was so absolute it rang in his ears.

The night had teeth now; he could feel them in the wind that skittered trash along the curb, in the way the sidewalk trembled with every passing gust. He kept walking. On the next block, a strip of houses sat above the street, each one perched on cinderblock and hope. He climbed the slope, the weed-choked path slick under his boots. The scent of wet earth rose up, mixing with the chemical sharpness of the mine's breath, drifting in from the shaft at the edge of town. He could see the mine lights in the distance, a string of dull golds and reds, blinking like signals from another world.

He paused at the first porch, running his hand along the loose boards. They moaned under the weight of memory. He pressed harder, listened to the hollow creak of wood settling, the same way it always did after the sun went down and the town exhaled. He tried to remember the last time he'd heard laughter here, something real, but all he got was the echo of the pharmacy cross and the hum of empty streets.

He kept climbing, the guitar case heavier now, until he reached the top of the hill and his own rented room. The house was a shotgun, narrow and deep, the front stoop held together with faith. He stepped onto the porch and stopped, looking back down the length of Main. The view from up here was supposed to be something, miles of hills, the river in the valley, maybe even the promise of another life if you squinted hard enough. But tonight, all he saw was the dark, the neon from The Farmacy cross burning a hole in the night, the rest of the town lost in shadow.

He sat on the stoop, setting the guitar case at his feet. The cold worked through his jeans, settling into the bones. He flexed his hands again, letting the wind dry the sweat on his palms. He didn't want to go inside just yet. The room was small, just a bed and a hotplate, and the walls were thin enough to hear the neighbors talking in their sleep. Out here, at least, he could pretend there was a little space.

He leaned back, eyes on the strip of moon above the ridge. He traced its shape, thought about the stories his father used to tell him, how the miners had followed the moon out of the hollers, how every man carried his own patch of darkness behind him, no matter how bright the night. Danny tried to hum, but the words caught in his throat.

The wind rattled the eaves, stirring something deep

in the tin roof. He let the sound settle over him, a lullaby of rust and longing, and wondered if anyone else was awake to hear it. He listened for footsteps, for laughter, for the bright, brief noise of something breaking through. But the only thing that came was the buzz of the pharmacy sign, three blocks down and never sleeping.

He closed his eyes, and for a moment he could almost hear the old song again, "pills on the move and the move is here to stay," and he wondered if maybe that was all any of them could hope for, just to keep moving, night after night, through the dust and the dark, until the end of the street.

He listened until the wind stopped and the town held its breath, then he stood, shook out his hands, and stepped through the door, into the hush and the hollow of home.

THE MINE AND THE MUSIC

Danny woke up choking on a mouthful of blood and coal dust. The blood was his own, from the back of his throat where the tissue grew thin and raw. It always had. The dust was a gift from the mountain. A souvenir that survived the cheap sheets, shut windows and the faded flower-print curtains the landlord's wife insisted made the place homey. He lay there for a minute, eyes open, watching the water stains on the ceiling change shapes with the sun, gray veins against the aging plaster, a map of some world no one would ever visit.

He hacked up black spit into the tin wastebasket by the bed. It hit with the sound of a small bug dying. He wiped his mouth with the back of his hand. The clock on the table glared 4:12, or maybe 4:17. He rubbed his eyes and counted back how many hours it had been since he'd seen behind that clock or cared.

The room had gone cold overnight. He pulled on his pants in the dark, toes curling against the cracked linoleum. The boots by the door were still wet. He slid them on, sucking in a sharp breath as the chill bit through his socks. The guitar case waited in the corner, open-mouthed and empty. It was just the way he'd left it. He reached toward it but let his arm drop mid-stride. The morning didn't want music.

Out on the porch, the sky was already stained by dawn. The river valley filled with fog so thick it hid the shape of the town, just the neon cross from The Farmacy hovering above the milky soup. It looked holy from up here, a lie so big you almost believed it. He shivered, flexed his hands, and headed down the steps.

At the mine, a crowd of shapes loitered by the entrance, most of them hunched over cigarettes, faces lit from below. Their breath steamed white and quick, mixing with the rolling smoke and the ever-present sour of sulfur. The air vibrated with the low hum of waiting. He recognized the men by silhouette, broad, stooped, or birdlike, and by the music of their talk, nothing more than a run of vowels ground down by the rock and the grind.

Earl was already there leaning against the guard shack, one boot up on the concrete block with his arms crossed tight around his chest. He looked at Danny with a smile that was more confession than greeting. "Look like death warmed over, son," he said. "You been practicing for the afterlife?"

"Just keeping ahead," Danny said, voice catching on the dust.

A few others grunted as they shared in the sentiment. One, the wiry new guy with a birthmark shaped like Kentucky crawling up his jaw, lifted a hand but didn't speak. The rest smoked and flicked their ashes into the same wet spot on the pavement, years of habit pocking the concrete with tiny scars that weren't already filled in by the coal dust.

When the shift whistle split the morning, the men

filed in. Boots thudding the metal grate, helmet lamps winking alive. They passed through the lipless wound in the hillside, and the light of the world narrowed to a single ribbon behind them, then vanished.

Inside, the ceiling hunched lower with every step, and the walls seemed to pulse with the memory of all they had swallowed. The timber supports sweated condensation, creosote, and old sap running in black tears. The floor was a memory of mud, packed down by boots and the slow shuffle of iron rails and heavy hearts. A hundred yards in you forgot there was ever an outside.

Danny let the darkness take him. It was easier that way. He focused on the rhythm of the walk, the shuffle and drag. Breath echoed off rock and skin. He thought of a bass drum, the slow thump of a marching band, then let the thought drift.

They reached the main shaft and lined up for the cage half a dozen at a time. "Nut to butt" the old-timers barked. The old steel meshes around the cage biting through coats. When the operator dropped the lever, the cage dropped, too, sudden and with purpose. The air screamed up around them, and every man gripped the rail or the man beside him, because letting go was not an option.

At the bottom, the mine branched into fingers. Each one lined with pipe and cabling, glistening hope of something left to take. The men scattered, peeling off in pairs or solo, each to his assigned station. Danny was a face on the north wall, given a vein that ran thin and brittle, but still worth time in the accountant's eyes. He swung his pick from the rack, felt the balance of it, the way the grip rolled easily in his palm. There was a knack to the swing, a trick to making muscles last twelve hours. The old men knew it. He learned by watching.

The first strike jarred the whole arm. It felt like hitting bone. The second and third blended into one long note, the clink of steel on coal ringing up the tunnel and back. He settled into a rhythm, breath in, pick back, breath out, pick forward. The sound of work was melodic if you forgot what it was doing to your body.

He tried a tune, low in his throat, just above the drone of air movers. It was a song he hadn't finished, a thread of melody about a willow and a sky. He sang it without words, humming so soft he could taste the dust vibrate in his mouth. The wall in front of him seemed to lean in, curious, or maybe just hungry for more.

Sweat rolled into his eyes. He blinked it away, then kept swinging. His fingers slipped on the pick handle, and in the slick moment between chords he imagined the neck of a guitar, the perfect arc of callus on string, the way the sound trembled out into nothing and left a tinge of pain behind. He stopped for half a second and thumbed the handle as if tuning it, then laughed at himself and swung again.

Time distorted in the mine. Seconds were minutes and minutes, hours. Breaks came and went. Earl passed by once. He was dragging a cart of scrap out of the finger and paused at the knuckle. He watched Danny for a long beat, shook his head and moved on. At some point, the new guy slipped in to ask about something, but Danny couldn't remember the question when it was over. All that mattered was the noise, the work, the strum of blood behind his ears.

He pushed through until the lamp on his helmet gave a blink, battery nearly out. He moved to adjust it, drawing his hand up to his face. His knuckles were split, and his fingernails were blue to the quick. He stared at the hand. When he tried to flex it into a C major, he laughed at the attempt.

Toward the cage, someone coughed a deep, tearing sound. The day crew was changing out. Danny set the pick on the rack and stepped into the tunnel wiping his palms on his pants. The light behind him faded and for a moment he walked by memory alone.

The men gathered at the main shaft, their faces smeared with dust, and their eyes ghostly bright in the helmet glare. They didn't talk much. Some looked at the floor, some at the ceiling, a few at the nothing in between. Danny leaned against the wall, watching the veins of salt and mica shimmer in the rock.

After a time, a voice: "What you always humming, kid?" It was Earl, the old man's voice flat and tired.

"Song I'm working on," Danny said, not looking up.

"Sounded like a funeral march," Earl said. A couple of the men snorted.

Danny shrugged. "Maybe it is."

They loaded into the cage. The door clanged shut, and the world lifted, then shuddered, then paused halfway. For a second, the darkness was total. In the cage, no one breathed.

Then the power kicked in and the cage lurched upward. Danny felt the weight of everyone pressing down on him. He kept his eyes closed, letting the song finish in his head. He heard every note as if he was the only soul left in the mine.

At the top, the men spilled out into the light, blinking, squinting, like they'd forgotten what the sky was for. The sun burned overhead, and the wind scraped their faces clean, or at least tried.

They stood for a minute on the platform. As each man reclaimed his own weight, the dust settled on their boots and in their hair, making them identical again.

Earl gave Danny a look, something between a warning and an apology. "Don't let them songs get in your way," he said. "Mountain don't care for melody."

Danny watched the old man go, then turned back toward the shaft, feeling the echo of the tune still working in his bones.

He spat black into the dirt, wiped his mouth, and let the rest of the day carry him, note by note, into the quiet.

The next shift fell on him before his bones had cooled. Time in White Oak Hollow could loop like a noose around your regrets or snap like a cable under too much strain; for Danny, it always took the hard route down. He drifted through the house in the blue just before dawn, sipping at cold black coffee. The taste was raw on his tongue, he headed out. The streets were empty, except for the dogs, shadow shapes nosing at garbage bags, tails low, ribs prominent, and eyes bright with hunger.

At the mine entrance, the sun barely grazed the ridgeline. Frost clung to the rails, and the whole landscape looked embalmed. Danny didn't greet the others this time. He kept to the edge, watching them. The same faces, new dust on some.

The foreman read off assignments, his voice cracking through the air like a tire iron on an anvil. Danny filed in with the rest, through the wet stink of the mouth, helmet lamp tunneling out a path no wider than his palm.

Inside, the temperature rose, and the walls pressed closer. The corridors bled water. It slid down timbers and glistened in the hairline fractures making the rock look alive. Danny wiped sweat from his nose. The smell of oil and ozone mixed with the old, wet rot of something long buried already coating his knuckles. The group moved as one, boots scuffing, backs hunched. The passage narrowed, and in places the ceiling dropped to chin height. Danny's helmet scraped more than once, sending a shiver down his neck.

He let his mind slip, as if it could float outside the skull and find some patch of blue, silent sky. Instead, it hovered on the thin edge between what the mine was and what it could never be, a place of music, or light, or anything unbroken. The sound of picks and shovels, the grind of a powered auger, the tap-tap of steel on coal, all of it built a kind of rhythm. He found the downbeat and added his own counterpoint with each breath. The song came back: "willow in the sky, sky in the willow."

They reached the end of the spur, and each man took his place. Danny's job was to loosen the seam, break off slabs by hand and load them into the battered old carts. He swung the sledge in tight arcs while using more wrist than shoulder. In the mine, you're always saving muscle for the long haul. Chips flew and dust blossomed, filling the lamp light with a haze that made the air hard to swallow.

It was an hour in before he noticed the wall breathing. At first, he blamed it on the heat, the pulse in his ears, the slow starvation of oxygen. But the illusion held. The wood supports creaked and flexed, sucking in and out. The sound was somewhere between a heartbeat and a groan. The blackness between the lamps seemed to move, too. The void rolled back and forth, alive as river fog in winter.

He swung and caught his knuckle on a sharp edge. It split, a thin red line instantly drowned by black. He gripped the sledgehammer tighter. The sting was sharp, but he didn't slow down. Instead, he let the music fill his mouth, humming low and steady, barely more than a vibration in his chest. He pressed his thumb to the wound and watched it smear over the handle, a wet, shiny bruise.

Earl was in the next drift over, close enough to hear. He must've been listening, because he shouted, "You got breath for humming, you got breath for working." His voice echoed, doubled by the rock. The words bounced back uglier each time.

Danny kept at it, sweat pouring and his arms numb to the bone. He hummed a little louder, just to see if Earl would say it again.

He did. "Waste of breath, son. Them songs don't put beans on the table."

Danny let it hang to ponder the thought. The silence after was heavier than the coal. It pressed down in the small of his back, knotting his shoulder. He choked on the next line, but the tune kept circling in his head, stubborn as an Appalachian mule.

The cart filled slowly. Each chunk weighed more than it should. He heaved the last piece in, slammed the gate, and signaled to the runner. The runner was a kid, maybe sixteen, wide-eyed and twitchy, hair too long, plastered to his face with sweat. He nodded at Danny, took the handle, and vanished up the tunnel, his head bobbing to his own rhythm.

Now alone, Danny crouched down and pressed his spine to the wall. He let his arms dangle as the pain throbbed, sweet and deep. He closed his eyes. He imagined a stage, a battered stool, a crowd not looking to him for anything but song. The fantasy, vivid at first, faded to emptiness with his slowing pulse.

When he opened his eyes, Earl was standing there blocking out the lamp light. "You want to die in here, keep singing. That's how the mountain knows to take you when you ain't mindin' your work." His face was a mask, coal dust painted over every wrinkle, but his eyes were sharp as splinters.

Danny swallowed. "What's it matter, dying quiet or dying loud?"

Earl shook his head. "Don't matter to the dead. Matters to the rest of us."

He walked off, boots splashing in a band of runoff. Danny looked at his hands. The blood had stopped, but the coal had worked into the cracks. It made a map of black lines and smudges. He flexed his fingers and tried to form a chord, but the skin pulled tight. He let his hands drop, then pushed himself to his feet and followed the tunnel.

The rest of the shift blurred. He worked until the ache turned to something like numbness, until the only thing he could hear was the ghost of his own voice and the scrape of metal on stone. He fell into the rhythm, gave himself over to the machine of it. Each swing of the sledge was another link in the chain that binds.

When the end bell sounded, he trudged back through the passages, past the places where the water dripped and the timbers cried. Past the places where men left their initials burned into the wood. At the cage, the others waited with hollow eyes and black-rimmed boots.

Earl stood at the edge of the group, arms folded, not

looking at anybody. The runner kid leaned against the wall, eyes half closed, mouth open as if catching flies. Danny joined them, feeling every bruise and cut. The weight of the day sat on his chest.

They loaded into the cage, the door shutting with a metallic shudder. The rise was slow, the shaft winding up forever. Someone farted and the whole crew nearly laughed, but the sound died before it got far.

At the top, Danny coughed once, then spat into the dirt, watched the gobbet melt into the frost. The air was crisp and cold. His boots left prints behind him, ghost steps already filling with new dust.

Earl was waiting at the clock-out shed. "You got a ride?" he asked.

Danny shook his head.

"Then walk with me." Not an order or request. Just an empty beckon.

They walked the road in silence, past the old truck graveyard, the sagging houses and the painted-on hope. Earl never spoke, but he didn't need to. His presence was a revelation: This is it, kid. This is the world. Make your peace.

When they reached the fork, Earl peeled off in his direction. He tipped his head once as Danny watched him go. He stood in the road for a long time, counting his own heartbeats. The sky sprouted pink ribbons at the edge, and soft clouds boiled with a storm waiting to happen.

He flexed his hands, feeling the grit in every line. For a second, he made the shape of a chord, just to remember the motion, and let the memory linger.

When he started down the hill, his boots raised little dust storms with every step, and the tune found its way back into his throat. It was softer now, but still there, working its way out from under all the day's weight.

Danny, exhausted, trudged through the dim streets, the day's labor etched in every muscle. As he reached his doorstep, the world around him hushed into stillness, offering a brief reprieve before the dawn of another day.

The drudgery of mining never seems to instill hope. The energy to find coal is hardly worth the energy it gives back.

At the end of a shift, time did not pass as much as it dissolved. All the men had to show for their hours were ruined shirts, bruised hands, and a hunger that bit through any other ache. The bell that signaled the end of work sounded hollowness, as if someone had rung it inside a coffin.

Danny set his sledge in the cart and tried to wipe his forehead. His sleeve only smeared the sweat and coal into a paste. He felt old, though his ID still said twenty-one. He lined up with the rest, waiting for the elevator to drag them up into the world. The crew shuffled in circles, trading jokes, insults, and the scraps of gossip that kept memory alive.

He heard them before he saw them, two old-timers, thick in the chest and thin at the hairline, standing just out of lamp range.

"You see her yet?" said the first, voice bubbling with mischief.

"Who?"

"That Boone girl. Out at the diner. She's a looker, makes the whole joint glow. Heard she pours coffee like she's pouring gold."

The second man grunted. "They all pour gold when you ain't had a drink in twelve hours. You ask her name?"

"Hell, I don't need to. Every fool in town knows it. Shelby Boone." The man drew the words out and made them sound fancy. "She got the kind of smile that makes you forget what's wrong with your life."

The other whistled low. "Ain't nothing can do that, not around here."

"Maybe not, but she tries. Saw her last night, served up my corned beef with a wink. Near made me believe in God again." The two men snorted, harsh and hollow.

Danny stared at the floor, but the name burned a hole in his chest. Shelby. He'd heard she was back, working nights. She was saving for something or running from it. From the next county over, a rumor made flesh. He'd seen her once, years ago, playing piano at a school assembly. Her fingers danced over the keys like she owned them. He'd thought about those hands more times than he'd admit.

The line crept forward, and the men loaded into the elevator cage. Six at a time, pressed close, nut to butt, all the hope in the world pinned between steel mesh and the stone that would not let them go. Danny let himself be squeezed in, his back to the cold bars, hands folded in front.

The cage shuddered, then jerked upward. The lamp above them swung, painting the faces with sickly light plunging them into darkness every few seconds. The men said nothing. Everyone was listening to the clicks and whines of the winch. The shaft was so narrow the air pressed in on all sides. Danny tried not to think about what would happen if the cable snapped.

He looked down at his hands. They were ruined, swollen knuckles and scabs traced with the black of coal, the skin under the nails forever stained. He flexed them and remembered the way they could glide along a fretboard, pulling music from nothing. Now, even the thought of it hurt. But in the pitch-black, he let himself believe for a moment that they were clean again, nimble and sure, that all the scars were just the map to something better.

The cage crawled, then stopped so suddenly his teeth clicked together. Then, with a last groan, it jerked up. The mouth of the mine yawned open and flooded with pale afternoon light.

The miners tumbled out, blinking, cussin' the light. Most lit cigarettes before they even stepped off the ramp. Danny stood apart from the others with his hands in his pockets, watching the way they shook themselves out to shed the mine like a bad coat.

The two old men kept talking, voices pitched enough for him to hear. "You gonna see her tonight?" one asked.

"Wouldn't miss it," said the other.

Danny tasted jealousy, sour and bright. He didn't know if he wanted Shelby Boone or just the idea of her, something soft and untarnished. In his mind, she was still playing piano, all fingers and grace, untouched by The Hollow. He wondered if she'd even remember him, or if he'd become just another black-lunged ghost in her rearview.

Earl stomped over, flicking ash from his cigarette. "You got plans, kid?" he asked.

"Maybe."

"Don't waste time dreaming on things that don't want you back," said Earl, voice not unkind. "Ain't no salvation down at the diner."

"Maybe I'm just hungry," Danny said.

Earl snorted. "We all are." He walked away, whistling an old miner's hymn.

The miners drifted off, some to the lot, some to Percy's, a few straight home. The sun had painted the landscape while they were below, gold slanting through the mist and making the cars shine with frost. Danny lingered by the fence, watching his breath make clouds in the air.

He tried to picture the road into the next county, the way it curved around the ridge and dove through thick woods of river birch and black locust. He wondered if Shelby Boone would be at the diner, if she still played piano, if the rumors were true about her impact on the soul. He imagined walking in, shaking the dust off his coat, ordering coffee just to see her pour it. Maybe she'd smile, maybe she'd remember.

He looked at his hands again, the memory of music fighting with the pain. He flexed his fingers slowly and carefully, making the shape of a chord. The tune he's working on hummed in his chest, a stubborn spark under all the ruin.

He turned toward town, every step raising a cloud of black behind him. The mountains rose in the distance, blue and hungry. Between here and there, a thousand miles of nothing.

Danny started walking.

BY THE CREEK

He changed his mind about the diner, its sign buzzing and flickering like a dying lightning bug against the coal-dusted evening. Earl's words still rang in his ears, sharp as the mine's whistle. "No way she'll remember me, or even care," Danny mumbled to himself, his voice lost in the rumble of empty coal trucks passing. His gaze drifted toward Percy's Bar, where yellow light spilled from grimy windows and silhouettes of miners hunched over their glasses like mourners at a wake. "Whiskey don't want me either." The thought settled heavy in his chest. Too many sorrows to drown, too much pain to numb. Like trying to put out a forest fire with a teacup. He turned away, boots crunching on gravel, and headed toward the edge of town where the streetlights ended and the hills began to swallow the horizon.

Danny followed the cut of the creek where it left town, the last of the mine's breath chasing him down the switchback road. Boots still wore the day's dust; it turned the grass gray where he stepped. If you looked back, you could trace the route by the grit alone. He didn't. The sound of the shift whistle still echoed under his ribs. Every step hurt in a different way.

White Oak Hollow disappeared behind him, its last lights swallowed by twilight. The forest grew dense ahead, birch and pine standing shoulder to shoulder like old men passing judgment. He followed no marked trail, only the worn impressions left by generations of deer and wild boys, then emptiness after they grew up and fled. The darkness had thickened until he couldn't make out his boots, only feel how the ground guided his steps. But vision didn't matter here. This place would pull a blind man forward.

The air changed near the creek. It always did. Cooler, sweet with rot and wild mint. Danny slowed, careful on the muddy bank. The slope was slick, pocked with rocks and the knuckled roots of trees. A frog launched itself from the shadows, arcing through a cloud of gnats before disappearing into the black. Fireflies floated above the water, their lights slow and uncertain, blinking on and off like a broken sign.

At the bend where the creek widened, mist curled up from the surface. Danny ducked under a willow, let the branches stroke his hair and face, fine and cold as wire. His hands trembled. It was the blood sugar crash, or the nerves, or both.

He heard her before he saw her. Not a noise, just the absence of it. There was no sound but the whisper of water rolling over stone, and the way the hollow wind carried and then cut out. Even the cicadas seemed to hold their breath.

Shelby sat at the edge, half-shadow, feet dangling in the water. She wore a skirt hiked above her knees; bare legs pale in the weak moonlight. Her hair, white-blonde, almost colorless, was unbound, a mess of loose strands haloing her face. Danny stopped dead, heart swelling in his throat. He watched her for a beat, then another, afraid that if he moved the whole scene would shatter. There was no reason for her to be here. None but the one he'd prayed for.

He saw the rise and fall of her breath, the slow splay of her toes in the water, the way her hands pressed into the wet dirt at her sides, keeping her anchored. In the half-dark, Shelby looked less like a person than an apparition. Danny tried to swallow, but his throat was sanded raw.

He wiped his palms on his jeans, then checked the move, embarrassed by the gesture. She didn't know he was there. He liked it that way. For a moment, the world held still. Danny felt every beat of his heart, every tick of his pulse in the tips of his fingers.

He shifted his weight, and a stone rolled underfoot. The noise was small, a click, but it was enough. Shelby's head snapped up. Her eyes caught him and didn't let go.

Her eyes widened just enough to catch the moon-light. Three years since she'd seen that silhouette, shoulders hunched against invisible weight, hair still cut short above the ears like his mama had done it with kitchen scissors, but her pulse jumped like it was yesterday. While other boys from the hollow had eyes dulled to river-stone gray, his still held that blue flame, bright as a gas stove even in this darkness.

"Danny Wallace," she said, voice as low as the creek. She smiled, small and slant. "I thought you was a ghost."

He took a breath, let it out shakily. "I get that a lot."

"You look like hell," she said, not unkind. She scooted over, patted the bank. "Sit."

He did, careful not to crowd her, folding himself onto the bank with all the grace of a worn-out animal. He looked at her, then at his hands, then at the water. The fireflies drifted closer, their glow catching in her hair, lighting her from the inside out.

Shelby kicked at the creek, toes stirring the surface. "Ain't you ever take off your boots?" she asked.

He shrugged. "Never found the time."

She laughed, a quick burst that startled a heron from the reeds. Danny felt it roll through him, sharp and sweet. He braced his hands behind him, pretending to stare at the current. In truth, he watched the way her knees flexed, the cut of her jaw, the way she squinted at the world as if seeing it twice.

"Thought you moved off," he said, voice barely above a whisper.

"Didn't take," she answered. "I'm like a weed The Hollow won't let go."

They sat in the hush. The wind combed through the pines, carrying the scent of pitch and wet earth. Danny could feel the cold leeching through his jeans. It was a good cold, honest, nothing like the damp rot of the mine.

Shelby traced circles in the dirt with her heel. "You still playing?" she asked.

Danny stared at the water, watched the reflection of the fireflies bob and break on the ripples. "Just for myself. Some things ain't worth sharing."

"Bet they are," she said, voice gone soft. "You always had something in you. Wasn't like the rest."

He didn't know what to say to that. He wanted to ask her why she was here, if she missed the world outside, if she ever wished she was someone else. But the words snagged in his throat.

The creek ran on, smoothing over everything. In the distance, a dog barked twice, then fell silent. The fireflies thickened. Danny found his hands had stopped shaking. He let the quiet hold him, tried to remember what it was like to feel less alone.

He turned, found her watching him, eyes the color of distant storms. She smiled again, softer this time, and then leaned back on her elbows. "You ever think about running?" she asked.

He shook his head. "Only every day."

Shelby nodded. "Same. But where would we go?"

He didn't answer. Didn't have to.

The moment held. The moon slid higher, and the mist rose off the creek, wrapping them both in silver. Danny listened to the water and the girl and his own uneven breath, and for the first time in years, the darkness didn't seem so heavy.

Shelby flicked her ankle in the creek, sending rings of moonlight skittering away. The gesture was casual, but Danny caught the way her eyes darted sideways at him, coyly. She gave a little smile, like she was letting him in on the joke.

"Ain't many folks come out this way after dark," she said. "What's got you spooked from town?"

Danny shrugged, picking at the cuff of his jacket. "Didn't feel like drowning in the bar, that's all. Air's better out here."

Shelby snorted. "Air's nothing but mold and mud. Better than whiskey, though."

She dipped her toes deeper. The water ran cold even in summer. It numbed the skin. Danny risked a glance at her, the way her hair curled damp at her neck, how her lips parted when she was thinking. He tried to memorize it, knowing the moment would slip away.

They lapsed into a hush, listening to the creek gurgle. The current was slow tonight, so soft you could almost hear each pebble tumble. On the far bank, something rustled the underbrush. Possum or stray cat, maybe just the wind. Out here, the animals had more right to the land than people did.

Danny pulled his knees up, crossing his arms over them. He didn't know what to say, so he let the silence spool out. Shelby seemed content to sit with the quiet wisps of breeze. She stretched out her legs, then flexed her feet so the water flicked up little drops that caught the fireflies. They orbited her shins like tiny satellites.

She looked over, eyebrow up. "You ever think of leaving? Like, for good?"

Danny considered it. "Sometimes," he said. "Then I remember I ain't got nowhere else."

She nodded like she understood. "This place is a trap. You get used to the ache." She bit her lip, then added, "You remember that tree at the edge of the field? By the old Harlan barn?"

He nodded. "The one with the tire swing. Used to run past it after school."

Shelby smiled, quick and true. "They cut it down last year. Said the roots were wrecking the foundation. Like the building mattered."

Danny laughed, a low scratch. "That barn's been dead longer than we've been alive."

"Roots don't know when to quit," she said. "Keep digging even after everything else is gone."

He watched her profile, sharp as the sparkle on a coin in the moonlight. He could see the fine hairs on her arm, the uneven tan line from her sleeve. Her hands rested in her lap, fingers laced, mostly clean, except for the smudge of wet dirt at one knuckle. He tucked his own hands behind his knees, ashamed of the stains.

Shelby caught him looking. "Let me see," she said,

nodding at his hands.

He hesitated, then held them out, palms up. The black was deep in the creases, nails rimmed in gray. It didn't matter how hard you scrubbed. It was part of you.

"Pretty," she said, tracing one finger along the scars.

"You know, they say miners have the best hands. Strong, but gentle. Like you could crush a rock or play a violin."

Danny grinned. "More likely to crush the violin."

"Still. I bet you could do both if you tried."

She brushed her fingertip over his thumb, soft as silk. The touch sent a line of heat straight to his chest. He wanted to grab her hand, hold it, but he let it fall away.

Shelby leaned back, resting her weight on her elbows. "You still play?" she asked, eyes on the stars above the tree line.

"When I can. Don't got an audience, though."

She closed her eyes, as if feeling the notes in her own head. "I'd listen."

The admission sat between them, quiet and complete. Danny didn't know what to say, so he watched the way the fireflies tangled in her hair, the way her breath made little clouds in the air.

A frog croaked nearby, breaking the tension. Shelby snorted, then grinned. "See? Even the frogs got more to say than we do."

He looked at her, emboldened by the darkness. "You always talk like this?"

She shrugged. "Only when the sky's black and the world's asleep. Less risk of making a fool of myself."

He grinned. "You could never be a fool."

She made a face. "Tell that to every boy in White Oak

Hollow. Most figure I'm broken, or dangerous, or both."

Danny shook his head. "They're idiots."

Shelby rolled onto her side, propping her chin in her hand. Her bare foot swung in the current, almost touching his. The water glimmered between them, reflecting their faces back in soft fragments.

"Tell me something true," she said.

He thought. "Alright. My first memory is falling off the back porch, hitting every step on the way down. Broke my collarbone."

She laughed. "That's it? Nothing profound?"

He shrugged. "I remember the pain more than anything else."

She was quiet, then said, "Mine's watching my mama brush her hair. She did it every night, a hundred times, said it kept away bad dreams. I tried it once, pulled out a whole clump. Never tried again."

Danny tried to picture it, the little girl Shelby, blonde hair wild, hands clumsy on the brush. He wanted to reach over and smooth the stray strands from her face, but he stayed still.

Shelby sat up, feet now pressed flat to the ground. She smiled, the reminiscence gone from her voice. "Ain't much to see in White Oak Hollow 'cept the folks you ain't met yet."

He almost said her name, just to taste it, but he held back. Instead, he kicked off his boots, pulled off his socks, and dipped his feet in the water next to hers. The mud sucked at his toes, cold and real.

"See, that wasn't so hard," she said, bumping his ankle with hers.

"Just needed a push," he said.

They sat like that, side by side, letting the creek

numb their feet. The night pressed in, but the circle of light from the fireflies held it off. Shelby's laughter echoed in the woods, and Danny felt lighter, less haunted.

They watched the water drag the world downstream. Above them, the moon broke free of the clouds and floated, yellow and full, mirrored in the black surface of the creek. The bank stank of river mud and old leaves, sharp and thick. Every now and then, a curl of wind would bring the scent of honeysuckle from the far side, and Danny breathed it in, trying to bottle it for later.

He started humming. Just a note at first, then a line. He hadn't meant to, but it leaked out of him anyway, the way water finds a crack in stone. Shelby tipped her head, listening. The song was new, barely a skeleton, just a shape of melody. But she sat quiet, not talking, not even looking at him, as if she understood that the song needed room to grow.

"Was that one of yours?" she asked after a bit.

He nodded, embarrassed. "Not finished."

"It's pretty. Like something you'd play to a baby, if you wanted it to sleep and dream."

Danny grinned. "Maybe that's what I want."

She turned, folding her legs under her. "What do you dream about?"

He thought about it. "Never the same thing twice. Sometimes it's the mine, but not how it is. Brighter, cleaner. Sometimes I'm somewhere else, don't know the place, but it's empty, and I can hear my own music echoing for miles. Other times, I'm just floating. No gravity. Like a ghost."

Shelby nodded, like that made all the sense in the world. "I dream about running," she said. "Not away, just running. Fast as I can. Like I'm chasing something, or it's chasing me, don't matter which. Then I wake up and I'm still here."

Danny picked at a scab on his knuckle. The quiet pressed in. Somewhere, a whippoorwill sang its name into the dark. "You ever wish you was somebody else?" Just then he wished he had a rabbit's foot or a couple of coins to rattle for good luck.

She laughed, soft. "All the time. But then I think, hell, what if that other person's wishing they were me?"

"Can't blame them," Danny said.

She gave him a look, half-teasing, half sad. "You don't know nothing about me."

"I know enough."

Shelby laid back, hair fanning over the ground, eyes on the sky. Danny followed suit, the earth cold and soft beneath him. They stared up, fireflies tracing wild, slow loops above their heads.

The conversation drifted, loose and aimless. They talked about the old school, about whose parents still lived in the Hollow and who'd vanished for good. They traded names, most of them half-remembered, now just echoes in the woods. Shelby wondered if the woods ever missed them, or if the trees didn't care who came and went.

"People think trees are quiet," she said, "but they're always talking, you just got to know how to listen."

Danny smiled. "What's this one saying now?" He reached out and touched the nearest trunk, fingertips rough on the bark.

She closed her eyes, as if reading a message sent up from the roots. "Says we're idiots, sitting in the mud with wet feet."

He laughed, loud and honest. She opened her eyes and laughed too, their voices tumbling together, richer than music.

Danny rolled over, propping himself on his elbows. Shelby did the same, noses almost touching. The space between them was thinner than before.

"What happens now?" he asked, meaning it.

Shelby shrugged. "We dry off, go home. Pretend we never came out here."

Danny felt a pang, but it was gentle. "You want to?"

"Not really," she whispered.

He watched her eyes, searching for the lie. There was none. He reached out and tucked a strand of hair behind her ear. She didn't pull away.

Shelby leaned in, slow, letting him see it coming. Her lips touched his, quick and light, more the idea of a kiss than the thing itself. It caught him off guard. She tasted like river water and smoke, sweet and new.

She pulled back, grinning. "You're a mess, Danny Wallace."

He wiped at his face, left a coal smear on his cheek. "Better than being clean and hollow."

She ran her finger down his jaw, tracing the line. "I'd argue with that, but I don't want to."

The world was smaller now, just the two of them and the circle of light from the fireflies. Every sound was amplified, the pop of frogs, the rush of water, the soft wet sound of their own breath.

They lay there, arms touching, saying nothing for a long time. The cold seeped through Danny's shirt, but he didn't care. He wanted to bottle the feeling, keep it for the next day, and the next. Shelby reached over, entwined her fingers with his, squeezing tight.

She closed her eyes, head on his shoulder. "Sing to me," she said, so soft he almost missed it.

He started to hum, the same song as before, but now he let it run out, filling the spaces in the air. Shelby relaxed, her body sinking into his. The tune bent and shifted, changed to fit the moment, as if it had always been meant for this.

The fireflies flickered above, blinking out and back in, the darkness gentler for their company. The moon, the creek, the girl beside him; Danny wanted to make a memory so strong it wouldn't ever fade.

At some point, Shelby sat up, shivering. "We should go," she said, regret in her voice.

He nodded. Neither moved.

"I'll walk you back," he said.

Shelby gathered her shoes, standing at the edge of the bank. Danny followed, boots squelching in the mud, hands shoved deep in his pockets. They climbed out, into the woods, and found the path by the sound of their own footsteps.

Near the edge of the woods, they stopped, facing each other in the weak light.

"I'll see you," Shelby said.

He wanted to ask, "when?" but didn't.

Instead, he said, "Yeah. You will."

She left first, moving silent as a thought. He watched her go, until she was just a pale shape among the trees, then gone.

Danny stood there, letting the night and all its creatures fold around him. He could still smell the honeysuckle, still feel her lips on his.

He walked home slow, letting the song carry him, the sound of the creek lingering behind, gentle and steady.

If there was a promise made, it was stitched in the silence, in the way the darkness didn't scare him so much anymore.

Maybe that was all he'd needed, just a single night when the world wasn't all hollow.

He let himself believe it.

BARTENDER'S WISDOM

Danny showed up at Percy's before daylight even thought about dying. It was the hour when the sun, if there was one, just glowered behind the hills and clouds and didn't bother to finish the job. Coal dust stuck to Danny's skin in greasy whorls, made dark rings at his neck and wrists, and left a print on the door glass as he stepped inside. Nobody looked up; nobody needed to. The bar was thick with the sort of men who knew exactly how much a door weighed and who was desperate enough to push it.

He took the end seat at the bar, the one where the wood dipped low from a century of elbows. He pressed his forearm into it and felt it stick. The bar was lacquered pine, aged and patterned with a million slow leaks of sweat, whiskey, and maybe blood. There was a crust at the edge, and if you cared to look, you could track the years by it.

Percy Harlan shuffled out from the back, moving with the precision of a man who's never dropped a glass in his life. He wore the same shirt as yesterday and likely the same apron. His beard was more gray than black, and it caught the overhead bulbs like cat hair on a couch. Percy set a glass in front of Danny and filled it with two fingers' worth of Old Grand Dad 114, never spilling a drop, his eyes not once leaving Danny's.

"You're early," Percy said, voice sanded down to the grain.

Danny didn't bother replying. He slid the glass toward himself, watched the light from above catch in the brown-gold, the way it refracted into odd little prisms, dirty as the rainwater that dripped from the mine roof. He took a sip and let it burn its way down, then coughed and set the glass back hard.

"Rough day?" Percy asked, more statement than question.

Danny shrugged. "No rougher than usual."

From the other end of the bar came a sound, somewhere between a cackle and a groan. That would be the Gutter Choir, three men posted like scarecrows at the corner table, ringed in empties and pill bottles. They drank whatever Percy poured cheap, and sometimes what he didn't, and their laughter was a thing to be gotten used to, like the mine rats or the taste of rust in the water.

"You hear about No.4?" one of the Choir called, mouth stained dark around the gums. "Laid off half the night crew. By tomorrow, it'll be down to a foreman and his canary."

Percy nodded. "No.4's been dying since before you were born, Billy. They keep patching it up because they got nothing else left."

Another of the Choir, Tommy, still mostly upright, scar down one cheek from a bar fight he won, lifted his bottle in mock salute. "I heard The Farmacy is hiring. You get a script, they'll give you a job, too."

The last man didn't speak, just shook his head slow,

as if it hurt to agree with anything.

Danny watched all this from behind his glass, head angled so the overhead bulbs lit only the bottom of his face. He didn't want to see himself reflected in the mirror behind Percy. He knew what he looked like: black crescents under the eyes, one cheekbone raised a little higher from the break last year, lips cracked at the corners. The hands were the worst. On a good day, he could flex all ten fingers, but today was not that day.

Percy finished drying a glass and leaned in, arms folded on the bar so close Danny could count the brown spots on the old man's knuckles. "You still chasing that Boone girl?" Percy asked, low.

Danny stiffened. "Just asking if she wants to see a show. Ain't nothing to it."

"Ain't nothing to it," Percy repeated, slow and careful. "If you mean Shelby, her daddy'll twist your head off and use it as a yard light. That Boone man don't cotton to folk finding trouble around his girl."

The Gutter Choir heard it, because of course they did. Words go in their ears clearly. It's when they speak that the alcohol fumes change the sound. They snickered, then went back to their grumbling.

Danny swirled the whiskey in his glass. "She's grown," he said.

Percy nodded, but his mouth pinched up like he'd bit a lemon. "Lot of things grow in this town. Don't mean you want to be the one to pull 'em up."

He wiped the bar with his rag, trailing a clean patch that closed behind him as if erasing the warning. Danny sipped again, more careful now.

Out the window, the sky was already fading to twilight. The Farmacy's green cross buzzed across the street, cutting through the dusk. From inside the bar, you could watch the townsfolk limp in and stagger out, none of them smiling. The sign read 24 HOURS and nobody had ever seen it dark. Even the bugs avoided its glow.

Over Danny, the only light came from the lamps above the bar and the red digits on the clock behind Percy. The clock was always a little wrong, or else everyone's memory of the hour was off. Sometimes Percy would tap it, but it never kept better time for the abuse it took.

The Gutter Choir started singing, low and off-key. They'd taken to reworking old hymns, twisting them until the words didn't mean anything anymore. Tonight it was "Will the Circle Be Unbroken," except the only part they cared for was the refrain. They left the verses empty, like teeth knocked out for fun.

Percy ignored them, kept his attention on Danny.

"You got a song in you, don't you?" Percy asked, eyes narrowed.

Danny grunted. "Maybe. Never finished one worth a damn."

"That's because you sing with your hands, not your throat. You gotta let it out somewhere or it'll eat you up inside." Percy refilled his glass before Danny asked. "Look, I'm not saying you can't chase after Shelby, but you'd better have a plan. Her old man's got a mean streak and a memory like a safe. You get on his bad side, you're finished."

"Maybe I'm finished anyway," Danny said, but quietly.

A laugh erupted from the Gutter Choir, loud enough to pop a vein. "We're all finished!" Billy shouted. "Just waiting for the dirt to fold in over us, and maybe a little rain for the weeds."

Danny gave them a look, but it was a tired one.

He nursed the second pour slower. The edge came off, but not enough to make it sweet. He tried to think about the words for a new song, but all that came up was the tune from the Choir, the circling refrain and the space where the verses should be.

More miners drifted in as the shift changed, each one coated in a different vintage of dust, some with the look of men who'd been underground too long, eyes so wide the color washed out. The bar filled with the smell of bodies and machine oil and cigarettes. Talk turned to the layoffs, to the imaginary girls they dated, then to the price of heating oil now that winter was coming in hard.

But under it all, The Farmacy's light pulsed. If you looked right at it, it hurt. If you looked away, it haunted you from the edge of the eye. Nobody talked about it, but every single man in there knew the taste of something ground up, prescribed, bottled, and swallowed just to sleep. Some of them wore the shake in their hands, some hid it behind their teeth, but the bar was as much a confession as anywhere in town.

Percy's voice cut through again, gentle but not soft. "You ever think of leaving?"

Danny shook his head. "Not in a way that could matter."

"You ever think maybe you got more to do than die here, underground?"

Danny finished the whiskey, set the glass down. "No," he lied.

Percy smiled, faint. "Didn't think so. That's why I

keep a seat open for you."

He should have left right then, but the night pushed him down in the seat, insistent as a toothache. The Gutter Choir was still at it, now slurring their way through "Swing Low, Sweet Chariot," and every note sounded like it was being buried alive.

That's when Jimmy "Half Pint" made his entrance. Nobody ever saw Jimmy approach, but they all felt it. The air went hot and thin, the hairs on your arms stood up. Even Percy stiffened, then loosened his grip on the bar rag, pretending not to care.

Jimmy was small, maybe five-five in boots, but he walked like a man twice his size and half his weight. The nickname came from the flask he carried everywhere, though he was rarely seen drinking from it. Rumor was, he kept something better than whiskey inside. A rumor nobody wanted to test.

"Wallace!" Jimmy sang out as he wove through the crowd. His voice sounded like a knife drawn down a fence wire.

Danny ignored him, staring into the bottom of his glass through the whiskey he had left, but Jimmy was a heat-seeking missile for silence. He slid onto the stool next to Danny and leaned in, close enough to smell the salt and nicotine on his skin.

"Look at you," Jimmy said, toothy and sharp. "Already pickled and the night's still a fetus."

Danny said nothing. Jimmy laughed, then reached across Danny's front to snag a bowl of pretzels from the next spot over, jostling his arm. Whiskey slopped onto the bar, bleeding down the glass in quick rivulets. Jimmy didn't apologize. Instead, he held up a pretzel, examined it with great seriousness, and then ate it whole.

"Some folks don't know when to call it quits, eh, Percy?" Jimmy said, not taking his eyes off Danny.

Percy set down a glass too hard, making a hairline crack in the rim. "Don't see you turning in early either, Carter."

"I work hard, I play hard," Jimmy said. "Ain't that right, Wallace?" He jabbed Danny's arm again for emphasis.

The Gutter Choir had gone quiet, three pairs of eyes fixed on the new drama. Even the clock on the wall seemed brighter, and at the right time.

Danny finally looked up. "You need something, Jimmy?"

The question landed like a stone in the well. Jimmy leaned back, surveying the bar as if he owned it, then leaned in so only Danny could hear. "Just saying, heard you was sniffing around that Boone girl. Word travels fast."

Danny's jaw set, but he didn't bite. "Maybe I was just being polite."

Jimmy smirked, tobacco teeth shining under the bar's cloying light. "Polite can get you killed in this town, or had you forgot?"

Percy appeared between them, hand braced on the bar. "Ain't worth the trouble, boys." His tone left nothing to discuss. He wiped up the spilled whiskey with a swipe so neat it could have been magic.

Jimmy raised both hands, palms out. "See? No harm done." But his eyes never left Danny's, and there was something ugly in them, a tension that might break a man or make him break something else.

He slithered off his stool, gave Danny a final shoulder

bump, then drifted to a corner table where the Gutter Choir waited. They welcomed him with hollow laughter, all of it too loud and too thin, echoing off the bottles and walls like a coyote's yip. Danny watched him go, the prickle of unease not fading. Jimmy sat with his back to the wall and one eye on the door, same as always.

Percy poured Danny another, on the house this time. "Don't let him get to you," Percy said, voice low. "He's looking for a fight, but he'll take a scare if that's all you got."

Danny nodded, but his hands shook a little as he lifted the glass. "He ever kill a man?"

Percy wiped his hands clean, then thought about the question. "Not that I know. But he's made plenty wish they was dead."

They drank for a moment in silence, the world outside closing in with the dark. The neon cross burned through the window, bleeding into every reflective surface, and inside the bar the air grew thick enough to chew.

The Gutter Choir started up again, Jimmy's voice rising above the rest, slurring out new lyrics for old songs, each one worse than the last. But every so often, the corner would go silent, and Danny could feel Jimmy's eyes back on him, cold and watchful.

He finished the whiskey, then stood to leave. The bar had gotten smaller since he arrived; the voices denser, the faces meaner. On his way out, he glanced once at the mirror behind the bar and saw Jimmy watching through the glass, a grin painted on his face like a threat.

He left without another word. Outside, the Farmacy's light was the only thing that moved, pulsing in time with his heartbeat.

He walked, letting the cold slap the sweat off his skin, knowing that if Jimmy wanted trouble, he'd find it. But for now, all Danny could do was move forward, one step at a time, following the cracks in the sidewalk, each one a silent hymn for the men who'd already slipped through.

Danny kept to the street's edge walking down Main, guitar case in one hand, jacket zipped up to the chin. The night was a stranger's embrace, neither warm nor cold, but alive with the possibility of turning on you. His boots slipped a little on the blacktop, grease and dew making the surface slick. He liked the risk. It felt like proof he still had some skin in the game.

He passed under a streetlight where the Gutter Choir sometimes nested, but tonight the sidewalk was bare except for a couple of empty pints and the dried-up foam from a long-ago spill. The only sound was the shuffle of his own steps and the slow, wet grind of a truck on the next block over. Nothing human. Nothing else at all.

The light at The Farmacy was pressing out like a fever. He saw two figures at the counter, the pharmacist in his white coat and a woman he recognized by the way she leaned, always ready to flee or fight, never just standing. He made a mental note of her face, then moved on. He didn't want to linger, not under that glow.

The diner was two doors past the pharmacy, its old neon sign stuttering between EAT and nothing at all. Through the window, he saw the same four booths, each one painted with a thin coat of sadness. The stools at the counter were all empty but one. Shelby was there, back turned, cleaning off the last table, her reflection warped in the cracked glass.

He pulled open the door and felt the slap of heated air, heavy with fryer oil and burned sugar. Shelby didn't look up right away. She moved slowly, wiping in careful circles like each crumb was a small sin to be erased. Her hair was pulled back in a loose knot, and a lock had come undone to frame her cheek. The uniform was the same as every waitress in every small town, pale blue, two sizes too big, sleeves cuffed twice, name tag crooked and a little sad. But on Shelby it looked like a pageant costume.

Behind the counter, her father stood with arms crossed, wide chest filling the space between two coffee urns. His jaw was set in concrete, the eyes above it twin gun barrels. He wore his old miner's jacket over a flannel, even inside. The sleeves were rolled up, and his forearms were latticed with the scars of someone who'd argued with more than one machine. He tracked Danny from the second the bell over the door rang.

Danny nodded at him, but got nothing back. He went to the counter and set the guitar case on the floor with a hollow thud. The father's gaze dropped to it, then back to Danny's face, as if the instrument was a rival or a weapon.

Shelby finished with the table and came over. Up close, the gray-green of her eyes burned with an almost unnatural brightness, like living embers set against the ash of her pale, tired face. She smiled, but not all the way.

"Hey, stranger," she said, voice pitched low enough for just him.

He tried to find something light to say, but nothing came. "You working doubles now?" he asked, instead.

"Since the new girl quit. Can't say I blame her." She smirked. "Less folks in here at night, though. Calms things down."

Danny eyed her father. "You don't get lonely?"

She shrugged. "Ain't exactly fond of fending off coal-dusted men who think a smile means more than it does."

He caught the glance she tossed over her shoulder, the way her body tensed and loosened in a wave as she spoke. He wanted to touch her wrist, reassure her, but there were rules to these encounters, and her father was all the rules at once.

"What can I get you?" she asked, louder now. She had her pen out, pad in hand, the mask of waitress slipping over her features.

"Just coffee," he said.

She poured from a pot left too long on the burner, black and burnt, not that she knew but just the way he liked it. The mug was chipped at the rim, and the handle bore the marks of someone with nervous hands. She set it down in front of him, close enough for her fingers to brush his. He felt the spark, then the retreat.

"Thanks," he said, not taking his eyes off her. "Listen, I was thinking" he stopped himself. The right words never sounded right when you spoke them.

Shelby cocked her head, lips tight. "Go on."

He tried again. "You remember that spot, out by the creek? Where the willow bends low?"

She looked at him like he was crazy, then nodded. "Of course I do. We was just there the other evenin'."

Danny smiled, weak but true. "Meet me there tomorrow night? After you're done here. Just… just to talk."

She hesitated. He could see the gears turning, her

eyes flicking past his shoulder to the figure behind the counter. Then she nodded, once, quick. "Okay. After close, I'll come."

Her voice caught on the word, as if she'd nearly swallowed it. The moment was over before it started. Her father grunted, loud, and pretended to wipe down a carafe that didn't need it.

Shelby stepped back, put the pot on its burner, and looked everywhere but at Danny. He watched her for a while, memorizing the way her shoulders squared when she poured milk into a small pitcher, the gentle arc of her neck when she leaned down to grab a cup. All the grace of someone who'd never been allowed to move freely.

Danny sipped the coffee. It was acid, straight to the bone. He drained half the mug and set it down hard, just to feel the jolt in his arm.

Her father came around the counter, slow, deliberate. The boots he wore left black imprints on the faded checkerboard linoleum. He leaned in, bracing both hands on the edge of the counter so his body formed a wall.

"You still working the mine?" he asked, not blinking.

Danny nodded. "Yes, sir."

The man grunted. "You still think you'll outlast it?"

Danny shook his head, honest. "No, sir."

The father stared for a long moment, then looked away, as if the answer had disarmed him. "That's good," he said, voice low. "Nothing worse than a man who believes his own story."

Danny wanted to say more, but Shelby was there again, refilling his cup without asking, the tremor in her hand barely noticeable. Her face was a mask, but her eyes told another story, one of nerves pulled thin, of wanting to speak but not daring.

He set his last five on the counter, more than enough for the coffee. "Keep the change," he said.

Shelby met his gaze, held it longer than was safe. He saw the hope, the fear, the silent apology. He stood, picked up the guitar case, and let himself out with as little noise as possible.

Back on the street, the green neon was brighter than before, the cross now doubled in the glass of the pawn shop window around the corner and across the way. The town was dead but for that light, and for the first time in months, Danny felt the shape of a future opening up. It was thin as wire, brittle as the ice that forms in the shadow of a car, but it was real.

He took the long way home, passing the path to the creek willow. He pictured Shelby's face, the way she'd looked at him when she said "okay." The word rolled around inside him, new and dangerous.

He never saw the shape watching from the diner window, never felt the suspicion and disdain radiating out from behind the glass.

He walked on, the green glow painting his hands as he gripped the guitar case. Every step felt lighter, and for once, the night did not press so hard. The promise thrummed under his ribs; sweeter than any song he'd ever learned. He let it carry him, step by careful step, all the way back to his room in the hollow.

UNDER THE STARS

Suggested Listening: Before diving in further, cue up Creek Don't Rise by Raleigh Keegan and let its rhythm carry you into the heart of what's to come.

Shelby was already there, curled on the creek-bank like she'd grown from the moss and dew. Dusk hadn't quite finished falling, but enough of it had pooled at the bottom of the hollow to wet the grass and smudge the colors. Danny stepped out of the tree line with the air of a boy arriving late to his own funeral, sure he'd find the world gone or else changed entirely while he wasn't looking.

He scanned the creek once, twice, but saw only the willow and the fog, the long tongue of water catching the last light of the sun. For a half-beat, panic nipped at his throat. She'd been intercepted, maybe, or her father had guessed and snapped her up like a trout on a worm. But then a bird started up in the branches overhead, and Shelby's pale head lifted from the grass, a ghost-light blinking in the dim.

He let out a breath, shallow. She was perched right on the edge, her knees drawn to her chest, arms wrapped tight. Her shoes were off, set in neat tandem on the bank, and her bare feet glowed against the clear but dark water, toes dipped and flexing like she was testing the world's temperature.

"Thought you got lost," she called, not turning.

"Thought maybe I got stood up," he answered, trying for a grin but coming up short. His voice cracked on the last word, made it sound younger than he meant.

She looked back then, moonlight catching the angle of her cheek. "I'm not that easy to lose," she said.

He slogged through the wet, boots swallowing more dew than grass. The chill sank fast, but he made a point of not wincing. He let his eyes linger on her, tracing the cut of her silhouette, the way her dress hiked high on her thighs, the sprawl of hair loose and wild as creek foam. He swallowed, and the sound of it echoed in his ears.

They sat together, knees almost touching, a silence opening up between them like an itch wanting to be scratched.

She spoke first. "I almost didn't come," she said, voice low.

He didn't answer. The truth was he'd expected that. Maybe even hoped for it a little, to save himself the pain of whatever came next. He picked up a pebble and rolled it in his hand, feeling the edges bite into his skin.

"Daddy was in a mood," Shelby went on. "Came home talking loud, cussing at the television. Said he'd disown me if I left after supper." She shrugged. "He fell asleep with his face in a plate of fried chicken. Didn't notice a thing."

Danny tried not to smile. "That's a hell of a guard dog."

"Better than most," she said. "At least when he's drinking."

The creek sang its endless, empty song, and somewhere a woodcock started up, sounding peent...peent...

peent, dancing for a prospective mate in the evening. Danny watched the ripples at their feet. "You want to get out from under your Daddy's eye?"

She wrinkled her nose. "I think about it. But where would I go? All I know is right here." She glanced at him, sidelong. "I know you think about it?"

"Sometimes," he lied feeling a constant pull.

The willow hung low, branches trailing in the water like hands searching for something dropped long ago. The moon rose, fat and creamy, and the mist over the surface of the creek softened everything it touched. It was the kind of night that made secrets seem holy.

"You ever swim here?" Shelby asked, sudden, as if the idea had landed right on her tongue and needed out before it died.

He looked at her, then at the water. "Not since I was little. Used to come with my cousin, back when we both fit on one tire swing."

She arched an eyebrow. "You scared?"

He snorted. "Not of the water."

She stood, dusting the wet grass from her thighs. "Then let's do it." She stripped her dress off in one motion, bare legs shining under the moon, the white slip underneath clinging to her in the damp air. Her arms were thin but strong, the muscles at her shoulder tensed and ready.

Danny flushed hot, tried to pretend he didn't notice. He set his boots side by side, peeled off his shirt and undershirt, hands shaking enough to tangle the buttons. He left his pants on, just rolled them to the knee. Shelby grinned.

"You're modest for a miner," she teased.

"Don't need to get arrested for indecency on top of

whatever other laws we are breakin'," he said.

She kicked her toes in the mud, then stepped into the water, sucking in a breath at the chill. "It's not bad," she lied.

He followed, letting the mud pull at his feet. The water was a live wire, sharp and mean, but Shelby moved fast, wading deep until the current licked her thighs. Danny hesitated, then splashed after her, the ache of it washing over him all at once.

They were two dark shapes against the lighter surface, pale skin and coal shadow, bodies half-submerged and shivering. Shelby laughed, sudden and wild, the sound carrying across the hollow. Danny watched the way the water wrapped her, the slip clinging see-through against her hips, the gold of her hair slicked flat and gleaming.

He tried to keep his gaze above her collarbone but failed. "You're going to get pneumonia," he said.

"Worth it," she said, and lunged at him, fingers cold as a dare, grabbing his wrist and yanking him off balance.

He went under, swallowing a mouthful of creek, and surfaced sputtering, eyes stinging. "Damn," he coughed. "You trying to drown me?"

She wiped the water from her face, then smiled, slow and wicked. "Not yet."

They circled each other, feet kicking up mud, the creek bed soft and uncertain. Every now and then their hands brushed under the water, accidentally at first, then on purpose. Shelby drifted in the current, letting it catch her and pull her downstream, then treading back, hair streaming behind her like a banner.

Danny floated on his back, letting the water hold

him. He looked up at the sky, at the slice of moon, the low drift of clouds. For a minute, the ache in his bones left him, replaced by the clean sting of cold and the softness of Shelby's laughter.

She ducked under and came up beside him, close enough that he could feel her breath, smell the sweet scent of honeysuckle and wet skin.

"Want to see something?" she said, and before he could answer, she dove, legs flashing in the moonlight, toes pointed and then gone.

He panicked for a moment, scanning the surface. Then Shelby erupted downstream, splashing and gasping, hair plastered to her forehead. She spun in a slow circle.

"It's better here," she called. "The water's deeper. You can't touch."

He swam as best as he could after her, kicking clumsy, swallowing more creek. He made it a few yards, then lost his bearing and sank. Shelby's hand found his in the black, her grip strong.

"Take my hand," she said, laughing and solemn all at once.

He clung to her, heart racing, the cold now a distant thing behind the rush of blood and fear and some other feeling he'd never had a name for.

They floated together, side by side, legs brushing, hands tangled. For a while, they just drifted, letting the current do the work, the only sound the lap of water and the slow measure of their breath.

Danny looked at her, really looked, and saw the way the moonlight followed every line of her face, how her lips parted when she breathed, the freckle at her jaw. He wanted to say something, anything, but the words felt too small.

Shelby spoke first, voice quiet now. "I used to come out here at night, just to listen. Sometimes it sounded like the creek was talking."

"What'd it say?" he asked.

She shrugged, water beading on her shoulders. "Depends. Some nights it says I'm not alone." She smiled, but there was an old pain behind it. "Other nights it says run. Get out while you can."

Danny nodded. He understood. The world could be loud that way.

The cold started to bite again, and they waded back to the bank. Shelby pulled herself up onto the grass, body shivering, arms wrapped tight. Danny flopped beside her, breathing hard, skin prickling with gooseflesh.

For a long time, neither spoke. The willow dripped water on their backs, and the fog thickened over the creek, hiding them from everything but the moon.

Shelby looked at his hands, black even in the silver light, and reached out. She traced the lines of coal marred along his fingers, the old scars and new calluses. "You got the hands of a man twice your age," she said, almost sad.

"They hurt like it, too," he said.

She held his palm to her face, pressed it there, the heat of her skin leeching through the cold. "You have a chance to start over. You have a dream, don't you?" she asked.

He shook his head. "I do on occasion, but I can't see it in the daylight...not yet" he said and meant it.

She let his hand fall, then leaned into him, shoulder to shoulder, her body warm and trembling.

They sat like that, waiting for the water to dry and

the world to start again. The night was thick around them, but for the first time in memory, Danny didn't mind. The future could wait. Here, in the hush and the dark, she was enough.

He said it out loud, not meaning to: "You're enough."

Shelby laughed, not mocking, but sweet. She kissed his cheek, brief as a firefly. "You're a mess, Danny Wallace," she said.

He smiled, teeth chattering, and let her rest her head on his shoulder. The two of them, damp and ruined, hidden in the hollow, waiting for something neither could name.

Above them, the willow kept their secrets, and the creek ran on, careless and clear.

They sat quiet for a long while, two figures outlined against the silvered wash of the creek. Shelby pulled her knees to her chest and wrapped her arms around them; chin pressed to the bony crown. Danny shivered beside her, both of them still dripping, their shadows stitched together by moonlight and fog. The rocks were slick with lichen, the cold biting up through their bones, but neither made a move to put on dry clothes. To move was to admit the night could end, and neither wanted to be the one to break it.

Somewhere up the creek, a thrush called, fluting out notes that twisted through the branches and faded into the hush. A woodcock answered from deep in the woods, the whistle high and lonesome. Drops of water clung to Shelby's hair, dripped slow down her temple and across her jaw. She caught them with her fingertip and wiped them away, leaving a shiny trail down her cheek. The rest of her hair clung to her back, pale and fine, picking up every stray gleam the moon offered.

Danny tried to memorize the scene, every sharp angle and curve of it. He wanted to file it away, something to keep for later, when the world closed in again. But the ache in his chest threatened to overtake him, and the words crowded behind his teeth.

Shelby spoke first, voice soft and steady, as if talking to herself. "Sometimes I wish I could just work at the elementary school. Teach first grade. Or maybe open a little shop, sell old books and candies. Just...just something to keep me out of the house and that diner." She looked at him, lips quirking into a half-smile. "That probably sounds dumb."

He shook his head. "Doesn't sound dumb at all. Sounds peaceful."

She laughed. "Peaceful. That's the dream, isn't it?" She let her knees drop and leaned back on her hands. "What about you? Coal mining ain't peaceful."

He shook his head, the movement slow, uncertain. "Can't see myself doing it forever. Not even for a little while." He scrubbed at his jaw, felt the grit there. "I think about music. About playing somewhere big, not just bars with sticky floors and a crowd of drunks yelling for soul-sucking 'Free Bird.'"

She grinned. "You want to be a star."

He snorted. "Not a star. I just want to know what it feels like. Maybe go to Nashville, try my luck. Write songs that make people feel things." He shrugged, embarrassment coloring his words. "Stupid, right?"

She didn't answer, just watched the water eddying around the rocks. Her hand found his, a simple, clean motion, no drama to it. Her fingers were cold, but the touch set his skin on fire. She squeezed his palm, and he squeezed back, tighter than he meant to.

"You could do it," she said. "If anyone could, it'd be you."

He wanted to believe her. Wanted it more than anything. But the world always found a way to keep him small, to remind him of where he came from. He looked down at their joined hands, the contrast of her skin against his, pale on black, soft against rough. He thought about the people at the bar, the way they watched him when he played when he did play there, hungry for something they'd lost but never dared admit.

He thought about his father, how he'd wasted away coughing up coal dust and lies, how he'd died in the same room where he'd been born, nothing changed but the bed sheets. Danny didn't want to end up like that, but he didn't know if he had it in him to run.

Shelby let go and leaned into him, head resting on his shoulder. "You ever think maybe we're just..." She trailed off, then started again. "Maybe this is all there is. Just one night, here, and then the world snaps back and we pretend nothing happened?"

He nodded. "Maybe. But it's still something."

She made a soft noise, not quite a sigh. "I don't want to forget this," she said.

"Me neither."

Danny drew his knees up and wrapped an arm around her, pulling her close. Her skin was slick with cold, but her body fit against his perfectly, like it had always known the shape of him.

He wanted to kiss her then, but the moment was too perfect to risk breaking it. Instead, he rested his chin on her hair and listened to her breathing, the soft, even rhythm of it. They stayed like that until the numbness in his toes climbed up to his shins, until the only things left in the world were the sound of the creek and the pulse of her heart against his ribs.

After a long time, Shelby shifted and turned her face to him. "You're not going to stay here forever," she said, half-question, half-statement.

He shook his head. "Don't think I can."

She nodded, as if she'd known all along. "Promise me something?"

He met her eyes, the color of river glass, sharp and clear. "Anything."

She hesitated, searching for the right words. "If you go, take something with you. Something that means you'll remember." She touched the spot over her own heart, then his. "Or leave something that means you won't be gone forever."

He smiled, gentle. "You want a lock of my dirty hair?"

She laughed, a real one this time, bright and alive. "I want you to remember this." She gestured at the creek, the willow, the sky. "Remember me, even if you don't come back."

He swallowed, the promise catching in his throat. "I will."

She leaned up then and pressed her lips to his, brief but electric, a spark running through the hollow of his chest. When she pulled back, her cheeks were flushed, eyes bright with something unnamable.

They sat like that, Shelby's head tucked against Danny's shoulder, until the sounds of the woods grew bolder and the world inched closer to dawn. His shirt hung over his shoulders and clung to his back, wet and cold, but she was warm under his arm. He tried not to think about how soon he'd have to let go.

Shelby stirred first, sitting up straight, then digging in the pocket of her jacket, which she'd laid across a branch to dry. She fumbled a second, brow creased, then held out her hand, palm open.

Resting in the center was a silver key, dull but with a shine in the moonlight, threaded onto a chain.

Danny blinked, unsure what he was seeing. "What's that for?"

She stared at the key like she was afraid it would vanish. "It's my grandma's. To her front door." Shelby ran the chain through her fingers, holding it up so the key swung, a soft, gentle arc. "I always used to hide it from her when I was little. She'd get mad, then laugh and tell me the house was already mine anyway." Shelby drew a breath, voice steady but small. "First place I ever felt safe."

Danny didn't move; afraid a misplaced motion would spook her or send the key tumbling into the dark water.

She leaned in and, with careful hands, looped the chain around his neck. The metal hit his chest, cold, and lay there, heavier than it should have been. Shelby's fingers lingered at the back of his neck, brushing the fine hair. She let her hands fall and then held his face between her palms.

"You're leaving," she said. Not a question.

He didn't answer. Didn't have to.

Her thumb traced his jaw, the smudge of coal dust coming away on her skin. "I want you to remember. Even if you make it big and never come back. I want you to know there's somewhere you belong." Her voice caught. "Even if it's not here. Even if it's just a memory."

He closed his eyes, and for a moment, the cold and the ache and the dread were all washed away. The only thing left was Shelby's hands, Shelby's breath, the press of the key against his chest.

She kissed him, a real kiss this time. Slow at first, searching, tasting the night on his lips. Then she pressed harder, arms wrapped tight around his neck. He pulled her close, nearly crushing her in the hug, hands knotting in her hair. The desperation of it scared him, the way her body shook in his arms, the way his own heart battered at the bones of his chest.

When she broke away, her face was wet. He didn't know if it was tears or just water from her hair, and it didn't matter. The key lay between them, gleaming like a promise neither of them was sure they could keep.

Shelby wiped her face, gave a shaky laugh. "Look at me," she said. "I'm a mess."

He smiled, thumb smearing another streak of coal across her cheek. "You're perfect," he said.

They sat on the grass, side by side, not touching now, both staring out at the moon's reflection in the creek. The mist covered their feet, a thin and shifting veil.

After a while, Shelby spoke again. "If you go," she said, voice low and raw, "I want to go with you. But I can't. Not yet. I have to take care of Mama, at least for a while longer." She paused, wiping her nose. "Promise you'll come back."

Danny heard the terror in her voice, the need. He didn't know if he'd be able to keep that promise. But he nodded anyway, felt the key dig into his skin, the weight of it anchoring him to the moment. "I promise," he said.

She pressed her forehead to his, and they sat like that, breathing the same air, each pulse a new promise.

The chill grew as the night wound down, and somewhere behind them, a blackbird woke up and started its own song. Danny slipped his arm around Shelby, pulled her close again. She curled into him, hands finding his, fingers laced tight.

They sat there, waiting for the world to change.

When the sky paled and the first morning birds called, Shelby stood and shook herself dry and grabbed what remained of her things minus one. She looked back at him, eyes clear and hard. "Don't lose that key," she said.

He tapped his chest, where the key hid under the shirt. "Never."

She smiled, then turned and walked up the hill, shoes slung over her shoulder, hair a tangled banner behind her. Danny watched her go, every step farther and farther until she vanished in the trees.

He sat alone on the creek bank for a long time, listening to the water, to the new day coming. The key pressed cold to his chest, but he liked the weight of it. Liked that it hurt just enough to keep him awake.

Danny looked up at the willow, its branches now gray in the dawn, and thought of how roots held even when the trunk was gone, how the memory of what you were could anchor you long after the world turned you loose.

He closed his hand over the key.

Life hands you pieces without the box cover,
so you build the image as you go.

NEW TO NASHVILLE

Suggested Listening: Hit play on this cameo song, New to Nashville by Raleigh Keegan, and walk the line with a Lower Broadway musician chasing the spotlight. It's a tune that knows running ain't just about where you're headed, it's about what you're leaving behind.

D anny woke to the sound of the phone buzzing through the splintered wood of his night-stand. He let it ring out, once, twice, three times, until the noise became the only thing in the world. No one called this late except bad news or wrong numbers. But the voice on the other end wasn't either. It was Nate, the kid from high school who left for the city and never looked back, the one who said he could always find a way if you just gave him a night and a reason.

"Wallace," said Nate, voice run through with static and neon. "You ever been to Nashville?"

Danny rubbed the black from his eyes, the taste of sleep like copper in his mouth. "I been close," he said, though he hadn't.

"Well, you're going. They got a spot at Hank Williams Jr Boogie Bar. You've heard of the Boogie Bar? Down on Broadway, rooftop, next to AJ's place? They got an afternoon slot they need to fill, somebody fresh who don't suck. You still got your guitar, right?"

Danny looked at the guitar case in the corner, the strings wanting to curl off the headstock like fishing line. "Still got it," he said.

"Good. Don't screw the pooch on this. I told them you could do it."

Danny hung up before Nate could say more. He sat on the edge of the bed, breathing in the silence, letting the words sink down to the marrow. The room was dark except for the stripe of moon on the floor, but the walls buzzed like they were alive.

He dragged himself up, tripped over his boots, and sat cross-legged with the guitar in his lap. It was a cheap guitar, laminated spruce, the wood nearly splitting at the bridge. The action was high enough to take your fingerprints off. He picked up a flat pick and started with a G chord, the sound full and ugly. Then C. Then D. The three chords every song ever written in this town was built from.

He played them over and over until the tips of his fingers split and bled, red seeping into the ridges of the fretboard. He wiped it on his jeans and kept going. Thinking to himself that mining and playing have two different targets to callus. Each time he hit the G, it buzzed with the old familiar ache, the same note he'd been chasing since he was a kid. He played until his hands cramped, then he played some more.

The world outside was dead quiet, the kind of hush that only came after midnight and never lasted long enough. He tried not to think about Shelby, tried not to remember the shape of her in the creek, the way her breath had tasted sweet and scared. He tried not to see the key she'd hung around his neck, the dull shine of it against his chest.

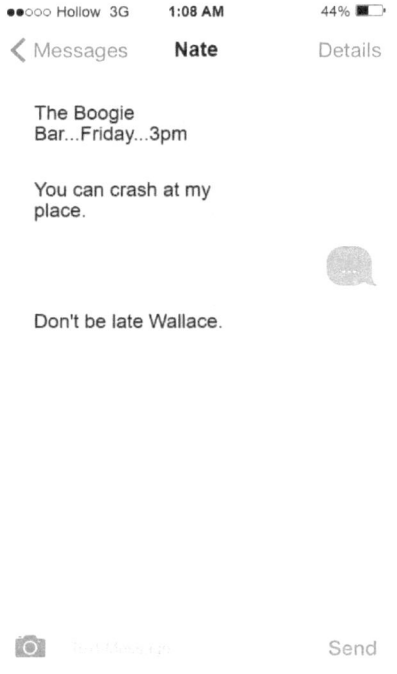

He played until the room filled with the smell of old sweat and coal dust, and the strings turned slick under his hands. Every now and then, the phone buzzed with messages again, but he ignored it. He knew the only thing on the other end was expectation, the chance to be bigger than this hollow, but the price of it was all the air and all the time in the world.

When the sky outside turned the color of lead, Danny put the guitar aside and stared at the ceiling. There were cracks up there, lines running wild and hopeless, crossing each other until the pattern stopped making sense, a reflection of the truth in life. He watched them until his eyes blurred. He wondered what it would feel like to leave for good, to walk away and never look back. He wondered if Shelby would forgive him for breaking the one promise she'd asked him to keep.

He didn't sleep.

In the morning, the coal dust was back, settling on his skin like a verdict. He showered and pulled on clean jeans and a shirt with no holes, but it didn't matter. The black worked its way through, a stain that didn't give a damn about soap or water. He stood at the window, watching the sun claw its way over the ridge, and felt the weight of the key dragging at his throat.

He heard her footsteps before she knocked. The tap on the door was soft but insistent, the way rain falls when it wants to be noticed.

He opened the door, and there was Shelby, hair tied back and face scrubbed raw. She wore a dress the color of wet limestone, and her arms were folded tight across her chest. Her eyes found the guitar first, then his hands, then the key. She looked at him like she'd already read the ending.

He tried to smile, but it didn't land. "Hey."

Shelby didn't step inside. She kept one foot on the porch, like she wasn't sure the floorboards could take the truth.

"Got a call," he said, and the words stuck.

She nodded. "Nashville?"

He blinked. "How'd you know?"

Her mouth twisted. "Don't take a genius." She pointed at his fingers, "You only play like that when you're scared, or when you think you're never coming back."

Danny looked at his hands, the dried blood in the

cracks of his skin. "It's just a show. One afternoon."

She stared through him. "Is it?"

He shrugged, then gave up. "Don't know."

For a long time, neither spoke. In the yard, the sun hit the morning dew and turned the grass to shards of light. From down the road came the sound of miners' boots, hard on gravel, the beginning of another shift. The air was thick with it, the promise of the day already choking out the hope of anything better.

Shelby reached out, brushed the sleeve of his shirt. "You said you'd tell me."

He nodded. "I wanted to right away but only got the call last night."

She pulled her hand back. Her voice was steady, but the way her fingers dug at her elbow gave her away. "When do you leave?"

He checked the clock. "Couple days. Maybe less, if I can bum a ride with the Gutter Choir."

She laughed, a sharp, surprised sound. "They'll drink you under the table before you get ten miles out."

He managed a grin. "That's the plan."

She reached for the key at his neck, touched it with one finger. "You taking this with you?"

He looked at her, then at the key, then at the sky. "Don't know what else to do with it."

Shelby's finger hovered on the key, drawing circles in the air before she finally let it fall against his chest. "You could leave it with me," she said, but her voice was cracked glass, half-joke, half-dare.

Danny wanted to say something to fill the space. He tried to think of how many days had passed since that first night by the creek. He tried to count the mornings she'd brought him coffee, the afternoons she'd laughed at his dumb jokes, the nights she'd curled up beside him on the chipped steps of his rented porch, both of them watching the sky for storms that never came.

He'd lost track. He'd thought that was a good thing, finally, time measured in Shelby instead of shift bells. But now he heard every tick in her silence, the way her eyes went flat, the way her arms folded her in.

Shelby let her hand fall. She looked at him for a long time, like she was memorizing the shape of his face. "Promise you'll call," she said, and it wasn't a request.

"I'll call," he said, but his voice was so quiet he wasn't sure she heard.

She stepped away, then stopped. "I hope it's worth it," she said. "Whatever you're running toward."

Danny wanted to tell her he wasn't running, that he was chasing something better than the hollow, but the words felt weightless. He nodded, and the gesture said everything.

Shelby watched him for a moment, then turned and walked off the porch. He watched her go, the shape of her shrinking with every step. He felt the ache in his chest, deep and mean, but he didn't fight it.

He closed the door and leaned his forehead against the cool, dirty wood. The smell of coal dust lingered, even here, even now. Outside, the sound of boots on gravel faded, then returned, then faded again as the waves of workers filled the mountain's gizzard. The world kept moving, whether or not he was ready. But Danny wasn't going to the mine, not anytime soon.

He sat on the bed and picked up the guitar. He played the G chord, then the C, then the D. It sounded the same as always, but felt different now, charged with a new kind of sadness, an unvarnished truth. He played until the sun climbed high and the cracks in the ceiling turned to veins of gold.

He wondered if he would ever play for anyone who cared the way Shelby did. He wondered if leaving would make a difference, or if the world would just swallow him up and spit him back.

He played until his hands bled again, and this time, he let the blood stain the strings.

He played until he forgot what it felt like to stop.

On his last night in White Oak Hollow, Danny wandered the streets with the hollow ache of someone already half-gone. He took the slow route down Main, boots dragging, guitar case slung heavy at his back. It thumped him with every step, as if to remind what was waiting on the other side of the world.

The shops were shuttered. Every window was blind with plywood or dust. Percy's Pawn still had lights on, a sick yellow glow bleeding out from behind the security grate. Down the block, The Farmacy's sign flickered green as usual, stuttering through the names of pills and six-packs, the cross outside buzzing so loud it masked the silence. Each time Danny passed a streetlamp, his shadow doubled itself, then melted away at the next patch of dark.

He met Shelby on the bridge over the creek, the spot where the water lost its name and became part of the river. She stood on the parapet, arms out, balancing against the slip of the concrete. When she saw him, she hopped down, feet finding safer dirt, and wiped her palms on her skirt. The night had cooled her skin, left her face pale and drawn.

They walked without talking. He tried match her stride, but she moved faster, as if she was chasing the moon through the sky. Danny let the distance stretch, then caught up, the case booming him like a cajon center-hit. The air carried the smell of honeysuckle, sickly sweet, and the deeper tang of river mud. It wrapped around him, clinging to his clothes along with the ghost of coal dust still coating him from his last shift in the hole.

They passed the hollow's empty heart, the post office closed, the two-pump gas station silent. It hadn't seen a car in nearly three years.

At the church, she stopped. The building squatted on the edge of the rise, white paint blistered and sagging, the steeple leaning toward collapse. A string of Christmas lights wrapped the railing, though it was only October, and most of the bulbs were blown out. Shelby sat on the bottom step and waited for Danny to follow.

He set the guitar case on the sidewalk. His hand shook a little as he fumbled the latch, but he didn't open it. He just looked at Shelby, at the way the lamplight caught her hair and the way her fingers gripped the edge of the concrete.

She glanced at his chest, at the place where the key pressed under his shirt. "Still got it?" Asking as if this was the only solid link between them that would ever be.

He tapped his chest. "Didn't let it go."

She nodded, then scooted over, making space for him. "They ring the bell every night at ten," she said. "Don't know why. Ain't nobody left to hear it but the drunks and the dogs."

Danny tried to smile. "Guess I'm both."

Shelby leaned in, shoulder pressed to his. Her skin was warm now, alive with the charge of her nerves.

"You scared?"

"Yeah," he said. "Terrified."

The bell went off, a single low peal that rolled down the street and shook the windows. Danny felt it in his teeth. Shelby reached for the key at his throat and curled her hand around it, thumb tracing the edge. The touch was gentle, but it pinned him to the step.

"So you remember the way back," she said, voice barely a whisper.

He covered her hand with his own, knuckles raw. "I'll call," he promised. "You'll see me in the news, maybe. Or on a record."

She rolled her eyes. "You don't even like country music."

He laughed, but it caught. "I'll play what they pay me to play."

Shelby's smile was small, sharp. "You always did."

The bell tolled again, and somewhere a dog barked, the sound carrying through the trees beckoning normal folk to bed. Danny tried to memorize it all, the blue of the moon, the shape of her face, the weight of her hand on his chest. He wanted to take it with him, but already it felt thin, a copy of a copy.

Shelby tilted her head. "You'll come back for me?"

He nodded, but she didn't let go of the key.

"You don't have to lie," she said. "Just say goodbye if that's what it is."

Danny couldn't meet her eyes. He let the silence fall, and in that gap, he felt the world shrink. He wanted to tell her he'd stay if she asked, but she never would.

She pulled his head down and kissed him, soft and slow, her lips salty with tears he hadn't seen her cry. The kiss was quick, but it stayed on his skin after she let go.

She pressed her forehead to his.

"Don't forget," she said. "Not for a second."

He shook his head, the weight of it making his neck ache.

Shelby stood and dusted off her skirt. "I gotta get home before Mama gets worried." She turned, took three steps, then looked back. "You're a damn fool, Danny Wallace."

He smiled, sad and perfect. "Always was.'

He watched her walk away, arms swinging loose. He wanted to follow, but he stayed where he was. Sitting on the church steps until the bell rang again each note a nail in the coffin of the life he was leaving behind.

When he finally got up, the world felt empty. He picked up his guitar case that now felt like a fouled anchor stifling progress in one direction but pulling him in another. He walked home through the dead streets, the air thick with honeysuckle and heartbreak.

Morning came. Danny woke to a town that didn't know was losing him. Pale blue, every house still asleep, the smoke from a hundred invisible breakfasts already starting to rise above the roofs. He stood at the window for a while, watching the first light ooze up over the edge of the hollow, then got ready for the day, slow, each motion a funeral for something he'd never get back.

He packed what fit in the duffel; a pair of jeans, two shirts, a few odd socks. He wiped down the guitar with a rag, careful not to leave any more blood, then slipped it into its case, the handle taped and glued, ready to break with the next hard pull. The key sat cold at his chest. He thought about leaving it on the nightstand, but in the end, he tucked it under his shirt, pressed to the bone.

He ate a stale biscuit and drank water straight from

the tap. The pipes groaned, shuddered, then spat out a mouthful of iron. He finished it anyway. When the hour struck seven on the cracked clock above the stove, he slung the bag over his shoulder and stepped out into the damp.

The air tasted clean for once, the usual coal dust beaten down by the night's rain. His boots scuffed wet gravel as he crossed the empty yard, the world so still he could hear his own heart above the slow grind of the mine in the distance.

He walked Main Street, passing the shops and the bar where the Gutter Choir nursed last night's sins. On a stoop, a single member of the Choir lay sprawled, half-conscious, clutching an empty bottle like a baby. He looked up as Danny passed, eyes squinting through the hangover.

"Go get 'em, boy," he mumbled, then rolled over and threw up into the gutter.

Danny smiled, then kept on.

At the end of town, the road forked left to the mine and right to the depot. He paused, staring at the cross-roads, the cinderblock sign still advertising a circus that came and went before he was born. He looked to the mine first, out of habit, and saw Earl McKinney at the gate, hands braced on his hips.

Earl raised one arm, a wave as sturdy as a goodbye could get. Danny answered with a nod, not trusting himself to speak. The old miner spat into the dirt, then turned back to the darkness.

A dog padded out from under a porch, ribs counting out the days between meals. It sniffed the air, then fell in beside Danny, trotting two steps ahead, then two behind, never quite looking at him but never leaving.

At the depot, the dog sat on its haunches, watched as Danny shifted his weight and set the guitar down.

"You can't come," Danny told it. The dog whined, then got up and wandered back toward the houses, tail down.

Shelby was there, alone on the platform, hands in her pockets. She wore a flannel shirt that hung too big, sleeves rolled and rolled until they swallowed her wrists. Her hair was pulled back in a low knot, but loose pieces drifted in the wind, gold in the sunrise.

Neither of them moved for a minute. They stared at the tracks, at the weeds pushing up between the ties, at the way the sky got brighter with every breath.

He went to her, close enough to see the sleep still caught in her lashes. She looked up, eyes steady.

"You got everything?" she asked.

He nodded, then shrugged. "Enough."

The train was late, as always. They sat on the cold bench, their shoulders not quite touching, the guitar case between them. The morning passed in slow motion, every sound drawn out, the crows in the trees, the whistle of the shift change, the clatter of a single car down the road.

When the train finally came, it announced itself with a banshee wail and a cloud of diesel that erased the sun. The brakes screamed as it slowed to the platform. Shelby stood first, her hands balled tight.

He picked up the guitar, the bag, and the hope he might be good enough for the world waiting outside.

She hugged him, hard, the key digging into her collarbone. Her hands found his face, cold fingers tracing the line of his jaw, then settled on his shoulders.

"Call every day," she said.

"Every day," he said, and wished it could be true.

She let go, and he felt her absence like a tooth pulled from his mouth.

They kissed, just once, enough to mark the moment but not enough to satisfy anything deeper. Her lips were dry, her breath all honeysuckle and grief. She stepped back, arms folded now, bracing herself.

He climbed the steps to the train, found a window seat, guitar case wedged under his legs. When he looked out, Shelby stood where he'd left her, arms wrapped around herself. She didn't wave. She just watched as the train started moving, as the windows blurred, as he was carried away from the only world he'd ever known.

He pressed his palm to the glass, leaving a smudge, fogging it with every exhale of anticipation, or regret.

The ride was quiet. Fields rolled by, then woods, then more fields, each one the same as the last. The train stopped twice, letting on people who didn't look up from their phones, didn't smell like home, didn't care about a boy with calloused hands and a guitar. He dozed, woke, dozed again. Each time, he clutched the key under his shirt, afraid it might disappear if he let go.

After three hours, the fields gave way to houses, then highways, then the silver slice of a city rising out of nothing. Nashville shimmered ahead, the lights burning even in the late morning, every promise alive and feral.

Danny sat forward, face almost to the glass, watching as the city got bigger, closer, more real. The last of the coal dust drifted from his hands onto the seat. He watched it settle, then brushed it to the floor.

He opened his shirt and looked at the key, cold and shining. Closed his hand over it, and this time, he smiled.

He didn't know if he was free, or just hollow, but he kept his eyes fixed on the lights ahead, and let the train carry him forward.

Behind him, White Oak Hollow shrank to a memory, sharp as the ache in his chest, but smaller now, easier to hold.

Ahead, the world waited, wild and hungry.

ROAD GIGS

Recommended Listening: The Hollow may have shaped him, but Broadway's about to test him. Hear the calm before the chaos with Raleigh Keegan's Bluegrass State of Mind.

By the time Danny saw the sign for the Hank Williams Jr Boogie Bar, his hands had already started to shake. The sign was not subtle, eight feet of neon script, the kind of blue that hurt to look at. He watched the letters flicker and burn into the wet sidewalk, watched the way the light stretched out and split across the slow river of beer and rainwater that pooled at the curb.

Inside, the air was thick enough to taste, a stew of cigarettes, old whiskey, the sweet rot of fryer grease. The bar curved around the left like a broken spine, the tables clustered together so tight you had to shoulder your way through. The stage was a two-by-four riser, painted black but worn to the wood at every corner. There was a mic, a single amp, a stool with the stuffing clawed out by years of nervous hands.

Danny stood at the edge of the room, guitar case in one hand, nervous energy in the other, and tried not to look lost. He counted the crowd. Maybe fifty people, maybe more if you added in the ghosts. Every one of them staring at the band already playing, a three-piece in matching t-shirts, their harmonies so clean it made

Danny want to hide.

A guy in a snapback and branded polo found him. "You Wallace?" he said, not really asking.

"Yeah."

"You're up next. Set's four hours, with two fives and a fifteen. Any original shit, clear it with Jake." The man's eyes lingered on Danny's boots, then the guitar case, then the hands. He looked at the nails, the skin, the scars. He made a little face, then said, "Go set up. Crowd's not too rough, long as you keep it hot and mostly country."

The guy vanished. Danny drifted toward the stage, heart slamming. He wiped sweat off his palms. The guitar case clicked open with a sigh, the hinge already loose from the trip. He pulled out the instrument, tuned by ear, then tuned again, just to have something to do. When he looked up, the three-piece was unplugging, and the middle one, a woman with hair the color of wild honey, winked at him.

"Break a leg, blue eyes," she said, and meant it.

Danny climbed onto the stage. The lights were set low, just enough for the crowd to see your face, not enough to read it. He perched on the edge of the stool, adjusted the mic, and tried not to think about the first note. His right thumb split open his second week in the mine, and it never really healed right. Now, resting on the E string, under the blue of the bulbs, he could see the thin white line, a fault under the ridge of callus.

He touched the key at his throat. The metal was cold, even here, but the chain was warm where it lay against his skin. He let the feel of it settle him, then took the first breath, then another, and then he played.

The first song was an easy one, "Family Tradition,"

the only Hank Jr he could sing without losing the tune. The chords came simple, muscle memory, and the crowd knew it before he was two lines in. Half the bar sang along, the other half shouted requests. He kept his eyes low, let the sound roll over him. The wood under his boots buzzed with every stomp, and the voices in the room blurred into one. For a minute, he forgot the city outside, forgot the key, forgot everything but the song.

He finished the first set with Merle, a run of Haggard deep cuts. The tip jar filled slow but steady, bills folded around loose change, all of it already slick with beer and sweat. The manager, Jake, he figured, gave him a nod from the bar, then held up two fingers, tapped the watch. He took the break, ducked into the alley, and let the cool air scrape his lungs clean.

He called Shelby. It rang twice before she picked up, her voice soft and quick as a sparrow.

"You make it?" she asked.

"Yeah."

"You on yet?"

"Back on in five."

She laughed, low. "You nervous?"

He looked at his hand. The split on the thumb was bleeding now, but he liked the way it looked. "Not at all."

"Liar," she said, and he loved her for it.

He heard the clatter of dishes in the background, the TV on low. Shelby was probably sitting at the kitchen table, coffee going cold, face turned toward the window like she could see the whole state from there. He wanted to ask her to come, to drive all night just to see him on a stage no bigger than a bathroom mat, but he didn't. She had her mother to take care of, and the world didn't always let go that easy.

"You'll do great," she said, voice steady. "Sing something for me."

"I'll play your favorite," he said, and meant it.

"Good," she said. "Don't screw up."

He hung up before she could say anything sweeter.

The second set was harder. The crowd was bigger now, the room twice as loud. He played what they wanted: "Folsom Prison," "Mama Tried," even "Wagon Wheel" though he secretly hated the song. The air grew dense, and the sweat pooled at the crook of his elbow, ran down his neck, and glazed other parts unseen. The blue lights made his skin look dead, but the eyes in the crowd were alive. They watched him, really watched, even when he missed a chord, even when his voice cracked.

Someone shouted for a song he didn't know. He said, "Sorry, brother," and the whole place laughed, then shouted louder, as if testing him.

Halfway through, Jake came up, handed him a Bud Light with the cap already off.

"How you doing?" Jake asked.

Danny smirked, "Fair to partly cloudy," and took the offering from him.

He drank half the bottle in a swallow, wiped his mouth, and went back to the music. The key slipped free from his shirt, swung out and caught the stage lights, throwing a little silver star onto the mic stand. He smiled, and the woman with honey hair saw it, nodded once, as if she understood exactly what it meant.

On the third set, he played his own song. Not on purpose; it just came out. The shape of it was familiar to his hands, the melody so plain and clean he thought no one would notice. But the room got quiet. The words hung over the bar like a new kind of smoke, and for the first time all night, no one shouted or sang along. Even the bartender stopped wiping the counter, just listened.

The chorus was simple: "Mouth to the moonshine, nose to the grind." He played it rigidly but let it roll out slower than usual, then stopped before the last verse, afraid he'd mess it up. But the crowd didn't care. They clapped, and someone even whistled.

After four hours, his fingers were raw, the inside of his palm stained with string grease and blood. He packed up, counted the bills in the jar, over a hundred, not counting the coins. Jake handed him another stack, cash from the bar, all of it real and heavy. Danny felt it in his bones, the weight of it, more than he'd ever made in a day at the mine.

Jake said, "You're good. Come back next Friday."

Danny nodded. "I will."

He called Shelby again, this time from the front door, where the neon from the sign bled onto the bricks. She answered first ring.

"How'd it go?" she asked.

"Good," he said, and this time he didn't have to lie. "They want me back."

She made a sound, half laugh, half something else. "I knew you could do it."

He listened to her breathe, and for a second, he could almost feel her hand on his cheek, the way she'd done when they sat by the creek, the way she touched the key and said it was proof he belonged to something. He closed his eyes, felt the night settle.

"I wish you were here," he said.

"Me too," she said, and nothing else.

After, he walked Lower Broadway, the street a river of

light and sound. Every bar pulsed with a different song, every window full of people chasing something very few would ever catch. Danny felt the music in his teeth, in his ribs, in the hollow of his chest. The key thudded against his heart with every step, a metronome for the life he was building, piece by stubborn piece.

He stopped at the end of the block, looked back at the Boogie Bar, watched the neon letters stutter and burn. He thought of home, of the creek, of the girl who told him not to screw up. He touched the key, closed his hand around it, and smiled.

This was the start. He could feel it, deep and sure, the same way you felt a storm before it hit.

At first, the city was a song. Every night, Broadway lit up for Danny, and every face in every bar was a new subject waiting to listen. But Nashville had a mean memory, and its songs turned quick from hymn to dirge.

The first time he noticed was at the Boogie Bar, third Friday in. The crowd was thinner, office guys, a couple of tourists with the dead-eyed look of folks who'd lost their luggage and hope at the same layover. Danny ran through the set, the same songs, the same jokes between, but the room was heavy with waitstaff and nobody else. The applause was two hands and a cough. The tip jar held a ten and some nickels.

He tried to laugh it off, blame it on the rain or the new construction down the block. But it happened again, and then again, at a dozen bars lined up like dominos on Lower Broadway. He'd play his heart out for rooms that couldn't care less, singing to the backs of heads, to shadows huddled over whiskey, to the TVs that played silent sports and ate the attention whole.

Bar managers, started coming by more often, tapping their watches before Danny even made it to the bridge of "Folsom Prison." "Keep it tight, kid," they'd say, voices low enough for only Danny to hear. "Covers only, none of that homegrown shit. Tourists want to drink, not think."

Danny wanted to fight back, but the only thing worse than playing "Wagon Wheel" was not playing at all. So, he played it, three times a night, each time a little hollower. When he slipped in his own verse back at one bar, the song Shelby liked best, a manager appeared from the dark like a bad thought, draw his finger across his throat, then disappear back behind the bar.

By December, he could see his own ribs in the mirror. His clothes hung off him, the denim gone soft at the knees, the shirts sour with sweat and nicotine. The city wore him down from the outside in, bit by bit, until all that was left was nerve and guitar string. It was like the mine but black and ashy on the inside. The grind soiled his soul.

He still called Shelby. At first, it was every night, after the last set, when the street sweepers hosed vomit off the curb and the drunks wandered in circles, looking for their next best mistake. He'd call, and she'd answer, her voice bright and sweet even through the static and distance.

"How's it going?" she'd ask, and he'd tell her about the crowd, about the bachelorette who tipped him with a glow stick and a kiss on the cheek, about the guy who threw up during the third set and then asked for an encore.

She'd laugh, and for a while, the ache in his chest would ease. But as the days blurred, the calls got shorter. Sometimes she'd be at work with her dad, or her mom would need something, or the line would go dead before he even said hello. He'd try again, but more often than not, he'd get voicemail, her recorded voice soft and careful, promising she'd call when she could.

He started leaving the same short messages, sometimes two or three a day, just to hear himself say the things he couldn't say to anyone else. "Miss you, Shel. Wish you could see it. Wish you were here." He left them like breadcrumbs, hoping she'd follow them back to him.

Once, in a bar so empty he could count every body from the stage on one hand, he saw the honey-haired singer again, the one who'd told him to break a leg. She was at a table near the door, nursing a whiskey and staring at her phone like it was a lifeline.

Danny played his set, tried to catch her eye, but she never looked up. After, he sat at the bar, counting out change for a Miller Lite, when she slid onto the stool beside him.

"You're still here," she said, voice flat.

"Nowhere else to be," Danny answered.

She traced the rim of her glass. "You ever think about home?"

He shrugged. "Not much there for me now."

She made a sound, half-laugh, half-sigh. "That's the trick, isn't it? Home ain't a place, it's whatever you left behind that still hurts."

He looked at her, at the streak of dirt from playing guitar under her fingernails, the raw skin at the cuticle. She wore her pain with the same rough pride he did, and she was no further on her path than he was, and she'd been there years.

She nodded at the key around his neck. "That from a

girl?"

He nodded. "Shelby."

"Good name," she said. "Hang on to it. Everything else out here's just noise."

She finished her drink, left a bill under the glass, and vanished out the door.

He played three more gigs that week. Each one was worse than the last. The tip jar grew lighter, the managers grew meaner, the crowd grew thin and glassy-eyed. By February, he was down to one set a night, sometimes none at all. He pawned a spare guitar he had managed to score for food money, then borrowed against the next gig to cover the motel.

It was always the same: gray walls, a coin-op TV, a bedspread with stains older than he was. He'd count his tips, line them up by denomination, then call Shelby. Sometimes he'd get her, but mostly not. He'd lay back on the bed, the key cold on his chest, and listen to the empty ring of the line.

One night, a guitar string snapped mid-song. The sound was sharp, a whip-crack that silenced the room for half a second. He stared at the broken end, the way it curled like a dead bug on the wood, and finished the song with five strings, voice ragged.

After, in the dressing closet that passed for a green room, he tried to fix it, but his hands shook too bad. He found an old string in the case, black with sweat and tarnish, and wrapped it on, not caring if it held.

He sat in the dark for a long time, the phone on his knee, Shelby's number glowing on the screen. He didn't call. He couldn't. He stared at the number until it faded, then closed his eyes and let the dark wrap around him.

On the walk back to the motel, he saw his reflection

in a bar window. He looked like a man who'd survived a war, but lost everything in the process. He touched the key, pressed it to his lips, and tasted metal and memory.

The next morning, he woke with the world spinning. His head pounded, mouth dry as chalk. He tried to remember if he'd eaten, but all he could recall was the bitter beer and the taste of regret.

He showered, dressed, and packed the guitar. The string held, barely.

He thought about calling Shelby again, but didn't. He wrote a text instead.

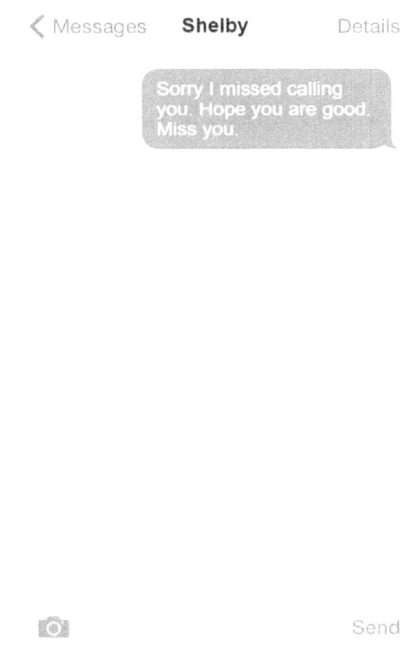

He deleted it before sending.

That night, he played his last set in Nashville. The bar was half-full, but the sound was pure. He played "The

Farmacy," the whispering willow song Shelby liked, and for a minute, he swore he could hear her voice in the room, singing along with every word.

When the set was done, he took his pay at the bar. He walked out into the night, the air cold and clean, and let the city fall away behind him.

He wandered the streets, not sure where to go. He ended up at the train depot, the same brick-faced depot where he'd first stepped off the train in Nashville, with its high-arched windows and wooden benches worn smooth by a thousand restless bodies. Now it was full of strangers going nowhere fast.

He bought a ticket with what was left, counted out the bills and coins, and waited for the train.

In the polluted light of dawn, he climbed on, found a window seat, and watched the world blur past.

He pressed the key to his heart, closed his eyes, and listened for a voice that would never come.

Two days of the Southeast landscape, Savannah hit him like a wet fist. The air was heavy, full of salt and sugar, and it stuck to the inside of your lungs whether you wanted it or not. He stepped off the train with his guitar slung over one shoulder, the duffel hanging limp at his side. The station stank of urine and desperation, and the concrete steamed in the morning heat.

He walked the city for hours before the sun even started to break through the clouds. He found River Street by accident, following the tug of music and the smell of roasted peanuts. The river looked brown and angry, churning between its banks like a tongue chewing on loose teeth. The buildings were old brick, their windows rimmed in black mold, the alleys thick with trash and lost time.

Every bar he tried turned him out the same way: "Booked through Spring, kid," or "We got our guy, try down the block." The managers didn't bother to learn his name, didn't care that he'd played every joint in Nashville until the music bled out of him. He showed them the calluses, the way his fingers could wrap a G chord blind, but they only shrugged, pointed at the next guy in line.

So, he drifted to the end of River Street, where the buskers worked the crowd like hungry dogs. There were two of them on every corner, each one louder and more desperate than the last. Steel drums, fiddles, harmonicas, every noise in the world except quiet. Danny found a patch of shade under a wrought-iron staircase, set down his case, and started to play.

No one stopped. The tourists walked by with cameras and neon fruit flavored drinks, the locals never even slowed. The music vanished into the humid air, swallowed up by the river and the noise. After two hours, he counted three dollars in the case, all of it in coins.

By dusk, his hands shook so bad he had to steady them between his knees. The hunger clawed at his stomach, but he'd long since stopped noticing. He played anyway. He played until the sweat ran into his eyes and the skin split open on the side of his thumb. He played until the shadows grew long and the other buskers packed up, one by one, leaving him alone with the last scraps of sunlight.

The final song was a broken lullaby, the one Shelby liked to sing under her breath when she thought no one was listening. He made it halfway through the chorus before the string snapped, the sound a sharp twang that echoed down the empty street.

He stared at the guitar, at the ragged wire curled like a tongue, and then at his hands. He could have cried, but the tears wouldn't come.

He packed up, shouldered the case, and walked until the streets emptied out and the sky turned black. He found a bench near the river, the wood warped and slick with old rain. He set down the case and sat, elbows on his knees, head in his hands.

The key around his neck burned against his skin. He held it between his thumb and forefinger, rolled it until the chain cut into the flesh. He looked at his phone, at Shelby's name blinking in the missed calls. He hadn't called her in days or weeks, he wasn't sure and hadn't heard her voice since the night he left Nashville for good. Time seemed to melt away.

He wanted to dial her number, to say he was sorry, to say he missed her more than food, more than air. He wanted to tell her about the river, about the way the city looked at you like it already knew how you'd end up. He wanted to ask if she'd wait for him, just a little longer.

Instead, he turned off the phone and set it in the guitar case, tucked safe under the strap.

He lay down on the bench, arms crossed over his chest, guitar hugged close. The world spun slow, and the city hummed with secrets. He watched the stars blink on, one by one, then drifted into sleep, the sound of the river in his ears.

He dreamed of White Oak Hollow, of the way the mist rolled off the creek and the trees whispered his name. He dreamed of Shelby, her hands in his, her breath warm and alive. He dreamed of a place where the music might matter, and the pain of it didn't last forever.

When he woke, the sun was already up. The tourists were back, the buskers too, and the day smelled of coffee and old bread. He picked up the guitar, felt the empty spot where the string should be, and started to play anyway.

Three months passed in a blur of broken strings and calloused fingertips. On Tuesdays, when the riverboat cruise ships docked, he'd count out wrinkled bills for a motel off Montgomery, room 112 with its flickering lamp and dated, Old-South furniture. Other nights, he'd curl against the curved slats of the riverfront bench, jacket bunched under his head, while raccoons rustled through nearby trash. Whether on stained sheets or splintered wood, he'd stare upward, the hollow beneath his ribs expanding with each breath, Shelby's name caught somewhere between his throat and tongue.

The key pressed hard against his heart, a weight that didn't get any lighter.

THE CALL

Suggested Listening: Turned 22 by Raleigh Keegan. A coming-of-age anthem about turning loose too soon and realizing what you left behind.

Rain hammered the thin glass of the motel window, the sound a low, ceaseless snare. Danny hunched on the corner of the bed, elbows to knees, hands dangling like broken instruments. The room stank of bleach and something older, a rot behind the clean, the way a graveyard smelled in early spring. The wallpaper peeled in curls, yellowed at the seams, and the bulb above him strobed and guttered with every shift in the wiring. It lit the cracks on his knuckles, the city grit mashed into every line, the half-healed scabs where his blood had blistered out between frets.

When he walked in the room, he'd left the guitar case open on the bedspread, a blue-lidded coffin holding its meager dead: five-dollar bills, all singles, curled and damp, and a scatter of coins that looked like they'd been dredged from the river. He counted the money twice, then shoved it into the pocket of his jeans, the coins so heavy it pulled the fabric off his hip. The bills were soft as tissue, stinking of spilled beer.

He hadn't eaten in twelve hours. His hands shook, not from hunger, but from the sudden loss of adrenaline. Busking was a kind of dying, he'd decided. You could lose your life in plain view, and nobody would notice except for the kids who came to gawk, maybe a woman who thought you looked like somebody she used to know, and the old men who pretended not to listen.

He lit a cigarette, drew in the smoke, and let it out slow. The nicotine sat mean on his tongue, made the hunger sharper. The bedspread was stiff under his thighs, probably boiled to sterilize some unknown sin. The rain on the window hit a beat, fast, like fingers drumming on a casket.

The coal stains on his hands had faded, replaced by the black from the city; street tar, bus exhaust, and whatever the bars left behind. He flexed his fingers, testing the pain. He felt the cut open again, wetting the old string callus with a new seam of red.

He set the cigarette in the chipped ashtray, let it burn, and picked up the phone from the nightstand. The display was cracked, but he could still read the time—9:42 —and the number glowing underneath; Shelby's, the only one that ever called anymore.

He stared at it, the way you look at a wound you don't want to touch. The phone shuddered in his palm, the ringer set low but insistent. He felt the pressure behind his eyes, a migraine brewing from the day's failures, and thought of letting the call run out. He imagined the slow fade of her name from the screen, the ghost of her voice bottled up in the voicemail, waiting for him to be brave enough to press play.

He slid his thumb across the glass, then stopped, the screen smeared with his blood. He let his head fall, the damp of his hair clinging to his forehead. With his free hand, he touched the key at his neck, the one she'd given him that last night by the creek.

The key had become more than a piece of metal; it was a constant reminder of something he couldn't quite touch. He carried it, turned it over in his hand, felt the ridges press into his palm, yet the memory it belonged to wasn't his. She said it was something from somewhere else. It lived in her mind, anchored to a moment he had never seen, a truth he could never claim. All he held was the artifact; cold, unyielding, and heavy with meaning he was meant to have but forgotten or lost.

He closed his hand around it, squeezing until the ridges bit his palm.

The phone kept ringing.

The rain battered the window harder, like it was trying to get in. The city still hummed outside, the river close enough to feel in the air, the promise of salt and brine and a thousand dead things floating out to sea.

He thought of Shelby in her kitchen, maybe standing in the yellow light by the sink, her hair twisted up, her hands cradling her own phone like she was afraid it might break. He thought of her father, the way the old man would glower at him from behind a newspaper, or the way he'd sneer when the TV got too loud.

He wondered if she'd answer if he called back, or if this was the last ring before the line went dead for good.

He sucked in the air, the taste of smoke and rain and all the things he couldn't say. He pressed the key to his lips, then let it fall, landing cold on his chest.

He answered the phone.

"Hello," he said, voice raw and thin.

Shelby's silence on the other end was heavy, louder than the rain, thicker than the smoke, and for a second, he couldn't tell if she'd hung up or if the connection was just too far gone.

She spoke at last, but her voice was faint and far, as though she'd fallen into a well and called up from the bottom.

"Hey," she said. "You get my message?"

Danny's mouth was dust. "Been out all day. River Street, you know. Played 'til my hands cramped up."

A pause, then, "You're working too hard."

He tried to smile, but there was nothing in him that could make that journey. "Can't make room and board sitting pretty. Gotta keep a dry place to stay. How's White Oak?"

Another pause, longer this time. "Same. Nothing changes, unless you count more folks gone. They put up a sign at the church, says we're 'United in Hope.' Ain't nobody buying it."

He laughed, a short bark, then let the silence return. The line hissed with static, the cell towers straining in the rain.

"I miss you," he said.

She didn't answer at first, then: "I miss you, too." Her voice a little less certain. "You eating okay?"

"Like a king," he lied. "Had a sandwich from this little place by the river. They fry the bologna on the griddle, get the edges crisp. Taste almost like home."

She made a soft sound, then coughed. "Mama asks about you. She says you should call more."

Danny dug his thumbnail into the meat of his forefinger, watched the half-moon bloom pink. "I will."

"Daddy's the same," Shelby went on. "He's fixing up the Impala, won't let me so much as touch a wrench. Says girls are only good for holding the flashlight, which

I guess is something."

He pictured her there, crouched on cold concrete, the work light in her hand, trembling, her father scowling through a haze of cigarette smoke. He'd always hated how the old man talked down, but Shelby just let it slide off, like rain she'd walked through all her life.

"He still asking when I'm coming back?" Danny asked, voice light.

"Sometimes," she said, but her tone was thin as air. "Mostly he just wants to know when I'll stop calling you."

Danny let out a low whistle. "That's harsh."

"It's not so bad. He's used to winning, and I don't let him." She went quiet, the only sound the distant drip of the rain.

He wanted to tell her something true, something that would bridge the gap, but everything felt counterfeit. He thought of his room, the smell, the lonely rain, the ache in his hands. He thought of the men who stood outside the bars and never bothered to listen. He thought of the song he'd written for her, the one nobody ever wanted to hear.

"You still singing songs for me?" Shelby asked, as if she'd read his mind.

He nodded, forgetting she couldn't see. "Every night. Place here outside of Oglethorpe's, can pay twenty bucks a set and a meal ticket if the crowd stays sober," he carried on the charade built on fragments of the truth.

"Do they?" she said.

"Not once," he said, and they both laughed, real for a moment.

"I wish I could see it," she said. "You, up there on a stage. Bet you look taller."

"Only from the back," he said. "From the front, I still slouch."

Another silence, softer now, like they'd run out of things to say but didn't want to hang up. The static on the line was a heartbeat, uneven.

She spoke next, and her words came with a hitch, like she'd rehearsed it all day. "Daddy had someone over for dinner last night."

Danny frowned, not sure where the story was going. "Who?"

She hesitated. "Boy from the church. Said he could fix our boiler, ended up staying for supper. Daddy called him 'a real good man,' which is the highest compliment he's ever paid anyone, including you."

Danny felt his ears burn. "You like him?" He tried to keep it light, but the words came out splintered.

"He's nice," she said, the words dropping like cold water. "Smart. Studies business at the community college about an hour away. Mama says he's polite. He brought me flowers, which was strange, but sweet." She paused. "I didn't know what to do, so I put them in a jar."

He squeezed the phone, his palm slick with sweat. "Sounds like you had a good time."

Shelby laughed, but it was brittle. "He's not you."

He didn't know how to take that, so he just nodded again, useless. The rain battered the window, and the room felt smaller with each breath.

"I miss the creek," she said, changing the subject. "I went out there last week. The willow's gone, somebody cut it down, left the stump like a gravestone. I sat on the rock anyway. Didn't feel right without you."

Danny thought of the creek, the cold water, the curve of her body in the night. He thought of the key around his neck and how it used to mean something.

He tried to joke, "You carving my name into the stump?"

She was quiet, and then: "You remember the night you left? I said I'd wait, but I don't know how long I can."

The line was thick with static. For a second, he thought she might be crying, but then he realized it was just the connection, breaking up with the storm.

He wanted to scream, to punch the wall, to run out into the rain and let it drown him. Instead, he pressed his lips together and said, "I know. I'm sorry. I just need more time."

"I know," she echoed. "I do, I promise."

He listened to her breathing, the small clicks and pops of the phone, the way her voice rose and fell.

"I turned twenty-three today," he said, out of nowhere.

Silence.

"Oh, Danny," she said, her voice cracking. "I forgot, I'm so sorry. I've been so—"

"Don't worry about it," he said, forcing a laugh. "Birthdays are for kids. I'm too old now. The city's aged me out."

She sniffed, then laughed, the sound raw and lovely. "You'll always be a boy to me. Even when you're ninety."

He smiled, then felt the smile die. "Wish you could see me," he said as a longing wrapped in a question.

"I do," she said. "Every time I close my eyes."

They let the silence sit, long and deep.

"I gotta go," she said at last. "Mama's making pie, and she'll kill me if I miss it."

He nodded. "Alright."

"Don't forget me," she said.

"Never," he whispered.

He waited for her to hang up first, but she didn't. So he pressed end, and the world fell back into rain and the hum of old lights.

He looked at the phone, at the number still bright on the screen, and felt the ache in his chest settle in for good.

After the line went dead, Danny just sat there, phone cooling in his hand, the blue of the screen staining his palm with fake light. His breath came thin, as if the room had lost its air when Shelby's voice blinked out. The rain doubled, hard against the glass, wind driving it sideways so it sounded like a thousand coins tossed against a headstone.

He set the phone down, slow, and watched the screen fade to black. His hands dropped into his lap, fingers splayed wide and empty. He leaned forward, elbows digging into his knees, shoulders hunched like he was trying to fold himself small enough to fit inside a pocket, or the crack in the drywall, or the slit in the cloth edging where the mattress bled its stuffing.

He stayed like that for a long time, not thinking, just letting the world run itself out. At some point, the bulb overhead flickered out for good, leaving him in a shade of darkness that hid nothing.

The only light was the neon outside, leaking through the cheap curtains, drawing lines on the walls and up his arms. The sign out there buzzed and stammered, half the letters burned out so it just said "INN" in stuttering red. He could see it reflected in the window, superimposed over the black of the night.

He stood, legs numb, and crossed the floor. The air by the window was cold, wet and alive with mildew. He drew back the curtain, then pressed his forehead to the glass. It was slick and cool, and it steadied him, made the throb in his head recede a little.

Outside, the rain churned in the gutter, made rivers of the parking lot, washed out the old cigarette butts and bits of broken glass. The neon splashed itself over the puddles, painting the world in blood and nothing.

He watched the water crawl down the pane, the drops racing each other in crooked tracks. Some merged, some vanished, some just hung on until gravity peeled them away. He tried to remember the last time he'd cried, but couldn't. He didn't even know if he could anymore.

He looked up, caught his own face in the glass. The city had starved him, hollowed out the jaw and deepened the lines under his eyes. He looked like someone halfway through becoming someone else, or maybe like two ghosts fighting for the same space. The key at his neck glimmered, and he reached up to touch it, expecting it to burn, but it was just cold. Heavy as always.

A thought of ripping it off, throwing it in the gutter to let the rain have it crossed him, but his hand fell away before he could. He pressed his palm flat to the glass instead, the wet chill biting through.

"Shelby," he mouthed, but the glass caught the breath and left a clouded stain.

He stood there, unmoving, until the rain slackened and the world outside slowed to a trickle.

When the sun came up, pale and sickly through the storm, he was still at the window. The neon switched off at dawn, but his reflection stayed, looking back at him, a stranger in his own eyes.

Alone had never felt like this. Not even in the mine,

not even on the road, not even on the first night in Savannah with nothing but the guitar and the promise of a future he'd already lost.

He let his hand fall, watched the condensation on the window bead around his fingerprints, then slide away.

For a long while, he just sat on the edge of the bed, hands in his lap, the key digging into his chest. The city buzzed beyond the walls, relentless, alive, but nothing in the room moved except for the slow, even rise and fall of his breath.

EMPTY STREET, EMPTY PROMISE

Suggested Listening: Before you walk with Danny through these empty streets with empty promises, cue up Raleigh Keegan's Love Dyin' Young. Its raw ache of love cut short will echo against the choices Shelby faces, and the silence Danny carries home.

White Oak Hollow always looked better in memory, but even the rot was worse than Danny remembered. He stood at the edge of Main Street, boots sunk in clay, guitar case in one hand, duffel bag in the other. Nine months out and nothing had changed except the last flicker of hope had been blown out and left to smolder on the breeze.

He walked. Each step forward brought more evidence that the world, or at least this part of it, was meant to fail. Where once there'd been a bakery, the windows were gone, the sign drooping by one bent screw. The hardware was a hollow shell, shelves stripped bare, the counter half-collapsed, yellow price tags still clinging to the edge like barnacles. The thrift store limped on, but its awning flapped loose, the red letters faded to a dirty pink, the glass front sprayed with white paint: "EVERYTHING MUST GO." Under that, a smaller hand had added graffiti, "INCLUDING YOU."

Porches were crowded with emptiness. Wicker chairs collapsed under the weight of their own disuse, the seats rotten through. Mailboxes sagged, some with bills spilling out, sodden and gray. He counted three old cars in various states of decay on the short walk, two up on blocks, the third buried to its axle in weeds, windshield starred by a rock or maybe a fist. The further he walked, the less he wanted to see.

Nobody said his name. Nobody looked up from the drag of their feet, the dull shuffle to and from the general store, or the rumble of battered trucks up the gravel roads. The ones he passed had the eyes of ghosts, unseeing or else refusing to see. A woman in slippers watched him through a slit in the door, hands clutching a plastic jug of something orange. She let the door swing shut slow, as if expecting him to come knocking, then thought better of it.

He checked his reflection in the pawn shop window. He looked like a man recently paroled, cheeks hollow, skin stretched over the bones of his face, a beard that had failed to fill in. The clothes, heavier than the weather called for. Sleeves rolled but hanging loose, made him look shrunken inside himself. He flexed his left hand, watched the tendons run under the skin. The calluses had never left, just grown over, the old miner's hardness now a musician's too. He liked the way it felt... or told himself so.

A banner above the pawn shop read "WELCOME HOME CLASS OF 20??" The last two numbers had been spray-painted over. Across the way, Percy's Bar was still open, the neon beer sign buzzing even in daylight, but the front door was propped by a cinderblock, as if daring the wind to try its luck. He thought about going in, but the weight of the duffel and the ache in his knees told him to keep moving.

He made it as far as the Farmacy before he stopped. The neon cross throbbed in the window, same sick green as before, but weaker, the light stuttering every few seconds as if fighting a losing battle with the dark. Inside, three people waited at the counter, faces drooped, eyes unfixed. One of them clutched a paper sack with both hands, rocking in time to some inner metronome. The pharmacist, the same old man from before, worked the register with one hand while the other massaged his temple, eyelids at half-mast.

He wanted to go inside, ask about the medicine that kept half the town from falling apart, but the thought of having to explain himself, to admit he'd come back to anyone, was too much. Instead, he walked on, past the town square, the church with the leaning steeple, and the gas station where, a gallon cost less than a bottle of painkillers, if they had any gas to sell.

There was graffiti everywhere, more than before. Some of it was just curse words, the kind of stuff high school kids used to scribble on desks, but there were new ones, too. Strange phrases, shapes, loops of red and black paint layered over the bricks. On the side of the old post office someone had drawn a crown, and beneath it, "NO KINGS." The words stuck in Danny's head. He laughed once, a short, dry bark, "not since 1776" he mumbled to himself.

He ran his thumb along the edge of the key at his neck, the metal cool even through the fabric of his shirt. He tried not to think of Shelby, but it was impossible. He pictured her walking these same streets, maybe on her way to the diner, hair pulled back, eyes set on the sidewalk to avoid the neighbors. He wondered if she'd recognize him, or if she'd even want to.

On the next block, the diner's sign still flashed OPEN, though the E and N were dead. Through the window, he saw a handful of regulars hunched over coffee, the waitress leaning on the counter, face bored to glass. Danny thought about going in, saying hello, but he didn't have the heart. There was nothing inside for him but the memory of better meals and the echo of Shelby's laugh in the back booth.

He kept on. A pickup passed, engine knocking, bed rattling with buckets and old tools. The driver didn't look, just spat out the window and kept going. Danny watched the spray hit the blacktop, then disappear.

At the end of Main, the houses turned small and close together, shacks at first, then just trailers patched with tarps and sheets of plywood. Here, the road was more mud than anything, potholes big enough to hide a man's foot. He slowed, dragging the duffel now, the guitar case shifting numb fingers. His shoulder burned. He welcomed the pain.

Danny halted at the overgrown path leading to where the old willow once stood, its absence a gaping wound in the landscape. He trudged down the familiar trail, weeds brushing against his legs, memories flooding back with each step. The stump loomed before him, jagged and splintered, a ghost of what had been. The grass around it lay unkempt, gone to seed, as if mourning the loss of its sentinel. He knelt beside the weathered wood, the rough texture grounding him in the moment. His fingers traced the surface, discovering a new carving that snaked across the bark, a chaotic jumble of letters, foreign and cryptic, not the initials he thought might be there. A pang of nostalgia twisted in his chest. Kids, he surmised, or perhaps the tree had simply given way under the weight of time and secrets. He sank down onto the cool earth, resting against the stump, allowing the quiet to envelop him, the air thick with whispers of a past he couldn't quite reclaim.

He sat, legs folded under him, and let his head drop. The sky pressed down, solid and gray, air thick with the taste of coal and rain. The wind carried the sound of the town, engines, a screen door slamming, the echo of a dog barking somewhere distant. Danny listened to it all, eyes shut, the key at his neck pulsing like a slow heartbeat.

He stayed that way until the cold found his bones. He picked up the guitar, slung it over his back, and stood. The duffel felt heavier, but he was used to weight by now.

He took the last steps to his old, rented room, each one measured, each one counted. The landlord's wife promised she would hold the room for him, but the house looked smaller than he remembered, paint curling off the siding, roof patched with pieces of tin. The porch was empty but for a milk crate, the remains of a cigarette pack, and a nest of bees under the eaves. He stood in front of it for a long time, the world on his shoulders.

He didn't go in. Not yet.

Instead, he turned, walked to the edge of the yard, and looked back up Main Street. The neon cross flickered behind him, the pawn shop light gone out, the world settling into a deep, uneasy quiet.

He wondered if anyone knew he was here. He wondered if it mattered.

He sat on the step, set down the guitar and duffle, and waited for the Hollow to notice he'd come hcme.

The old path to the mine was rutted deep, the clay packed so hard it might as well have been cast in iron. Danny's boots found the groove easy, the muscles in his legs remembering the way before his mind caught up. He'd meant to stay away, but something about the silence at the house made the thought of the tunnels almost comforting.

The mine itself looked the same, only less alive. The corrugated shed at the entrance had lost half its siding, the windows gummed with black. A sign that used to read "White Oak Consolidated" now hung sideways, dangling by a thread of rusty wire. Danny could hear the slow whine of the belt deep in the slope, but no men gathered outside, no laughter, no fire barrel, no nothing. The parking lot was a graveyard of old pickups, a few with four flats.

Earl McKinney stood at the head of the path, hands braced on hips, chin up, a living fossil if ever there was. His coveralls were a second skin, dusted at the seams, but the color of them had been scrubbed out long ago by years of bleach and sweat. His hair was gray and thick, grown wild at the edges, and his face was scored with lines so deep you could lose a coin in them. The eyes, though, were sharp as ever.

He caught Danny in his gaze, then gave a slight nod.

"Knew you'd show up sooner or later," Earl said, voice tuned to a perfect rasp. "Figured you'd be back before the thaw, but then again, Hollow's not got much to offer a man with ambition."

Danny stopped, toeing the line between respect and regret. "Just passing by. Thought I'd see if the slope was still holding."

Earl grunted. "Still holds, though it's about all that does. They got us running skeleton crews, 'cause the ones left either too old to quit or too stubborn to die." He spat, thick and black, then wiped his lip with the back of his hand. "You got taller. Or maybe just skinnier."

Danny tried a smile, but his mouth didn't know the shape. "More time above ground, I guess."

Earl studied him, as if measuring a slab of meat at the butcher. "You look like shit, son."

"Good to see you too."

They stood that way, silence thick between them, until the sound of machinery floated up from the dark: a deep, shuddering groan, followed by the snap and catch of gears eating at stone.

Earl jerked his chin at the mine. "You hear that? Used to be I couldn't sleep without the racket. Now I don't sleep at all. Miss the men, mostly. Even the dumb ones." He squinted, then added, "Especially the dumb ones."

Danny shrugged, wanting to change the subject but not sure where to steer it. "Anybody left worth remembering?"

"Not many." Earl's eyes narrowed. "Bobby's gone. Overdosed in January. They found him behind the storage shed, arms all purple. Left a girl and two boys." He ticked off the names. "Gutter Choir's down to one, and Percy's closing early now. Nothing but sad old men and sadder liquor."

Danny's fingers twitched at the mention of the bar. "Heard things got bad."

Earl made a noise, almost a laugh but with no humor in it. "Ain't been 'good' since Watt worked for Reagan. But yeah. This place is running out of men, and the ones left are running out of time." He nodded at Danny's neck. "That key new?"

Danny's hand flew up before he realized it. "Old, actually. Just forgot to take it off."

Earl watched him a moment longer, then let it go. "You get any further than Nashville?"

Danny tensed, felt the air thicken. "Made it all the way to Savannah. Lotta good it did."

"Never cared much for the ocean," Earl said. "Too wet. Too much sky." He scratched his chin, black dust crumbling off his nails. "What brought you back?"

Danny hesitated, unsure if honesty would buy him anything. "Wasn't much left out there for me. Even less than here."

Earl nodded, as if he'd already figured that out. "You lose her?"

Danny blinked, caught off guard by the question.

"Shelby," Earl said, voice softer now. "Girl had you wrapped up tight. Last I heard, she was working at the diner, doing night shifts for her daddy."

Danny looked away, the world narrowing to a pinhole. "She's still here?"

"Don't know. Don't go out much." Earl's face creased deeper. "You ought to call on her. Heard her daddy tried to set her up with some muck, but if she's still waiting, she'll let you know."

Danny tried to imagine the conversation: Shelby at the counter, pouring bad coffee, her eyes bright and hard as always. He pictured her looking up, not surprised, just disappointed.

"Maybe I will," he lied.

Earl slapped him on the back, hard enough to pop the air from his lungs. "You do that. Maybe bring her something nice. Girls always like that."

Danny coughed, then grinned. "You still working doubles?"

"Only when they need a man who won't quit. You hear that, boy?" Earl jabbed a finger at Danny's chest. "That's what's wrong with your whole damn generation. Everybody quits."

It became apparent Danny had hit an exposed nerve. "Go ahead. Ask any of them turds if they'd rather work hard or hardly work. Six one half dozen the other, they'd say. Shit on a math machine, what is that?" He drowned out his own voice with the gruffness in his delivery. As the tirade came to a close, "Idiots…," he lingered for a moment looking for Danny to respond.

Danny wanted to argue, but what was the point. Earl was right, even when he was wrong. He stood there, letting the smell of coal and oil settle on his clothes, letting it soak through to the skin.

"I gotta go," Danny said.

Earl watched him turn, then called after, "Don't let the mine get in your lungs. That's the part that kills you."

Danny raised a hand, not sure if he was waving or just brushing off the past. He walked back up the path, boots kicking up the same old dust, the engine noise fading with every step.

He didn't look back, but he could feel Earl's eyes on him, all the way to the edge of the ridge.

When he reached the main road, Danny stopped. He put his hand to the key, felt the old weight settle there. The world smelled like coal and rain, and underneath it, something sweeter, almost lost.

He wondered if Shelby's heart had blurred the edges

of him into something almost forgotten.

The bell over the door rang in a way that made Danny flinch, not from the sound but from the memory of all the times it had marked his entrance before. He waited a beat, letting the echo settle, then stepped in. The air was thick with fryer grease and the syrupy reek of too many cheap pies baked one after the other for a thousand years. The floorboards remembered him, groaned with each step, the dust swirling up to coat the toes of his boots.

He kept his eyes down, let the layout of the place draw him forward. The jukebox by the window was dark, its plexiglass cover smeared with years of handprints, the song list inside faded and curled. The booths were mostly empty, though one had a man asleep over a half-eaten plate of eggs, and another held a pair of kids with matching buzzcuts, faces blank, heads bowed over battered cell phones.

Behind the counter, Shelby stood arranging the mugs around the coffee makers. Her hair was pulled tight, no loose strands, the color more gold than he recalled. She wore the uniform, light blue, frayed at the collar, the sleeves rolled to show her arms. The name tag still said Shelby, but the font was smaller, like the world had made her shrink to fit it.

She turned to restock sugar packets, the fluorescent light catching something on her left hand. A white stone winked at him, perched on a band that slid halfway to her knuckle when she tilted her wrist. His lungs seized mid-breath. His fingers found the key at his throat, cold metal warming against his skin, before he forced them back to the sticky countertop where they left damp prints.

He cleared his throat.

She looked up.

Their eyes locked, and for a moment, the old spark was there—a quick flash, then gone, replaced by a wary chill. She set down the coffee carafe, wiped her hands on a towel, and squared her shoulders.

"Hey, Danny," she said, voice flat and careful. "Didn't expect to see you here."

He tried a smile, felt it twitch and die on his lips. "Just got in. Place looks the same."

She shrugged, lips pinching. "Nothing changes around here except the paint. Even that peels off in time."

He sat at the counter, set his hands flat on the laminate. The surface was sticky, and he left twin prints in the residue. He waited, but she didn't move to pour him coffee.

"How you been?" he asked.

"Fine," she said. "Busy, mostly."

He nodded, watched as she rearranged the salt and pepper shakers, a pointless exercise. The ring caught the light, made a small rainbow on the metal counter. He swallowed, felt the skin in his throat catch.

"Congrats," he said, gesturing at her hand. It had only been a little while since Earl made the suggestion, "I heard."

Shelby's face flickered, not quite a smile, not quite a wince. "It's new. Just happened a month back."

He wanted to ask who, but that would mean admitting he hadn't kept up, that her life had moved on without him. "He treat you good?" he managed.

"He's fine," she said, then, "Thomas Wilcox. He's working at the bank now. Daddy's happy."

Danny let that hang. The sound of the coffee brewing filled the air, a slow drip, the glass pot half-full and steaming.

"Glad for you," he said, not sure if he meant it.

Shelby wiped at a spot on the counter, then stopped. "You staying long?"

He shook his head. "Just passing through. Thought I'd say hello."

She met his eyes, and for a second, the old sadness was there. "That's probably best."

He felt the urge to say more, to confess everything: the failure, the hunger, the way he'd thought of her every night from Nashville to Savannah and back. But the words died before they reached his lips. Instead, he glanced at the ring again, and the silence between them swelled until it threatened to break the world in half.

"I thought I saw your name on a poster," she said at last, her voice cracking like old glass. "But I guess I was mistaken."

A short, humorless laugh escaped him, dry as the dust in the Hollow. "Yeah, that wasn't me. Must've been some other Wallace."

Shelby didn't smile. "You always were better than this place."

He wanted to tell her that was a lie, that he belonged here more than anywhere else, but the look in her eyes stopped him. She didn't need comfort. She needed distance.

He stood, the stool scraping loud against the tile. "Guess I should go."

She nodded, her hand drifting up to touch the ring, a nervous habit already etched in her bones. "Take care of yourself, Danny."

He hesitated at the door, half-turned, but she was already wiping the counter, eyes down, body angled away.

Outside, the day had gone gray. The Farmacy's neon flickered overhead, painting the street in queasy green. Danny walked slow, hands deep in his pockets, the chill working up through his sleeves. He passed the thrift store, the pawn shop, the gas station. He walked until his legs went numb, then stopped, breath billowing out in white clouds.

He looked back once, before losing site of the diner. Through the window, Shelby was still at the counter, the ring on her hand catching the sick light, bright as a wound.

Danny's head sunk low, his shoulders hunched forward, he let the Hollow swallow him whole.

THICKER THAN WHISKEY

Percy's was built before the world learned to want for more, and the world left it behind soon after. The windows were painted shut and glazed with tar, so the only light came from a few jaundiced bulbs dangling naked over the bar and the flicker of a dying flatscreen wedged into a far corner. The rest was shadow, thick as syrup, hugging the booths and the stretch of floor where the miners liked to line up after a double shift. Most nights, the air hummed with the static of lost bets, cheap whiskey, and the slow rot of men who'd learned to drink hope out of themselves.

Danny sat at the end of the bar, his hand curled tight around a glass. It was his second, or maybe his third, and the burn of it was all that kept his guts warm. The whiskey hit the tongue like poison, but it was a poison he'd missed. The ice in the glass melted to nothing, so now it was just brown and mean. He liked the way it stung. He liked how the numbness started at his lips and radiated in, a little death marching in a steady parade toward the center.

Percy watched him over the counter, arms braced on the bar sink, eyes as bloodless as the rest of him. The old man didn't say much, but every wipe of the rag, every slow sweep of the glass, had an opinion in it. Danny figured he was running out of customers worth the trouble, and he wasn't wrong.

"You been in here every night this week, son," Percy said, voice barely raised above the hiss of the ice machine. "Might be time to ease up, before you rot through."

Danny tapped the glass on the bar, listening to the thud on wood, the only beat in the room. He knocked it back, killed the rest, and set the glass down with a thump.

"Just pour another, Percy. I ain't looking for no sermon," Danny said.

Percy didn't move right away. His hands gripped the bottle at the neck, but his knuckles whitened, like he was about to wring it dry. For a second, Danny thought the old man might refuse, that he'd stand there with the bottle in hand and let the silence turn the moment sour. But in the end, Percy's face softened, or maybe he just got tired.

"You're the boss," he said, and the whiskey splashed in. Percy pushed a glass of water toward Danny with the back of his hand, so it was less an offer than a gesture, a habit he'd picked up after too many funerals. The water wobbled, left a trail of rings on the bar. Danny didn't touch it.

A few regulars hunched over the nearest table, playing hands of a familiar game with a deck of cards so bent they looked like paperbacks run through the wash. The miners wore their coveralls even here, the dust ground in so deep that you could never tell if they were freshly off shift or if they'd finally bought a new set of dark ones. The men didn't talk much, just grunted at the cards, but every once in a while, a burst of laughter would echo out, too sharp and too loud, like a joke nobody heard but everyone still got.

By the pool table, Billy stood alone, save for a couple trying to ignore him, cradling the dregs of a pitcher as he bumped against the pool cue stand. The laughter of the Gutter Choir had faded, leaving only echoes of their raucous camaraderie. He wiped his nose with the back of his sleeve, a habit born from years of dust and drink, and muttered something about the price of heating oil that drew a few half-hearted chuckles from a group of drunks huddled nearby. The weight of loss hung heavy in the air, an unspoken reminder of the two who had slipped away last year, leaving Billy as the last note in a song long forgotten. In this dimly lit bar, where shadows danced like memories, Danny watched him, wondering if Billy even remembered the sound of laughter without the haze of whiskey clouding his mind.

The whole place was falling in on itself, and the only thing propping it up was the stubborn routine of men who had nowhere else to go. Danny liked it that way. The sameness. The way even the rot was predictable.

He caught Percy watching him again.

"You ever consider eating something?" Percy said, real quiet. "A sandwich maybe. Or hell, even a plate of fries."

Danny shrugged. "Whiskey's got calories."

"Not enough to keep a man alive," Percy said.

Danny smiled, but it was a crooked thing. "Not the plan. A man don't drink for living. Drinking is for living with somethin'."

Percy wiped down the bar with the rag that had once been white, his swollen knuckles pressed it into the wood grain. His eyes lingered on the empty seats where Tommy and Floyd used to sit before the stress of the mine and life took them both last winter. When he looked up at Danny, his gaze paused at the yellow tinge creeping into the whites of Danny's eyes, then dropped to the tremor in his left hand. It was the same tremor Percy's brother had developed six months before they found him cold in his truck.

The whiskey bit harder on that last round, or maybe it was just the nerves catching up. He let it ride out, the heat, the slow fade. On the TV, a commercial for a car dealership played on repeat, the volume down but the colors so loud they burned out the corner of his eye.

The miners at the card table hit a lull, the quiet thickening as the hand ended. One of them, face scarred with an old burn, glanced at Danny and nodded, just once, then went back to the game. A nod of solidarity. Or maybe just a nod of "I see you, and I know what you're going through." It was the only connection Danny wanted.

He looked down the bar, past the bottles lined up like headstones, to the door. The light through the glass was purple-black, the kind of night that only happened this time of year, when the sun gave up and let the dark have its way. Every time someone came in, the temperature dropped ten degrees, a little winter backhand just to remind you that the outside world was even less forgiving.

Danny sipped at the fresh glass, slower now, just enough to get the charred barrel and vanilla on his tongue. The taste took him back, not in a good way. He remembered his father at this same bar, back when the town was less dead, when men could still buy a future here if they had enough credit or the luck to work a long seam. His father never drank to numb. He drank to sharpen, to get meaner, to outlast the day. Danny hated that about him. Hated it so much he made a whole life out of doing something different. But sometimes, in the way his jaw set or the way he licked the rim of the glass before every sip, he saw the old man looking back.

Percy caught him in the memory. "You know," he said, voice soft, "I watched you grow up in here."

Danny grimaced. "I tried to forget."

Percy's mouth twitched. "You ever hear from Shelby?"

Danny flinched, just enough for Percy to notice. The question was a knife. "No," Danny said.

Percy didn't push. He knew better.

Billy started up a song, as if the rest of the Gutter Choir could join in from the grave, his voice rising in a drunken, ugly harmony with the neon sign outside. "Take you home, country boats," all the verses wrong, all the timing off. Danny stared at the cracks in the bar, the way the lacquer had peeled back to bare wood in a dozen places. He traced the lines with a fingertip, wondering how many more nights it would take to wear it down to dust.

After the last glass, the world started to numb a little. Danny welcomed it. The sick comfort of it. He let the voices in the bar blur together, the conversations and laughter mixing into a white noise that held him in place. It was like being underwater, but the pressure was on the inside, squeezing all the empty out.

He caught a reflection of himself in the mirror behind the bar. His face carried the years. Cheeks carved shallow, eyes shadowed in ashen rings. At his throat, the key caught a dull glint in the wan light. He reached up, thumbed the edge, and wondered what it would take to let it go.

The water glass sat untouched, sweating a puddle onto the bar. Danny pulled it toward him, then watched as the droplets slid down the glass, merging and then breaking apart again. He remembered the rain in Savannah, the way it drummed on the windows and drowned out every thought. He missed that sound. He missed anything that could make him forget.

Percy dropped a few ice cubes in the water, "You ever think about leaving again? Changing somethin' and givin' it another shot?" the old man asked.

Danny laughed, a short bark. "Got nothing left to chase."

"Sometimes that's when you need to run the most."

Danny let that hang in the air. He didn't have a reply. He drank some of the water, pushing the whiskey glass to the side for now.

The miners at the table started up another hand, the slap of cards sharp in the hush. Someone lost a bet, tossed a nickel into a growing pile at the center, then grumbled about the game being rigged. The others just snorted and played on.

Billy had run out of song, but not out of voice. He started telling a story, something about a deer he hit on the way back from Lexington. The story had gotten wilder with each time Danny heard it, the deer turning into a moose, then a bear, then finally a state trooper who tried to ticket them for "animal endangerment." The punchline made the table shake, but Danny didn't even crack a smile.

The whiskey had warmed him, but only on the way down. The water sent a chill to the rest of him.

At some point, a man in a brown jacket, like his father used to wear came in, ordered a beer, and sat at the far end of the bar. He nursed the bottle like it was a child, never looked up from the label. Danny didn't recognize him, but it was hard to tell these days. Everyone looked the same in the Hollow, especially after dark.

Percy made his rounds, checking on the miners, clearing the empties, topping off Billy's pitcher with a practiced tilt. He made it a point to skip over the man in the brown jacket, like he was invisible. Or maybe just already gone.

Danny's water glass was empty. He slid it across the bar, careful not to tip it over. Percy filled it with a steady hand.

"You sure you don't want to eat something?" Percy said, one last try.

"Not tonight," Danny said.

Percy nodded.

Danny raised the glass in a silent salute, then drained it in one go.

He let his head fall forward, chin to chest. Not out of a drunken stupor, more like a drained soul. The buzz he had going was less than the slow buzz of the light above the bar. The world moved different here, slower and heavier, like it didn't want to get to tomorrow.

He closed his eyes, the whiskey and water settling like sediment at the bottom of a creek and waited for to hit, anything.

He could have stayed that way forever. Or at least until closing.

But then, something changed.

The door creaked open, letting in a gust of cold air and the smell of wet asphalt. There was laughter in it, bright and sharp, the kind of laugh that didn't belong in a place like this.

Danny looked up, and the whole bar turned with him.

Daisy Whitaker walked in like she was arriving at a party thrown in her honor, and maybe she was. She wore a denim jacket with faux fur on the collar, a dress the color of clear skies. Her hair was gold spun up high, held in place by a ribbon that used to be pink and was now the faded blush of old lipstick. She carried a purse that was more rhinestone than fabric, swinging it like a dare. Behind her trailed two boys; brothers, maybe.

She stopped just inside, gave her hair a little pat, and scanned the room. The miners tried to look like they hadn't noticed, but every one of them sat up a little straighter. Even Billy, drunk as a stone, stopped mid-joke to take her in. Daisy smiled at the attention, then let it go, as if she was used to being the last real thing left in a dead town.

She picked her way across the floor, boots clipping hard, and chose a booth along the back wall. The brothers tumbled in after her, knocking elbows and jostling for space. She slid in, took center, and let the men arrange themselves as best they could. The table filled up with noise: the clink of glass, the shuffle of cheap cigarettes, the undertow of longing that always followed her like a bad scent.

Danny grabbed his refilled water and watched her, trying not to stare, but every time he blinked, his eyes drifted back. The way her shoulders squared, how she lifted her chin just a little when she laughed, the curve of her mouth when she said something that made the brothers flinch. She owned every second, every inch of the booth, every gaze in the place.

He felt something stir in his chest, a pulse of heat he'd thought he'd left behind in Savannah or maybe buried for good after seeing Shelby at the diner. It scared him, how easy it was.

Percy noticed the shift, saw the way Danny's water glass hovered just short of his lips.

"That there's trouble walking," Percy said, low and steady. "Daisy Whitaker. Pretty as a picture and twice as expensive."

Danny didn't answer. He just watched her, the way she let the men argue over who'd buy her next drink, the little flick of her hand that signaled the winner. She leaned in, close enough to whisper, but kept her eyes on the mirror behind the bar, tracking every move, every glance.

"You know her?" Percy said, not looking up from the glass he polished.

Danny shook his head. "Didn't know anyone still lived anywhere near here with that much light left in them."

Percy huffed, a sound halfway between a laugh and a cough. "She's got more sense than any of the boys she runs with. None of 'em last long, though. She'll use 'em up, toss the shells, move on. Never the same one twice."

Danny's fingers tightened around the glass. "What's she want?"

"Same thing as the rest of us. Not to be here."

Daisy's head tipped back in laughter, the ribbon catching the bar light. The brothers talked over each other, but it was clear she'd already picked the favorite. She let him scoot closer, pressed her thigh to his, made a show of brushing his arm with her hand. The other brother scowled, nursed his beer, and sulked. Daisy ignored him. Or maybe she liked it that way.

Danny lost the thread of time, just watched the scene unfold in fragments: Daisy's lips around a straw, her eyes flicking up to catch him in the mirror, the way she twisted her ankle in the boot so the heel tapped out a nervous rhythm. He felt the itch in his palms, the old compulsion to write it down, but there was nothing to capture in a song that wouldn't sound fake.

Percy filled the water glass again, insistent. "Might want to keep your wits about you, boy. Daisy's not for amateurs."

Danny smiled, not breaking his gaze from the booth. "Don't worry, I'm out of the game."

But even as he said it, he knew it was a lie. The truth was in the way his heart sped up when she looked his way. The truth was in the throb in his jaw, the itch in his teeth. He was already in, whether he wanted it or not.

At the back booth, Daisy leaned in and whispered something in the favorite brother's ear. The man grinned, but it was the nervous kind, the grin of someone who didn't know what he'd just agreed to. Daisy let the silence stretch, then laughed again, loud enough for everyone to hear.

She caught Danny's eyes then, right in the mirror. She didn't look away. She just smiled, slow and sure, and raised her glass to him.

Danny lifted his own in response, the water cooling down his throat. He set it back on the bar. The miners at the card table had turned to watch, their faces slack with awe or maybe dread. Billy, not to be outdone, started up another round, louder this time, but nobody cared.

The bar was hers now. Everyone knew it.

The clock above the bar counted the minutes, slow and stubborn. Outside, the wind howled against the glass, trying to get in. Inside, everything was illuminating, and sharp, and dangerous.

For the first time since he'd come home, Danny felt something in his chest besides cold.

He didn't know if it was hope or hunger, but he wanted to see how far it could go before it broke him.

He felt Jimmy Carter before he saw him; a stink of cigarettes and cheap beer, the rattle of a half-empty flask being thumped on the bar. The name on the birth certificate was James, but nobody called him that since grade school, not even his mother. "Half Pint" suited him better, a man who never measured up to a full one.

"Hey, looky here," Jimmy slurred, breath thick as engine grease, "White Oak Hollow's favorite son, returned from the big time. I'm honored. Should I take my hat off, or my pants?"

He dropped onto the barstool next to Danny, bringing a halo of bad spirit with him. A half-drunk glass of beer, still sweating cold, sat just beyond Danny's elbow. Jimmy came in from the left, snatched it up like it had been waiting on him, and dragged it close. The pull tipped the rim, sending a thin spill down Danny's arm. Jimmy watched it run, then met Danny's eyes with a grin sharp enough to cut, mocking, like the spill was the punchline he'd been waiting to deliver.

"Sorry, friend," Jimmy said, not sorry at all. He wiped the spill with his bare hand, then licked the foam from his palm.

Danny took a breath through his nose and stared forward. "You need something, Half Pint?"

Jimmy let out a cackle, a bark more than a laugh. "Just company. I figure misery ought to stick together. Maybe start a club." He flagged Percy with a two-finger wave. "Get my pal here another, yeah?"

Percy eyed Jimmy, then Danny, and poured one for each, slow. Jimmy's hand hovered over his own glass, waiting for Danny to pick his up.

"On me," he said. "Least I could do, given how the world's gone and all." Danny grabbed his water.

He took a long swallow from his own glass, then leaned in, elbow bracing on the sticky surface. "So, what brings you back? Homesick for the smell of failure, or just missed your parole officer, Earl?"

Danny let the insult glide off. "Just passing through."

Jimmy rolled his eyes, the whites gone yellow. "Bullshit. You don't 'pass through' the Hollow, not unless your car breaks down or your luck runs out. And I heard you left your luck in Savannah, Tennessee, or somewhere, maybe with some waitress and a bottle of Jack."

The air in the bar dropped a few degrees. Danny felt it, the whole room pressing in, waiting for someone to make the first move.

Jimmy kept going, voice getting lower. "Saw you staring at Daisy. You got a thing for that, don't you? Broken toys. Used to be Shelby. Now it's the girl who can't keep her purse strings or her bedsheets tied shut."

Danny's jaw tensed so hard he thought he'd crack a tooth.

Jimmy leaned closer, breath hot and foul. "Let me give you a tip, straight from the heart. She don't want you, Wallace. Not unless you got money, or a truck that ain't held together with hope and spit. She wants out, and she'll ride whatever's got the biggest engine."

Danny turned to face him, slow. "You done?"

Jimmy grinned. "Not even started. You know how many men she's run through? Hell, I been on deck a couple times myself, and I guarantee you she'd pick me over..."

Danny's hand came up, fast, catching Jimmy's wrist mid-air as he pointed. The bar went silent. Even Billy shut up, waiting.

Jimmy's face changed, the bluster crumbling for a second. He tried to yank back, but Danny held on, grip like a vise.

"Say one more word about her," Danny said, voice cold as the night outside, "and I'll pour the rest of that drink down your throat, glass and all."

Jimmy pulled back, but there was nowhere to go. The men at the card table froze, not sure if they should intervene or let the show play out.

Percy stepped in, hand landing heavy on Jimmy's shoulder. "That's enough, Half Pint. Go sleep it off."

Jimmy tried to protest, but Percy's grip was stronger than Danny's. He wrenched free of Danny's hand, half-falling from the stool, and staggered back. He glared at Danny, but it was a weak thing now, nothing behind it but old jealousy.

"You think you're better than us?" Jimmy spat, voice shaking. "You're just a broke miner who couldn't cut it. You'll die here like the rest of us."

Danny watched him go, the echo of his words hanging in the air like smoke.

Percy stayed a moment, then gave Danny a look, half

warning, half apology, and went to settle up Jimmy's tab. The room buzzed with whispers, but no one looked Danny's way. They all knew what Jimmy was, and they all knew what Danny was, too.

Danny pushed away the glass Jimmy bought him. That whiskey would've carried the taste of spite and sour grudges, not the memory Danny wanted to tie to Percy's tonight.

He glanced at the back booth. Daisy was watching, her eyes dark and wide, her mouth curled in a smile that could have been anything, pity, pride, invitation. She held the gaze, then raised her glass to him, same as before. This time, she tipped it back, emptied it in one long pull, and slammed it on the table. The brothers stared at her, then at Danny, unsure what had just passed between them.

Danny smiled, just barely. He didn't move. He let the moment stretch, let Daisy watch him, let the whole bar feel the electric charge in the air.

Billy started up a new song, something sad and slow, and the world seemed to settle back into its rut.

But for Danny, nothing felt settled. For the first time in a long time, he felt alive, blood hot and sharp under the skin.

He wiped the wet from his sleeve and stared across the bar at Daisy Whitaker.

She stared right back, fire in her eyes, the space between them sparking like a fuse.

He knew it was stupid. He knew it was dangerous.

But in that moment, Danny Wallace wanted nothing more than to see what happened next.

*A face is just a record sleeve for
the soul's soundtrack.*

CURRENCY OF DESIRE

Danny nursed the last inch of his water and watched Daisy in the booth. The brothers looked like men who'd paid for more than a pitcher and were starting to realize they'd bought nothing at all. She let them hover; one on her left, already slumped with an arm half-behind her, the other sharp-eyed and waiting for his turn. Daisy sat dead center, her back straight as if she owned the whole damn bench, one leg crossed over the other, heel tapping out a message in Morse code no one else could read.

The bluntness of her stare shifted, recast into a coy disguise. She seemed to know exactly how long to make a man wait, how long before he started to sweat. Danny tried not to play the part, but by the time he got up and crossed the floor, he could feel the blood in his face, the tremor in his hands.

He moved through the bar like he was late for a funeral. He could feel Percy's gaze at his back, the regulars at the table going hush, the air flattening around him as the whole room recalibrated to Daisy's gravity. He'd never been good at walking into things. He just hoped his knees wouldn't betray him before he made it to her booth.

She looked up only when he was close enough to count the smudges in her mascara. Her eyes cut through the low-lit haze, unblinking and blue as a bruise. The corner of her mouth bent into something between a smile and a warning.

"Evenin'," she said. The word hung in the air like a lure.

The left-side brother made a noise, cleared his throat, and straightened up. "You need something?" he said to Danny, trying for menace but landing closer to wounded. His fist clamped the beer glass, steady but shaking at the edges.

Daisy didn't break eye contact with Danny. She patted the cushion to her right. "Sit, if you've got a mind to." She didn't look at the brother that had been sitting there, didn't even flick her wrist to excuse him, but he got the message. He shrank back, lips pressed in a line.

Danny sat. He left a respectable gap between them, but Daisy fixed that by scooting closer. Her thigh pressed warm through his jeans, not quite a touch, but close enough to call it a dare.

"You're Wallace, right?" she said, her gaze flicking to the key at his throat. "Heard you were good with a guitar."

Danny felt the scar on his thumb tingle. "Not as good as the stories."

She laughed, not the bright thing from across the bar but a private, low-slung sound that made him feel like he'd already passed a test. "They say you left for Nashville. Didn't think you'd come back."

"Couldn't cut it," Danny said, truth ugly in his mouth.

She let the silence stand. The brothers were watching, waiting for her to throw them a bone, but Daisy ignored them. She reached across Danny, plucked the sweat-ringed glass from his hand, and drained it. When she set it back, her fingers lingered, tracing the rim before sliding off and brushing the back of his hand.

"You still working the slope?" she asked, eyes narrowing.

"Yeah, when I can. Not much else pays."

Daisy's hand drifted to his wrist, her thumb finding the black under his nails, the old burn scars. She looked at his hands the way you'd look at a tool, or maybe a pet, something useful, something that might bite. "Strong hands," she said. "My daddy always said you could tell a man's worth by the shape of his grip."

Danny pulled his hand away, but she caught it, pressed it flat on the table. The brothers exchanged glances, unsure if they should be jealous or just embarrassed. The left one tried to recover his spot, leaning forward, but Daisy shut him down with a single look.

"Why'd you come back?" she said, her thumb riding the tendon in his wrist. Her nails were painted a chipped red, ringed with tiny flecks of gold. "Most don't."

Danny considered lying. But the weight of her hand made it impossible.

"Didn't have a choice," he said. "Got to where the city felt like a bad joke." Shifting focus back to her, "You ever get past this place?"

She shook her head, hair sweeping over her collarbone. "Not for long. I got close once. Had a ride lined up and everything but something kept me." Her voice dropped half an octave. "You believe in fate, Wallace?"

Danny almost said yes. He almost said he'd spent the last two years convincing himself there was some reason to every bad turn, every shit card he got dealt. But the truth was, he believed in nothing except the next shift and the bottom of the glass.

"Maybe," he said.

Daisy's eyes went soft for a second, as if she was listening to a song only she could hear. Then she let go of his hand, leaned back, and signaled Percy for another round with a snap of her fingers. It was the kind of move that would look cruel on anyone else, but on Daisy, it felt like a performance. A man couldn't get mad at her for it. Not really.

The right-side brother tried again. "Daisy, you gonna introduce us to your friend?"

She didn't even look at him. "You boys know Wallace, don't you? He used to play at the county fair when we were younger. They say he could make you cry with a single chord."

Danny tried but couldn't remember ever having seen Daisy at the fair, or anywhere for that matter.

The right-side brother looked like he wanted to disagree, but he just grunted.

"Bet you can't play worth a damn anymore," he said.

Danny shrugged. "You're probably right."

Percy brought the new drinks. He set them on the table with a nod to Daisy, then retreated quick as a mouse.

Daisy picked up her glass, swirled the whiskey, and watched the way the ice orbited inside. "I always thought music was a waste of time," she said. "You can't buy anything with a song."

Danny smiled, first real one of the night. "You can buy something," he said. "Just not for yourself. Every song seems to take something away."

She raised her glass to that, sipped, then licked the moisture off her lips. "Maybe you can give me that something someday."

It was a threat and a promise. Danny felt it ripple through him, tight and electric.

She set her drink down, then reached over and straightened the collar of his shirt, fingers lingering on the edge of the key.

"I like that," she said. "It suits you. I was wondering who you were keeping a secret for."

Danny didn't answer. He could smell her perfume now, a clean citrus that cut through the rot of beer and old smoke. He let her hand rest on his shoulder.

"Tell me a secret, Wallace," she said. "Tell me something you never told anyone."

He wanted to say he missed Shelby, that he still dreamed about her hands, the way her breath would hitch when she was about to laugh, that the only reason he kept the key was because it was the last thing he had that belonged to her. But Daisy didn't want to hear that, and he didn't want to say it.

"I sometimes wish I'd never left," he said, quiet.

She laughed again, eyes glittering. "Everyone here wishes they'd left. Except you, I guess." She cocked her head, studied him. "You're different than I pictured."

Danny looked away, embarrassed. "You're exactly what I was hearing around," he said, then regretted it immediately.

Daisy's mouth curved, pleased. "I hope so," she said. "I work hard at it."

The brothers were restless now, glancing at each other, then at Daisy. The left one mumbled something about having to work in the morning, stood, and left the booth. The other hesitated, then followed, shoulders hunched. Daisy didn't say goodbye.

She edged closer to Danny, her knee pressing hard against his. "You ever wonder what your life would've been if you'd made different choices?"

He wanted to say yes, that he spent every night doing nothing but that, but he just shrugged. "Everyone has regrets."

She nodded, leaned in until her cheek almost grazed his. Her breath was warm, alive. "What's yours?" she whispered.

Danny felt the answer wedge itself in his throat, heavy as coal dust.

"Don't know...yet," he said.

She smiled, touched the spot just above his heart. "Let me know when you figure it out."

He didn't trust himself to speak. Daisy's fingers drummed a little pattern on his chest, then slid down, slow, to the flat of his stomach. She sat back, eyes never leaving his.

"You got anywhere to be tonight?" she asked, voice easy.

"No," he said. "Not really."

"Good," she replied. "You can buy me another drink."

He didn't argue. He flagged Percy, ordered two more. The rest of the bar faded away. Just a hum of voices, a flicker of light on glass, the slow melt of ice remained. Daisy stretched her legs out under the table, her boots running the length of his shins. She talked about the Hollow like it was a punchline, told stories of the women who'd raised her, of men who'd promised the world and delivered nothing. She punctuated her tales with a laugh that had edge to it, like a knife honed for cutting off hope at the neck.

Danny found himself talking more than he meant to. He told her about the mines, about the time he'd nearly lost a finger, about the weight in his chest that never went away. She listened with that same flat-eyed focus, nodding only when he said something that made her smile.

"Why don't you play anywhere anymore?" she asked, near midnight.

He looked at his hands, flexed them. "Hasn't felt right since I came back."

"That's the saddest thing I ever heard," she said. But her hand slipped into his, and she squeezed it hard.

They drank. They talked. At some point, Daisy's head fell onto his shoulder, and she left it there, warm and heavy, as if it belonged.

He didn't want the night to end. He didn't want to go home alone.

When the bar thinned out and Percy started stacking chairs on tables, Daisy nudged his ribs, then slid from the booth. She pulled him up after her. "Let's walk," she said.

He followed her out into the night, the Hollow so quiet he could hear rodents scurry into the storm drains.

She didn't take his hand, but she didn't have to. He'd have followed her anywhere.

At the corner, she turned, planted her feet, and looked at him. She reached up, traced the line of his jaw with a thumb.

"I like you, Wallace," she said. "You're not what I expected."

She stood on her tiptoes, kissed him hard, then

pulled back and grinned.

"You can see me again, if you want. Tomorrow, earlier though. Bring something nice. Give Daisy her due," she said trailing off to a whisper.

She walked away, hair a gold banner with a pink streamer in the streetlight.

He stood there, heart pounding, the world tilting under his boots.

Danny wondered what tomorrow would cost him, and if he'd ever find the bottom of the well she'd just thrown him into.

He wasn't sure he cared.

The next night, Percy's felt emptier, though the regulars were all there. Maybe it was the way Daisy slid into the booth before the sun was even down, or maybe it was the color of her dress. Plum this time, not blue, tight enough at the waist to make the room seem smaller. Danny walked in, hands shoved in his jacket, the black from the day's shift still under his nails.

Daisy raised a hand, called him over. No brothers in tow tonight, just the space she'd reserved for him, marked by two drinks already sweating on the table.

He sat, and she leaned in, her perfume heavier than before, sharp enough to bite. She fixed on him with a smile that showed every tooth. "Wasn't sure you'd show."

"Couldn't keep you waiting," he said, and hoped it sounded like a joke.

She laughed, just once. "Good. I can't stand a man who's slow."

Danny picked up the glass, let the ice numb the tips of his fingers. Daisy watched him, her head tilted, eyes darting from his face to his hands and back again.

"So," she said, "how's the slope? You working doubles yet?"

"Starting tomorrow, I think," Danny replied. "Pays more. Less people to trip over on the second shift."

Daisy pursed her lips, then reached across the table and caught his wrist. She turned his hand palm-up, thumb grazing the old split scar and the new calluses. "I bet you're strong," she said, her voice lower, for him alone.

He felt the tremor start in his fingers, ripple up to his shoulder.

She held on, didn't blink. "You know what I admire most in a man?" she whispered, as if anyone cared to overhear. "Work ethic. A man who doesn't quit when he's tired or broke or sad. My daddy used to say you could tell the winners from the rest just by how they held a shovel."

Danny flushed. "Never figured myself for a winner."

Daisy laughed again. "Oh, honey. Winning is just about surviving longer than the other guy."

She set his hand down, then traced a finger along the rim of her glass. "You get paid every week, or every other?" she asked.

"Every Friday, if the checks clear right away," he said. The question caught him off guard, but the way she asked made it sound almost innocent.

She smiled. "Good. That's how you know it's real work." Her gaze flicked to his jacket, the threadbare sleeves, then back to his face. "You ever think about what you'd do if you had real money?"

Danny shook his head. "Never had enough to consider it."

Daisy leaned closer, the light from the bar catching

her pink ribbon, throwing shadows across her cheek-bones. "If I had it, I'd be gone. New York, Miami, somewhere the air doesn't taste like burnt hair and regret."

She ran her finger along his wrist again, nails scraping just enough to raise goosebumps. "What about you?"

He thought of Shelby, the time they'd dreamed out loud about getting away. How they'd laughed at the idea, knowing neither would ever leave for good. He shoved the memory down, focused on Daisy's hand.

"I'd buy a better guitar," he said. "Maybe a car that didn't sound like a dying animal."

She grinned, all satisfaction. "That's a start."

She let her hand slip from his, then raised her glass, catching the rim with her mouth. Her tongue lingered a heartbeat too long, tasting the bourbon like it held a secret.

"A woman like me," she said, almost idly, "doesn't settle for little...and never leaves empty-handed."

Danny almost choked. "You looking for a provider?"

She gave him a look that could have meant anything. "I'm looking for someone who can keep up," she said. "Someone who won't choke when things get hard."

The word hung there. Danny coughed, tried to laugh it off. "Don't know if I'm your guy."

She shrugged, but her eyes said otherwise. "You could be."

She finished her glass, then ran both hands back through her hair, resetting it. The movement drew every eye in the bar, but she only looked at Danny.

"You see, Wallace, I don't have time for games. If you want me, you'll have to earn it."

He tried to meet her stare, but it felt like staring into

a headlamp. "How does someone do that?"

She smiled, slow and wide. "Start by bringing me something nice, pretty. A gift. Flowers, or a trinket, or maybe just something that proves you've got skin in the game. My love language is gifting. My lust language is being gifted to."

He nodded, not trusting himself to speak and not really knowing where to go with that information.

She laughed, softer this time, and let her hand settle on his knee under the table. "You're cute when you're nervous."

He gripped the edge of the bench, knuckles white. "I'm not nervous."

She squeezed his knee. "You're a terrible liar," she said, but she liked it.

For a while, they just sat, the hum of the bar smoothing out the awkwardness. Danny stared at her hands, the way her fingers toyed with the hem of her dress, the shape of her wrist. He remembered Shelby's hands, the way they'd tremble when she was happy, and felt a flash of guilt. But Daisy's hand was real, now, and she knew exactly how to get what she wanted.

She leaned in again, voice just above a whisper. "Tomorrow night. Same time. Don't disappoint me."

He felt the breath catch in his chest. "I won't."

Daisy kissed his cheek, left a print of bourbon and lipstick. "You better not," she said.

She stood, gathered her purse, and glided out of the booth. For a second, he thought she'd leave without looking back. But at the door, she turned, caught his eye, and winked.

The door swung shut behind her, and Danny sat there, the warmth of her touch burning through his jeans. He reached for his drink, and found his hands shaking.

He finished both glasses, then sat in the empty booth, staring at the grooves in the table. The world seemed small and mean, but Daisy's words echoed, louder than anything else in the room.

He wanted to see her again, needed to. But he knew the cost would be more than he could pay.

He didn't care. Not yet. He felt like a kid in a candy store who just needed a fist full of dollars to buy all the happiness he wanted.

Danny left the bar in a haze of hunger and cheap whiskey, the ache in his hands outdone only by the ache somewhere lower. The street was empty, the houses along Main closed up, lights off, like everyone had agreed to sleep through whatever storm was brewing inside him.

He didn't go home. He didn't want to face the room with its cracks in the ceiling and the mattress that reeked of old sweat and older hope. Instead, he headed for the mine, letting the rhythm of his boots on the wet pavement set the pace. Every step, he heard Daisy's voice, the edge of it, the way she'd curled her hand around his knee and told him to bring her something nice. He wanted her to want him. He wanted it so bad he could taste it, salt and iron, same as the air around the mine.

Percy must've watched him go but didn't call after. Maybe the old man knew there was nothing left to say.

The road to the slope was all ruts and puddles, the kind that sucked at your boots and threatened to leave you barefoot if you didn't keep moving. The mine's floodlights flickered at the far end, painting the world in yellow stripes and black voids. The only sign of life was the hum of the conveyors and the lonely figure on the bucket outside the shed.

Earl McKinney sat there, smoking a hand-rolled cigarette and staring at nothing. He wore the same coveralls as every other night, sleeves up, collar open, a flash of white T-shirt underneath. The gray in his hair caught the light, made him look older than the dirt he worked.

Danny stopped just outside the glow, letting his eyes adjust. Earl saw him, raised a brow, and flicked the cigarette butt into the mud.

"Wallace," Earl said, voice barely above the noise of the mine. "Didn't expect to see you tonight."

"Need to talk," Danny said.

Earl gestured at the barrel next to him. "Sit."

Danny didn't. He crossed his arms instead, tried to steady the shake.

"I want double shifts," he said. "Starting tomorrow."

Earl stared, then spat. "You got a death wish, or just a gambling habit you ain't told me about?"

Danny shook his head. "Just need the money."

Earl squinted at him, then grinned, a slow, ugly thing. "Some girl got her hooks in you? I figured you'd last longer than most."

Danny bristled. "Ain't about a girl."

Earl laughed, deep and wet. "It's always about a girl. Don't lie to an old man, Wallace." He stood, flicked dust from his hands. "You know what double shifts do to a body?"

"Yeah," Danny said, voice flat. "You've told me every day."

"Didn't slow you, either," Earl said, almost admiring. "Alright. You show up at six, I'll put your name down for the double. Just don't pass out in the muck like Billy did. Took two men and a backhoe to fish him out."

Danny nodded. The noise of the slope wound up for a new cycle. He glanced at the black opening in the hillside, the lipless mouth of it, the way it never seemed to change no matter how much rock they pulled out.

Earl followed his gaze. "That's what's waiting for you," he said. "A hole you'll never fill, no matter how hard you try. The mine, the road, and what has you baited...it sucks the soul out of you if you ain't paying attention."

Danny tried to think of something smart to say, but all that came out was, "It's work."

Earl grunted. "Ain't nothing else, is there?"

He patted Danny's shoulder, hard. "Don't let her bleed you dry, son. Get what you want, but don't give it all away."

Danny watched as Earl ground out another cigarette, then went back into the light, boots tracking mud. He stood alone for a long time, listening to the steady whine of the mine, the shiver in his bones slowly going quiet.

He looked into the dark, felt the hunger open inside him.

If Daisy wanted proof, he'd bring her the world, one double shift at a time.

He'd never felt more alive...or more empty.

He walked home in the wet, hands raw, the taste of her on his lips, and every footstep counting down to the next paycheck.

THE WEIGHT OF WHAT WAS

Earl promised him all the shifts he wanted, and Danny clung to the promise like it might drown out Daisy's sly smile, knowing that she wasn't good for him. She vowed to fill the hollow with something real, though it was desire, not devotion, that set the terms.

She'd spoken of a county fair long gone, of a boy with a guitar who'd never seen her. The memory wasn't his, but the weight of it pressed down all the same.

Danny thought work would smother the past, but the past had its own timetable.

❊ ❊ ❊

Back in White Oak Hollow, nine months earlier, Shelby Boone's father was already laying the stones for a future she hadn't chosen. And miles away from Pulaski County, Daisy Whitaker was already moving toward the Hollow, carrying secrets of her own.

The Boone house wasn't much from the road, two stories gone to mildew at the gutters, porch swing chained more for show than use, but inside, everything shined. The walls glowed with the patina of old wood polish, every nail hole filled, every corner scrubbed. The dining room was set for four, table stretched with a starched runner, the good plates and the little crystal salt cellars Shelby's mother only dusted for guests. Tonight, Thomas Wilcox was the guest. He sat at the end of the table, hands folded over his napkin, watching Shelby with the polite intensity of a man who'd been warned about her before he'd ever spoken to her.

Shelby's father orchestrated the evening like a man conducting a slow parade. He worked through the main course with stories about local politics and the price of seed, every sentence swinging back to Thomas and his steady promotion at the bank.

"People need a man of numbers, especially with this economy," her father said, nodding to himself. "It's honest work. Not like those new schemes on the internet, all smoke and mirrors."

Thomas smiled, but only because he thought it was expected. "Well, sir, we're just trying to keep the community afloat."

Her father beamed, satisfied, and started in on his second drumstick. Shelby's mother, at the other end, hovered between the kitchen and table, tucking flyaways behind her ear, checking the biscuits, pouring sweet tea before you realized your glass was low.

Shelby looked at the roast chicken on her plate, then at her hands. She hadn't even cut into it. She pushed the peas around with her fork, watched them roll and cluster, then split apart under gentle pressure. She wondered if it was possible to vanish by will alone.

"You still painting, Shell?" her father asked, the question an accusation. "Or are you done with that phase?"

She shrugged. "I still paint."

Thomas perked up, seizing the thread. "What do you like to paint?"

She considered lying, say landscapes, or dogs, or some other thing a bank man could approve of, but said, "Faces. Not real people. Just ones I make up."

Thomas nodded, thoughtful. "That's nice. I wish I had a creative bone, but I guess I'm more of a numbers guy."

Her father clapped the table, making the silver rattle. "It's a good thing! Artists don't eat steady."

Her mother shot him a look, a small frown that traveled the table and landed in Shelby's lap. "Not everyone paints to be famous, Bill. Some people do it for the joy of it."

Her father chewed for a moment, then said, "Sure. But the world don't run on joy."

Shelby listened to the rhythm of their voices, the scrape of fork on plate, the hollow thump of her own pulse in her ears. She tried to picture herself across from Thomas Wilcox every night for the next fifty years, his hair going thin, his shirtsleeves rolled exactly two times, his laugh even and contained. She thought of Danny's hands, the way he picked at a guitar string until it broke, the way he could never sit through a whole dinner without saying something to make her mother blush or her father bristle.

Her mother brought out a pie, blackberry, still hot. "You like blackberry, Thomas?"

"My favorite," he said, polite to the end.

Shelby took a slice, let the color bleed into the white plate. She touched her tongue to it and tasted only sugar and memory. She wanted to tell her mother about the time she and Danny picked wild berries out past the hollow, hands purple to the wrist, both of them so sticky they had to wash in the creek, how they'd laughed at the cold, and how she'd never felt more alive than that summer. She wanted to tell the story, but she knew how it would be received, the hush that would follow, the way her father would mutter "delinquent" and her mother would change the subject to the weather.

So, she said nothing.

After dessert, her father set down his fork and declared, "It's a nice night for a walk. Why don't you kids stretch your legs before it gets too dark?" He didn't wait for an answer, just got up and excused himself, leaving a trail of aftershave and authority in his wake.

Her mother stacked plates with a quiet efficiency. "Take a jacket, Shell. The wind's coming up."

Outside, the sky had faded to a dusky blue. The porch light flickered, chased by moths. Thomas walked beside her, careful not to step ahead, matching her pace as if she'd set it for both of them.

"I hope you don't mind your dad inviting me," he said, hands in his pockets. "I think he's worried you'll find somewhere else and forget all of us here."

Shelby laughed, short. "I doubt that. Most people forget me before I leave."

He stopped, looked at her. "Not me," he said. "I mean, you were the smartest in our year. Most people thought you'd end up a doctor, or a lawyer, or...something." His voice trailed. "I guess the bank is just another kind of prison, huh?"

She shrugged. "Guess it depends who holds the keys."

They walked in silence past the edge of the yard, out toward the strip of trees that shielded the Boone property from the town. The grass tickled her ankles. She felt the wind thread through her hair, lifting it away from her face, and thought of how Danny used to say her hair always smelled like rain, even in August.

"I heard from my dad you were with Danny Wallace for a while," Thomas said, not unkindly.

She looked at him, tried to read the angle. "I was."

"He's a legend at the barbershop. Whole town says he could be big someday."

She smiled, small and sad. "Whole town's never left the county line."

Thomas looked at her, and there was something like longing, but it was gentle, even apologetic. "You don't have to tell me," he said. "It's just...I know how it is, when you want out. And I'm sorry if this," he gestured to the house, the town, the sky, "feels like a cage."

They walked a little further. Thomas picked a seed pod from a bush and rolled it in his fingers. He watched it break apart, the little seeds scattering on the wind.

"My dad's already got me signed up for the church young singles club," he said. "He wants grandkids before he's fifty-five." He laughed. "I don't know if I want that, but I don't know what else there is."

She stopped, looked up at the darkening clouds. "You thinkin' about doing somethin' else, somewhere else?"

Thomas nodded, once. "All the time. But every time I try, something pulls me back." He shrugged, awkward. "Guess I'm just not brave enough."

Shelby felt the edges of herself blur, the sky bleeding into the trees, the world slipping between possibilities. She wanted to say she was sorry, that she understood, that she didn't blame him. But mostly she wanted to run, to fling herself into the creek and float down until she hit the river, then the ocean, then some place where nobody cared who she'd been with or what her father thought of her.

Instead, she walked beside Thomas, feeling the warmth of his arm and the easy cadence of his steps. She tried to imagine a life with him. Dinners like this one, kids who looked like him but maybe had her hands, Christmases spent in rooms like the one she grew up in. The thought was both comforting and suffocating.

They circled back to the porch. The lights inside were on, her mother's silhouette moving past the curtains, already resetting the table for breakfast. Shelby stood on the step, hands cold.

"Thanks for walking me," she said.

Thomas smiled, earnest and a little lost. "Anytime, Shelby. I mean that."

He hesitated, then said, "You ever want to talk about art, or music, or anything, let me know."

She nodded, and he walked off, the crunch of gravel under his shoes the only sound for a long time.

Shelby stood on the porch, letting the wind tear at her hair, watching the lights flicker down the road to where Thomas would disappear. She thought of Danny, of the letters he'd sent from Nashville, the way his handwriting grew smaller and sadder with each envelope. She wondered if he was thinking of her, if he could feel the weight of her indecision all the way down the tracks.

She closed her eyes, tried to breathe, and told herself she could live with the ache.

Inside, her mother waited at the kitchen table, a cup of tea in her hands, eyes gentle but sharp.

"You could do worse," her mother said, not unkind.

Shelby nodded, but didn't answer.

She went upstairs, left the light off, and sat on the edge of her bed, waiting for her heart to settle. In the dark, the world shrank to the square of window and the thin line of sky.

She listened to the wind, the house shifting, the slow tick of the clock, and wondered which part of herself she'd have to kill to survive this place.

Shelby's room was painted a soft green, but the color had faded to the shade of lost hope. Every inch of wall was claimed by posters, snapshots, and slivers of her old life. The rest of the space was cluttered with evidence of what she couldn't give up: the battered Polaroid of her and Danny in the parking lot at the Fourth of July fair, ticket stubs lined up by date from his shows on the road she couldn't go to, and the CD he'd made for her, "For When You Miss Me" scribbled in the margin in his sharp, nervous print.

It was past midnight and the house had gone quiet. She sat cross-legged on her bed, comforter pulled up to her chin, ringed by the stack of letters that had once arrived weekly, then monthly, then only when the guilt overcame him. The last envelope was thinner, the paper inside ragged at the edge. She'd read it four times since yesterday, but each word still felt new and wrong.

Hey Shell,

I know I said I'd call, but the gigs got longer and I've been working doubles at the bar to have enough for room and board. Sorry. I broke the screen on my phone, so it doesn't work as well as it used to. The guys I was playing with are gone, all of them. Manager says there's no room for original songs. I'm playing covers in a place called the Boogie Bar. Sometimes the tips are good, but mostly they're not. Last week I saw a guy get stabbed for a pitcher of Miller Lite. The city's meaner than all the papers make it out to be. Thinking maybe I'll head down to Savannah. I hear it picks up this time of year.

I want to come back, but I don't know if there's anything left for me there. Or if you even want me. I hope you do.

I think about you every night. I hope you're doing okay.

—Danny

She held the page to her face, tried to conjure his scent. Cigarettes, coffee, maybe the glue from the tape he wrapped around every broken thing he owned. There was nothing left but the faintest dust of old cologne, a smell so thin it broke her heart.

She wanted to cry but the tears wouldn't come, not yet. So, she set the letter down and played the CD, letting the old mix fill the air with scratchy guitars and three-chord confessionals. She played the first track on loop, the song they'd danced to that one winter night in his rented room, feet bare, the world outside lost under two feet of snow.

She let the memory in. Danny's voice in her ear, telling her he'd never seen anybody move like she did, that she was the only good thing he'd ever had. The way he'd held her, careful but sure, the keys to the future in his pocket and the whole world waiting if only they could hang on.

It hurt to think of him like that. It hurt worse to think of him sitting in a motel room, eating ramen and counting the days since she'd last written.

She pulled out a sheet of stationary, the last page with the bluebells in the corner, and uncapped the pen. Her hand shook as she pressed it to the paper.

Danny,

I read your letter three times and cried all three. I guess I never told you, but my mom used to say that crying was proof something mattered. I think she's right. I think you matter to me more than I know how to say, and that's why it hurts so bad.

I want you to come home, but I'm scared you'll come back and hate it, hate me for being the reason. I want to see you happy, I want to see you whole, but all I've ever done is wait for you to come back. I can't build a life on maybe. I can't wait forever.

I still love you. That's the worst part. I hope
you find what you're looking for, even if it's
not me. Please write if you can. I'll always
read them.

Love,

Shell

The pen leaked, smearing her signature. She left it
that way. It felt honest.

She folded the letter, slid it into an envelope, and
wrote his name on the front. She carried it to the window, let the breeze lift the flap open, then sealed it with
a breath.

For a long time she sat there, the envelope in her
hand, thumb running over the paper, over his name.
She pictured him alone, reading it, the way his face
would fall, the way he'd close his eyes and pretend it
didn't sting. Maybe it was better not to send it.

She pressed the envelope to her lips, then tucked it
deep in the back of her dresser, under a stack of shirts
she hadn't worn since high school. It felt like a burial.
She told herself that was the end, that she could move
on now.

She didn't believe it.

She lay on her back, eyes to the ceiling, the music still
running on repeat. She let the sadness fill her, waited for
it to crest and fade, but it just stretched out, long and
unbroken, like a highway with no turns.

She watched the sun come up.

When her mother came in to wake her, she pretended to be asleep, face turned to the wall, hands clutching at nothing.

* * *

The white Cadillac hit every pothole on Main, but inside, Daisy Whitaker rode high and unbothered, ankle swinging, hand tight around the wrist of the man beside her. He was new, or at least new to the Hollow, all jawline and cologne, his shirt too starched for the way the roads curled through the old hills. The car's paint job was so clean it glared in the late afternoon sun, turning every passing eye their way, as if the town itself couldn't believe it had drawn such luck.

Daisy had always liked an audience. She leaned out the window as they passed the pawn shop, waved at the old men lined up like crows on the stoop, then flashed a smile at the boys on the bikes who'd stopped to stare, jaws loose, hands limp at the handlebars.

The man's name was James Earl, and he hated it here. She could smell the sweat on him, under the expensive aftershave, and it thrilled her. He gripped the wheel like he could strangle the town with it.

At Percy's Bar, Daisy made her entrance. The Cadillac idled, humming low, while she fussed with her lipstick in the side mirror, then pulled her hair up into a knot and tied it off with her trademark pink ribbon. The jewelry at her wrists and throat glittered in the sickly bar light as she swept through the door, James trailing like a bodyguard or a man on parole.

Conversation died at the sight of them. The miners at the table dropped their cards. Percy raised one eyebrow and reached, automatically, for the better whiskey.

Daisy let James order first, some imported nonsense,

which Percy met with a flat stare and a dust-coated bottle of Evan Williams. Daisy took a seat at the bar, crossed her legs, and tapped her nails on the surface until the whole room got used to the noise.

The air in Percy's was wet with old beer and old secrets. Daisy tasted both in the way the men looked at her. She didn't smile back, not yet. She let the eyes settle, let them measure what had changed since the moment she walked through the door.

She ordered whiskey, neat, and when Percy poured it, she winked and slid a folded twenty across the bar. He left it, untouched, and busied himself with a rag.

James leaned in, whispered through gritted teeth: "Do you think they always stare like that?"

She grinned, teeth perfect and bright. "Only if you look like you got something worth taking."

He scowled, turned back to his drink.

Daisy uncoiled from her seat, drifted along the bar, hips rolling slow, and started talking to the boys in the corner, the ones who'd been too nervous to look at her directly. She knew how to pace the conversation, just enough sweetness to draw them in, just enough acid to make them sweat. She asked about the mine, about the layoffs. She laughed too loud, made sure her voice carried.

James grew tighter with every minute. His jaw ticked, his hand a white ghost on the glass. Daisy saw it, and she liked it. She let her laugh ring out; let it slice through the low hum of the bar.

After an hour, when the crowd was deep and the air thick with smoke and envy, James grabbed her arm. His grip was hard, his breath sharp with resentment.

"Can we go?" he said, not waiting for an answer.

She leaned close, brushed her lips against his ear. "We just got here."

He stiffened. "I don't like it here."

She pulled away, loud enough for the whole bar to hear. "Then go wait in the car. I'm not finished."

James' face burned red. He threw a wad of cash on the bar, turned, and stalked outside.

Daisy watched him leave, let the silence resettle. She fixed her ribbon, smoothed the front of her dress, and reclaimed her spot at the bar.

Billy, drunk already, tried his luck. "Hey, you bringing that fancy man home for the wedding?"

She smiled, sweet as arsenic. "He's not my type. I like men who can hold their liquor and a conversation."

The whole bar erupted. Even Percy cracked a smile, thin as it was.

Daisy let the warmth wash over her. For a minute, it was enough to be wanted, even if it was only for the joke of it.

It didn't last. James' shadow loomed at the door, then his voice: "You coming?"

Daisy let the room watch as she slid off the barstool, slow and deliberate. She kissed Percy on the cheek, left another bill on the bar, then walked outside.

The air was cold and clear. James paced by the Cadillac, lighting a cigarette with hands that wouldn't stop shaking.

"You made a fool of me in there," he said.

She shrugged. "You did that yourself."

He flicked the cigarette away, stepped in close. "You're not better than me. You're just a little girl playing dress-up in the dirt."

She looked him in the eye, unblinking. "Then leave.

Go back to your city."

He did. Dropped her suitcase, slammed the car door, peeled off down Main, tires screaming, dust blooming behind him. Daisy stood in the empty street, her suitcase at her feet, the tail-lights already gone.

For a second, her breath caught. Just a second.

She bent, picked up the bag, brushed the grit from her dress. She untied her ribbon, then retied it, tighter this time.

She walked back into Percy's with her head high, her smile brighter than ever.

The miners at the table made room for her. She sat, poured herself a drink from their pitcher, and let the world see she was still standing.

She would always be standing. Never takes a fall.

* * *

The days slipped by, slow and heavy as syrup. Shelby kept her job at the diner, pouring coffee for the same men who'd known her since she was knee-high, and spent her off-hours with Thomas Wilcox, who had the decency to never show up at the counter without a tip and a quiet smile. They didn't talk much, but it was a good kind of silence, the space between their words filled with the clatter of dishes or the drone of the radio in his truck.

Sometimes he met her outside after her shift, the two of them sitting on the back steps and sharing pie straight from the tin, the sky above stretched thin as eggshell. He'd ask how her day was and really listen, brow furrowed in a way that made her want to reach out and smooth the worry lines with her thumb. She never did.

On Sundays, she rode with him to church, sat stiff in the pew next to his mother and sisters, singing the hymns with a voice barely above a whisper. She watched the way Thomas closed his eyes during prayer, head bowed, hands folded, the picture of a man who believed in something. Sometimes she wondered if she could ever believe like that again.

They started walking together, out along the creek, but she never let him take her as far as the willow stump. That place was still marked off in her mind, roped with caution tape and old pain. Instead, they wandered the back fields, the borders of the town, talking about anything except the future.

One night, after the kitchen closed, Thomas took her hand and led her out behind the parking lot, where the world was nothing but grass and stars. He stopped at the edge of the field, cleared his throat, and pulled out a ring.

It wasn't much, just a slim gold band with a tiny white stone set crooked in the middle, but it glittered under the moonlight all the same.

"I know it's soon, four months," he said. "But you make me feel like I could be more than what I am. Maybe I could make you happy, too."

He went down on one knee, the whole thing straight out of a catalog. His eyes were shiny and scared.

Shelby felt her heart hammer in her chest, wild and uneven. She looked down at him, at the ring, at the place where his thumb trembled against her knuckles.

She thought of Danny, the way he'd never asked, the way he'd always said someday but never today.

Thomas was waiting. The night was waiting.

Shelby nodded. Just once. "Okay," she whispered.

He slipped the ring on her finger, stood up, and hugged her so hard it hurt. She let herself be held. She let herself imagine it could be enough.

They walked back to her house, her hand sweating inside his. The porch light was on, her father waiting in the doorway. When he saw the ring, he whooped and clapped Thomas on the back, nearly knocked him off the steps. Her mother hugged her, but the touch was gentle, hesitant, as if she were afraid Shelby might break apart right there in the glow of the bug-zapper.

Her father started talking about wedding plans before they'd even closed the door. He wanted a spring ceremony, full of people and music and cake. He wanted the whole town to know his daughter was marrying up, that she'd picked a good man with a future.

Her mother just watched her, eyes soft and searching.

That night, after the house had gone still and her father's snores filled the hallway, Shelby crept into her room and opened the box under her bed. She sifted through the old letters, the photos, the CD with the label worn thin. She read Danny's last note one more time, tracing the loop of his signature with her fingertip.

She didn't cry. She just sat there, the past pooled in her lap, and felt the weight of every choice she'd made, every word she'd left unsaid.

When the clock struck three, she put the letters back in the box, pushed it deep under the mattress, and wiped her hands clean.

She lay down, watched the slow blink of the streetlight through her window, and tried to convince herself that this was what happiness looked like.

She wore the ring to work the next day. Nobody commented, but everyone noticed.

Time moved on, the future assembling itself piece by careful piece.

But in the quiet of her room, with only the sound of her own breath to keep her company, Shelby knew that a part of her would always be waiting for something that never arrived.

* * *

Daisy took the apartment above the Farmacy, a squat two-room with windows that looked out over the dumpster in the alley and Main Street in the other room. It smelled like old soap and older onions, but she liked the vantage. She could see half the town from her perch, and from that height, White Oak Hollow almost looked alive.

She moved in with a single suitcase and a box of costume jewelry, nothing more. The landlord gave her a skeptical once-over, but she charmed him with a laugh and a story about her time in Oneida, working at the shoe store and running a pageant circuit on the side. He believed it, or at least wanted to.

By the end of the first week, Daisy had the place fixed up. She thumbtacked velvet scarves over the windows, laid the prettiest hand towels on the battered sink, and set her perfume bottles in a neat row along the sill. She kept a single mug on the counter, pink ceramic with the handle shaped like a heart. She sipped instant coffee from it every morning, watching the men stream into the mine, counting which ones looked worth the trouble.

It wasn't long before the town had opinions. The old women at the post office called her "fast," but with a kind of awe, as if they admired the velocity. The younger ones at the salon watched her walk past, heads tilted, waiting to see who she'd claim next.

Most nights, she held court at Percy's. She'd glide in at dark, hair done up, lips painted blood red and take her spot at the bar. Billy always bought her the first drink, and she'd let him talk her ear off, laughing at his stories even when she knew they were lies. She flirted with the men who sat close, batted her lashes, made them feel seen.

But Daisy's real talent wasn't in her looks or her laugh, it was the way she listened, how she made you think your words were the only ones that mattered. She'd draw out their secrets, their hurts, their pay stubs, then smile like she'd never heard better.

She cycled through prospects with a surgeon's precision. First there was Steve, who worked maintenance at the mine and drove a Mustang that barely ran. Daisy rode with him to Lexington, once, and let him buy her dinner at the steakhouse. When the car broke down a week later, she was already on to Luke, who owned a little trailer and had a TV in every room. She spent a few nights there, let him buy her cigarettes and scratch-offs, then moved on to Randy, who worked the night shift and spent his days fixing up a '67 Chevy that never seemed to get finished. Even Jimmy Carter made it into the lineup, but he struck out pretty quick, a little too drunk even for Daisy.

She never left a mess behind. Just a note, or a kind word, or a thank you for the good time. The men pretended they weren't hurt, but everyone knew better.

She told wild stories at the bar, about her family's mansion back in Eastern Kentucky, about the cousin who'd been a finalist for Miss America, about the summer she spent as a lifeguard at Lake Cumberland. Sometimes she'd let the truth slip in, a detail about her mother's hospital bills, or her brother's run-in with the law, but mostly she kept it shiny, easy to swallow.

Every man in town thought he could be the one to tame her. None of them could.

She always paid for her own drinks or at least acted like she did. She kept track of who owed her, who was flush and who was dry. Payday at the mine was her favorite night. Percy's would be packed, laughter and music thick in the air, and Daisy would make her rounds, collecting compliments and phone numbers like bouquets.

She wore her heartbreak like a brooch, pretty and visible, but never once let it slow her down.

Sometimes, late at night, she'd sit on the stoop behind the store, smoke a cigarette, and watch the world wind down. She'd listen to the freight train in the distance, the hum of the highway, the buzz of her own mind spinning out what she wanted next.

She didn't think about the Cadillac, or James Earl, or the men who'd left her behind. She didn't think about the future, either.

Daisy just lived, full and fast, soaking up every look, every laugh, every small victory.

And if she was lonely, sometimes, she never let it show.

Not once.

THE WHITAKER
DEBT

Listening Suggestion: Stop here for a moment. Go find Raleigh Keegan's song Danny Loves Daisy and give it a listen before you move on. I wrote the next four chapters with that melody in my head, and it'll put you right where I want you before the story continues.

D anny felt the mountain still on his back as he pushed through the door of Percy's. His second double shift in as many days had scraped him empty like a coal cart at the end of the line, but Daisy was already there in the booth near the pool table, her legs tucked beneath her like the town didn't have claim on her the way it did on him.

She was playing with the pink ribbon tied through her hair, rolling its frayed end between her fingers, gaze far away until she saw him.

"Look at you," she said, grinning. "Like the mine spit you out for last call."

Danny slid into the booth, sweat dried to salt on his shirt, his hands cracked and rimmed in black. He nodded at the ribbon. "You always wear that."

Her grin softened. "That's 'cause it ain't just cloth. It was my grandma's. She tied it in my hair the day I turned five. Told me as long as I wore it, I'd never be alone in this world." Daisy's eyes flickered, half teasing, half daring him to laugh.

"I'm not laughing," Danny said. He reached across the table, touched the ribbon where it looped against her blonde hair. "It's the cleanest thing in this whole town."

She leaned back quick, smile crooked. "Careful. Coal dust stains worse than sin. You'd ruin the last innocent thing I've got."

Danny smirked, but she was already tapping her earrings, the ones he'd picked out of a pawnshop case last week. "Now these, though…" she tilted her head so the light caught the rhinestones, "these make a girl feel like someone sees her."

He caught the shift. The ribbon was hers, sacred. The trinkets were his duty. He didn't say it, but he felt it. The difference was the size of a mountain.

Daisy traced the rim of her glass, round and round, until the condensation smeared away. The first few minutes she kept it light, recounting the parade of fools who'd tried to fix her sink that week, how the landlord's nephew managed to flood her entire kitchen with a pool of rusty water, but it was only a warmup to something else. Danny could tell by the way her leg jiggled under the table, the rhythm out of key with her voice.

"Listen," she said, after a lull, "Can I tell you something, and you swear you won't run off or get all weird about it?"

Danny wiped his palms on his jeans. "You know you can."

She hesitated, eyes darting to the pool table, to the regulars hunched around their beers, then back to him. "You ever hear the story about the mine being cursed?" She said it low, almost swallowed by the hum of lights in the bar. "How the Whitaker boys brought it down when they dynamited the third shaft, and every Whitaker since has owed a death to the rock?"

Danny nodded, slow. He'd heard it in a dozen versions, none worth much after the third round, and none that would have made him thought Daisy Whitaker was part of that family, but she looked serious as she said it. He waited for the turn; a joke, a wink, something, but Daisy just stared at the melt in her glass, thumb pressing a white half-moon in the wood.

She went on, "My daddy used to say it was a blood debt, not just a run of bad luck. And that's why..." but before she could finish, a crash like a dropped anvil split the bar.

At the pool table, two miners stood nose to nose, both of them with sleeves rolled, faces streaked in black. One held a cue snapped clean in half; the top end pointed at the other's chest as if they'd rehearsed for a duel. There was shouting, but the words slurred out mostly as wet noise, threats melting back to laughter before the broken cue could aim at anything but the floor. Percy had them apart in two steps, one hand on each man's shoulder, voice pitched so low and mean Danny couldn't make out the words. The bar's tension snapped, the regulars sinking back into their seats like nothing had happened. The pieces of cue stick clattered onto the table, and the two miners slouched off to opposite corners, each lapping his wounds with a shot of well whiskey.

Daisy didn't flinch. She watched the whole thing with a look like disappointment, as if the real show was still waiting in the wings.

"My daddy used to say," she started again, and now

her voice was sharp, "that every Whitaker who tries to leave mining country just ends up swallowed by it." She drummed her fingernail against the glass.

"Thing is," she said, "that's not how I want it to be. My grandpa took his last breath coughing up black, my uncles all either dead early or gone mean as hell, and now every time I close my eyes, I see myself getting smaller and smaller inside this mountain, any mountain from Oneida to White Oak Hollow matters not, until there's nothing left but coal dust and the sound of someone else's boots on the floor above me. You know what I mean?" She called the last line like a challenge, not a question.

Danny hunched over the table. The sweat between his shoulder blades hadn't dried. He watched the rings form around her glass and thought about his old man's hands. How they tremored when he tried to lift a cup, how the cough never shook loose. He stared at Daisy, the lines of her knuckles, the ribbon faded at the ends.

He shrugged. "Different family, same script."

Two nights later, Danny showed up at Daisy's room, body aching from the mine, black dust still in his pores.

She opened the door with a laugh. "No way you're sitting on my bed like that. You'll turn the sheets to soot." She tossed him a towel and pointed at the bathroom. "Shower's on the fritz but it runs hot if you give it a minute and jiggle the knob."

Danny stripped down, turned the faucet until it rattled, and stood under the spray as coal-black water curled around the drain. He scrubbed until his nails bled pink under the cuticles, until his skin felt almost borrowed. By the time he stepped out, towel slung low, Daisy was sprawled across the bed, waiting with the half-patient look of someone used to getting what she wanted.

"You clean up nice, miner boy," she said, eyes lingering too long.

Danny tossed her a box. A thin scarf he'd picked up for a dollar because it felt like thirty. She squealed, tied it around her neck, kissed him so hard he forgot his lungs for a moment. Then she pulled him down, laughter muffled against his throat.

Later, when their breaths slowed, Daisy flopped onto her back, scarf glinting in the lamplight. She stared at the ceiling, tracing cracked paint with her finger. "This place is killing me," she muttered. "I wasn't made for two-room apartments with mildew."

Danny propped himself up on one elbow, but she didn't look at him. He tried to joke, "Could be worse. You could be the one crawling through the mine."

She didn't laugh.

She rolled to face him, the gravity of her mood shifting the night colder. "Do you ever wake up and feel like you're already dead, or is that just me?" she whispered, voice creaking on the edge of a joke, but Danny could see her jaw clench, the muscle tight right under his hand.

He didn't answer. There was nothing to say to that kind of confession except maybe "me too," but he doubted she'd want to hear it. She rolled away and he kissed between her shoulder blades, the salt still there from her skin, and watched the slow rise and fall of her back, the way she held her breath like a secret.

Daisy turned again and buried her face in his chest. "You don't talk much when it's just us," she said. "Are you always thinking, or just empty?"

He looked down at his calloused hands, then back at

her. "Maybe if I'd brought those flowers from the road-side stand like you mentioned last week, we wouldn't be talking about dying in this town."

The days blurred after that. Black dust smeared into the cracks of Danny's hands day in and day out, into the weave of his shirts no matter how many times he scrubbed them. He worked doubles back-to-back, the foreman barking for more carts, the whistle sounding like a threat instead of a promise. Sleep never seemed to catch him; when it did, it was shallow, broken by coughing fits and the echo of picks striking coal.

The mine had a way of stealing time. Hours bled together until he couldn't tell if the shift had just started or was about to end. His body told him, though. Knuckles split, back knotted, a weight in his chest that refused to loosen. When he tried to pick up the guitar in his room, his fingers trembled too much to shape a chord. What came out wasn't music, just a reminder of what he couldn't do anymore.

Daisy noticed. Or maybe she didn't, not in the way he hoped.

The first evening he dropped by without anything in hand; no earrings, no scarf, not even a candy bar from the drugstore, she was distant, distracted. She let him kiss her cheek, but her eyes stayed on the magazine in her lap, an old Cosmo she'd read a dozen times. The perfume of her hair didn't bend toward him; her laughter was saved for some thought she kept to herself.

"You look beat," she said flatly. "You oughta rest."

He knew what she meant, "come back when you got something that shines."

The next time, he came with a thin bracelet he'd bartered for at the pawnshop. The metal was on the edge of tarnish, but Daisy's face lit up as if it were gold. She slid it onto her wrist, held it up to the lamp, and suddenly she was all warmth again, laughter spilling, hand tracing circles on his chest.

"You always know how to keep a girl shining," she purred.

Danny smiled, but it caught in his throat. He wondered if she realized the pattern, or if it was just instinct. Affection bought in small pieces, as regular as the mine's whistle.

Later, sitting on the stoop outside her building, Daisy stared off toward the dark road that ran out of town. The night air smelled of coal smoke and honeysuckle.

"Sometimes," she said softly, "I think I was meant for a place where the lights never go out. Where night looks like day, and nobody ever shuts their eyes just to make it through. But I might just have to shut my eyes forever."

Danny followed her gaze but said nothing. He didn't have to. Her words landed heavy, carving out another hollow inside him. He wanted to tell her he understood and that he thought of running again, every day, but the thought of saying it made the chains around his chest pull tighter.

Instead, he squeezed her hand. She let him, but her eyes were already far down the road, past anywhere he could take her on a miner's pay.

On his next day off, the first in nearly a week, Daisy grabbed his arm as they walked through town. "Come on," she said, her eyes dancing. "I've got someplace to take you. We need a happy place. Something better than Percy's stale beer and this apartment with the same ole' view."

He followed her through back roads and trails until

the woods opened on a swimming hole at the far edge of town. The water was clear and cold, fed by some spring that hadn't yet surrendered to coal dust. Moonlight glazed its surface silver.

"This," Daisy said, slipping the ribbon from her hair and setting it carefully on a rock, "is my place. First time I've let the ribbon off in years. But maybe it deserves a night off."

Before Danny could answer, she tugged her dress over her head and tossed it onto the grass. The slip underneath followed, a puddle of pale cloth at her feet. She didn't rush; she moved like she wanted him to watch.

Danny's throat tightened. He bent to untie his boots, his fingers clumsy, and by the time he looked up again, Daisy had waded in, water kissing her thighs, then her waist. Moonlight traced her shoulders as she dove under. She surfaced with a gasp, slick hair plastered against her cheeks, laughing like the water had been waiting for her.

"What're you waiting for?" she called, voice echoing across the hollow. "Afraid it'll scrub the coal clean off you?"

Danny stripped down, the night air cold against his skin, and rushed in. The water swallowed him whole, sharp, clear, cutting through the ache in his bones. When he came up, Daisy was already circling him like a cat.

They splashed first, chasing each other through the shallows, laughter breaking over the stillness. But when she closed the space between them, laughter thinned into breath. Daisy brushed against him, shoulder to chest, her skin warm even in the cool water.

"See?" she whispered. "Not so cold if you move close."

Her legs tangled with his under the surface, not accidental. Her hands slid across his chest, exploring the ridges the mine had carved into him. She pressed her palm against his heartbeat, then trailed it downward, pausing just enough for him to feel heat rise under his skin.

The water made everything slow. Every brush of her thigh against his carried weight. Every slip of her hand was amplified, lingering. Danny cupped the back of her neck, kissed her hard, the taste of spring water and something sweeter. She answered with a laugh that caught halfway into a gasp, her body pressing against his like she was testing how far they could go before the water itself blushed.

She wrapped her arms around his shoulders, and for a moment they floated together, half tangled, half fighting the current. Her breath hitched when his hand traced the line of her waist, dipping lower. She nipped his jaw with her teeth, playful, then drew back just enough to look at him, eyes shining in the moonlight.

"You burn hotter than coal," she said softly.

Danny's answer was another kiss, softer this time. She melted into it, then slipped free suddenly, kicking away with a splash, laughing breathlessly. He lunged after her, caught her wrist under the water, pulled her back. Their chests collided, water slicking between them, the contact nearly enough to undo him.

"Careful," she whispered, lips brushing his ear. "We'll end up drowning each other."

But she didn't let go.

They hovered on that edge. Every touch an invitation, every retreat a tease. The night was thick with crickets, the hollow holding its breath. Danny felt both starved and full, a hunger that was more than the body, though his body screamed loud enough.

Finally, Daisy slipped from his arms and swam for the bank. She climbed out slow, deliberate, water sheeting off her skin in silver rivulets. Moonlight turned her into something otherworldly. She bent, tied the ribbon back into her hair, and when she glanced toward the road that wound out of town, her smile faltered.

"One day," she murmured, "I want someplace where water always runs clear. Where you can wash something off, and it stays gone."

Danny stayed waist-deep, watching her silhouette against the dark. His chest rose and fell with something he couldn't name; longing, fear, maybe both. He wasn't sure if he was drowning or learning how to breathe again.

He walked her home in silence. She hummed a tune under her breath, light as if nothing had passed between them but a swim. Back in his own room, Danny collapsed onto the bed, his body spent but restless.

Through the thin walls, he heard the mine whistle blow for the night shift, a reminder of where he belonged. But in his mind, he saw the ribbon drying in Daisy's hair, and felt her heartbeat pressed to his under the cold water.

He couldn't tell if she was pulling him closer, or hollowing him out, piece by piece.

The days between were thick as coal dust. He worked double shifts, the heat and grit searing his lungs, the clang of metal on rock gnawing at his brain. He dreamed of water and the hush of her skin against his, something not as dark as this. But the dreams drifted into the walls of the mine, echoing back at him like a curse.

Nothing tasted as sweet as Daisy's laughter, but nothing soured as fast. It left him hungrier, emptier, the void Shelby left growing all the while. He stumbled from the mine each day, knowing she was waiting but never knowing for how long. Each night was a rush, a fever, wild and heady, but he could feel the strain like a fault line, deep and spreading. His body ached from the work, but more from the want. He burned through paychecks and gifts, his own hunger, and still never caught up.

Daisy's eyes were on the distance, already gone before they closed together in sleep. He couldn't take her where she wanted. He couldn't even take himself. The crash waiting for him was worse than any rockfall.

A week later, Daisy showed up at Percy's in a white sundress, hair plaited tight, and lips painted a shade of red that could have gotten her arrested in three counties. She beckoned Danny to her booth with two fingers, ignoring the looks from the regulars lined up at the bar. When he eased in beside her, she tugged the collar of his flannel straight and leaned close enough to give him heart palpitations.

"You're late," she said, but her eyes said she'd waited.

He tried to explain the extra hour at the mine. Something about a loader breaking down, Earl cussing up a storm, but Daisy wasn't listening. She toyed with the straw in her drink, wound it round and round until it bent double. "You ever notice," she said, "that nothing in this town gets fixed, just patched till the whole damn place is more patch than town?"

Danny nodded. The bar smelled of spilled whiskey

and mop water and something fresh out of the hole.

"Let's get a bigger place," Daisy said confident. It wasn't a question, but more of a statement. Danny felt what muscle he had left in his back tear under the weight of the thought.

BIGGER DIGS

The darkness down the Number Four tunnel was near perfect, broken only by the arc of a bare bulb that left more shadow than light. Danny pressed his chest to the wood of the support beam and wormed through, knees and elbows sinking in black slime. Above him, the seam was thin, not worth the effort but still called for on the chart, and he could hear the slow drip of water somewhere ahead, counting time in irregular ticks.

The cart behind him was loaded heavy, tailing on a rusted chain. Each pull set the metal to squeal and the rock overhead to dust. Sweat stung his eyes, coal gritted between his teeth, and every breath sucked at the wound in his lungs, the old one, the one the nurse said was "just scarring." He didn't mind the hurt. It was the silence that worked at him. The further he dragged into the seam, the more the mine closed off the world above, until it felt like even memory couldn't find its way down here.

He set the pick into the coal, sparks running in the dark like a secret. It took three swings before he got a bite, the vibration singing up through his wrists. He worked fast, not because there was quota but because every minute down here was time stolen from somewhere else. The days had taken to sliding together, the same bruise on his knuckles, the same ache in his back, the same face in the locker mirror at the end of shift, black ringed eyes and a smile that couldn't keep its shape.

The tunnel was so narrow he sometimes lost the sense of up and down. The rock pressed on his shoulders, and sometimes he thought the whole mountain wanted to fold him flat, erase the space his body took. He worked through it, found a rhythm in the scrape and crash of coal, lost himself in the old music of labor, the hymn of men gone before and men still in the black.

He worked until the battery in his lamp faded to a sick yellow and the seam was picked raw, then hauled the cart back, scraping it on every outcrop. At the junction, he wiped his eyes with a sleeve and spat a black slug on the floor. He stood in the mouth of the drift and listened to the world above, faint and distant, the grind of the fan house, the shift bell, the far-off whine of a loader.

When he climbed out, the day had gone blue and mean, a wind cutting up the hollow and slicing the heat off his skin. The world above stank of rot and old rain, but it was a good stink, a human stink. He wiped his face in the crook of his arm, then took the rutted trail down to town, boots caked and body howling for rest.

The new place crouched at the far end of Main, past the hardware store, past the gas station that hadn't had gas in months. It was two stories, pitched roof, narrow, paint still tacky from the last coat, but the sign out front had the word "RENT" scrawled with such desperation you could smell it. Daisy's idea, of course. She'd signed the lease before he could even see the place, "because it's got a view," she'd said, though the only thing you could see from the kitchen window was the fire escape and the power lines, sagging like tired veins to the commercial building next door.

He let himself in, braced for the smell of primer, but Daisy had thrown open every window. The rooms were barely furnished, sound bouncing from wall to wall, and he found her in the living room, spinning circles with a strip of fabric in each hand.

She saw him and stopped dead. "Don't move," she said, grinning. "I'm checking the light." She held up a swatch, bright gold, let the light hit it, then compared it to another, green as pond scum. She looked from one to the other with a frown, as if her whole life depended on picking right.

Danny dropped his bag by the door. His muscles quivered. He looked at Daisy, her hair up in a quick knot, t-shirt that made her look like the 'girl next door,' cheeks flushed. She looked better than anything in the room. Better than anything in town.

She held both swatches up, blocking her face, and said, "Which do you like?"

He shrugged, wiped his hands on his jeans. "Whatever you want," he said, voice hoarse.

She made a face. "That's no answer. You've got to care, or it's just walls and windows."

He tried to care. He tried to picture the room done up in color, the couch that came with the place, the rug she'd circled in a catalog for weeks, the little touches she always talked about as if they could fix what was wrong in a place. But all he could see was the light bulb overhead, flickering in a way that said it would die first thing in the morning.

"Gold, then," he said.

She brightened, twirled, and tossed the green aside.

"Knew you'd pick right." She drifted to the window, held the gold up to the glass, and watched the wind press it flat. "Makes it look like a real home," she said.

Danny didn't answer. He watched her move, the way she owned the air in the room, the way even the light seemed to bend around her. She'd hung lace curtains in the kitchen already, the kind with little flowers stitched in, and they swayed when the wind got in, breathing like living things.

She turned and looked at him, her eyes wide. "You look like hell, Wallace."

He grinned. "I am hell."

She crossed the floor and put her arms around his waist, pulling him in like she could squeeze the hurt out of him. She pressed her cheek to his chest, ignoring the sweat, the dust, the stink of twelve hours buried alive.

He rested his chin on her hair, let her soak up whatever she needed.

She tilted her face up, eyes half closed. "It's perfect," she whispered. "Just needs some fancying up."

He wanted to tell her that nothing was ever perfect, that every nice thing got ruined by use or time or bad luck, but she kissed him before he could open his mouth, and her lips were so hungry he thought maybe she was the one being hollowed out, not him.

They stood like that a long minute, the world quiet but for the creak of the building and the far-off bark of a dog. She let go first, stepping back, her eyes shining. "Let me show you the rest," she said, already walking, upstairs, toward the bedroom. "I moved the bed around, but we'll need a real dresser soon. And there's a tub! Not one of those moldy stand-up showers, but a real one you can sit in. Like the ones you see in movies."

He followed her, half dazed, half dead on his feet. The bedroom was smaller than the old one, but the window faced east, and the last of the sun made the walls glow. The bed sheets were tidy, and Daisy had already thrown a blanket over the end, blue and frayed but cleaner than the rest of his life.

She looked at him, uncertain now, and said, "Do you like it?"

He nodded. "It's good."

She bit her lip, then smiled. "It'll be better, once we get settled. Once the smell's gone. Once you're not so tired."

He let himself fall to the mattress, the springs giving way all at once. He closed his eyes, felt the world spin. He heard Daisy in the other room, humming a song he'd never heard, her footsteps light, her voice lighter.

He tried to feel safe, or happy, or something, but all he felt was the weight of the shift, and the emptiness it left behind.

He drifted, somewhere between sleep and nothing, and in that space he dreamed he was still in the tunnel, dragging the cart, only now the chain was wrapped around his chest, and every step forward pulled his heart tighter.

He woke once, maybe twice, to Daisy's hand on his face, cool and gentle, her voice whispering, "Sleep, Danny, sleep."

When he woke for real, it was dark, the window filled with streetlamp glow, the air thick with the perfume of cut grass and fresh paint. Daisy was curled next to him, breathing slow and even, her hand tucked under his arm.

He watched her for a minute, then traced the line of

her jaw with his thumb, the way he used to when they first met, when the world hadn't started closing in. She didn't stir. He listened to her breathe, listened to the house shift and settle.

He wondered how long it would take before the shine wore off.

He lay awake, counting the shadows on the ceiling, listening to the night. In the dark, the house felt bigger, emptier, like a shell. There were a few furniture pieces throughout but not enough to fill all the voids. He thought of the mine, of the tunnel, of the way the dark pressed in to fill those voids and never let go.

He wondered what it was that Daisy saw in him, or in this place, that made her want to stay.

He wondered what it would take to fill the hollow she'd made.

He turned to her, pulled her close, and breathed in the smell of her hair, the hint of dust, the ghost of paint, the salt of her skin.

He closed his eyes and let himself fall.

The days came in a narrow groove. Danny woke before the alarm, body trained to the slope's hours, and got dressed in the dark, careful not to wake Daisy. She always slept light, curled around his side, a tangle of hair and old flannel, but somehow he managed to slip away without breaking the spell. The air outside was colder now, even in early autumn, and the walk to the mine numbed him clean to the bone. The building at the pit mouth glowed like a lantern, all yellow light and the stutter of diesel, and when the whistle blew at six, the world condensed to noise, motion, and the simple, stupid fact of survival.

He lost himself in the work. The mine was a god,

jealous and greedy, and it took everything you brought with you, and then your dreams for good measure. Some days the dust was so thick it gritted between your teeth. He coughed it up at the end of shift, spat it into the sink, and watched the flecks swirl down the drain.

The new place was only half a mile from the mine, and he came home filthy, uniform stiff, face raw from the grit. Daisy met him at the door most nights, hair done up with the pink ribbon, the same faded jeans she'd worn on their third date. She made a game out of it, locking the chain and forcing him to stand on the porch while she asked, "Password?" like she was running a speakeasy. He always answered, "Please, ma'am, let me in." She always did.

He would strip off in the entryway, let the dirt fall on the mat, and walk to the shower on feet so tired they felt like something borrowed. Sometimes Daisy watched from the doorway, eyes soft, or sometimes she'd vanish into the next room, humming or talking to herself.

After a week, the first real change came. He came home, half-dead, and found Daisy on a stepstool in the kitchen, a length of lace bunched between her teeth, fingers nimble as she tacked it to the window frame. The kitchen didn't need more curtain, but Daisy's kitchen did. Sun caught in the new curtains and turned the room white. She stood back, admired her work, and then turned to him with a look of pure, feral pride.

He wiped his hands on his shirt. "Where'd you get those?"

She grinned. "Picked them up from Percy's. He was gonna let them rot in the back room." She ran her palm over the edge of the curtain, smoothed it like it was a living thing. "Don't it look better?"

He nodded. "Yeah. Looks good."

She looked at him, serious now. "You like it?"

He tried to muster something in his face, but it was all he could do to stay upright. "Yeah," he said again, softer.

She beamed, kissed him hard, the taste of cigarettes and sugar. "Go clean up," she said, slapping his ass, and then she was off, already rearranging the cups on the counter, moving through the kitchen like she owned every atom of it.

Danny rinsed off, the water running black, and watched the new curtains billow in the wind as he toweled dry. He stood in the kitchen, still damp, and stared at the way the late sun laced through the white. It was too nice for a place like this. Too good to be real. But Daisy was already dreaming up the next change, already talking about new paint for the bedroom, a better table, maybe even a potted plant if she could keep it alive.

That night, she pulled him onto the mattress before he could protest, hands hot and insistent. She pressed him to the sheets, fingers tracing the shape of his ribs, tongue flicking at the salt on his neck. She wanted him, wanted to claim him, as if she could write her name into his skin with every touch. He let her, lost himself in the ache, the quick sharp of her teeth, the electric hum that always ran under her laugh when she finally broke. Afterwards, she sprawled across him, her hair fanned out, the ribbon tangled around his wrist.

She whispered, "See, that's the good thing about new starts. You get to make your own rules."

He stroked her hair, unsure what rule he was supposed to follow.

She slept easy, always, while he lay awake, every

nerve in his body tingling from the shift and the after-glow. He tried to picture tomorrow. All he could see was the same groove, the same dirt under his nails, the same hunger in Daisy's eyes.

The next day he came home to find the living room different. The couch was moved. In its place, Daisy had laid out a rug, the kind with colors so bright it hurt to look at them, patterns wild and coiling, every edge stitched in gold thread. She was on her knees, running her hands over the fringe, as if she'd found a lamp with a genie inside.

He stared at it, the blue and red and gold a shock in the drab of the house. "Where'd that come from?"

She looked up, hair loose, eyes alive. "Got it from the antiques place up in Hazard. Wasn't even expensive, they wanted it gone. Look." She patted the rug, then flopped down on it, legs crossed, back straight. She looked like a queen on a throne.

He walked in, careful not to step too hard. "How much?"

She shrugged. "You worry too much. Less than it's worth."

He ran a hand over his jaw. The rug was nice, maybe too nice. The rent check still needed cashing. The mine paid on Friday. "We gotta be careful, Daisy."

She smiled, dreamy, and tugged the pink ribbon tighter around her ponytail. "A man takes care of his woman, don't he?"

He wanted to argue, but she patted the spot beside her, and when he sat she pulled him down, wrapped him in her arms, and bit at his ear until he forgot why he was mad. She was good at that, at making the world shrink down to just the two of them, the rug under their backs, the spinning of the fan, the taste of her on his tongue.

He lay with her until he felt the world stop, until the weight in his chest eased enough to let him breathe. But even then, the worry gnawed at him, low and constant.

That night, he woke in the dark, head buzzing. He found the old coffee can where they kept their cash, thumbed through the bills. There was less than before. Not enough to matter, not enough to survive a week if the mine shut down. He stared at the money, the ragged edges, the thin stack, and tried to imagine how many rugs you'd have to sell to cover rent.

In the morning, Daisy was up before him, making coffee. She wore the new curtains like a shawl, swirled the lace around her arms, then draped it back onto the rod, giggling at her own show.

He sipped the coffee, watched her flit around the kitchen, and tried to picture the future. All he could see was more rugs, more curtains, more bright things in rooms that couldn't hold them.

The next week was more of the same. He worked doubles, came home dead. She greeted him at the door, sometimes naked, sometimes in a dress she'd borrowed from a friend just to spice it up a bit. She'd pull him into bed, or onto the rug, and strip the work out of him, laugh as he gasped her name, hold him tight enough to crush the doubt for a while.

But every day, the hands got rougher. The cough in his chest dug deeper, and his eyes took on a shadow even Daisy's laughter couldn't bleach. He counted the days until payday, watched the numbers on the bank slip, and felt the old panic start to rattle in his bones.

But he never said no. Not to Daisy, not to the mine,

not to the need that ate at them both. He just kept moving, kept filling the hole, one double shift at a time.

He was bone tired, down to the marrow. But every time Daisy wrapped herself around him and whispered, "You're my man, my only man," he let himself believe it.

Even as the rug frayed and the money thinned, he let himself believe it.

The days went on, Danny breaking and Daisy building. He came home particularly down. Daisy asked him, "Something is wrong today," as if this was the first day she had seen him tired.

"Another double," he muttered, staring at the window. His reflection looked like someone half-remembered. "They said we're getting cut next week, maybe two shifts less a month."

She rolled her eyes, pushed away, and went back to the bags on the table. "We'll make do. You always do. That's why I picked you." She winked, voice gone syrupy. "You're not a quitter."

He watched her pull out a glass vase, the kind nobody in town would ever use for real flowers. She set it on the counter, turned it this way and that, checking it in the lamp light.

"You want to help me pick something for the bedroom?" Daisy said. "There's a special surprise in the second bag."

He hesitated, then followed. Inside, she'd packed a new set of bedsheets, blue with little gold stars, and a blanket so soft it nearly slipped through his hands. There was a card, too, "To Us," scrawled across the front in fake calligraphy.

"Feels like Christmas," she said, tossing him the blanket. "You ever have Christmas with real presents before?

Not just stuff your family found at the Dollar General?"

He shrugged, not wanting to say that most years, he hadn't had Christmas at all.

Daisy flopped onto the bed, arms and legs stretched wide. She patted the spot next to her, and he sat, sinking into the mattress.

"You know what I like about you, Wallace?" She pulled his hand onto her stomach. "You don't pretend to be anything but what you are."

He wanted to tell her she was wrong, that he pretended every day, but the words stuck. She pulled him closer, her lips finding his, her body a magnet. He gave in, even as his muscles screamed for sleep.

Later, she lay curled in the crook of his arm, breath warm against his chest. "We're gonna make it out, you know," she whispered, as if she was talking to herself.

He stayed awake long after her breathing steadied, listening to the hum of the fridge and the wind scraping at the windows. He stared up at the curtains, ghostly in the lamplight, and felt a new, sharper emptiness. He thought of the hours he'd spent under the mountain, the black dust caked in his lungs and wondered how much of himself he'd have to sell before Daisy felt at home.

Then he got up, dressed in the dark, and went back to the mine.

Pay week was shorter, hours cut. Danny got home in daylight now, and it was like seeing his own life under a microscope, every flaw, every debt, every spot he'd let Daisy fill with color that wasn't his.

The first thing he saw was the mirror. It was taller than Daisy, gold leaf curling off the frame like vines about to strangle it, the glass so polished it threw back all the light in the room. She'd propped it against the wall by the window, where the curtain flapped in the breeze. She stood in front of it, arms above her head, hair loose and wild, watching herself with the focus of a surgeon.

"Look," she said, twirling. "I got it for nothing, practically. The guy at Percy's let me have it for a song."

Danny stared at the glass. He saw Daisy's reflection, bright and whole, and then his own, slouched behind her, the dark rings around his eyes swallowing the rest of his face.

"What do we need a mirror for?" he asked, the fatigue creeping into his voice. "You're the only thing in this place worth seeing."

She turned, hand on her hip, and laughed. "Don't be such a martyr. It'll make the space look bigger." She stepped toward him, slipped her arms around his waist, pressed her body close. "You like it, don't you?"

He wanted to say no, that every time he looked at himself, he saw his father's ruin in the set of his jaw, the hollow of his cheeks. But Daisy's fingers slid up his back, kneading the knots at his spine, and he just nodded.

"It's fine," he said. "It's great."

She grinned and gave him a peck on the cheek, already bored, then darted to the other side of the house, where boxes of potential decor covered the dining room floor. Danny followed, the ache in his lower back radiating through his legs. He noticed the rug was already stained in two places, the bright pattern muted by grime from his boots and a splash of Daisy's nail polish.

She tore at the packing tape, nails sharp, and revealed a complete serving set of four plates, bowls, saucers, cups you couldn't get an ounce of coffee in, fake silverware, and all the placemats and napkins one might never need.

"We can host dinner parties now," she said. "Or at least eat like civilized folk."

Danny knelt to help her with the tape, the movement sending sparks down his legs. He watched Daisy skim the packing slip.

"Let me," he said, reaching for the knife to open another box. His hands shook, but the years of working with tools in the mine had taught him the patience to let the tool do the work. He climbed into the chair.

She plopped into his lap, wrapped her arms around his neck, and laughed. "See? You can build a life from scratch, if you just try."

He smiled, but his lips didn't remember how.

The house was full now. Every surface crowded. The kitchen table sagged under the weight of unopened mail, catalogs, bills with red stamps on the front. Danny tried to keep track, but they arrived faster than he could open them. He started hiding the worst ones in the drawer, telling himself he'd deal with them later.

Daisy dressed for dinner that night, slipping into a short, black dress that hugged her sharpest bones. She ran lipstick twice over her mouth, checked herself in the new mirror, and called Danny to join her.

He came; hands still covered in dust. Daisy poured two glasses of wine, cheap but strong, and set the table for just them, candles flickering at the center.

"Isn't this better?" she asked, tucking her feet under the chair. "Doesn't it feel like we're making progress?"

He nodded, staring at his glass. "You always know how to get what you want."

She touched his hand, her skin warm and electric.

"That's why you love me."

He let it hang, the answer stuck somewhere he couldn't reach.

After dinner, Daisy went to the bedroom. Danny stayed at the table, stacking plates, wiping the crumbs into his palm. The pain in his back was a constant now, a dull, living thing. He watched the candle burn down, the wax running onto the wood, pooling at the base.

He got up, went to the window in the front door, and stared at the hollow. Streetlamps painted the road orange, but nothing moved out there. He pressed his forehead to the glass, watched his breath fog the pane. In the reflection, he saw Daisy behind him, tying the pink ribbon in her hair, her face bright and eager. He saw himself, hunched and small, almost out of frame.

He turned away, hands fisted at his sides.

He went to the kitchen, pulled out the drawer, and counted the bills. The stack was thick. He ran his thumb over the edges, feeling the weight of each one.

He heard Daisy laugh, a high, wild sound from the other room. He wondered if she was laughing at something on TV, or at him.

He leaned on the counter, shoulders folding in, and let the sound fill him.

He stayed there until his legs went numb, then he went to bed.

He slept badly, the dreams restless and mean.

In the morning, Daisy was gone. He wasn't sure where she'd taken off to. The smell of her perfume lingered. The new mirror caught the sunlight, throwing it in shards across the walls.

He sat at the kitchen table, staring at the space where the bills used to be, and thought about how nothing ever filled the hollow. Not even her.

The mine let him out at dusk, throat raw from the dust and a cough stitched deep in his chest. He had nothing left but the ache in his spine and a single crumpled bill in his pocket. He walked past the pawn shop, past the Farmacy with its lights flickering green, and let the doors of Percy's swallow him whole.

Inside, it was loud and sharp, the air torn by laughter and the sour stink of men who hadn't bathed since last payday. He slid onto a barstool, nodding at Percy, who poured his whiskey without a word. Danny nursed it, counting every second between the burn in his throat and the slow hush it brought to his nerves.

The regulars were already there. Billy, with his head tipped back, singing off-key at the end of the counter. Two others hunched over cards, flicking glances at the mirror behind the bar, like they could catch time moving if they looked fast enough.

It would have been easy to let the world fuzz out, but the voices to his left got sharper, the words pushing through the fog like broken glass.

"Saw Daisy Whitaker yesterday," one said, voice low and mean. "She was all over Half Pint in that booth, joking and laughing. Didn't care who saw."

The second one snorted. "That girl's got a taste for lost causes. You'd think she'd aim higher but guess the bottom's the only place left."

They laughed, the sound soft and ugly.

Danny stared at his glass, fingers curling tight around it. He tried to remember the last time Daisy mentioned Jimmy Carter, the way she'd wrinkle her nose and call him a dog, the stories she'd told about how he used to get so drunk he'd piss himself behind the Farmacy. Danny always thought she was above that, above him. But the words lodged in his chest, splintered and raw.

He finished the whiskey in two gulps, then motioned for another. Percy poured it, the sound of the bottle a kind of mercy.

"Rough day?" Percy asked but didn't wait for an answer.

Danny wiped his mouth with the back of his hand. "You hear about Daisy?"

Percy shrugged, eyes flat and distant. "Ain't my business what people do when they're bored."

Danny wanted to argue, but all he could do was drink.

The voices at the end of the bar kept up, loud enough now for the whole room. "Saw her cutting up with him the day before, too. Thought he was gonna puke on her shoes, he was laughing so hard."

"She's a wild one," the other said. "Gonna chew up every man in this town before she's done."

Danny felt his pulse jump. He didn't want to believe it, but the memory of Daisy, her smile, her hands, the way she looked right through him when she was bored, made it too easy to picture.

He paid with his last twenty-dollar bill and left the change on the bar. The walk home was slow, the night air thick and wet. The lights in the house were on, every window glowing.

Inside, Daisy was curled on the rug, painting her toenails a fresh red. The new mirror caught her from every angle, a whole room of Daisies all watching themselves. She looked up, saw him, and smiled, bright as the first day.

"Hey, stranger," she said. "Thought you'd run off with the coal dust."

He stood in the doorway, hands in fists. "You see Jimmy Carter last night?"

She went still, the smile dropping. "Why?"

"Heard you were with him. At Percy's." He tried to sound angry, but it came out small.

Daisy set down the brush, wiped her hands on a towel. "Are you seriously jealous of Half Pint? He's a joke, Danny. He's nothing."

The words should have soothed him, but her face stayed flat, eyes bright and cold.

"I just…" he started, but Daisy cut him off, her voice already trembling.

"You think I'm not lonely?" She grabbed the pink ribbon, twisted it around her finger until the skin turned white. "You think I like sitting here waiting for you to come home every night, covered in someone else's dirt? You think it's easy, being with a man who can barely look at himself in the mirror?"

Danny's heart thudded. He wanted to tell her he was trying, that everything he did was for her, but she pressed on.

"A girl needs attention, Danny. If you can't give it to me, if you're too tired or too sad or too busy with your own misery, then what do you expect me to do?"

Tears sparked in her eyes, but she didn't let them fall. She stared at him, daring him to argue.

He didn't.

He crossed the room, dropped to his knees in front of her, the pain shooting up his legs. He took her hands in his, rough skin against soft, and squeezed.

"I'm sorry," he said. "I'll do better. I promise."

She let him hold her, but her body was stiff, her face turned away. The tears dried, and she pulled the ribbon free from her finger, tying it back in her hair with shaking hands.

"Don't let it happen again," she whispered. "I don't like feeling like a fool."

He nodded, shame burning in his gut.

That night, she let him into the bed, let him hold her until the dawn. But when he woke, she was already gone, the smell of her perfume a ghost in the sheets.

He stared at the ceiling, the weight in his chest growing by the hour. "Where'd she go," he thought to himself not sure if he even cared.

He got up, dressed, and went back to the mine.

He didn't stop at Percy's that night. He worked an extra shift that came available, then came home to the empty house, the mirror reflecting the hollow of his face.

He poured himself a drink of cheap bourbon, sat on the edge of the bed, and watched the world turn blue outside the window.

He thought about Daisy, about Jimmy, about the stories that traveled faster than truth in a town like this.

He thought about the promise he made and wondered if it mattered. Daisy still wasn't home.

He finished the bottle and waited for morning.

The next night, Daisy was waiting. She wore a dress he'd never seen, something shimmery and bright. She greeted him at the door with a kiss, the taste of whiskey sweet on her lips, a slur in her voice.

"I made dinner," she said, leading him to the table. The meal was nothing; cold pasta, canned sauce, but she lit candles and poured the cheap wine, and for a moment, it almost felt real.

They talked about nothing, the way people do when they're trying to hide what matters. Daisy laughed, her voice louder than the walls could hold. She told him stories about people at the salon, the women who hated her, the men who watched her walk by. She acted like the world was just waiting for her to take it.

After dinner, she danced with him in the living room, bare feet on the rug, the mirror catching them as they spun. She pressed her body against his, kissed him hard, and pulled him down onto the floor.

For a while, he let himself believe it would be enough.

But when she slept, Danny sat up in the dark, the pain in his back grinding against his ribs. He watched her breathe, the ribbon splayed on the pillow, her hand curled in a fist.

He thought about the way she'd looked at him, the way she'd made him promise, the way her words never quite matched the way she held him.

He closed his eyes and dreamed of the mine swallowing him whole.

Morning bled pink across the ridge, the fog clinging to the hollow like a hand that didn't know when to let go. Danny walked the road slow, hands shoved in his jacket, the world just starting to stir. He passed the mine, silent at this hour, and made his way up the gravel to Earl McKinney's house, the old man's porch light still burning against the dawn.

Earl was there, planted in his swing, pipe smoke curling from the corner of his mouth. He wore the same coveralls as always, patched at the knees, and a sweater that might have been blue once. The porch sagged under his weight, boards creaking as he rocked.

"Wallace," Earl said, not turning. "You look like hell."

Danny took the steps slow, sat on the far end of the swing. He braced his arms on his knees, watched the pink light creep up the valley.

"Couldn't hardly sleep," Danny said.

Earl grunted. "Never could myself. After Nam, the only sleep I got was drunk sleep. The kind where the crackle of a fireplace could wake you from the dead ready to fight." He tapped the pipe, ash falling onto the boards. "What brings you up this early?"

Danny hesitated, picking at a blister on his palm. "Just needed to talk."

Earl nodded, waited.

"It's Daisy," Danny said finally. "She's bleeding me dry. I keep thinking, if I can just make her happy, maybe she'll stop looking past me. But every time I get close lately, she's already dodged me." He stared at his hands, the evidence of sacrifice, the harsh words the mountain wants you to remember.

Earl smoked, silent. The only sound was the wind through the trees, the slow ticking of the porch settling.

"She ever talk about leaving you?" Earl asked.

Danny shook his head. "She talks like we're building a future. But all I see is her taking pieces out of me, one at a time, to build hers."

Earl smiled, just a twitch at the edge of his mouth. "You ever hear about my brother? Man loved a girl so much he dug her a rose garden with his bare hands. Didn't matter that she was allergic, that she hated the smell. He just wanted to give her something nobody else could."

Danny looked up, brow furrowed.

"She left him anyway," Earl said. "Found a boy who

didn't care about flowers, just liked to watch the stars."
He let the story hang, pipe clamped between his teeth.

Danny didn't say anything.

Earl leaned forward, elbows on his knees. "There's two kinds of hunger in this world, son. One you can feed, with enough sweat and money and time. The other…" he waved his hand at the morning fog, "it just grows. No matter what you pour into it, there's always more room. Nothing fills it but the wanting for more."

Danny felt the words settle inside him, heavy as stone.

"Which kind is she?" Earl asked.

Danny opened his mouth, but the answer wouldn't come.

Earl patted his knee. "Don't take it hard. It's just how some folks are made. Don't mean she's evil. Just means you'll die trying to make her full."

They sat in the quiet for a long while, the sun barely above the hills. Danny watched the light creep over the trees, turning the dew to gold.

"You ever wish you'd done things different?" Danny asked, voice low.

Earl shrugged. "Wishing's free, but it don't buy back a minute." He drew on the pipe, the tobacco glowing red. "I figure, if you're gonna bleed for someone, you ought to know if it's livin' blood or dyin' blood."

Danny nodded, the ache in his chest spreading. He thought of Daisy, her laughter, the way she'd curl into him at night and then be gone by morning. He thought of the mirror, the new rug, the bills stacked up like bad news on the table.

He stood, joints cracking, and looked out over the hollow. The world seemed smaller from up here, like you could see the end of it if you squinted.

"Thanks, Earl," he said.

The old man nodded. "Any time. You know where to find me."

Danny started down the steps, then paused. "What happened to your brother?"

Earl grinned, all teeth. "He's still planting roses. Hasn't figured it out yet."

Danny smiled, the first time in weeks.

He walked home slow, the sun on his back, the mountain taller than ever.

He knew what kind of hunger lived in Daisy, and he knew it would never be fed.

But he also knew he wasn't ready to stop trying.

That night the sky pressed down so heavy it felt like the world had collapsed into the hollow. Danny walked home with his shoulders hunched, sweat cold on his chest, the ache in his bones louder than the sound of his boots on the stairs. Daisy wasn't home yet. The house was dark except for the light in the bathroom, the only place Daisy hadn't claimed for herself. He squinted against the glare and stared at his own face in the mirror.

The eyes that looked back were rimmed in black, the skin bruised and slack. His cheekbones stuck out, cut sharp by hunger and sleeplessness. The split in his lip was new, a gift from a slip of the hammer at work, and his right knuckle was an open wound, black blood caked into the lines. He peeled back the tape, watching the scab lift, and felt nothing.

He washed his hands slow, letting the water run pink and then clear. The sink filled with black grit and shavings of his own skin. He thought of Daisy, her laughter ringing in his ears, her smile stretched wide as she spun through the house, ribbon streaming. He thought of how she'd said, "Don't let it happen again," and how she didn't mean the joking, or the drinking, or even the other men. She wasn't talking to herself. She meant the way he made her feel alone, the way he couldn't fill the air with enough of himself.

He dried his hands and opened the drawer beneath the sink. The old lock pick set was still there, wrapped in an oil-stained rag. He turned it in his fingers, the metal familiar and cold. He took it, along with a cheap pair of gloves, and slipped out into the night.

The street was empty, the only sound the drone of the neon cross over the Farmacy. Danny kept to the alleys, head down, steps soft. The windows in Percy's were dark, the blinds pulled, the sign in the door flipped to CLOSED. He waited in the shadow of the dumpster, heart stuttering in his chest. He listened for voices, for the shiver of a car passing on the main drag, but there was nothing. The hollow was asleep.

He crouched at the door, gloves tight over his hands, and set to work. The pick slipped into the lock, the tension bar behind it, and he felt for the pins, listening for the tiny click of each one giving way. His hands shook, the tremor running all the way up his arm. He gritted his teeth and worked slower, counting under his breath, the numbers steadying him.

He had a movie playing in his mind. He knew what he needed to do to up the ante, to get the girl. Danny thought about what he'd take: maybe the necklace with the emeralds in it, or the ring Daisy had admired, blue stone sharp as a tear. Maybe just enough cash to keep her happy for a week, to buy a meal that wasn't bread and bologna. He told himself it was for her, but he knew better.

The lock gave a soft pop, the deadbolt sliding free. Danny's hands went still. He looked over his shoulder, the street unchanged. He reached for the handle, then stopped, the weight of the moment pinning him to the step.

He had visions of himself, in the mirror behind the bar, face drawn and empty. He saw Daisy's eyes, bright and cold, waiting to see what he'd bring home. He saw Earl, shaking his head, the words echoing: "You'll die trying to make her full."

He let go of the handle, breath shuddering out of him.

He backed away, the lock pick rattling in his pocket. He stood in the alley, staring at the door, the world silent except for the thud of his own heart.

"She needs to be gone," he whispered. "I'll die trying...," the whisper trailed off.

He turned and walked home slow, hands buried deep in his pockets. The neon sign buzzed overhead, its light painting the street. He stared up at it, the letters flickering.

He stood there a long time, listening to the hollow breathe.

When he finally climbed the stairs, Daisy was asleep on the couch, TV still playing. She'd left the door unlocked, trusting the world to leave her alone.

He sat beside her, watched her chest rise and fall, the ribbon loose in her hair. He reached out and touched her neck, gentle, as if she might break.

He waited for her to wake, not knowing if he'd ever be enough.

He waited, because that's what he did.

And the hollow waited with him, patient as the end of the world.

DIAMONDS ARE FOREVER

T he first time Danny put his hand around an- other man's throat, he half expected it to feel different. But it was only skin, hot and pa- pery, and the blood underneath thudded with the same terror as his own.

It started slow, always did, with Daisy curling her legs under the booth at Percy's, making a show of not looking at the bar. Danny hated how easy she made it, the way she could slide her glance along the rail and catch every man in the net, but pretend it was all just chance. He sat with her, picking at the label on his bot- tle, watching the clock creep toward his next shift.

Half Pint Carter sat three chairs down, alone but never lonely, the kind of drunk that survived on hear- ing his own voice bounce off anything with ears. He watched Daisy, eyes peeled wide, drinking her in the way men did when they had nothing else left to drink. Danny saw it, felt the way it crawled up his neck, but said nothing.

He wasn't scared of Half Pint, nobody was, not really, but the man's laugh stuck like a bad splinter. Daisy never let on, just twirled her pink ribbon through her hair, making it glint under the neon. The ribbon was old, maybe as old as her dreams of leaving, and Danny wondered if it was the only thing about her that ever got to stay.

Percy ran the bar with the silence of a warden, barely blinking as the hours ground through him. He poured for the regulars, wiped the same spot on the counter until the finish went dull. When he got to Danny, he poured heavy, maybe out of pity, maybe just to keep the peace.

The place was nearly empty. Billy and his shadow leaned over the pool table, eyes glazed, chalk dust smeared on his jeans. Two miners, not from the day crew, sat at the end, heads together, plotting either theft, escape, or street work depending on their bill.

Daisy ordered a rye whiskey, neat, and Percy handed it over with a glance at Danny. "You want another?"

Danny shook his head. He watched her knock it back, the liquid, spiced caramel gone in one snap of her throat. She didn't cough or make a face. She just set the glass down, wiped the edge with her thumb, and waited.

Half Pint was on his third, maybe his fifth, when he made his play. He sidled over, standing just close enough to let the sour of his breath creep onto Danny's skin.

"Never understood what you saw in her," he said, not to anyone, just to the air. "Nothing but a pretty neck and a taste for trouble."

Daisy didn't look up. Danny kept his eyes on the TV above the bar, where a weatherman in a cheap suit pointed at a line of storms rolling through the hollow.

Half Pint tried again, voice rising like he wanted everyone to hear. "Bet she screams if you pull it hard enough. Girls like that always do."

Danny turned. "You got something else to say to me?"

Half Pint smiled, teeth all edge and tobacco. "Just that I hope you're getting your money's worth. Wouldn't be the first time she's made a man pay through the nose, now would it?"

The words landed like a punch. Danny felt every eye in the bar flick his way, even Billy's, who'd stopped mid-shot to listen. Daisy said nothing, just stared at her empty glass, the ribbon in her hair like a flag for surrender.

Percy's hand paused on the register.

Danny stood. His boots squeaked on the wet patch of floor where someone had spilled a beer hours before. He moved without thinking, one motion, no grace. One hand on his neck, the other caught the front of Half Pint's shirt and lifted, not far, just enough to make the man's feet come off the ground for a second.

"Say that again," Danny said, voice flat.

Half Pint didn't blink. "Go to hell, Wallace. She's not worth it."

Danny shoved. Not a punch, not really, just a raw, mean push that sent Half Pint back onto a chair, the legs shrieking against the floorboards before the whole thing toppled. Half Pint hit the floor, beer and spit flying from his mouth, and for a second he looked like a child, lost and furious.

One of the miners laughed, the sound cold as ice. Billy whistled, low and slow.

Daisy didn't move.

Percy set the bottle down, walked around the bar, and stepped between them. He put his hand on Danny's shoulder, the weight of it more warning than threat.

"Let it go, son," Percy said. "Ain't nothing here but the ghosts you make."

Danny took a breath. His hands were shaking. He didn't remember making a fist, but his knuckles throbbed, white and bloodless. He opened his hand slow, feeling the hurt bloom down his arm.

Half Pint sat up, rubbing his throat, a wild smile on his lips. "That's it?" he said. "That's all you got?"

Danny wanted to crush him, to see the light go out in those eyes, but Percy's hand was steel. "Go home," Percy said, voice low. "Both of you."

Daisy slid off the bench, her body liquid, eyes unreadable. She didn't look at Half Pint, didn't look at Danny. She just walked to the door, ribbon trailing behind, and waited for Danny to follow.

He did.

Outside, the air was cold and wet, a haze of fog rising from the street. Daisy lit a cigarette with hands steady as a surgeon. She offered one to Danny, but he shook his head, the burn in his chest already enough.

They walked home in silence, the distance between them a live wire. Danny tried to catch her eye, but she stared ahead, the glow of the cigarette tracing her every exhale.

When they reached the house, Daisy went straight to the bedroom, dropped her bag on the floor, and stripped to her slip in one motion. She climbed onto the bed, pulled the blanket up, and waited.

Danny undressed slow, each button a battle, the bruise on his knuckle already spreading. He crawled in beside her, the sheets cold, her body colder. She rolled to him, pressed her mouth to his, and bit down just enough to draw blood. He kissed her back, not with tenderness but with the need to prove something, to make her feel it, to make himself real again.

She dug her nails into his back, scoring lines down his ribs. His movements were rough, with purpose, each an apology for what he couldn't fix. She didn't moan or cry out, just gritted her teeth and took it, eyes open, staring over his shoulder at the ceiling.

He finished quick, rolling off her before the ache in his chest could get worse.

She didn't reach for him. She didn't even close her eyes.

They lay side by side, the width of the bed between them, the only sound the slow bleed of rain against the window.

Danny stared at the ceiling, the shadow of the fan slicing the dark into ribbons. He listened to Daisy breathe, the hitch in her chest almost gone, and wondered if either of them would ever be enough for the other.

He reached for her, once, but stopped short, the space between too wide, too final.

Sleep was slow, heavy, and full of dreams he wouldn't remember.

In the morning, Daisy was gone again.

By late afternoon the world had shrunk to the size of a headlamp's halo. The wind off the hills had teeth in it, but inside the old No.3 drift, the air was still and heavy, thick enough to drink. Danny's boots slipped on the black moss at the mouth, and the stench of wet rock and mildew hit him in the sinus cavity like an infection.

He liked the hush here, the way sound died a few feet in, and the light behind you never made it past the first bend. He'd walked this seam a hundred times in a prior life he convinced himself, but the place felt changed, as if the mountain had grown meaner now that it was dying for good.

The entrance was caved on the left side, a jumble of beams warped and slick with brown rot, and the right hung open like a cut that wouldn't scab. Danny ducked through, headlamp flickering, hand skimming the old rail that led carts to the main drift. His gloves were thin, and the chill in the metal burned straight to bone.

Past the first turn, the air tasted like nothing, just the twinge of old stone and your own spit. The walls slicked in places, bleeding water where the rock wanted out. He ran his fingers along the ribs, counting the echo of each step, letting the dark swallow the sound behind him.

It didn't take long to lose sense of distance. He moved deeper, marking time by the way his breath plumed in the beam, by the drop in temperature, by the way the floor gave underfoot. The timbers creaked, but he trusted them, trusted the math and the history in the way they leaned.

After the fourth crosscut, he found the place he re-membered. The side tunnel slumped into black, half the supports gone or broken. It looked worse than before, as if the years had chewed it hollow, leaving only the rind. He stood in the arch, listening for the wet tick of water at the bottom, but heard only his own pulse, loud and hard.

This was it. The spot. The room at the end of the cut. A round void centered in the space. The shaft dropped straight, no grating, no fence, just a sign staked to the slush at the edge: DANGER, UNSTABLE, NO ENTRY. The shaft's mouth was maybe six feet across, rimmed in moss and old rust, and you could see nothing past a few feet down. He loosened a rock and dropped it, counting off the seconds, but there was no sound, not even a tap. He'd heard it went a thousand feet, maybe more, all the way to the water table. He pulled up the warning sign and sent it to the abyss as well.

He fished the spare flashlight from his pocket, thumbed it on, and aimed the beam into the hole. The circle of white vanished after a second, the dark eating it alive. He held it for a moment, then let it go, watching the pale ghost of the light tumble, spin, and then vanish. He waited for the sound, for anything, but it never came.

Danny crouched at the lip, boots pressed into the mud, and pictured Daisy here, her hands on her hips, eyes rolling at his stories, face lit up with the greed that made her beautiful. He imagined her leaning close, all focus on the wall, never seeing the fall until it was too late.

He rehearsed it, down to the words. There's something in the rock, he'd say, a shine behind the shale. He had to push her to take the bait. You ever seen a real diamond? Biggest you ever saw, just out of reach. He'd tell it slow, let her get hungry for it, let her want it more than she wanted him.

He thought of the ribbon, perfect and untouched, and knew she'd wear it till the day she died.

He stood, dusted his palms, and took one last look into the hole. The urge to spit in it, to mark it, crawled up his throat, but he swallowed it down. Better to leave no trace. Better to let the mountain keep its secrets.

He turned back, lamp tracing the slick walls, counting the way out by memory. Each step felt lighter than the last.

By the time he reached the daylight, his hands had

stopped shaking.

Percy's on a Thursday night was nothing, just the static hum of men who'd forgotten what day it was. The crowd sat thinner than blood. Half Pint hunched in the crook of the bar, Billy and his new tagalong still fighting the same game of eight ball from yesterday. Even Daisy seemed worn down, the string of her laughter pulled tight and ready to snap.

She showed up late, hair down for once but still adorned with the pink ribbon, lips a bruised plum color that made her look almost innocent. Danny flagged her over with a nod and bought her a drink before she even sat. He took the booth near the pool table, Half Pint planted close enough to hear but far enough to pretend he didn't care.

Daisy curled in beside him, pressed closed, and exhaled cigarette smoke in slow blue arcs toward the ceiling. "You look like you got news," she said.

He grinned. "You ever hear about the Hollow diamond?"

She rolled her eyes. "That's an old wives' tale. Billy says the only thing under these hills is more coal and regret."

He leaned in, close enough that she had to listen. "That's what they want you to think. But my daddy said there's a real one. Big as a hen's egg, clear as spring water. They pulled it from No.3 drift, back when the mines still ran. Only the boss man got greedy, tried to hide it, and the shaft caved, damn near killed him."

Daisy's eyes narrowed. "What's that got to do with us?"

Danny lowered his voice and pushed her to believe. "The shaft's still open, if you know where to look. Some nights, when the night's right, and your headlamp ain't dull, you can see a shine in the wall of the shaft. It's just sitting there. But nobody's ever gone after it, not since they tried to dynamite the cave. Some say it's cursed. Whitaker curse, to be exact."

She snorted, but her fingers tightened on her glass. "My daddy always said the real Whitaker curse was being born broke and mean. All that stuff about the mine was just to keep us out of the business."

Danny smiled. "This ain't about curses. It's about being the first to get in, before they shut it for good." He took a drink, letting the lie settle in the space between them. "I can show you. Tomorrow night. If you're ain't scared."

Daisy sat back, weighing him. "What's in it for you?"

He shrugged. "Just want to see your face when you hold a fortune in your hands."

For a second, she almost softened. "You know I could leave if I had money like that."

He let her think it. Let himself believe it, too, for half a breath.

Behind them, Half Pint's voice cracked like ice. "Bet you a hundred bucks there's nothing down that shaft but bones and broken dreams."

Daisy turned, sharp, but Danny just waved it off. He pushed her further, "Don't take my word. Come see for yourself."

Billy drifted over, leaning on the pool table. "You two plotting to rob the company store?" He grinned, missing three teeth in front.

Daisy ignored him, her gaze on Danny. "Why now?"

He glanced at the clock. "They're sealing the old drifts next week. After that, no one's getting in."

She chewed her lip, then nodded. "Alright. Let's do it. You'll owe me if it's just another ghost story."

He took her hand, felt the pulse thrumming there, and gripped it hard.

Across the room, Half Pint smiled into his drink, eyes pale and bright.

They left before closing. The cold hit hard, pulling tears from Daisy's eyes. She walked fast, dragging Danny by the wrist, the two of them trailing shadows down the alley to their house.

Inside, she tore off her coat, flung it at the chair, and turned to face him. "You really think it's real?" she asked.

He lied without blinking. "I do."

She kissed him, hard and open, teeth scraping his lower lip. He pushed her against the wall, the hunger in them back, ugly and alive. They made it to the bed in a tangle, her nails raking his chest, his hands in her hair. For once, it wasn't cold, wasn't empty, just raw and desperate, both of them clawing for something that would outlast the night.

After, she curled on her side, back to him. He watched her shoulder rise and fall, slow and even. In the dark, she looked like a normal woman, loving and honest. He wanted to reach out, to hold her, but didn't dare.

Instead, he stared at the ceiling, replaying the story he'd sold her. The diamond, the shaft, the promise of escape. He wondered if the lie would hold. He wondered if he could do what he'd planned, when the moment came.

He wondered if the Hollow would forgive him, if it ever forgave anyone.

Near dawn, Daisy rolled over, hair wild, eyes sharp.

"You promise you'll show me?" she whispered.

He nodded. "I promise."

She smiled, and for a second he saw the girl she must've been, years before he'd met her, before the mine or the town or any of it had ground her down.

He almost wished the diamond was real. He almost wished he could give her everything she wanted.

But in the end, all he had was the hole in the ground, and the hope that it would take her farther than he ever could.

In the early afternoon, they walked back to Percy's, hand in hand, shift cut short at the mine. Half Pint was there, same seat as before, eyes bloodshot but alive. He watched them, expression flat, and raised his glass.

"To fortune," he said.

Daisy laughed, brushing it off like he thought he knew what he was talking about. "To fortune."

Danny drank to it, feeling the words burn all the way down.

He didn't see Half Pint slip out the back door. He didn't see the way the his hands shook, or the way he palmed the old switchblade from his boot.

He just watched Daisy, watched the shine in her eyes, and waited for night to fall.

*Those who believe the last piece will complete
them rarely notice the ground giving way.*

SHE'S STILL FALLING

Dusk dragged itself down the hollow in a ragged heap, snagging every rusted signpost and dead sycamore from the old rail spur up to the mouth of No.3 drift. There, the mine's entrance hunched behind a curtain of thorn and switchgrass, as if the ground itself had spent years trying to choke the wound shut. The warning sign, caution in sun-bleached black, bolts twisted loose, sat half-swallowed by mud and burdock. Most didn't even notice it anymore. Most never got this close.

Jimmy "Half Pint" Carter got closer than most.

He came up the incline like a possum nosing for eggs: slow, sideways, with his left hand jammed in his jacket and the right trailing the slope, catching on briars for balance. It was still warm enough to sweat, and he did, the runoff tracking through the coal dust on his cheeks until his collar was streaked grey and salt. The smell of the place hit first. A standing damp of rot and mold mixed with the memory of ozone from when the fan house still spun. There'd be less than an hour before true dark, he figured. Enough.

He crouched behind the rib of a cut-stone loading dock, let his breath settle, and studied the black eye of the main shaft. He'd spent his first summer at this mine, running mule and cart, learning the pattern of cuss and silence that passed for communication underground. All that ended the year the Whitaker brothers lit the dynamite too wet, packed it anyway, and caved the Number Three crosscut on themselves and the shift boss. Three bodies, two recovered. The last one, so the stories went, was still down there, smothered in slurry and chunks of busted iron, waiting for a payday that never came. Since then, the place had been dead, but not unvisited. Nothing in White Oak Hollow ever truly quit.

Half Pint spat into the dirt, rolled his shoulders, and checked the knife at his ankle. His hands trembled, but only a little, the way they did before a fight or some pretty girl paid him attention. He liked the charge it gave him, like licking a battery, only meaner. He'd brought a half-pint of Evan Williams in his back pocket, and he unscrewed it now, the glass cool and sticky from the fridge at Percy's. He drank deep, not caring about the bite. Tonight was about more than comfort.

He pictured Daisy Whitaker the way he'd last seen her; hair wound tight in a twist, the pink ribbon trailing like a dare, lips painted so wild they looked lit from inside. He'd watched her all last summer, watched her move through the mine camp and the bars, always just out of reach, always looking for the next pair of eyes to drown in. She had a way of laughing at a man from a room away, turning every glance into a secret. Danny Wallace fell for it, poor bastard. He followed her without question. Like a pup with his paws still too big for his heart.

But Half Pint saw her. Knew her. Underneath the polish and the hungry, she was hollow. He'd seen it in the way she clutched at the gifts, the way she wrapped her fingers around her whiskey glass, the way she held herself apart, even when she pretended to let you in.

"She's been teasin' me for a year," he muttered, voice thick with dust and bourbon. "Thinks she's too good. Tonight, she'll learn different."

He took the knife from his boot, tested the edge against his thumb, and tucked it back. Not that he needed it for her, not really, but a man never could guess what shape the dark would take once you got inside. He checked his fly, spat again, and wiped both hands on the seat of his jeans. The anticipation sat under his ribs like a drumbeat, steady and growing.

Somewhere off in the trees, a nightjar started up, the whistle rising and cutting out like a bad light switch. He listened to it, imagined it was the whistle at shift change, a soul stealer all the same. He imagined that all the old crew would come pouring up the drift, dirty and laughing, ready for supper. Most were dead or gone now, except for Earl, Wallace, and a few others too dumb or stubborn to leave. He'd always hated Wallace. The way he made even the filth of the job look like a choice. The way he carried the guitar to work, played for tips on Friday, got pretty girls even when he couldn't afford to keep them. Wallace was weak, but lucky. And Daisy, she was his last jackpot, or so she thought.

Not after tonight.

Half Pint shifted in the weeds, the thorns tugging at his jacket, and pictured how it would play out. He'd wait for her to come, with the loser. They'd be dumb, probably drunk, talking loud, never thinking anyone would be out here this late. She'd go first, always did. Never let a man have the lead unless she wanted him to think he had it. He'd let them get deep enough to feel safe, maybe halfway to the Number Four crosscut, where the beams dripped with mold and the air was thin as a dream. Then he'd step out, say her name, and watch the panic bloom. He'd always been good at that. Sometimes, if he timed it right, she might even smile at the surprise.

He rolled his head back, watched the clouds bunch up behind the ridge. The sun was a smear, just a trace left above the trees. Good. The dark was always an advantage.

He unscrewed the bottle again, drained it, and let the warmth coil through his stomach. "Gonna be a hell of a show," he whispered, and let himself grin.

The mine was a living thing. He felt it every time he got close. The way the wind at the mouth pulled at your lungs, the way the ground thrummed under your boots like a heartbeat. He stood and stretched, knees popping, then slipped around to the side entrance, where the old cable winch still leaned against the wall, half-collapsed. He crouched behind it, eyes on the main drift, and settled in to wait.

A bat skittered out of the hole, wings catching on a shard of light before vanishing. Half Pint counted backwards from a hundred, then again, just to keep the nerves in line. He flexed his hands, knuckles swollen from old breaks and new work, and let the time slide over him.

He thought about Daisy again, about the way she'd smiled at him at Percy's that night, how she'd taken his hand, real soft, when he'd offered to walk her home. She'd let him touch her, once, out behind the Farmacy, lips sweet and sticky with cherry, her body hot against the brick. She'd pushed him away after, but he remembered the sound she made, a gasp like she was scared of her own wanting. He'd thought about it all summer. It made him frenzied.

He thought about the shaft, about the story Wallace spun. The diamond. It was bullshit, everyone knew, but the kind of bullshit that made sense if you needed it to. Daisy needed it. Maybe Wallace did too, though Half Pint doubted it. What Wallace needed was to be punished. To see his pretty prize get taken. To see what happened when you played hero in a world built for wolves.

He licked his lips, the taste of sweat and whiskey strong in the dying light. He pictured how he'd take her, how he'd hold her so tight she couldn't breathe, how she'd fight and then give in, because that's what girls like her always did. She'd pretend to hate it, but she'd thank him after. He'd make her remember.

He waited, patient, while the hollow held its own.

And somewhere down the switchback, in the clutch of evening, headlights flashed once and then disappeared.

It was time.

❋ ❋ ❋

By the time Danny parked the truck outside the Farmacy, the moon was a dirty thumbnail over the ridge. The store's neon cross flickered between green and dead, and inside, every light made the pills and packages look toxic. He squinted against the glare, worked the list in his head: fresh batteries, a cheap first-aid kit, maybe something for the ache that had started up behind his eyes three days running.

Daisy waited on the curb, pacing short laps, the

heels of her sneakers leaving little arcs in the powdery dust. She checked her phone even though it was out of minutes, drummed her nails on the glass like she could rattle Danny into hurrying. The way she moved reminded him of a cat that wanted out, pure tension and no patience.

He found the batteries fast, in the aisle marked "Electronics & Oddities." The packaging was greasy, the price gouged, but he needed the headlamp for the tunnels. Daisy had made it clear; if they came back with nothing, she'd leave him before winter set in. He believed her. That was plan B.

He set the batteries on the counter. The kid behind it looked at him like he was trying to buy a bomb. "You know these don't last but two hours in a row?" he said, voice flat as drywall.

Danny shrugged. "Don't need more than that."

The kid rang him up, never breaking the stare, and when Danny paid he could feel the judgment like a slap. He pocketed the change, shouldered his way back through the door, and nearly collided with Daisy, who'd started her own orbit just inside the vestibule.

She hooked his arm, voice a whisper: "You got 'em? I'm dying here."

"Here." He handed over the package. "But you gotta let me fix the light. Last time you changed batteries, it broke on you…"

She snatched the headlamp from his hand, ripped the batteries open, and jammed them in without looking. "I know what I'm doing," she said, though it took her three tries to get the cap twisted on right. When she clicked it, the bulb jumped to life, slicing a cold white circle onto the sidewalk. She grinned, a wild little animal.

"We should go now. C'mon." She didn't wait for him to answer, just started for the old truck. Danny followed, the taste of guilt mixing with new fear in his throat.

They hit the bottom of the switchback in less than ten minutes. The mine entrance was lost behind curtains of wild grape and chicory, the mud at the threshold churned to a soup by deer and smaller things. Danny cut the headlights and killed the engine. "You sure you want to do this?" he asked, but Daisy was already out the door, the headlamp bobbing as she scrambled up the path.

He halted at the tunnel's mouth and cursed under his breath. He'd left the knife in the truck. "Go on ahead," he called, fumbling with his jacket. Daisy didn't look back. The lamp's glow swallowed her as she stepped through the black arch.

Danny jogged back across the slick red clay, heart pounding in the silent night. The world outside the lamp was pure void. He found the knife by the tailgate, hefted it, then sprinted back toward the shaft, breath steaming in the cold air. But by the time he rejoined the mine entrance, Daisy was gone and all he had was a weak penlight for guidance.

Inside, Daisy advanced alone. The beam carved ragged paths through iron-scented air, hot with mildew and old diesel mechanizations. Water dripped somewhere far off, steady as a heartbeat, and every footstep echoed twice. She ran a gloved palm along the tunnel wall. "Feels like crawling through ribs," she murmured, dust pluming on her fingers. She laughed, a bright tinkle that snapped the dark.

The ceiling sank, walls closing in. At a left fork, sagging timbers creaked over the yawning elevator shaft. Daisy leaned forward, lamp probing the void. "Bet it's full of bones," she said, delighted at her revelation. She stepped back, grip on the lantern tight.

She pushed deeper, shoes skimming oil-slick puddles. The dampness thickened. Once, she slipped, her arm brushing something cold, mud, or maybe old blood, but she caught herself on a rotten beam and kept moving. Her heart hammered, and somewhere behind her Danny's boots never arrived.

Finally, the tunnel flattened and opened into a small round chamber. Black crystals mottled the far wall, glass that ate the beam. In the center, a perfect circle of stone: the bottomless shaft. Daisy crept to the edge, knelt, and shone the lamp down.

"Holy shit," she whispered. The light vanished into darkness that seemed to breathe. She leaned closer, hair falling over her cheeks.

A cough cracked the silence. She jerked upright. From the shadows stepped a figure, Jimmy Half Pint. Small, wiry, in a jacket two sizes too big. His grin was white against the black.

"Well, well," he purred. He took a half-step forward, and his hand went to the fly of his pants, loosening them in slow anticipation. She froze.

"Jesus," she said softly, stepping back, heart hammering in her throat. Recognition flashed in her eyes. It was the same desperate hunger she'd seen last time. But she didn't bolt. She lifted her chin.

"Look," she said, voice steady. "You help me find the diamond, I'll split it with you, half and half. Then we can both get the hell out of this hollow, after we take care of Danny." She tipped her lamp so it caught his face. "Deal?"

He blinked, then laughed, a rough bark that echoed off the rocks. "You're something else, Daisy," he said, voice low. He shrugged out of his jacket, the sleeves slipping off. "All right. Let's find your bullshit rock."

She nodded, stepping toward the shaft again. He moved with her, boots splashing in the muck. She kept the lamp trained on the hanging crystals, as if mapping their angles. He watched her, hungry, eager, but she never met his gaze.

At the lip, on the other side of the shaft, she paused, lamp sliding across his face. Carter's eyes were bright. He reached out and, without warning, snatched the ribbon from her hair. The pink strip fluttered in his fist, a defiant slash of color in the gloom.

She gasped, then smiled, sharp, fierce. Danny's footsteps finally echoed behind them, but the two were already locked in a dangerous dance at the edge of nothing. The ribbon lay loose in Carter's hand, and his pants had started to fall, as the shaft yawned below, silent and patient, ready to swallow them all.

※ ※ ※

Danny lingered at the tunnel mouth, waiting for the sound of her voice or the bounce of her lamp off wet stone. But there was nothing except the slap of water and, somewhere deep, the metallic echo of his own pulse. He called her name: "Daisy!" It came back at him warped, stitched together with old shouts and the memory of other names shouted down these walls.

He stepped inside, boots sinking in the slurry at the

entrance, and braced his palm against the cold stone. He hated the feel of it. Always slick, never quite dry, like the place was alive and exhaling under your skin. The mine pressed in. Every foot forward felt like a dare.

He moved deeper, following the marks left in the wet coal dust left by Daisy dragging her feet. The air thickened. Water dripped from the roof, sometimes steady, sometimes a sharp, loud spatter. Danny's breath burned in his throat; he pressed on, heart clenching.

He passed the elevator shaft, the old boards groaning under his step, and listened for the hollow thump that would say she'd gone ahead. He tried to remember what she'd looked like moments before when he last saw her. What she'd said. But all that came to mind was the sight of her back, her hair wild, the pink ribbon flowing longer than usual.

He called out again, and this time the echo came back with something new.

A scream.

It started small, like a laugh, then tore through the dark, sharp and real, rattling every beam and bolt. It went on, longer than seemed possible, then cut off, abrupt, like the air got sucked out. The mine shuddered, the sound hanging after, like smoke.

He ran, feet sliding in the muck, skin alive with fear. Each turn in the drift got narrower, the ceiling lower. He half-crawled, scraping his elbows and knees, gasping in panic and pain.

He found the room at the end, where the shaft gaped wide. And there, at the edge, sprawled like a sack of laundry, was Half Pint Carter.

The man's jacket was half off, pants undone and tangled at the knees. His face was a mess, scraped and streaked with tears or sweat or both. His hands clutched at something, and for a second Danny thought it might be blood. But when the man rolled, dazed, what he held was Daisy's ribbon, twisted and limp, a smear of pink in all that dark.

Danny froze, his own hands shaking. He tried to speak, but no words came.

Half Pint looked up, his eyes wide and pale, and whispered, "She's still falling."

Danny's mind cracked open. He pictured her, caught between Jimmy and the hole, the edge behind, nothing to hold on to but pride. He pictured how close he'd come to pushing her himself, just to get it over with, to be rid of the want and the need and the hole she'd drilled in his life. Now she was gone, and he was empty.

He wanted to kill Carter. He wanted to drag him to the shaft and shove him after her, to erase the whole thing. But he didn't move.

The ribbon hung from Carter's hand, swinging slow.

"What happened?" Danny choked out. His voice was dust.

Carter stared at him, hollowed out. "She's still falling," was all he could muster.

Danny saw the scratch on Carter's cheek, the way his shirt was ripped at the collar, the bruise rising on his jaw. He imagined Daisy's nails, her heels, the wild way she fought when cornered. He tried to picture her begging, but it wouldn't stick. He saw only the back of her head, the ribbon bright against the black.

He looked at Carter again. "You piece of shit," he spat.

Carter flinched but didn't let go of the ribbon. "Ask the mine," he said, the words nothing but sound.

Danny stepped closer, but his legs quit on him. He

slumped against the wall, the cold crawling up his back. He pictured the shaft, how it ate the lamp's light, how it never gave anything back.

He wondered if she was gone for good, or just waiting somewhere down there, her voice lost in the echo.

He wondered if it mattered.

He didn't cry. The tears wouldn't come.

The only thing left was the guilt, hot and bitter and alive. It moved in his chest, in his lungs, made every breath a punishment.

He stared at the ribbon, wanting to take it, but knowing he didn't deserve it.

He backed away, hands out, and left Carter on the floor, whimpering.

He walked out of the mine, step after step, never looking back, the sound of the scream stitched into his brain.

Outside, the night was full and blank. He stumbled to the truck, sat behind the wheel, and let the silence bleed him dry.

He didn't drive. He didn't move. He just sat and listened to the hollow breathing.

He would never say what really happened. He couldn't say what happened. He didn't know for sure.

He would carry the weight, like the mountain carried every other secret in this town. He had pushed her...if not in his mind.

He would keep her alive, in his guilt.

And the ribbon, even now, in the whiskey pickled hands of Jimmy Half Pint, made loneliness more real than ever.

FROST ON THE FIDDLE

Suggested Listening: Before you step further, I invite you to pause and listen to Raleigh Keegan's Wishing Well. Its pull of longing and reckoning will set the tone for what follows in ways words alone cannot.

The mine had gone to five eights, and still it managed to swallow every sound in the valley. By seven, the sun barely cleared the ridge, but the yard at the portal was already packed, more men than jobs, most staring at the wall of chain-link or at their boots. A line of trucks, beds sagging under coolers and plastic crates, idled along the berm, each one holding a driver with hands braced white against the wheel, waiting to see if they made the cut that day.

Danny Wallace slid in with the morning crew, his hard hat scabbed in duct tape, lamp already burning a hole in the fog. He didn't talk, didn't bother with the greetings or the mumbled shit talk that drifted around the muster point. The men were hungover from worry, faces slack in the gray light, all of them listening for the blow of the whistle that would mean the foreman had picked his number.

No one looked up when the whistle finally let loose. Three dozen miners flinched as one. Old Earl McKinney barked the names, sometimes first, sometimes last, sometimes both if he liked you, and always in a rhythm that left the losers waiting an extra heartbeat. Danny's came fourth, just "Wallace," then a jerk of the chin toward the gear shack. Two behind him, a man with a baby-face and half a tattoo on his neck slouched away from the line, hands jammed in his armpits, shoulders shaking as if he'd just dodged a bullet instead of taken one.

There were no smiles. No talk of luck or second chances. The ones not called turned on their heels, headed back to trucks or to the vending machine inside the cinderblock break room, where they'd wait for the next round or just for the morning to pass.

Inside, the tunnel's mouth was a black lung. Danny found his spot, a wedge of coal seam marked by an X in orange paint. He shouldered his pick and set to work, muscle memory taking over before the nerves in his hands had caught up. Swing, dig, pull. The impact ran up his arms, a familiar ache. The rhythm made him calm, enough to let his mind drift, enough to lose track of what day it was or where the week had gone. He barely noticed the others, even when their laughter or cussing floated down the drift in brief gusts, like weather.

He was three hours in before his lamp started to dim. He'd meant to charge it, but the battery was old even when it was new, and the backup was out of reach in the dark. He worked by the glow of the last bulb behind him, the shadows bleeding out of the wall, stretching as the light faded. He didn't mind. The dark suited him these days.

He thought of Daisy, not as she'd been, but as she was

now: a rumor, a caution, something that hovered in the gap between something true and something told. Her face was hard to call up, but the sound of her voice cut through the dust, the shape of her hand on his back, the curl of the ribbon in her hair. He worked faster, like he could dig her out of the wall if he just kept swinging.

The pick rang out, louder than before. For a split second, the air trembled, and the coal face buckled, not as rock but as flesh: soft and giving, like a body pressed flat against the mountain's frame. Danny blinked, and in the faint lamplight he saw her, not Daisy as she was, but Daisy as he had imagined, arms thrown up against the wet wall, hair plastered to her cheek, a smear of blood at her lip. Half Pint's shadow loomed behind, pants down, eyes wild, smile a bare line.

The vision snapped him out of rhythm. The pick slipped in his grip, bit deep into the seam, and stuck. His pulse hammered so loud it drowned out every other sound. He jerked his head, expecting to see the shift foreman, or maybe even Daisy herself, risen up from the shaft to call him a liar.

But there was nothing. Just the coal, the dark, and the rattle in his chest.

He yanked the pick loose and forced his breath slow. His hands shook, so he set them against the wall until the tremor faded.

He heard laughter up the drift, not mean, just tired. One of the men, probably Billy, told a story about a rat that had learned to drink from a forgotten lunch thermos, how it staggered around the lunchroom for a full week before it finally died of joy. They all laughed, but the sound was a dry scratch, more memory than real.

Danny finished the cut, worked the wedge out and

stacked it on the cart. The X was gone, erased by new black. He moved to the next seam, hands going through the motions, but his mind was back at the shaft, at the way the air seemed to shift, just before the scream.

He didn't speak until end of shift. The lamp had gone to orange, then to a soft, dying red. He followed the others out, boots squelching in the mud, the scent of sulphur and sweat tangled in the air. The yard was empty now, most of the men already gone home or to the bar. Only the late shift stragglers and a few lost souls hung around, staring at the sun as if it was some animal they'd never seen before.

He scrubbed his hands at the wash station, water running black and then clear. He caught a glimpse of his face in the warped mirror above the sink. Eyes rimmed in blue, cheekbone gone sharp, lips split at the corner. He touched his cheek, pressed until it hurt, then let up.

He walked the road home slow, cutting across the lot behind the Farmacy. He passed the window, saw a pair of men slumped inside on the plastic bench, eyes on the news running silent on the mounted TV. The place smelled of bleach and failure.

He went up the sidewalk to his house, keys jangling. He had locked the door out of habit, but it wasn't necessary. Nothing in there was worth stealing.

He took off his boots, set them by the heater, and hobbled up to the bedroom. The air inside was stale, the window still covered by the lace Daisy had tacked up before she left. Her scent was mostly gone, replaced by the mineral stink of the mine, but he could still see her in the way the bed was made, the way the blanket curled under itself on one side.

He opened the closet, half expecting her clothes to

have vanished. But they were all there, hung on the cheap wire hangers: the sundresses, the cardigans some missing buttons, the coat with the rip in the lining. He ran his hand along the row, then let it fall.

The box was under the bed, where he'd shoved it weeks ago. Just a cardboard rectangle, taped at the corners, the word "STUFF" scribbled in black marker. Inside was stuff she'd left behind: a hairbrush with three blonde strands still caught in the bristles, a tube of lipstick worn down to a stub, a nail polish bottle dried shut. There was a single earring, not even real silver, and a pair of pantyhose in the packaging, never opened.

He set the box on the bed and sat down next to it. He stared at the contents for a long minute, mind blank. Then he pushed the lid back on, hard, and shoved it under the bed again. He stood and shut the closet door.

He went to the window, thumbed the lace curtain aside, and stared at the ridge. The sun was long on the horizon, but the shadow hadn't moved from the mouth of the Old No. 3. He wondered if it ever would.

At night, Percy's bar filled slow, the regulars moving like they were under water. Most men sat in pairs, hunched over their glasses, backs to the mirror behind the counter. The only ones who drank alone were the ones who didn't have a story worth sharing, or the ones who'd already told too many.

Danny was on his second whiskey when Sheriff Colton Hale walked in. The room hushed, just a touch. Hale's boots were clean, his jeans ironed, and he wore his badge loose on his belt, as if it was an afterthought. He moved up to the bar, nodded at Percy, and took the stool beside Danny.

Percy poured him a double, no ice. Hale drank it in

two slow sips, then set the glass down so gentle it barely made a sound.

For a while, nobody said a thing. Behind the bar, Percy stacked empty glasses, polished them with a towel, eyes down. At the far table, Billy and his shadow played cards, never looking up.

Hale broke the quiet. "Funny thing about folks vanishing," he said, almost like a joke. "No one files a report, no one calls in the dogs. People just say 'that's a shame,' and let the wind do the rest. Frost on the fiddle it seems."

Danny rolled his glass between his palms, the liquor already burning his tongue numb. "Don't reckon there's much to investigate," he said. "Daisy was always running. Half Pint, too."

Hale nodded, as if that was the answer he'd expected. "Town's full of rumors, though. Some say you and Daisy were planning to light out, maybe with a pile of money. Others say you and Half Pint were at each other's throats, and now you're the only one left standing."

Danny shrugged. "People say a lot. Doesn't make it true."

Hale studied him, not blinking. "Never does. Still, you'd be surprised how fast things unravel when you start pulling at loose threads."

Danny drained the last of his drink, let the burn cut a path down his throat. "What are you getting at, Sheriff?"

Hale smiled, but there was no warmth in it. "Just keeping an eye on things. Last thing I want is for folks to think I'm not doing my job."

Percy poured another round, set the glasses down and wiped the bar clean. The room got quiet, the only sound the clink of ice and the dull thump of cards on the table.

Hale leaned in, voice lower. "You miss her, don't you?"

Danny's hands went still. He stared at the whiskey, watched the way it caught the bar light, and wondered if he could ever say yes without choking on it.

"I miss a lot of things," he said.

Hale straightened, pushed his glass away, and stood. He put a twenty on the bar, nodded at Percy, and walked out without another word. The bell above the door gave a tired ring, then silence.

After he left, the room let out its breath. Billy laughed, loud and fake, and Percy went back to stacking glasses. Danny sat there, not moving, until the ice melted in his glass and the sweat from his hands made a little puddle on the counter.

He heard the whispers, just under the hum of the lights. "Whitaker Curse." "She's not the first." "Wonder what the boy did to her."

He wanted to yell, to break a glass or throw a punch, but all he could do was stare at the glass where the whiskey had waited to punish him.

Percy came by, eyes softer than usual. "You okay, Wallace?"

Danny nodded, but it was a lie. "Just tired," he said.

He finished his drink, stood on legs that didn't quite want to work, and let the door close behind him. The street was empty, the neon cross above the Farmacy flickering green against the sky.

He walked home slow, the world fuzzy at the edges. When he got to the house, he stood at the door for a long time, key in hand, staring at the lock like he'd forgotten how it worked.

Inside, the box was still under the bed. The closet was still shut. Nothing moved, nothing changed.

He poured himself a glass of water, drank it in one go, and laid down on the couch.

He closed his eyes, but sleep wouldn't come.

All he saw was the shaft, the dark, and the bright pink ribbon swinging in the air.

And all he felt was the weight of not knowing, and the guilt of pretending he never would.

A few nights later, the bar was nearly empty. Only Percy, who never left, and Danny, who had nowhere else to be. It was the slow shift, when the lights buzzed louder than the voices and the only music was the sound of ice shifting in an empty glass.

Danny sat at the counter, his elbows leaving smudges on the lacquer, fingers idly spinning a small silver key on its chain. It caught the light, flashed, and spun again, over and over, a nervous habit he hadn't had in a long time. The key was plain, nothing special, but the weight of it felt like a stone against his chest.

He remembered when Shelby gave it to him, and the last day he saw her. She'd pressed it into his palm, hands shaking. "You can come back, if you want," she'd said. He'd promised to write, to call, to be more than just a ghost in the rearview. But after Daisy, the ghost was all that was left.

The door creaked and a man walked in. Not old, not young. Brown jacket, clean boots, hands too clean to belong here. He slid onto the stool beside Danny, nodded at Percy, and waited. Danny had seen this man before, he vaguely recalled, but some time back.

Percy didn't even glance his way. Just wiped down

the bar, poured Danny another shot, and went to the far end where he started sorting receipts.

The man in the brown jacket smelled faintly of tobacco and rain. He didn't order, just sat, arms folded, watching the rows of empty bottles behind the bar.

Danny turned the key in his hand, then let it drop to around his neck. "You ever lose something so quickly, you forget what it felt like to have it?" he said, to no one in particular.

The man didn't answer right away. He leaned forward, eyes bright, and said, "Sometimes the things we lose find their way back to us. And sometimes they stay lost for good reason."

His voice was like gravel, but there was a warmth in it. For a second, Danny thought of his father, the way he used to sound when he was tired but not yet mean. The way he'd talk to Danny late at night, when the world had gone quiet and there was nothing left but the two of them.

Danny laughed, a weak thing. "Not much of a comfort," he said.

The man nodded. "Wasn't meant to be."

They sat in silence. The key caught the light again, the chain rattling faintly around his neck.

Danny tried to think of something else to say. But the man was already standing, already pushing back from the bar. He left no money, no glass, just a faint impression in the seat.

Percy reappeared, towel in hand. "You want another, Wallace?" he asked.

Danny looked up, surprised to see the man was gone. The stool beside him was empty.

"Didn't you see that guy?" Danny said.

Percy frowned, looked around. "Who?"

Danny shook his head. "Never mind. I'm fine."

He let the key drop heavy against his chest. The door to the bar was still swinging, but the street outside was empty. He watched the way the neon light bled into the dark, then turned back to his drink.

He was alone again. Maybe he always had been.

The house was empty and loud. Every floorboard complained, every pipe whined. The refrigerator cycled on and off like a distant thunder. But nothing drowned out the noise inside Danny's skull, a steady grind that started as soon as he closed his eyes.

He lay on the bed, arms crossed over his chest, boots kicked off but nothing else changed. He hadn't bothered with the covers. The sheets barely held Daisy's scent, faded and bitter. He stared at the ceiling, traced the cracks that spidered out from the base of the ceiling fan. He wondered how long they'd been growing. He wondered if he'd ever notice if they finally split wide and brought the whole ceiling down.

He tried to sleep, but every time he blinked, he saw the shaft. The endless dark, the sound of her voice echoing in the tunnel, not in words but in a sharp, bright shriek that seemed to cut through his bones. Sometimes he saw Half Pint, face twisted in terror, hands clutching at the pink ribbon, eyes hollow as the mine itself. Sometimes it was just the ribbon, twisting and snapping in a wind that didn't exist, or Daisy's mouth forming his name with lips too pale to be alive.

He rolled over, punched the pillow, tried to squeeze the air out of his lungs so he'd finally just pass out. But the dreams didn't stop. They came harder, more vivid. Now he was back in the drift, pick in hand, but the seam bled red instead of black. He tried to dig, but the coal crumbled and ran like water, filling the tunnel, flooding his boots, crawling up his legs. The only way out was forward, but every time he moved, the drift grew tighter, the roof dropping until he could only crawl on his belly, mouth filling with grit and ash.

He woke, heart racing, sweat cold on his neck. He checked the clock, saw that only twenty minutes had passed. The world outside was silent, not even a car on the road.

He sat up, swung his legs off the bed, and put his head in his hands.

He'd never believed in curses. Not until Daisy. Not until he saw what wanting could do to a person.

He crossed the room, pulled his old guitar from behind the closet door, and sat at the window. The strings were out of tune, but he didn't care. He strummed slow, the sound thin and weak, but the noise of it was enough to cut through the ringing in his ears.

He grabbed a pen, pulled his notebook out, the pages warped from rain and old coffee. He started to write, letting the words come as they wanted, not caring if they made sense or if they rhymed. "Fill my cup up in a dust bowl river."

He titled it "Wishing Well," though he wasn't sure what he was wishing for anymore. Every line bent toward Shelby, her essence threading through every verse, even though he tried to keep her out. He wrote about loss, about yearning, about the ache of not finding the things you are looking for though you know you are looking right at them.

He played the melody, soft and broken, then wrote more. The words fell onto the page, misspelled and crossed out and started again, but he kept going. He wrote until his hand cramped, until his eyes blurred, until the sun started to rise behind the curtain.

When he stopped, the world was quiet. The ache in his head was still there, but softer, distant, like a bruise instead of an open wound.

He closed the notebook, set the guitar in his lap, and let himself drift. The dream came again, but this time the shaft was empty, the ribbon gone. There was nothing waiting for him in the dark, except for the sound of his own voice, echoing off the walls, getting weaker with every turn.

He slept then and didn't wake until the house was filled with light.

GHOSTS OF THE HOLLOW

When Danny woke, the house was full of light but no warmth. He lay a moment in the numb lull after a hangover, eyes glued open, the crust of last night's sweat still cold along his ribs. The guitar sat by the window, where the sunrise hit it straight on. He ignored it. He ignored the coffee pot, too, and the slow-grinding ache in his hip. He pulled on a shirt and jeans from the floor, then stepped barefoot, down the stairs, over the dust, and the loose boards, out into the sharp blue dawn of White Oak Hollow. He needed some sunlight on his face before the mountain's agitated breath covered the sky; and willing to live for the day, he finished getting dressed.

The air still stank of burning, some mix of old brush pile and sweet rot. Danny walked with his hands jammed into his pockets, boots scuffing the pitted concrete as he moved. The town was caught in the hush between shifts, some miners already underground, school kids not yet emerged, housewives left alone with their guilt and the TV. He followed the sidewalk past the Farmacy, past the pawnshop with its grimy window, to Main. There, on the east side, sat the music store. Once, it had been the only reason he ever thought this town might matter.

He slowed without thinking, stopped in front of the boarded glass. The sign over the door, ANCHOR MUSIC, hung from a single rusted hook, and the ANC had peeled into humped, drunken letters. A plastic banner still clung to the bottom of the window, but the color was gone, and the corners curled like the lip of an old wound. He counted three planks across the door, each nailed in with fat, deliberate spikes, as if someone had meant it permanent. The posters in the window were fossils, one for the State Fair Talent Show, one for a high school jazz night, one for a bluegrass festival that had happened before he got out of school. Behind all that, dust caked so thick it might as well have been paint.

Danny flexed his hands. They still remembered the fretboard. Even now, the fingers twitched and shaped invisible chords as he stood there, muscles tight with memory. For a second, he let himself see it, the kid with the wild hair, the first guitar slung like a gun, the fever-dream of making it all the way to Nashville, playing the honky-tonks where the air vibrated with more than just cold or fear.

He reached out, knuckles brushing the glass. It trembled under his touch, and a fine line of grit peeled off onto his skin. He wiped it on his jeans, then stared into the reflection. The sunrise made a gold halo around his head, but the rest of his face was a ruin, eyes ringed black, jaw gone sharp with hunger. In the glass, his image doubled: the grown man, and behind him the boy, not so different, just less hollow. The overlay made his stomach twist. He pressed his forehead to the window, closed his eyes, and counted to five, hoping the pulse in his temples would settle.

He thought about the time his old man brought him here, after a week of double shifts, so tired he could barely stand. He'd handed Danny a twenty, said, "Pick what you want, but don't ask for more if you can't pay back." He'd spent an hour in the shop, running his fingers over everything. In the end, he picked a set of nickel-wound strings and a capo so cheap it snapped a string on the second use. Still, the memory glowed. He'd played until his fingers bled, and even then, didn't stop.

The door was never locked, back then. Now, the boards said what nobody needed to say: nothing here worth saving, nothing here worth breaking in for. Danny stepped back, hands curled tight, and tried to remember why he kept coming by, what he expected to see.

A sudden wind kicked up, swinging the sign hard on its hinge. The metal shrieked. Danny flinched, the sound shattering the spell. Across the street, an old woman in a housecoat watched him from her porch, eyes narrowed, as if she expected him to smash the glass or piss on the stoop. He lifted his chin, gave her a slow nod, then turned away.

He walked on, the memory of the guitar still tingling in his fingers. At the end of the block, a crow picked at something dead in the gutter; rat, maybe, or possum, and a slick of blood shone on the blacktop. Danny watched the bird work, relentless, not caring who saw. He thought of his relationship with Shelby for a moment, the way she warmed the room when she walked in, the way it had faded to nothing so fast you could almost doubt it had ever existed. He let the thought go before it soured with the gutter activity.

At the edge of town, the hillside sloped down toward the old rail spur, the air heavy with a fresh wave of coal dust from the early shift. Danny paused there, watched the cars inch along the ridge, the line of them barely moving. He remembered how, as a kid, he'd traced each car with his finger, counted them, wondered where they might go. Now, he just envisioned a chain of men going nowhere, locked together by habit and hunger.

His hands ached with wanting. For the guitar, for the girl, for something that would let him break the surface of this place. Instead, he walked on, boot soles thumping the earth, body pulled forward by nothing but the knowledge that standing still hurt worse.

He didn't know where he was going, but he knew he couldn't stay. The music store's reflection clung to him, a ghost dragging at his shoulders. It would always be there, waiting, a mirror for everything he'd lost and never learned how to replace.

He kept walking, but the music in his head never quit.

He took the back way, past the switch yard and over the rusted pipeline that followed the creek. Morning shift at the mine was already in full swing and another wave of miners lined up, the pit gate open. He stood at the fence and watched them go, one after another, helmets low, boots dragging, as if the mountain pulled them in with a rope.

The men didn't talk, not at first. They moved in silence, hands shoved deep in pockets, eyes fixed on the ground ahead. Every third or fourth step, one would cough or spit, a little mark of resistance before the mountain finished swallowing them up. The only color came from the hardhats, some white, some yellow, a few streaked in spray paint or stickers that meant nothing outside of the yard. Most of the faces were blank, already dusted with black, eyes rimmed red from the cheap light and the sleeplessness that never left. They looked like ghosts of themselves, shadows drawn too tight.

Then, as the line slowed at the man-cage, somebody started up a joke. The words were muffled, swallowed quick, but the laugh that followed was sharp, slicing the gray. A few more men joined in, each laugh a little louder than the last, until the sound carried all the way across the parking lot. It was not a happy sound, more a bark of defiance, but it made the yard feel less dead for a second.

Danny felt it hit him in the teeth. He stepped back, away from the fence, but not far enough that he couldn't still see. The laughter echoed, then faded as the men packed into the lift. He counted the heads, the sets of shoulders, the way the group pressed together and then vanished as the steel cage sank out of sight. He'd made that ride too many times. Knew the jolt as the cable jerked you down, the whine of the gears, the silence in the dark while you waited for the cage to stop moving. He tasted the air, thin and metallic, and tried to spit it out, but the taste never left.

He watched the last few stragglers shuffle in. One was a kid, maybe seventeen, acne scarring the edge of his jaw, hat too big for his skull. Next to him, an old man, Earl's age, or older, dragged a lunch pail by the handle, his body bent from the waist as if bowing to a god that would not let him go. Danny saw how they moved together, the old and the young, neither one sure who was leading. The pit boss barked at them, waved them forward, and the gate clanged shut.

Another group stood off to the side, waiting for the lift to come back up. They leaned on the tailgate of a battered pickup, trading smokes and stories. One of them saw Danny watching, raised a hand in greeting, the gesture slow and tired. Danny almost waved back, then stopped. He looked at his own hands, saw the dark crescents of coal under each fingernail, the skin raw and split at the joints. He clenched his fist, felt the grit grind between his knuckles.

For a second, he thought about crossing the yard, going in, joining the line. He could do it. The foreman wouldn't blink, wouldn't ask if he was on the roster or not. You belonged, or you didn't, and the mountain didn't care either way.

But he didn't move. He stood rooted, watching the next set of men disappear into the cage, the laughter thinner now, stretched to breaking. He waited until the yard was empty, until all that was left was the echo of boots on metal and the dull hiss of the fan house pumping poison out of the black.

He let his hand drop. The dirt under his nails would never come clean, no matter how many times he tried. He knew that now.

He turned away, boots heavy, and let the mine swallow someone else for a change.

The Farmacy always smelled of burnt coffee and old fruit, a stink that settled in the back of your sinuses and made you want to sneeze it out. Danny slipped inside, head down, letting the door's warped bell jangle his entrance. The place was long and narrow; two aisles split by a row of freezers that hadn't worked right since the Bush administration. At the back stood the real business: rows and rows of liquor, from the cheap plastic jugs to the stuff behind the chicken-wire cage that only the out-of-towners ever bought. The rest was afterthought; cans of beans, a shelf of wilted apples, a rack of Wonder bread that nobody touched except to check the date and put it back.

Martha Blackwood ran the register and the whole damn store, her hair in a bun so tight it pulled her face sharp. She kept her ledger open on the counter, jotting figures in pencil between each sale, eyes never quite leaving the customer. Danny set his things down, a loaf, a jar of peanut butter, a pint of Evan Williams bourbon, and waited.

Martha didn't look up at first. "You're in late today," she said, voice flat, the pencil never pausing.

Danny shrugged, tried to keep his hands from shaking. "Didn't need much."

She glanced at the bourbon, then back at him, eyebrow raised just a tick. "Thought you'd sworn off, after the last hangover." She rang up the items, slow. "Heard you're spending more time at Percy's, lately, maybe got yourself in a bit of a mess."

Danny didn't answer. He slid the money onto the counter, pushing it toward her. His hands shook a little more than he liked, so he stuffed them in his pockets, nails digging into the seams.

Martha counted the payment, then flicked her gaze at him, eyes bright with something like hunger. "You ever going to pay off your tab? Or is this just how you like it, floating between paydays making good on last week's bill while you run up this week's?"

The words landed like gravel. Danny opened his mouth, then closed it. He'd heard it before, worse, but from Martha it hurt. He waited for her to finish.

She did, tallying his payment in the ledger, then scratching a hard line under the balance. "If you keep going the way you are, there'll be nothing left for you to put back together. You know that don't you?"

He nodded, not trusting himself to speak. He took the bag, feeling the heat of her stare as he turned.

The two men in the back, splitting a six-pack between them, stopped talking as he passed. One of them, the old guy with the limp, always in here after five, mumbled something about "Whiskey Wallace," and the other snorted. Danny ignored them, kept his eyes on the warped tile and made for the door.

Martha called after him. "You give my best to Daisy, now. Tell her we're all praying for her." The words twisted at the end, a barb more than a benediction.

He walked out, the bell giving a last, angry shriek. He stood under the awning, letting the chill settle into his bones, the plastic bag biting into his fingers. Through the glass, he could see Martha marking debts in the ledger, pencil dancing with a speed that seemed almost joyful. The other customers lingered, watching him, faces blank as masks.

He flexed his hand, feeling the coins he'd kept in his pocket, the last ones. He wondered how many more days before the balance in Martha's book caught up with the one in his chest.

He started for home, the sun still up but already losing to the gray. Behind him, the Farmacy glowed with bad fluorescence, a beacon for all the things that never got better.

As he walked, he felt the stare of the whole town on his back. He didn't have to look to know.

He walked the rest of Main, took the path behind the cemetery, and followed it down to the creek where he and Shelby used to go when the world felt big enough to let them. The way was mostly hidden now, overgrown with thistle and trash trees, but the old fence posts still lined the trail, leaning together like drunks at the end of a party.

The creek had shrunk, same as everything else. Once, it was wide enough to swim, the banks lined with ferns and wild mint. He remembered Shelby picking a bunch of it, rubbing it between her palms and laughing when the smell stuck to her skin for days. Now, the water ran black with mine runoff, slow and heavy, leaving a slick on every rock. The air above it burned his nose with the sweet rot of things that never fully died.

Danny sat on the bank, letting the cold seep through his jeans. The spot was the same one where he and Shelby had first kissed, and later, where they'd held each other with a desperation he didn't know how to name at the time. He'd come here sometimes after she left him for her own life, to see if the memory had faded. It never did, not really. There was always the key.

The blanket was long gone, but in its place were beer cans, shattered glass, and a mess of plastic bags caught in the branches at the waterline. The sun caught on the trash and made a sick kind of rainbow. He watched the colors break and bend, then shut his eyes, wanting to burn the image away.

He leaned forward, knuckles digging into the dirt,

and thought about stepping in, just to see if he could still feel anything at all. He reached for the surface, but the stink stopped him. It was worse than the mine; rancid, chemical, not of any world he wanted to belong to. He pulled back, wiped his hand on the grass.

He picked up a stone, flat and gray, and flicked it into the creek. It skipped once, then dropped, sending a ripple that warped the surface. For a split second, he caught his own reflection with Shelby, a mess of angles and shadows, but beautiful and with an air about her. He wanted to smash it. He wanted to pull Shelby out of the water and ask if it was all his fault, if there had ever been a way to keep her.

The sun slid behind a cloud, and the world went blue.

He was about to stand, to go back and try again to be someone worth looking at, when he saw it, caught in a clump of dead grass near the shore, a streak of pink so bright it burned. He blinked, thinking it was a scrap of plastic, but it wasn't. It was a ribbon, tangled but still whole, the color exactly the same as the one Daisy wore in her hair. He stared, heart stuttering, as the wind tugged it back and forth, back and forth, until it seemed alive.

He reached for it, hands trembling. The ribbon felt cool and slick, not like silk but close enough to trick him. He untangled it from the grass, held it up, and watched the way it fluttered, even with the faintest breeze.

He thought of Daisy then, and of every girl who had ever tried to save themselves with something beautiful, only to end up caught in the same current as everyone else.

He held the ribbon in his fist, tight enough to leave

marks, and stared at the water. He didn't move for a long time.

When he finally let go, the pink strip floated back to the ground, settling in the mud just like everything else that had ever mattered.

By the time he hit town again, the light was leaking out of the sky, blue gone to iron. Percy's was already lit, the neon in the window buzzing "Open" over a drift of cigarette haze. Danny slowed, not wanting to go in just yet. He'd heard Billy and the new choir around the pool table, but tonight the music crawled up the block, thick and slow.

Outside, on the brick stoop, Billy, a guy in an orange vest, and an old man with his head shaved to stubble stood shoulder to shoulder, leaning into the wall for balance. The three of them were singing, no lyrics, just a low, rumbling hum that snaked in and out of harmony, sometimes splitting sharp, sometimes melting together so smooth you couldn't find the seam. Their eyes were closed. Nobody moved, except to breathe. It was the sound of waiting, of wanting something to come and break the spell.

Danny stopped in the street, feeling the music settle into his bones. The old man's voice had a shake in it, like wind through dead grass, and Billy's was pure smoke, rough but steady. The third guy, the one in the vest, filled in the gaps, his voice lighter but urgent, as if trying to stitch the whole thing together.

Nobody said a word. They just kept singing, the notes rising and falling, echoing off the glass and stone. For a minute, Danny wanted to join in, to let the sound pull him out of himself, but he didn't know how. He stood there, hands in pockets, letting the music scrub away whatever else was left inside.

After a while, Billy opened his eyes. He saw Danny, and just nodded, not missing a beat in the song. The others nodded, too, acknowledgment without welcome, as if they were all part of the same bad dream.

Danny lingered, watching the way their breath clouded in the cold, how the music shaped the air around them. He looked at the window, and saw not just his face but three, five, a dozen others superimposed in the glass. Old men, young men, a single mother holding an LA or bust sign. Every person who'd ever come through Percy's, every story that started and ended with a drink and a song. They all had the same look: tired, worn smooth at the edges, eyes dulled but not dead.

He saw himself in the window, and he saw the Hollow. The straight jacket they all wore, the way it fit too tight, but nobody bothered to take it off.

He waited until the song faded out, the last note lingering like a question that would never get answered. Then he pulled the door open and let the warmth and noise swallow him.

Inside, the music was different, just the TV and the hum of the cooler. But the other sound, the one from outside, stayed with him. It was stuck under his skin, a ghost that hummed every time he tried to forget.

He took a seat at the bar, nodded at Percy, and waited for the world to spin a little slower.

BLUE MOON

Recommended Listening: Pause here and listen to Ra-leigh Keegan's Kentucky. Raleigh wrote the song while walking through the hills, in solitude, it carries the ache of distance and the pull of home, both of which shape the heart of this chapter.

In the narrow crease of morning, before the heat and haze could spoil it, Danny sat with his boots in the grass at the edge of a creek not yet spoiled by life, guitar on his knees and a notebook spread open on the stone beside him. The mist still clung to the ridges, drawn thin and slow over the green. He watched it move, the way it wrapped the black trunks of oak and poplar, the way it made the whole hollow look washed clean, erased for a minute. No trace of the black-dust street, no memory of last night's misery at Percy's, just the dull hush and the glimmer of wet leaves.

He tuned the battered guitar by ear. The pegs slipped sometimes, wouldn't hold a pitch, but he worked them until the sound snapped true. He tested a C chord, then let it ring out over the water. The creek took it, mixed it with the rush of current and the static of cicadas ramping up in the weed-choked banks. He strummed softer, thumb picking out the melody line he'd been circling for days. It sounded raw, and maybe a little too much like the Carter Family songs his grandmother played while she cleaned house, but he didn't mind. That's what this place did, it chewed things up and spit them back with a layer of silt and memory. He scribbled the chords on the margin of his notebook, the pencil lead smudged, then went back to the half-finished line:

My first and last, forever on my mind

I've never seen somethin' like this, the mist...

He stared at it, felt the words settle in. It was honest, if not clever. He'd never been clever. He let the pencil roll away, then traced the calluses on his left hand with the thumb of his right. It was a comfort, that roughness, proof that something could outlast the hollowing.

He looked up and watched the mist slide over the rocks. There was a spot just downstream where the water widened, and the stones made a shelf. Shelby used to talk about a place like this. Not Daisy, but Shelby Boone, the one who had always seemed half-dream herself, hair catching in the willow branches, skin so pale the blue veins showed at her wrists. Shelby was gone, awhile now. Not all the way gone but gone to Danny. She came back sometimes in the gentle memory, the kind that didn't sting, the kind that just hummed under the ribs like a tuning fork, but only when he remembered the key around his neck wasn't just to open some door.

She'd laughed at his first attempt at a love song, told him he played too slow, too sad for a boy his age. She would say, "play a song you can clap to." But she'd stay beside him on that creek side, pressed her cold hand over his, and traced the map of calluses as if it meant something. "You ever notice how the world gets louder when you quit trying to listen for it?" she'd asked. He'd said no, but the question stuck. The whole summer stuck, every breath of it, even now.

He thumbed the next chord, let it hang, then tried the line again: "My first and last, forever on my mind." The phrase made him uneasy, like he'd said something mean without meaning it. He crossed out "first and last," tried "past and future," then "the whole of life," but the line wouldn't fix itself. He shoved the notebook away and played the run twice more, letting the rhythm drown the words.

The creek was loud here. Not enough to lose himself, but enough to mask the start of a hangover in his temples. He counted the flow, tried to guess how much water moved past this bend each hour, wondered how many secrets the hollow carried out to the Ohio River and how many it kept. He figured the ratio was close.

A pair of crows paced the far bank, black feathers puffed against the chill. They watched him, heads canted, never blinking. He thought of Billy and the new choir, the way their voices tangled in the early dark outside Percy's, the harmony so deep it shook the windows. For a moment he envied them. He envied the simplicity of their want. All they needed was a bottle and a song, nothing else, and most days that was enough.

He played softer, just the ghost of a melody. The grass wet his jeans through, but he didn't care. He remembered when Daisy had dragged him to the swimming hole, just upstream, on this creek. She'd worn her hair up in a tight bun, ribbon matched to her lipstick, shoes too nice for the mud. She looked out of place, and she knew it, but she laughed when he called her "Queen of the Creek" and let him pick the leeches from her ankles after she dared him to race her across the hole.

He wondered, not for the first time, if Daisy had

loved him at all, or just the idea of being wanted. If maybe he'd only ever been an empty space she could fill with her own noise and need. He wanted to hate her, but he didn't. He just felt tired, and a little desolate, like the creek after a dry spell.

He tried another verse, mumbled the words into the curve of his arm:

The high dollar horses

Brown bourbon so sweet

He laughed at himself; the sound cracked in the morning. He looked up, made sure no one was close enough to hear. The crows had moved on, replaced by the blue flash of a jay in the sumac. The air was warmer now, and the mist started to burn off. He watched the leaves dry in the sun, the green bright and glossy.

He looked at the creek and saw his reflection, stretched and doubled by the ripples. He saw the scar above his eye, the one Daisy said made him look "serious," the way his hair stuck out at the sides, the way his face seemed too thin for the frame. He didn't recognize the man, but he knew him. He was the same as all the others who'd spent too long in the dark, the same as the fathers and uncles who never made it out. He was the hollow, and the hollow was him.

He set the guitar aside, closed his eyes, and let the sun warm his face. He tried to think of nothing, to empty his mind, but Shelby came back again, not as a ghost, but as a memory so gentle he almost wept. He remembered one of the last things she'd said to him: "I hope it's worth it, whatever you're running toward."

He didn't know if it was, or if it mattered. But the

words made him lighter somehow, for a moment. Caring in the terseness, not for herself but for him, genuinely.

He opened his eyes and watched a water strider skate across the surface, all legs and hunger. He thought about the song, the unfinished lines, the way the music sounded different here than in town, pure and less desperate.

He picked up the guitar, started to play. The music wasn't good, but it was true, and for the first time since Daisy disappeared, that felt like enough.

He played until the sun burned off the last of the mist, and the whole hollow opened up, green and blue and wild. He played until his fingers ached, until the sound of the creek drowned the memory of every bad night, every fight, every lie he'd ever told.

When he finally stopped, the peace stayed with him, fragile and bright as the ribbon he'd found in the weeds, still pink, still alive.

He packed up the guitar, tucked the notebook under his arm, and started the trek back to town. The air was different now, cleaner, almost sweet. He knew it wouldn't last, but he took it anyway.

By the time the sun leveled out and caught the dust hanging over White Oak Hollow, Danny was driving the old truck back down Main, window cranked and radio off. The air felt denser in town. Coal soot from the morning shift hung over the storefronts and streaked the windows of the Farmacy like rain gone sideways. The boarded-up places seem to multiply every time he drove past, the paint chipping off signs, the black mold working up from the sidewalk, but he knew that wasn't possible. Danny took it slow, the truck's engine grumbling under his knees, watching the world roll by in gray stutters.

The Farmacy's neon cross buzzed its own liturgy, a flickering response to every call of the scavenging birds in the gutter. A couple kids in hoodies huddled by the door, sharing a cigarette and arguing over who owed who for a pack of rolling papers. Danny watched them in the rearview as he rolled on, their faces pale as ghosts. It felt like nothing had changed in town except the faces. Old vices, new hands.

He parked behind Percy's, gravel crunching under the tires. The back lot was empty except for the trash from last night: a spent lottery ticket, a crumpled energy drink, a shoe missing its mate. He sat for a minute, hands on the wheel, thinking about the creek, the music he'd made there, how it already felt far away. The old hope that he might get out, make a life somewhere the air didn't taste of ash, had faded, but something had taken its place. Not hope, maybe, but stubbornness at a slow, rolling boil.

The bar was dark inside, blinds pulled, but the smell of whiskey and spilled beer hit him the second he crossed the threshold. He blinked at the dimness, let his eyes adjust. Percy stood at the far end, stacking glasses, the veins on his hands blue and raised. He nodded as Danny entered, no smile, just the brief lift of an eyebrow.

Danny took his usual stool. He set the guitar case down, pulled out his notebook, and flattened it on the bar. The pages were still damp from the creek, the pencil marks smeared but readable. He ordered a whiskey by holding up one finger; Percy poured it without looking.

There were a few others in the bar, Billy and the

new choir hunched over a game of eight ball, a pair of women at the corner table, their faces made up for war, their laughter sharp and mean. Near the window, two miners from the day crew nursed beers, their hands trembling each time they brought the glass to their lips.

Danny sipped his drink, slow. He listened but didn't look. The bar talk was the same as always: which mine had cut hours, whose brother was back in jail, who'd gotten kicked out of church for touching the wrong person at the wrong time. But beneath that was another thread, softer, almost reverent.

"She's never surfaced, or been seen again," someone said.

"Not even a trace, not even a shoe."

"Maybe she's just waiting, like the rest. Maybe she'll haunt him, one day."

Danny felt the words brush past his ear, but he kept his eyes on the page. He wrote another line, the pencil biting into the paper:

Hollowed out and hungry, still I call your name

Better men have vanished here, but
all the ghosts sound same

He scratched through those two lines right away, recognizing the environment in the words, coming out through his pencil.

Percy refilled his glass without being asked, set the bottle down nearby. "That's the first time I've seen you write more than you drink," he said. It wasn't a joke. He wiped the counter with the side of his hand, then stood quiet, waiting for Danny to answer.

Danny didn't look up. "Got a song to finish," he said.

Percy nodded, then drifted away, the soft creak of his boots the only sign he'd been there.

Billy whistled, low and off-key, a fragment of "Oh Death," and the old man beside him joined in, voices merging for a bar or two before falling apart. The women at the corner table lit cigarettes, the match flare painting their faces hollow.

Danny wrote another verse, tried it against the rhythm of his thumb on the bar. He played the words out in his head, shaping them until they felt right. He wondered if Shelby would have liked the melody, or if she would've laughed and told him to make it a little faster, a little less sad, add some clapping.

The talk at the far table grew louder, more insistent. The Whitaker Curse had grown from gossip to legend, like an oil slick on water.

"Not the first time someone's vanished round here," a miner said, voice hoarse. "Not the last, either."

The other shook his head, eyes fixed on the glass. "But this one... this one's got teeth. The tale grew teeth, but the hollow bit first."

Danny smiled, just barely. He liked that line. He scribbled it in the margin, thinking maybe it could fit somewhere.

He hummed the new verse under his breath, letting the words curl in his mouth before setting them down. The whiskey was only half gone. The notebook filled up quick, page after page of lines crossed out and started over. Each word felt like digging through the seam, searching for the vein that would finally break through.

He heard his name, once, but ignored it. For the first time in months, the song came easier than the drink.

Percy glanced over from the end of the bar, eyes narrowed, but said nothing. Just filled Danny's glass when it got low, then moved on.

The night shifted slow. Outside, the green neon at the Farmacy finally burned out, and the street turned white, blue, and empty. Inside, the talk faded, the regulars drifted out, and the light grew softer, until only the hum of the cooler and the scratch of pencil on paper remained.

Danny set down the notebook, flexed his hand, and stared at the bar's old wood. The grain was blackened and slick, every groove a memory of someone else's bad night, or maybe his own.

He finished the whiskey, but it didn't taste the same as before.

He packed his things, nodded at Percy, and stepped out into the chill. The coal dust had settled on the sidewalk, coating the boots and the tires and the benches out front. But the air was clear, and the sky above the ridge glowed with the start of the stars.

He looked up, breathing in deep, and felt the music still ringing in his ears, a sound that was his and nobody else's.

He left the truck, walked home with the notebook in his hand, the page still open to the last line, the ink wet and waiting for more.

The street outside Percy's was blank and cold, every lamp drowned by the blue of the moon. Danny's boots skidded a little on the slick, coal-sprayed sidewalk, but he kept to the middle, hands clasping his notebook and the bottom of his empty pocket, guitar case bumping his thigh. It was late, closer to one than midnight, and every window was dark except for the glow of the Farmacy's sign, now just a pulse of white light where the green tubes had burned out.

He passed the hardware store, the pawn shop, and the empty shell of the old music store, its windows layered in grime and hope long since faded. In the dark, the town looked tiny and fragile, waiting for someone to come along and wipe the dust off. It was the kind of image a model train builder would appreciate.

His head was clear, clearer than it had been in months. The song hummed in his veins, louder than the ache in his jaw or the slow crawl of whiskey behind his eyes. He walked slower than usual, feeling every step, every shift in the wind. The cold made his teeth ache, but he liked the sharpness. It reminded him he was still here.

Somewhere down Main, a dog barked once, then silence.

He looked up. The sky was almost clear tonight, the haze blown off by some mercy of wind. A handful of stars poked through the black, and for a second, he tried to count them, but lost the thread at eight, maybe nine. He remembered how, when he was a few years younger, he'd lay on the hood of the truck outside the mine and pretend the stars were bullet holes, each one someone's shot at something better.

He wondered what it would feel like to leave the ground for real, to see the hollow from above. To fly up, out, past the ridges, past the dark vein of the mine, and just keep going until the world turned green again. He liked the thought. It stuck with him, even as he turned onto his street, the wind picking up, shaking loose a handful of dead leaves that rattled down the asphalt ahead of him.

At the house, he let himself in quiet, careful not to

trip over the pile of old boxes by the door. He flicked on the light, then off again, preferring the dark. The kitchen sometimes let loose a faint scent of Daisy's perfume, something sweet and sharp in the curtains, barely there now, but enough to catch him off guard if he breathed too deep.

Upstairs, he set the guitar down near the bed, went to the bathroom, and stripped off his jacket and shirt. The mirror was still cracked from last winter, a jagged line through the center like a scar. He splashed water on his face, watched more coal dust swirl down the drain, then peeled off the rest of his clothes and stepped into the shower.

He stood under the hot water, watching the night sluice off his skin. The grime ran in streaks, pooling at the drain, then twisting away. He stayed until the heat was gone, and the tiles started to sting his feet.

When he got out, he dried off with an old towel, threw on an old t-shirt he pulled from the hamper, and stepped barefoot to the bed. He left the guitar leaning on the wall, set the notebook on the nightstand, and stared at the page. The word "Kentucky" was underlined three times, the ink deep and ragged from where he'd pressed too hard.

He thought about Daisy, and about Shelby, and about the people who'd vanished from his life, some slow, some all at once. He wondered where they were tonight, if they'd see the same sky, if they'd remember the sound of the creek in spring, or the taste of snow when you caught it on your tongue.

He closed his eyes, the sound of the water still in his ears, and let himself drift.

He slept, and for once, the music followed him all the

way there.

MESSAGES

Recommended Listening: Before drifting into the dream ahead, listen to Raleigh Keegan's I'd Like to Be a Bird. Its lift of longing and escape will ready your mind to take flight into what cannot be explained, only felt.

Danny went under quick, bourbon in his blood like a fast train, eyelids heavy as dead coal. The room rocked once, then again, then settled. Somewhere in the distance, a car alarm coughed and fell quiet, leaving him in a hush thick enough to drink.

He did not remember closing his eyes, but in the next instant, the dark was waiting for him, expectant as an open grave.

First there was smoke. It came in slow, gray plumes curling from the baseboards and through the old vent near the ceiling. It was not the smoke of burning, no bite, no panic, but something older, richer. The air filled with the taste of cedar and char, a memory of long-dead fire, the crackle of timber in the bones. Each breath flavored the tongue, coated the teeth, seeped through the seams of his skull.

Beneath it, a drum began, distant, slow, but gaining. It mapped to his pulse, every thud sending a ripple through the mattress and up the length of his spine. He felt it in the jaw first, a blunt force that threatened to shake loose the molars, then in the chest, then finally in the fingertips, until it seemed his whole body was just one muscle, flexing and releasing to a time it did not understand.

The smoke thickened. It funneled tight, drew itself into ropes, then into cords, then into the shape of two arms crossed over his chest. For a moment, he thought he was dead. He remembered that corpses were arranged like that, hands folded, the posture of surrender. But these arms were not his own. They pressed down, firm but gentle, and when he tried to lift them, they resisted, then gave, then split at the wrist.

Feathers. They erupted from the skin, black at the roots, white at the ends, sharp as wire. They grew in fast, in pulses, each beat of the drum sending up another inch of quill, another brush of vaned texture. They coated his arms, his shoulders, his chest, until he could no longer see the skin beneath. It didn't hurt, not in the way he expected. There was just a tingling, a prickling, as if his body had been dipped in ice and pulled out new.

He sat up, slow, and the feathers rasped against the bedsheet, the sound soft but insistent. He flexed his hands. The fingers obeyed, but behind them was something more, a tension that wanted to unfold, to stretch wider than bone allowed.

The drum went silent. The smoke thinned. For a second, he was just a man in a bed, sweating bourbon, arms bristling with the impossible.

Then the ceiling unzipped. It did not break, or crumble, or vanish, it simply peeled back, a slow curling from the center outward, like the lid on a soup can. Beyond it, there were stars. Not the pinprick of stars you saw through light pollution, but the full tapestry, more stars than sky, layered in bands and wounds and distance, the shimmering blood of the milky way. The night above the hollow was not empty; it was crowded, pressing in, hungry to be seen.

He felt a pull, not from gravity, but from something else, a command in the ribs that told him to stand, then kneel, then crouch on the mattress. The feathers along his back flared, caught air that wasn't moving. He shifted his weight forward and felt himself grow lighter, the mass of his body draining out through the soles of his feet.

He was rising.

The floor fell away first, then the bed, then the cramped room and its yellowed walls, the windowless dark, the mess of laundry and the cheap guitar in the corner. He passed through the ceiling, the shreds of it brushing his face like cobwebs, and entered the new cold above. The air was thinner here, clean, and each breath scoured his lungs.

White Oak Hollow unfurled below him. He saw it for the first time as a shape, not a place. A bowl cut deep in the ridge, houses lining the inside like teeth. The creek, blue-black in the moon, traced the bottom, writhing between the sycamores and willows. Roads spiraled outward, veins of blacktop and gravel, terminating in dead ends or in the dark where the forest still ruled.

He floated higher, a slow and steady drift, the feathers keeping him aloft even as his feet kicked for show, on nothing. He did not panic. The view was clear, and each feature of the town burned with its own significance.

There was Percy's bar, the neon sign outside it struggling and half-lit, strobing in a pulse that didn't match any human heartbeat. The light bled into the street, painting a small circle of safety in an ocean of black. Danny saw through the window, saw the hunched men still nursing their wounds, the outline of Percy behind the bar, a ghost moving slow, and a rag that never quite finished its journey along the lacquered wood.

Beyond that, Shelby Boone's house, the porch light a steady, unwavering eye. It looked out of place, too bright, too innocent, a single beacon in a row of broken lamps and covered windows. Danny remembered the exact shade of that bulb, the way it flattered Shelby's skin, made her seem untouched by the rest of the world. From above, the light looked like a atonement, or maybe a promise.

He drifted higher still. The rest of Main Street diminished, the pawn shop and the Farmacy shrinking to thumbprints of color. The mine's portal was visible even in the dark, a perfect wound in the side of the hill, circled by mud and the silhouettes of old machinery rusted to the dirt. The slag heap beside it glowed faintly, the memory of fire and work never quite gone. It pulled at the eye, demanded attention, dared you to forget what had been buried there, and what still lay beneath.

Danny hovered over the hollow, and the wind found him. It tugged at the feathers, at the edges of his being, threatening to unmake him or to carry him further. He welcomed it. There was nothing left in the room below, nothing he needed from the old life. The air here was better.

He stretched his arms, wings now more than arms, and turned in the current. The stars above seemed to move with him, spiraling, dragging him higher. He saw the ridgeline, saw the way the clouds bunched behind it, heavy with threat or promise. He saw the creek's mouth, the swimming hole, saw where it emptied into the larger river, and the thin, shining thread that ran near his own house all the way to the next county.

It was all so obvious, from up here. The connections, the patterns, the ways people and pain and history braided together. He'd never seen it so clear, never known how close everything was, how little separated one man from the next, or one fate from another.

He thought about Shelby, about Daisy, about the voices that had brought him to this state of mind, each one a note in the long, unfinished song. He thought about his own voice, about how small it must sound from this height, and wondered if it would echo, or just vanish into the larger music of the world.

He did not fear falling. There was no direction but up, no force but the music in his own bones, no future but the one he could make with his own hands, feathered or not.

He might have stayed forever in that hush, a silent watcher above the hollow, if not for the gathering storm. The clouds rose sudden, blacker than crow feathers, stacking in tight, mean layers. He saw them, felt their weight build at the edge of the sky, then begin to roll, slow and deliberate, toward where he floated.

The air ahead was thicker, electric. He drifted forward, arms wide, and the wind took him faster than before, threading him between warm columns of updraft and the thin, blue gasp of empty space. The first bolt of lightning split the clouds a mile off, but the next came closer, bright enough to bleach the bones beneath his feathers. Thunder followed in a boot-kick, shaking his ribs, making his heart race.

He wasn't afraid. The storm was a vessel, not a threat. He banked left, then dove into the black, the air around him boiling with ice and wet. The lightning found him again, licking at his wings, singeing the new growth at the tips, but he welcomed the pain. It was proof he still had a body, still had some claim on the world of the living.

Through the next layer of cloud, the wind howled in a voice he almost recognized. It had the cadence of miners on break, the shouts and cusses echoing down the drift. It blended into song, not words but the rise and fall of breath, an inhale and an exhale, the kind of melody you only heard in the dark when all the machines were quiet and the only thing left was the sound of your own labor.

From that noise, the first voice broke through. It was old, cracked, but strong. The voice of his grandfather, gone twenty years but never really left. The cough at the end of each phrase, the wheeze and the laugh tangled up together. "You got your mother's stubbornness," he said, "you never could sit still long enough to let the dust settle. That's what I loved about you, boy."

Danny pushed through another wave of cloud. The feathers on his arms bristled with static. He remembered the old man's hands, thick and battered, remembered how he'd carried him piggyback through the same hills that now looked so small from above.

The next voice was smoother, deeper, steady as coal. Earl McKinney. He heard it clear, cutting through the thunder like a line of scripture. "You'll never fill every hollow, Wallace. That's not the task. The task is to make peace with what lingers and still find the light to walk forward." The words carried the smell of pipe tobacco, the warmth of the porch at dawn, the quiet dignity of men who never wasted a sentence.

Danny tried to answer, but the wind ripped the sound from his mouth, scattered it behind him like torn paper.

Then, through a gap in the cloud, the third voice: his father's, a thing he hadn't heard in years except at the bottom of a bottle, a figure on a stool not really there, or in the echo of his own cussing. It started soft, a whisper under the rain, then grew until it filled the sky.

"Trust your wings, son. The ground's had you long enough."

It was not a plea, or a curse, or a warning. It was a blessing, as true as any prayer. Danny felt it settle over him, like a hand on the back of the neck, guiding him forward, giving him permission to rise.

He punched through the top of the storm, into a clearing of light so sudden it hurt his eyes. Above, the stars were gone, replaced by a golden rim that ran the length of the horizon, sunrise and sunset mashed together in a permanent glow. Below, the world was new. The fields bent in waves, the river flashed silver as it turned. Every patch of darkness in the hollow was softened, made less by the warmth above.

He looked down and saw the hollow not as a wound, but as a cradle. Every scar and scrape and broken house was part of the pattern, a mark of what it took to keep living in a place that never promised anything but work and pain.

He hovered there, suspended between the storm and the golden light, and for a moment, he thought he saw the outlines of others, figures in the air, flying with him, all feathers and light. Some he recognized, some he didn't, but they all moved with the same urgency, the same hunger.

Then, from the rim of gold, a new shape appeared. It was not a solid image, not quite shadow, but something between. As it neared, the details sharpened: wings longer and thinner than his own, tail flared in a perfect fan, beak hooked at the end. Its feathers glowed red at the edges, as if lit from inside. The eyes were bottomless black, rimmed in fire.

The raven circled him once, then twice, then drew alongside, matching speed and rhythm. It did not speak, not with words, but Danny felt the meaning as if it had been stitched into his own bones.

"Know the season. Know when it's time to move. No cage could keep you bound."

He turned to follow the bird, and together they arrowed through the air, south, then east, then up again, always just ahead of the storm. Each time the lightning cracked, the raven grew brighter, as if feeding on the chaos. Each time the thunder rolled, Danny felt the inside of his chest swell, filling with a music he did not know he could make.

They flew until the clouds ran out, until the sky was only light. The ground below blurred, fields and trees and water all mixing together. He saw the ridgeline again, the hollow at its edge, but now it was smaller, just one of a thousand cuts in the skin of the earth.

Far below, on the edge of the tree line, a wolf stood. Gray and lean, it watched the sky, eyes reflecting the gold above. When the raven called out, the wolf answered, with a howl so clear it pierced the wind, threaded its way up to Danny's ears.

He felt it shake his body, vibrate the length of his

spine. It was not a lonely sound, not anymore. It was the sound of recognition, of finding your kin, even if only for a second.

Danny looked at the raven. Its wings burned brighter, the red at the tips now full flame, trailing sparks behind every beat. The bird tilted its head, fixed him with that endless gaze.

He opened his mouth, not sure what would come out, but what did was pure, raw, louder than thunder, higher than any note he'd ever tried to sing. The sound left him whole, left him clean, ripped through the remaining clouds and called every other voice in the world to answer.

He sang, and the sky sang back.

In that instant, he was everything he ever wanted to be...weightless, endless, free.

The raven peeled off, banking hard, diving down toward the horizon. Danny watched it go, felt the tug to follow, but resisted. He turned once more in the current, taking in the hollow below, the whole map of his life, every pain and every joy, all laid out and shining in the gold.

He woke as if spat out of the dark, chest heaving, collar soaked through, a sour taste of sleep on his tongue. For a moment, he could not move. The weight of the dream pressed him flat, each muscle screaming with the memory of flight. He blinked at the ceiling, expecting it to open, to reveal stars or storm or the slow curl of smoke, but it was just plaster, water-stained and unmoving.

His ears rang with the echo of thunder, but under it, the night had filled with cricket song, thick and insistent, a sound that reminded him of nights with Shelby in the field, just listening, saying nothing, letting the noise fill in what words couldn't. He heard a dog bark, distant, and then the silence between the barks, larger than the noise itself.

He flexed his arms. The ache in them was real, as if he'd spent the whole night digging fencepost instead of dreaming. His hands wanted to close into claws, but the bones weren't right; there was no fan of feathers, just the raw sting of yesterday's calluses, the old wounds that could split open again.

He remembered the dream, not in pieces, not as flashes, but whole, unbroken, each moment preserved as if in amber. The smoke, the feathers, the voice of his father and the way the wind bit at the tips of his wings. He tasted the gold of the morning above the clouds, saw again the way the river curved through the hollow, how the whole town looked from above, how the porch light at Shelby's burned steady even in the worst of the storm.

The words lingered, soft as a whisper. "I'd like to be a bird for a day." He found himself saying them aloud, quietly, but enough to prove the dream hadn't lied.

He sat up, groaning as his body protested, and looked around the room. It was smaller than he remembered, the ceiling lower, the bed narrower. The guitar by the window looked abandoned, unplayed. The air was hot, stifling, thick with the ghosts of everything he'd ever tried to forget. The contrast was cruel: inside, a prison; outside, a whole world waiting.

He swung his legs over the side of the bed, feet hitting aged, cold wood. The floor was sticky, one patch damp from a spill he couldn't recall. He ran his hands through his hair, felt the sweat cooling at his scalp, and waited for the dizziness to pass.

The bourbon was gone from his blood. What remained was a clarity he didn't trust, sharp as glass and twice as dangerous. He wondered if it would last, if it would outlive the sunrise, or if by noon he'd be hollowed out again, chasing the next drink or the next song, trying to fill the ache with something that never quite did the job.

He listened to the crickets, then to the distant call of a train whistle, the mournful way it drifted over the ridge and then was gone. He imagined the hollow from above, the lines of the roads, the river's bend, the open mouth of the mine. He wondered how it would feel to never come back down, to float forever in that hush, above all the hunger and hurt.

He closed his eyes, reached out with his hands, and for a second, he swore he could feel the air move around them, could feel the start of something new, just under the skin.

He thought of the raven, red-edged and impossible, its eyes blacker than the world, and he wondered if it had been a warning, or a blessing, or just the last joke of a mind too far gone for sense.

He decided it didn't matter. The message was clear enough: "Know the season. Know when it's time to move." No cage could hold him, not unless he let it.

He stood, knees popping, and made his way downstairs to the kitchen, past his old coat and the unopened mail. He poured himself a glass of water, drank it in three greedy gulps, then refilled and drank again.

In the window, he caught his own reflection, shadowed and split by the screen. He looked the same as ever, maybe older, maybe just tired. But the eyes were different, less empty, as if the thing that lived behind them had found something to hope for, or at least a reason to keep watching.

He touched the glass, traced the line of his jaw, and tried to imagine feathers there, sprouting new from the bone. It was easy, in the dim light.

He left the glass in the sink, wiped his hands on his shirt, and stepped out onto the front porch. The night was fading at the edges, a hint of blue rising over the hills. The air was cooler, and the smell of wet grass hit him in the throat, raw and beautiful.

He listened, not for words, but for music, for the hum that ran under everything, the song of the hollow, old as dirt and twice as persistent.

He heard it, then, in the rustle of leaves, the sigh of the creek down the block, the slow exhale of the world turning toward dawn.

*Only when the pieces fall into place does the
broken land reveal itself not as a wound,
but as the map of the soul's return.*

PERCY'S ADVICE

Percy's was dead after eleven, nothing left but the bones and the stains and the men who refused to go home. For two hours it was just Danny at the bar, Percy behind it, both of them keeping the same vigil, neither talking except for the ritual exchange of glass and bottle. Outside, the neon sign glared into the black, flicking to red every ten seconds, then to nothing, then to red again. It threw a sick glow across the empty booths, the ones with their seats ripped out or springs so tired you could lose a phone between the cushions and never see it again.

The chairs were up on the tables, legs tangled like ribs in a dry corpse pile. Percy moved them one-handed, the other hand gripping a rag as he swept, always in a tight circle, as if he could erase the evidence of a decade's worth of drunks just by wishing hard enough. The cooler in the back hummed with a bad bearing, and every few minutes it would rattle loud enough to make the shot glasses hop in place. The smell of lemon cleaner was sharp in the air, battling with the ghosts of cigarettes and the spilled beer that clung to the cracks in the tile. You could taste the history on your tongue if you breathed too deep.

Danny stared into the glass. The whiskey was cheap, and even cheaper by the bottom of the bottle, but it suited him. His hands shook, but only a little, only at the moment before he brought the glass to his lips. It was the same tremor he'd had since he was a boy, and it never quite left, not even on his best days. He'd learned to hide it by drinking slow and keeping his hands wrapped tight around the tumbler.

Percy finished the last of the chairs, wiped his hands on the bar towel, and came to stand across from Danny. He set his elbows on the wood, leaned in, and stared at the bottles behind the bar as if any one of them might contain the answer to every question he was never going to ask.

"You're burnin' holes in that drink, Wallace," Percy said. His voice was even, the words ground smooth from decades of use. "What's sittin' on you tonight?"

Danny rolled the glass between his palms, letting it squeak against the lacquer. He watched the way the neon light broke over the rim, how the red mixed with the brown until it was the color of bruised fruit. He considered not answering, considered just draining the glass and walking home in the dark, but the silence between them grew, thick as lard, and he knew it wouldn't break until he gave it something.

He traced a finger through the ring of whiskey on the counter, then wiped it away with his sleeve. "It's the shaft," he said, low, barely more than a rumor. "Keeps coming back, like I'm still there. Like I never left."

Percy snorted, but it was gentle. "You and a thousand others."

Danny shook his head, harder than he meant to. "Not like this. This is different. I see her face, every time I close my eyes. Hear the scream, even when I'm awake."

Percy grunted, a sound that could've meant anything. He reached for the bottle and filled Danny's glass to the line, then set it down careful, no splash, no mess.

Danny took the drink, but didn't raise it. He stared into the swirl, the way the light bled through it, and tried to find the words that might explain what the hell was happening inside his skull. "I don't know what happened in that shaft, Percy. I can tell you what I heard, what I saw, but that's all I got. The rest..." He stopped, pressed the heel of his hand to his eye until the sparks flickered. "The rest is just noise."

Percy waited, still as stone.

Danny let the words settle, then started over. "I was comin' up behind her. Slow, as usual. Always a step behind Daisy. She had the lamp and the bag, said she'd wait, but she never did. I figured she'd go as far as the third cut, maybe look down the old cart rails for a laugh, then come back out." He paused, looked at Percy as if to ask if he should keep going, but Percy didn't move, didn't blink.

"She went deeper," Danny said. "Past the warning signs. Past where the air gets thick and you can't see your hand in front of your face. I followed the sound of her steps, the echo off the walls, but it was already too late to catch up." He closed his eyes, remembering the feel of the mine, how the cold worked into your lungs, how the world shrank to the circle of your own breath.

"I heard her laugh, once. Then nothing for a while. Then I heard... I don't know how to say it. It wasn't a laugh, wasn't a yell. It was a scream, but not like fear. More like... like the mountain itself was opening up and pulling her in."

He shuddered, the memory running its claws down his back.

"I ran. I swear I ran so hard I couldn't breathe. When

I got there, she was gone. Just gone, like she never existed. The lamp was rolling on the floor, still lit, still burning, but nothing else. No blood, no bag, not even a hair. I called for her, screamed her name until my throat bled. But she didn't answer. She never answered."

Percy's face was unreadable, the lines cut so deep you could lose a secret in any one of them.

Percy filled the silence, slow and measured. "You sure she's gone?"

He drained the glass, the burn less than he deserved. "That's not the worst part. The worst part is, I found Half Pint Carter. Laying on the ground, pants around his knees, clutching at something pink."

He stared at Percy, the memory vivid as a wound. "It was the ribbon. Daisy's. The one she wore every day, said it kept her company, she'd never be alone. Half Pint was holding it like a lifeline, like a trophy. His face was..." He stopped, tried to find the right word. "I don't know. It was shock. Horror. Maybe just the face of a man who finally saw himself for what he was."

Percy's hand stilled on the bar. "What did he say?"

Danny's mouth twisted. "He said, 'She's still fallin'.' Said it twice, like he wanted me to understand. I don't think I ever did."

He let the words hang, the image of Daisy suspended in the black, forever tumbling, forever out of reach.

Danny rubbed his eyes, both palms grinding into the sockets until he saw stars. "It's my fault. I convinced her to go down there, told her about the diamond, made her believe it was worth the risk. I was joking, at least in my head I was, but she took it serious. She always did."

He drew a shaky breath, the next part harder to say. "I pushed her, but only in my mind. I wanted her to see the truth, to stop chasing what didn't exist. But I never thought she'd…" His voice cracked. "I never thought she'd vanish."

Percy set the bottle aside and looked Danny in the eye for the first time. "You didn't push her, Wallace. You just walked the same bad road as the rest of us."

Danny wanted to argue, to lay out all the ways it could have gone different, but the words curdled in his mouth. Instead, he watched as Percy poured himself a glass, raised it in a silent toast, then knocked it back in one swallow.

They sat in the neon haze, the red glow painting their faces with a wounded light and listened to the cooler rattle out its last gasp.

Danny let his head fall to the bar; forehead pressed to the wood. The world spun, slow and merciless. He wanted to sleep, to dream of a place where he could undo every mistake, where Daisy came back and the shaft was just a hole in the ground, not a grave for every bad thing he'd ever done.

But the night offered nothing.

Time passed. The bar was a cave now, lit only by the neon and the single bulb Percy kept over the till. Danny's cheek was slick where it pressed the wood, and he could feel every thud of his heart echo through the counter. When he sat up, the room spun, the taste of bile and old smoke thick in his mouth.

Percy wiped the bar, same slow rhythm, never glancing Danny's way.

Danny watched him for a long time before speaking, his voice small as a secret. "I never saw her fall, Percy." He rubbed the side of his face, trying to wake it up, trying to shake loose the memory. "I never saw her at all after that. For all I know, she's down there in the dark. Or she slipped past me and ran." He made a sound, half laugh, half sob. "Maybe she never wanted me to know the truth. Maybe she never wanted me, period."

Percy kept wiping, but the motion grew tight. His shoulders bunched, just a fraction, but enough to see it was all getting in.

Danny coughed, then cleared his throat. "And still, I carry it like it was my hands that shoved her. Like it was my voice that screamed."

The words floated in the air, hovered there in the blur of red and gold. Danny stared at his hands, knuckles split and raw. He wondered how many times you could scrape yourself open before there was nothing left to bleed.

Percy's rag stopped moving. He set it aside, folded it slow, the way you would a flag at a graveside.

Neither man spoke. The silence filled the whole place, leaking out the seams and into the empty street, until it felt like nothing else had ever lived in the hollow but guilt and the echo of lost things.

The cooler rattled again, but softer now, like it was tired, too.

Danny slumped lower on the stool, hands dangling in his lap. He let the weight of the story pin him there, his whole life compacted to this one bad night, this one confession.

Across the bar, Percy looked at him. He watched the confession hang in the neon, watched it settle, watched as it failed to make anything better.

He watched, and said nothing.

Percy picked up the glass he'd been drying for the last ten minutes, set it on the rack with a thunk. The sound rang out, sharp, final. He leaned his knuckles on the bar, watched Danny like he was sizing up a damaged wall, deciding if it was worth patching or just knocking out and rebuilding from the studs.

When Percy spoke, it was softer than usual, as if afraid the words might shatter something fragile. "Wallace, this place'll give you ghosts if you let it. Every man that's walked through that mine carried somethin' back out with him. Sometimes it's just coal dust. Sometimes it's worse."

He let that hang, watching to see if Danny would flinch. When he didn't, Percy went on. "But don't go claimin' blame for what you don't know. That hole in the earth's already taken enough without you feedin' it your soul too."

Danny tried to answer, but the words tangled up and died on his tongue. He swallowed, tasted metal.

Percy leaned in, elbows squeaking on the old lacquer. "The Hollow ain't just a spot on the map, son. It's in here." He tapped the center of his chest with two fingers, then held them there, like he was checking for a pulse. "Some folks spend their whole life tryin' to crawl out. Most never make it past the door."

He shrugged, shoulders loose, but his eyes stayed locked on Danny's. "You want the truth? There's not a soul in this town that doesn't have a story like yours. Not a one. But you got the power to climb out, if you want it. You just can't do it with your head stuck in the mirror."

Danny sat with that, the words humming in his bones. He remembered the dream, the storm above the ridge, the way the air felt clean and possible up there, even with the lightning snapping at his back. He wondered if it was as easy as Percy made it sound, or if it would take everything he had just to get a foothold on the rim.

Percy slid the empty glass down the bar, tucked the rag into his belt, and stepped back. "You don't have to do it alone," he said. "Nobody ever did."

Danny nodded, once, then again. He felt the knot in his chest loosen, just a hair. "Thanks," he said. It came out hoarse.

Percy gave him a long look, then nodded back. "Any time, Wallace. That's what I'm here for."

Danny stood, legs stiff, back bent from too long on the stool. He fished a crumpled bill from his pocket, but Percy waved it off.

"Go on. Get some air."

He did. He pushed through the door, the bell jangling overhead even though the sign outside had long since quit pretending they were open. The street was empty, the hollow dark and deeper than ever. But the air was sharp, clean, full of the scent of wet dirt and crushed grass. Somewhere, a whippoorwill called, its song thin and bright in the spaces between the houses.

He walked. Past the window of the Farmacy, past the shuttered hardware store, past the place where the music store used to be. He didn't notice the three wooden planks across the door were gone. He couldn't notice. He walked until the lights of town were just a memory, until the sound of the creek was louder than the blood in his ears.

He stopped on the old bridge, leaned on the rail, and stared down at the water. The moon floated there, stretched and broken by the current, but still shining.

He stayed until his fingers went numb, until the

world felt small enough to fit in his hands.

Then, for the first time in years, he straightened his shoulders, pulled in a breath that didn't taste like defeat, and headed home.

It was a start.

THE LETTER

Danny walked away from the mine, the shift shortened today and crossed Main with the afternoon air braided tight to his chest, as if the whole hollow meant to hang on to him a little longer. Like trustworthy Number Four was giving up the ghosts and sending them home with the living or barely living in some cases. He walked slow, letting the world seep in, every wet blade of grass and fresh mud print a lesson in staying present. The air carried the sharp tang of creek water and ozone, a clean aftertaste to the old bitterness that usually ruled these hours.

He worked his way up the block, not the shortest path home but the one that made him feel less like he was running. The road was almost empty, nothing moving but the vapor from the streetlights and the single man he saw up ahead, slow-walking the curb with a trash bag in each hand. Danny watched as the man stooped, picked a can out of the gutter, then tucked it in with the rest like he was collecting gold. He wore a hi-vis vest over coveralls, reflective strips catching the light with every stoop and bend. Danny thought he might know the man, but nowadays, everyone was just a shape moving in time with the failing shop signs.

He nodded as he passed, and the man returned the gesture, no words, just the kind of look that said "I see you, we're both still alive, let's leave it at that." Danny's boots scuffed the grit on the sidewalk, a steady, low rhythm that steadied his hands more than the whiskey ever had.

He turned onto the main drag and let his eyes adjust. The old shops were hunched in shadow, outlines gnawed by the lamps' pale blue. The windows had been dressed for fall, but the decorations were just paper leaves taped to glass, curling at the edges, giving up. The old music store, the one he used to haunt, had lost another pane since last week, but someone had duct taped a trash bag over the hole, and it billowed with the wind like a set of lungs. There was a new sign on the door. A permit for work. Odd in this town where all work stopped at the mine's mouth.

Percy's words replayed, not as advice, but as something older and truer: "The Hollow ain't just a spot on the map, son. It's in here." He pressed his fingers to his chest, the gesture so automatic he felt stupid for doing it, but the thump beneath was real and loud.

He let the sound of his steps fill up the street, unspooling slow and regular. Each footfall lifted the scent of wet dust and coal, the two things this town was built on. He walked past houses he'd never been inside, tried to picture the lives behind those doors. Someone on a couch, dog curled at their feet, TV flickering over the same episode of Friends they'd watched last Thursday. Someone washing dishes in silence. Someone sitting in the dark, phone glowing blue, scrolling and scrolling for a hit of something that might keep them going.

He passed the diner on the corner, the one he hadn't entered since the end. The sign out front was busted, so the word "EAT" flickered on and off, sometimes just "EA," sometimes nothing at all. Through the fogged glass he saw only shadows, tables stripped of their sugar caddies, chairs upended on the linoleum. He stopped outside, hands in his pockets, and tried to remember what it had felt like to belong here. He could almost see her, the way she'd twist her hair when she was nervous, the way her laugh would fill a whole booth and make even the deadest night feel warm.

He looked at his own reflection in the door, hollow-eyed, shirt untucked, hair sticking out in the places where it had dried after the shower. He could walk in, he thought. Just push the door, sit at the counter, order a coffee. But the idea stuck in his throat, heavy as a lump of river rock. He wasn't ready for that yet. Maybe tomorrow. Maybe never.

Instead, he watched the sign flicker for a full minute, the "EAT" stuttering through its cycle, casting weird, pulsing shadows onto the empty street. He felt the urge to laugh, but the sound died before it reached his mouth.

He moved on, past the diner, past the pawnshop, past the Farmacy. The buildings blurred together, edges softened by the damp, but today he didn't see them as cages. They were just part of the hollow, breathing and waiting.

He slowed as he neared the turn back to his own place, letting the steps last as long as they could. He stopped once to look up, hoping for early stars, but the sky had gone to gauze, clouds strung together so close they'd smother anything that tried to peek through. Still, he stood there, neck craned, waiting for something, anything, to break the surface.

The wind shifted, and for the first time in years, he didn't flinch from it. He just stood, breathing deep, feeling the air settle into his shirt, feeling the town press against his skin, not as a threat, but as a blanket.

He let himself smile, just a little.

It was not hope, exactly. But it was something close.

He walked the last block with his head high, boots loud, not hiding from anything.

The house was dark as a grave when he let himself in. Danny did not bother with the light switch. The old fluorescent in the kitchen made a noise like bees eating drywall, and even when it worked it only made the stains in the countertop more obvious. He preferred the dark, the quiet, the way the air changed when you moved slow and careful through a place you could navigate blind.

He set his boots by the door, left the jacket in a heap on the couch, and stepped barefoot to the kitchen table. The window above the sink caught a scrap of streetlight coming to life, silvering the rim of an ashtray, the edge of a chipped mug. The only other thing on the table was a half-burned candle, thick and pale, stuck in a jelly jar. He lit it with a match from the stove, watched the way the wax pooled before catching the wick. The flame was small, but it warmed a circle of space just big enough for one.

He went to the hall closet and dug out the notebook. The leather cover was cracked and flaking at the edges, but the pages inside were still mostly clean, a faint scent of dust. He thumbed the cover open, the sound dry and thin, and let his eyes slide down the first page.

There were songs here he barely remembered writing. Titles scrawled in pencil, lines of lyrics crossed out, started again, then crossed out twice more. The first was "Strawberry Moon." He smiled at the name, less at the song itself, which was a mess of clichés about summer, heat, girls, the whole business. Next came "Way Back," a quicker tune he'd written in the weeks after Shelby got engaged. The lyrics were thin but honest, more wishful thinking than art. This one was almost done. He lingered on a verse, reading it aloud under his breath:

Going way back to seventeen

Jump back skipping through a CD

Seats moved way back

Thinking we had more time with you and me

He skipped ahead, the pages growing looser as he went, finding "The Cover" about halfway in. That one he remembered best, because of the way it got him laughed at during camp. He was sixteen, working as a lifeguard for the rich kids up the mountain, and one of the counselors, city girl, studied Elementary Education at UK, sharp as a tack, had read the lyrics and told him, "You're as tough to read as the Book of Job, Wallace." She said it with a crooked grin, meaning he was all pain and no easy answer. He remembered wanting to argue but knowing she was right.

He traced the title with his thumb, then let the hand drop to the table. The skin on the pad was already raw from the way he'd rubbed it against his own jeans just to stay awake at the bar last night.

The chair creaked as he sat. The noise ran up the legs and through the floor, like a warning shot for any ghosts that might be listening. He rolled a pen between his fingers, the weight of it oddly comforting. It felt heavier tonight. Maybe it was.

He tried to start a line, but the ink caught on a ridge in the paper, leaving a blotch where the word should have been. He wiped it with his thumb, smearing it, but the mark stayed.

He leaned back, closed his eyes. The hush in the house was total, but not the old, empty kind that used to make him nervous. This was a different silence, full and ready, as if the whole place was holding its breath, waiting for him to put something down.

He swallowed, the movement audible in the dark, and bent to the page.

He let the pen hover, not touching the page. Then he made a note in the margin, in parentheses, but flipped to the next page to start fresh.

(what might be the last thing I'll ever say to you)

The next part was harder. He tried to form the words in his head before they made it to the line, but his mind was stuck, tripped up on the memory of that counselor, the Book of Job, the idea that maybe some things weren't supposed to be understood, only endured.

He pressed the pen harder, making the first letter deep and indelible:

Shelby,

> If you're reading this, it's because I found the courage to let it leave my hands. Truth is, I don't expect you ever will. This letter's more for me than you, because the words have been rotting inside me, and I need them out before they finish the job.

I never blamed you for leaving. I just blamed the hole it left in me, and the fact that nobody else could fill it, not the music, not even Daisy, not even the work.

That camp counselor was right about me. I am as tough to read as the Book of Job. I never learned how to speak my mind, only how to bury it and wonder why all the angst of the world came down on me. Maybe that's why you left. Or maybe you just needed more than I ever had to give.

You should know that I never stopped loving you, not even when I hated life the most. Not even when I wished you'd vanish so I could stop aching every time I saw your name on the diner door, or in an advertisement at Percy's, or in the songs I can't seem to quit writing about you.

I wanted to be the one to free you from this hollow. But in the end, you freed yourself, and that's the only thing I can admire without wanting to punch a hole in the wall.

I wish I had the courage to tell you all of this in person. I wish you'd come to me in my weakness, just once, so I could say it out loud instead of hiding behind a piece of paper. But I know you won't. You've always been stronger than that.

So, here's what I need you to know: I forgive you. I forgive myself, too, though that part's going to take longer.

If you ever think of me, I hope it's not as the boy who let you go, but as the man who finally learned how to walk through the mirror and beyond.

I love you, Shelby. I'll keep the music playing, even if it's only for the ghosts.

-Danny

He stopped, hand cramping around the pen, the muscles in his arm tight as fence wire. He let the page sit open, the ink still shiny in the candle's light.

He looked up, around the kitchen, at the shadow of his own head thrown onto the far wall. He imagined the silence breaking, imagined the front door swinging wide, Shelby walking in like nothing had ever happened.

He let himself sit in that possibility, just for a second.

Then he closed the notebook, tucked the pen inside, and blew out the candle.

The dark was softer now.

He carried the notebook to the bedroom, set it on the nightstand, and laid down without bothering to undress. He folded his hands over his chest, ready for the rapture, and stared at the ceiling, waiting for the hush to finally turn into sleep.

The words were out. That was enough for tonight.

Danny woke to the sound of rain, soft at first, then

harder, needling the house with a million tiny requests. For a while he let it wash over him, eyes closed, hands still folded. The air in the room was cool and damp, and the silence felt less like an absence and more like a held note, the last echo of a song before it faded. He listened to the wet hush outside, the slow drip of a gutter, the way the wind made the frame of the window flex and groan.

He sat up, the bones in his back cracking one after the next, a chord of discomfort that shook the last of sleep from his body. The notebook was still on the night-stand, right where he'd left it.

He went to the kitchen, poured water into a chipped mug, and drank it in greedy gulps. His hand shook, not from nerves but from the aftershock of writing. There was a memory in the muscles, a tightness that remembered the shape of every word, every letter.

He brought the notebook to the table and read the letter again. The ink had bled a little where the tears or the sweat had hit it, but the words held. Each sentence was a splinter, but none of them had worked free on their own. They needed to be pulled out, one by one, and set down where someone might see them, if only himself.

He ripped the page free, careful not to tear the edges, and folded it twice, creasing the paper sharp. He found an envelope in the junk drawer, the kind that came with bills he never paid on time, and slid the letter in. The sound of paper on paper was final, the way a door clicks shut on a room you know you'll never see again.

He did not address the envelope. He just set it in the middle of the table, as if it might walk out on its own. For a while, he stared at it, letting his mind go empty.

The rain kept up its work outside, relentless, cleansing.

He felt lighter, but not free. The ache was still there, but it was a clean ache, the kind you get after hard labor, or a long run, or a fight that leaves you both standing. He flexed his fingers, rolled his shoulders, and let the moment settle in.

He sat for a long time, just breathing. The house did not creak, the ghosts did not whisper. Even the old fridge kept quiet, as if giving him space to let the new silence grow.

He thought of Shelby, tried to imagine her reading the words. Maybe she'd laugh. Maybe she'd tear it up and feed it to the creek. Maybe she'd tuck it in a drawer, let it yellow with time. It didn't matter. The words were out. That was the point.

He gathered his guitar from the bedroom, set it on his knee, and strummed a single, open chord. The sound was rough, but true. He tuned it by ear, then played the first bar of "Way Back." The notes hung in the air, mixed with the rain, settled around him like a blanket.

He closed his eyes, played the next line, and the next. The music had new shape now, a different tension. It sounded less like longing, more like remembering. Like good times once had.

He played until his fingers burned, until the rain slowed and the world grew bright at the edges of the window. He stopped, sat back, and let the quiet fill him.

He looked at the envelope again, waiting for it to speak.

It never did.

He picked up a pen, wrote "Shelby" across the envelope in one swift, decisive stroke, then tucked it inside his jacket. The world outside was wet and green, the grass shining, the air sweet with rain-washed possibility. He stepped out, barefoot at first, then doubled back for his boots.

The diner's windows glowed amber in the late afternoon light. He approached the door, heart hammering against his ribs, and slipped the envelope through the mail slot before he could change his mind. The soft thud of paper hitting floor inside made his breath catch.

He turned away quickly, mud from his boots leaving tracks toward Percy's, where whiskey waited to wash away the taste of vulnerability, and where, for a few blessed hours, the silence might finally give way to something louder than memory.

SHELBY'S RETURN

Suggested Listening: Before stepping into Shelby's Return, pause and let River to Me, by Raleigh Keegan, wash over you. The song's current of longing and steady devotion flows straight into the heart of this chapter. Listen first, then read, and you'll hear her footsteps echo in every note.

Three sharp knocks at the door broke Danny's silence. He jerked upright, heart stuttering in the middle of a line he'd been scratching onto the back cover of his notebook. The pen left a slash of ink, and he let it, the mark trembling like a hand in cold water. Nobody came out this far after dark unless they needed something, and even then, need was relative.

The knocks came again, more insistent this time. He set the pen aside and crossed the living room in three strides, stepping over the tangle of guitar case and couch cushion he'd pushed to the floor. The light in the room was poor, just a crooked lamp with its shade taped up one side, so the window by the door only showed him his own face, a smudge against the glass. For a second he thought it might be a trick of memory, a ghost conjured by too much whiskey and too little sleep, but the third set of knocks was accompanied by a voice, soft and sure.

"Danny? You home?"

He hesitated, but only for a second. He unlatched the

deadbolt and swung the door wide, the hinge letting out a squeal that felt like a warning.

Shelby stood on the threshold, flashlight in hand, the pale beam raking up his chest and pinning his eyes. The night behind her was a wall of black, the kind that grew denser the longer you stared at it. Her hair was down, loose over her shoulders, and she wore the same powder blue jacket she used to wear back in school, the sleeves fraying at the cuffs. The only other color on her was the bright white of her sneakers, which shone even in the dirt of his front step.

He opened his mouth, but nothing came. Shelby clicked off the flashlight, letting his eyes adjust, and waited for him to recover.

"Shelby," he managed, voice raw. "Didn't expect…" He stopped. He hadn't expected anything, least of all her, and she could see the truth of it written in the hollow of his throat.

She smiled, tight but not unfriendly, and stepped inside without waiting to be asked. Her body brushed his as she passed, the sleeve of her jacket catching on his wrist. He sucked in a breath and held it.

Inside, the living room felt smaller than ever. An old coffee table took up most of the center, littered with empty bottles, the cheap kind that never made it into the recycling. The notebook lay open, a spiral of black and leather against the dirty yellow light. The couch slouched against the wall, springs poking at the upholstery like broken ribs. He scrambled to clear a spot, stacking bottles and pushing the notebook to one side.

"Sorry," he said. "I wasn't… didn't know you were coming."

Shelby shrugged. She dropped her bag on the floor

and sat in the only decent chair, a thrift store number upholstered in maroon vinyl. The chair had a wobble, but she didn't seem to notice.

"It's fine," she said, smoothing her hair behind her ears. "I just... needed to talk."

Danny perched on the edge of the footstool, the split cushion threatening to bite into his thigh. The distance between them was three feet, but it still felt like three counties, even in the cramped quarters.

They sat in silence for a minute. Shelby traced the seam of her jeans, her fingers moving in slow, even strokes. He remembered those hands, the way they used to push through his hair, the way they'd pressed a gauze pad to his lip the time he'd split it open at the creek. She looked up, caught him staring, and didn't look away.

"You look tired," she said.

He barked a laugh, too loud for the room. "Don't sleep much. You know how it is."

She nodded. "I do."

Another silence, longer this time, the air thick with all the things they weren't saying.

Danny cleared his throat. "You want a drink? I got..." He looked at the table, at the empties lined up like a losing hand. "Water, maybe?"

Shelby's smile softened. "Water's good."

He went to the kitchen; feet bare against the cold wood. He filled a glass from the tap and brought it back, careful not to spill. His hands shook, just a little. She took the glass, her fingers brushing his again, this time deliberate.

She sipped, then set the glass down and laced her fingers in her lap. "I read your letter," she said.

He felt his stomach drop, the world tilting under his

seat. "Oh."

Shelby cocked her head. "Why didn't you just come in the diner and hand it to me? I work there every night."

He stared at the floor, then at his hands, then at her. "Didn't think you'd want to see me."

"That's a lie," she said, not unkind. "You just didn't want me to see you. You're always hardest on you, Danny. That hasn't changed."

He swallowed, the sound loud in his throat. "Guess not."

Shelby leaned back, crossing her arms over her chest. Her eyes moved around the room, taking in the details. The faded photos on the wall, the guitar leaning against the couch, the heap of dirty laundry by the door. She didn't say anything about any of it. She just watched him.

He tried to hold her gaze, but the urge to fill the air with words was too strong.

"I'm sorry about the letter," he said. "It was stupid."

"No, it wasn't," Shelby said. "It was honest. That's more than most people manage."

Danny looked at the table, at the notebook open to a page of scrawled lyrics. He remembered the last time he'd written something for her, how she'd laughed and said it sounded like a John Prine knockoff. He missed that laugh.

"Why'd you come?" he asked.

Shelby took a long breath, her chest rising and falling slow. "I wanted to see if you'd say it to my face. The things you wrote. About me. I wanted you to tell me the truth, about the rumors around town."

Danny felt his jaw clench, a bolt of fear locking him in place. "I don't know if I can," he said, voice thin as air.

"You can," she said, and this time there was no doubt, no hesitation. "You just have to start."

He nodded, once. The silence stretched until it threatened to break.

He looked at her, really looked, and saw the set of her jaw, the way her hair fell in front of her right eye, the faint scar at the edge of her eyebrow that matched his own. He saw the woman she'd become, not the girl he used to hold at the creek, not the dream he'd been nursing for years.

"Can I..." he started, then stopped. "Can I ask you something first?"

Shelby nodded.

"Are you happy?" he said, the words tumbling out in a rush. "With him, I mean. With Thomas. I see you sometimes, walking home, and you look..."

He didn't finish the sentence, but she did. "I look what?"

"Sad," he said. "Or maybe just tired. Like you're somewhere else."

Shelby let the question hang, then set her elbows on her knees and leaned forward, closing the space between them.

"Everyone's tired," she said. "That's how you know you're from here."

They both laughed, the sound short but real.

He saw her eyes glisten in the lamplight, a hint of something unshed. She didn't blink it away. She just let it be.

"I don't know if I'm happy," she said. "Some days I am. Some days I remember how it was, and I wish it could be again. But mostly I just keep moving."

Danny nodded. He understood more than he could

say.

They sat like that for a while, the floor creaking under their weight, the only sound the hum of the fridge and the soft ticking of the crooked lamp's pull chain as the heat came on and off.

He wanted to touch her, to reach out and bridge the distance, but he didn't. Instead, he said, "Thank you for coming."

Shelby's mouth quirked. "I'm not leaving yet," she said.

He smiled, the first honest smile in weeks. "Good."

The air felt different now. Lighter, but charged.

Shelby tapped the water glass on the table, the ring of it loud and perfect. "You want to tell me what happened?" she asked. "Really happened?"

Danny exhaled, then nodded.

The confession began slow, like water working its way through a crack in stone.

Outside the wind had picked up, shoving little knives of cold through every seam in the siding. The lamp, half burned out, gave the room an orange dusk and painted their shadows large on the far wall.

Shelby's knees were pulled up to her chest, arms wound around them, eyes pinned to the floor. She didn't speak. She just let the silence press in, making space for whatever needed saying.

Danny sat on the edge of the footstool; the guitar had rested across his thighs like a shield. He tapped the headstock with a nervous finger, then set the instrument aside. The room smelled of old bourbon, river water, and sweat. He tried to start three times before the words came.

"She showed up like she owned the place," he said,

and the sound of his own voice startled him. "Not just the house, White Oak Hollow. The whole damned valley. She walked around like it was Nashville and everyone else was backup."

He waited for Shelby to smile or snort, but she didn't.

"She was pretty. I don't have to tell you that. She knew it. Wore it like a badge. Wore everything else like she meant to get a ticket out of here. Damn near on her first day she wanted a phone plan, a manicure, and a car with air that worked. I could barely afford the power bill." He paused, his thumb worrying the seam in his jeans. "So, I took double shifts. I said it was for the house, but it wasn't. It was for her."

Shelby was very still, but the lamp caught the edge of her profile, and he could see the muscle in her jaw tighten.

"She never liked to be alone at night. She'd stay up, waiting for me. Wouldn't go to sleep until I came home. Some days I'd find her sitting on the porch, just staring at the road. She said it calmed her, watching the blacktop. Said if you looked long enough, you could see the lights from another world coming to get you."

He swallowed. The lamp guttered, and for a second the whole room went dark before the bulb surged back.

"Every morning, she'd tie that ribbon in her hair. The pink one. She always wore that ribbon, said it was her grandmother's and that she'd never be alone as long as she wore it. I started seeing it even when it wasn't there. She'd say, 'It's a bow, not a leash,' but it always felt like both."

He didn't look at Shelby. He wasn't sure he could.

"I wanted to quit. I mean, I wanted to keep her, but I knew it was burning me up, digging me hollow. The money, the hours, the way she'd go cold when I didn't give her what she wanted. She started disappearing during the day. I never knew where she went. So, I came up with the story about the diamond." He almost laughed, but it caught in his throat. "The 'Big Find.' I thought maybe if she believed there was something better coming, she'd stay. Or if it all went to hell, she'd blame the mine instead of me."

He dug his heel into the rug, twisting it. "She bought it. Said she could smell the luck on me. At least that's what she called it, 'diamond luck.' Right out the gate, she started planning how we'd spend it. A car first, then a plane ticket, then maybe a house in LA." He spat the word, as if it tasted bad.

The shadows on the wall stretched longer as the wind whined under the door.

He moved to the edge of the story, the place where it always hurt to go.

"That day, in the shaft, she wasn't following me. She was running from me. I was behind her, forgetting my ass if it wasn't attached. I had to get something from the truck. I don't even remember what I'd said, just that I would catch up. She ducked the barriers and kept going. I thought she'd just get scared and give up. But she didn't."

He looked up then, met Shelby's eyes across the span of table and shadow.

"There's a trick in those tunnels. If you don't know how the sound moves, you think someone's a hundred feet away, but they could be just around the corner or a million miles away. I thought I'd lost her. When I heard the scream, I knew. She wasn't close, not even a little. I was already too late."

The bulb in the lamp blinked, a single beat, then steadied. Danny's voice fell to a whisper.

"I saw the headlamp. Right on the edge of the drop. It was like she stepped out of herself, left it behind, just to spite me. I called for her. I called so long my throat felt like it bled." He shivered, the words shattering on his teeth. "But the shaft took it all in. Didn't even echo."

He pressed his palm flat to the table, as if to keep from floating away.

"When I walked around the void, Half Pint was there. Pants undone, face like he'd seen the devil. He was holding the ribbon. Daisy's ribbon, the one I wished she would have just burned. He looked at me and said, 'She's still falling.'"

He flexed his hands, opening and closing them until the knuckles popped.

"I wanted to blame him. I wanted to blame the shaft, the mine, the air, the darkness. But all I saw was myself. Like I wasn't in my own body. All I heard was my own voice, pushing her down."

He let the last of the air leave his lungs. "I ran. I didn't try to save her. I just left."

The silence that followed was enormous. The lamp flickered, the wind howled, and the old house groaned under the weight of what had just been spoken.

Shelby blinked once, a single tear tracking down her cheek. But her voice, when it came, was steady.

"She was falling a long time before that, Danny. You just happened to be the one there at the end."

He looked at her, the line of her mouth, the strength in it. He wanted to say something, anything, but the words wouldn't form.

She reached across the table, her hand warm against

the chill, and laid it over his fist.

"You're not alone," she said.

He believed her.

The wind eased, the lamp burned steady, and the shadows on the wall relaxed their grip.

For the first time while recalling that event, Danny didn't feel like he was falling, too.

After the words emptied out, the house filled with silence, a new, thicker kind, like a room after a storm.

Danny wiped his face with the back of his hand and stared at the lines in the scarred coffee table, every knot and scratch a history he'd never bothered to memorize. He wasn't sure if it was morning yet; the window above the sink was black as a burnt-out headlamp, and the only way to measure time was by the ticks and whines of the old cuckoo clock in the kitchen. It hadn't worked right since he moved in, but every hour and a half, or so, it still made a show, the bird's cry coming out slow and hoarse, as if it, too, was running on borrowed years.

He waited for Shelby to speak, but she didn't. Instead, she stood, crossed the tiny room, and filled her glass from the tap again, the water glugging out in little gasps. She took a sip, then returned, placing her hand on his where it still gripped the edge of the table. She didn't squeeze, just let it rest there, warm and alive.

The clock coughed out its badly timed punchline, a whistle and a thud, then stilled.

"I don't know why you came back," he said, voice breaking open. "Not after all this. After all you'd heard."

Shelby watched him a moment, eyes unreadable. "Sometimes I forget, too," she said. "But then I remember you're the only one who ever told me the truth. Even when it was ugly."

He shook his head, a bitter little laugh. "You got a funny definition of truth."

She shrugged. "Truth's not always pretty. Sometimes it's just all that's left when you scrape away the rest."

Danny stared at the lamp, the shade burned through in three places, each hole leaking yellow onto the far wall. "I don't got much left, Shell," he said, not expecting her to answer.

But she did. "Maybe that's why I'm here. Maybe I wanted to see if there was enough to start over."

He didn't know what to do with that, so he let it sit between them, heavy and bright as the moon on wet asphalt.

After a while, Shelby turned her hand palm-up, lacing her fingers with his. Her grip was strong, but the skin was soft, clean, without the coal dust or the scars that marked his own. He felt the callus on her thumb and wondered what kind of work made it.

"Are you still writing?" she asked, voice low.

He looked at the notebook, its spiral spine worn, pages fat with crossed-out lines and confessions. "Sometimes," he said. "Mostly junk."

She let go of his hand, picked up the notebook, and thumbed through a few pages. The lines were messy, some dark with anger, some so faint it looked like he'd written them in the air. She stopped on a page near the end; the paper stained with soot.

"You never showed me this one," she said.

He tried to remember which song it was, but all he saw were the words: "Nothing to do and nowhere to be, sweet as the dew on a juniper tree."

"It's not finished," he said.

She read it twice, maybe three times, then set the

notebook down.

"Neither are we," she said.

For a second, he couldn't breathe. Then the weight in his chest melted, replaced by something light and dangerous, something he hadn't felt since the creek days.

"Remember the first time you sang for me?" she asked.

He nodded, barely. "At the willow. You said I was off-key."

"I lied," she said, a ghost of a smile on her lips. "I just wanted to see if you'd try harder."

He almost laughed, but the old ache caught in his throat. "I did."

"I know," she said. "I heard you, even when you thought I wasn't listening."

The words hung between them, tender and raw. The wind outside found a new seam in the siding and whistled through, colder now but easier to bear.

Shelby looked at the floor, then at him. "You want to know the real reason I didn't wait?" she said, and the question landed like a weight on the table.

He nodded, not trusting himself to speak.

"I was scared," she said. "Not of you, but of the way you made me feel. Like anything was possible, like the world might actually open up for us if we just kept running, together." She looked up, her eyes shining in the dull lamp light. "I've never felt that since. Not even with Thomas."

He felt a twist in his gut at the mention of her fiancé, but it faded fast.

"I thought you were happy," he said.

She shook her head, hair catching in the lamplight. "Thomas is a good man. Steady. He loves me, and I try to love him back. But it's not the same. It's never been the same."

Danny let the words settle, filling in all the cracks left by guilt and loss. He tried to picture her in the life her daddy wanted, with Thomas. The quiet dinners, the easy silences, the life built on steadiness instead of fire.

"I keep waiting for it to feel right," she said. "But it just... doesn't."

They sat in the hush, the only sound the ticking of the off-time cuckoo clock.

Finally, Shelby pushed the notebook back to him, her hand brushing his again. "Finish the song," she said.

He picked up the pen, turning it between his fingers, and set it to the page. He wrote, not thinking, letting the words come as they wanted.

Toe in the river damn it was swift

Jumped in together, started to drift

Swam through your veins with a passionate kiss

Time rolls by, and we don't mind

He set the pen down, felt the ache in his hand, and closed the notebook.

Shelby leaned forward, her face inches from his. "I've never minded," she said.

He believed her.

They didn't kiss, not yet, but the promise was there, curling in the air like smoke from a wood-burning stove.

Outside, the night pressed its face to the window, waiting. Inside, Danny felt the hush shift, softer now, full of possibility.

He stood, helped Shelby from the chair, and they walked to the door together, her hand finding his in the dark.

On the porch, the air was sharp and full of stars. The blacktop stretched empty in both directions, but tonight, neither of them looked for the headlights of another world.

They looked at each other, and for the first time in years, it felt like enough.

When Shelby left, she didn't say goodbye. She just turned and smiled, the kind of smile that stuck in your chest for years, the kind that could keep a man digging through rock and ruin for one more day.

Danny closed the door behind her, the quiet now clean and bright.

He sat at the table, opened the notebook, and began again.

A HOLLOW
RELEASE

Suggested Listening: Close the book for a moment, press play on Raleigh Keegan's Simpler Times and feel the release echo through the Hollow.

They walked side by side, no more than a yard between, but it felt like an arm's length, enough to keep their thoughts from bumping into each other. The hollow held its breath. Nothing moved but the hush of their steps on cracked sidewalk and the distant tremble of a coal train along the ridge. The sun hung low, squeezing syrup through the tree line, and the air was sharp with the promise of rain.

Danny didn't rush, and neither did Shelby. He wondered if she'd learned to move this slow, or if the world outside had always crept at this pace and he'd just missed it before. They turned onto a cross street, past a dumpster with its tattoo of last summer's campaign stickers that nobody cared about, and onto a street where the hollow kept some memories on full display.

The hardware store was first, Hollow Hardware, painted so long ago the letters bled into the warped clapboard. The front was still hammered shut, boards nailed into the frame with a kind of resentment. Only the sign in the window changed, a single white paper:

"For Sale. Owner Retired." He'd heard Jonah, the owner's son, had run off to Pikeville to sell insurance, left his old man alone with his ghosts and the rot. The door hung crooked on its hinges, and the inside, what you could see through the dusty glass, was stripped to the bones except for a shovel with a splintered handle and a row of paint cans so old the lids had rusted shut. It wasn't a store anymore. Just the shape of one.

Next door, the thrift shop surprised him. The window, once a rumor of mildew and faded flannel, now shone clean, the display crowded with "new" arrivals. Secondhand coats, some with buttons missing, others with sleeves too long, hung in a parade of colors that weren't quite right for the season. Danny saw a dress in the middle, pink tulle and sequins, maybe a relic from prom two decades back. It sparkled when the wind blowing through the door caught the sun just right, and Shelby smiled at it as they passed, as if she could see herself inside it, or maybe a daughter not yet born.

"You ever shop there?" she asked.

He shrugged. "They gave me a suit once, for court. Pants were three inches too short. Percy said it made me look honest."

She laughed, the sound small but real. "You probably were, for once."

He watched her out of the corner of his eye, the way she ran her finger along the iron rail between the shops, tracing the chipped paint. She noticed the world in fragments, just the tiny things everyone else left behind, but put them together like a puzzle, into a picture that wasn't their sum.

The diner came next, its sign still promising "Best Pie in the Valley," though everyone knew the filling came from cans, and the crust from a box. But the cracked window was gone. In its place, a new pane, so clear it almost hurt to look at. Shelby's daddy must have splurged for it; Danny guessed it'd take them a year of pie to pay it off. The glass caught a square of sunlight, bounced it up into his eyes.

They paused at the crosswalk, even though nobody really drove here after six. Danny looked back the way they'd come, the sag of the hardware store, the run of paint along the thrift shop rail. It all felt like watching your own face age in the mirror, nothing changed until it was too late to do anything about it.

Shelby nudged him. "You see that?" she said and pointed.

At the end of the block, the doorframe of Percy's Bar had been hit with a coat of white paint. Fresh, not even a hint of dust on it, and the brush strokes still visible if you squinted. Inside, through the glass, the same haze of whiskey and old stories, the same men with their heads bent over the same bad news. But outside, the white paint was defiant. A flag of surrender, or maybe the start of a surrender to hope.

He grunted. "Looks stupid," he said, but he didn't mean it.

"I think it's nice," Shelby said, and took a step into the street. "Looks like someone tried."

He wondered if she knew how that sounded, or if she just said things as they came, letting the words find their own shape. He let her lead, watched the way her hair moved in the wind. He remembered once, when they were still in high school, she'd wanted to dye it, begged him to buy a box of bleach at the old Foodland. He'd refused; said he liked it just how it was. He wondered now what would've happened if he'd said yes. Maybe nothing. Maybe everything.

On the other side of the street, the feed store was gone, closed for good, according to the cardboard in the window. In its place, a shop selling candles, prayer stones, and jars of local honey. The sign said, "Root & Ritual," the letters done by hand in gold. The air outside smelled sweet, and for a second, he forgot where he was. Thought he was in Berea or one of those towns where artists took over the wreckage and called it quaint. He almost laughed at the idea of White Oak Hollow as tourist bait, but the joke stuck in his throat.

Shelby stopped in front of the music store, or what was left of it. ANCHOR MUSIC, the letters still missing their ANC, now just HOR MUSIC. The glass door was taped shut, a yellowed construction permit hanging inside, corners curled with weather. He stared at it, the memory running under his skin like a low current.

He'd bought his first cheap guitar inside those walls. Spent half a summer stacking lumber for Earl McKinney, saved every dollar, walked into the store and bought the battered Yamaha with cash. The owner, a guy with hair past his shoulders and a patch over one eye, had tuned it for him, showed him three chords, said "Play it honest, kid." Danny had never forgotten the way the guitar felt in his hands, the weight and the promise.

Now the shop was dead, gutted of instruments and life, the only sound the buzz of a dying bee trapped between the panes.

He pressed his palm to the glass, felt the chill on the other side. Shelby stood close, close enough that her shoulder touched his arm.

"I heard Thomas talking," she said, voice low. "Said

someone from Nashville's coming to look at the place. A real A&R man. Wants to see if rural quiet is his next step. Might even reopen the shop."

Danny pulled his hand back, wiped it on his jeans. "A Nashville man, huh?"

She nodded. "Yeah. Thomas said he's got a heart for music. Guess he has to as an A&R big wig."

Danny tried to keep his face blank, but something in his chest rattled. He pictured the future: some stranger with slick hair, turning the shop into a studio or a school, filling the hollow with the sound of other people's dreams. The thought made him uneasy. He didn't want the store to change, but he didn't want it to rot, either.

"You'd be good at that," Shelby said. "If you wanted. Teaching guitar and selling instruments."

He looked at her, really looked, and saw she meant it. She saw something in him he hadn't, not since the days when he thought a song could fix anything.

They stood a while longer, letting the sun touch the ridge. The street cooled, the wind picked up, and the hollow shifted from gold to blue. In the windows down the street, lights came on, slow and reluctant. Danny watched the world shrink, watched it grow small enough to fit inside his chest.

He turned to Shelby, and she was already watching him.

"You ready?" she said.

He nodded. "Yeah."

They walked on, leaving the music store behind. The night didn't offer any answers, but it didn't need to. For the first time in a long time, Danny felt like he could walk through the changes without judging himself.

Shelby reached for his hand, not asking permission, just doing it. He let her, and they moved together, easy and sure.

They walked, and the world kept walking with them. Past the gas station, the old church with its stoop cracked by roots and its steeple out of plumb, the house where someone once hung Christmas lights on a July afternoon and left them rotting until the bulbs exploded in the next freeze. The hollow blurred in the twilight.

Danny looked at the ringless hand in his, the fine bones, the faint paint stain on the edge of her cuticle, and all the questions he'd meant to ask curled up in his throat. He made himself say the biggest one.

"So, you and Thomas…"

She didn't let him finish. "Not really. I mean, yes, but mostly no." Her laugh was almost a cough. "We split. Or he split, technically, but it amounts to the same thing."

He waited, giving her the space to fill. She did, but not right away.

"He wanted a wife," she said. "A real one, dinner on the table, someone to iron his shirts, remember his parents' birthdays, keep the house and life tidy. I did okay for a while but I couldn't get past being a fiancé. But it was like faking a limp for sympathy." She cracked a knuckle with her thumb. "Daddy liked him so I tried, but you know I can't do tidy. Not even for a man who tries to build you a world out of this," she waves her hand back toward where they had just walked.

Danny thought of her old bedroom, how the walls changed color with the season, posters and art and scraps layered over the paint until there wasn't a patch of plain left. He wanted to say she was better than tidy, but it felt like something out of a bad song, so he squeezed her fingers instead, felt the tips cold as river stones.

"He went to Cincinnati last month," she said. "His mother's place. Picked up a commercial branch of the bank. He'll stay through Christmas, maybe forever, if you want to know the truth."

Danny let the words hang, but the yoke was light. He let a smile build behind his eyes.

They left the last streetlight behind, the road turning to packed dirt, and the hollow closing in on all sides. At the trailhead, Shelby moved first, her stride sure despite the ruts and the web of roots snaking through the path. Danny followed, hands shoved in his jacket, shoes slipping on the slick clay. He was taller than her by a head, but she climbed the switchback with the muscle memory of someone who never left the hills.

The woods were loud with the season's leftovers, tree frogs shouting each other down, a whippoorwill calling from the ridge. At each bend, the air thinned, cooling, until Danny could taste the clean bite of moss on every breath. He lagged, heart knocking against his ribs, but she kept pace, not looking back, not slowing. He liked watching her this way, framed by the narrow trail, hair wild at the edges. For a while, he forgot to be angry at the world, or even at himself.

They reached the overlook just as the sun caught fire on the western edge. Shelby sat on the low stone wall and patted the space beside her. He hesitated, not wanting to break the hush, but the view demanded it. White Oak Hollow laid out below, every street and switchback, the roofs blurring from shingle gray to a velvet blue as dusk slid in.

He sat, shoulders almost touching hers, and stared at the sprawl. From this angle, the town was a stitched blanket. The river cut a crooked S at the edge, doubling back on itself before it vanished into the timber. The mine was just a scar near the water tower, and the lights along Main flickered on one by one, soft as distant lanterns.

"Doesn't look so bad from here," Shelby said, voice low.

Danny grunted. "Doesn't smell so bad, either."

She elbowed him, a gentle nudge, and they watched in silence as the shadow of the mountain crept over the town. The sun caught on the black dust coating the roofs, turning it to gold. For a minute, even the mine looked clean.

He let out a breath he didn't know he'd been holding. The pain in his chest eased, the hard lump of regret or memory or whatever was softening. Shelby dug a pebble out of the dirt and flipped it toward the treetops.

"When I was a kid, I thought the world stopped at that bend in the river," she said. "Everything past there was just cloud and old stories."

He watched the sincerity in her words. "It keeps moving whether you have strength for it or not."

She smiled. "Some are strong enough to go. Some are strong enough to stay...you can't have both."

He nodded, staring at her hands. She turned them palm-up, as if breathing out a prayer, and let them rest on her lap.

"I thought I'd end up like my mother," she said. "Never moving, never even wanting."

They watched a raven rise from the valley, wings catching the last light. It circled once, twice, then vanished over the ridge. Danny wondered if it would ever come back, or if this was just a stop on some endless trek. He liked the thought that maybe it was both.

The town below flickered alive: porch lights, the green cross of the Farmacy, the neon at Percy's now stuttering between "O" and "PEN." He could almost make out the music store, its window catching the purple of dusk.

"It's not much," he said.

"It's enough for now," Shelby answered.

He didn't reply. Instead, he closed his eyes, listening to the hush between frog calls, the pulse of his own breath. He felt her hand slip over his, fingers cold but steady.

For a while, neither of them moved. They just sat, letting the last of the light wash over, until the hollow below was only a rumor, and the ridge above held everything that mattered.

When the first stars poked through the haze, Shelby let go, stretching her arms over her head. "We should head back," she said, but made no move to stand.

He stayed a little longer, the smell of pine and clay thick in his nose, the ache in his lungs now edged with something sweeter than pain. The world was new, same as before, but different, too.

Below, White Oak Hollow glittered in the dark, and for once, he didn't see himself in its wounds. He saw only what was there: houses and roads and river, stitched together by stubborn hope.

He watched the town until he couldn't see it at all, and when he finally stood, the ground felt steady under his feet.

They walked down the ridge together, no hurry this

time, each step carving out a place in the hush. The night closed around them, cool and easy, and neither spoke until the trail gave way to the first yellow porch light at the edge of home.

For tonight, the hollow was enough.

GRAND OPENING

By the time the regulars drifted into Percy's that night, the air was already thick with rumors, cheap smoke, and the chemical reek of the urinal puck Percy dropped in the men's room when he knew it'd be a long day. The bar stretched thin and yellow in the fluorescent light, counters gone sticky in the creases, every square inch cross-hatched with names, dates, and curses carved deep enough to survive three generations of failed dreams.

Danny nursed a whiskey at the end of the bar, eyes set to the wood, but his ears soaking up every word. The crowd was more than usual for a Wednesday, the kind of turnout reserved for a wake or the return of a prodigal son. Except nobody had died, and the only thing come back was a rumor about Randy Cobb.

"Coal Creek Records, you believe that?" one man said, voice pitched high in wonder or maybe just disbelief. "A bigshot from Nashville, right here in White Oak. Man must have lost his damn mind."

"Nah, I heard his wife left him for a preacher. Man needed a change of scenery, lick his wounds. That or he's here to dry out. Percy, get me another…"

The second man cut in, elbows braced wide as if to claim his territory on the table. "I'm telling you, Cobb's got family buried up in Boone cemetery. That's why he bought the old music shop, gonna fix it up and run it himself."

"You're all full of shit," said the woman in the corner booth, her hair a helmet of ash-blond, holding a wine glass marred with cheap lipstick. "Nobody leaves Nashville to retire in White Oak unless they're running from something. Or maybe just waiting to die."

They all laughed, but it was a dry, hollow sound, and Danny caught the edge of it on his tongue. He didn't laugh. He traced the rim of his glass with a finger and let the talk move around him, a current he didn't have to fight.

Percy polished glasses behind the bar, each motion methodical, like he could wipe away not just the stains but the history that made them. He gave Danny a look and then moved down the line to handle an argument over whose tab was older.

Near the pool table, a cluster of miners straight off second shift were passing around a battered iPhone, reading some online post aloud and cackling at every line. "Says right here, Cobb's retired as A&R VP for Coal Creek Records and is looking at imprint possibilities, under the label. He's scouting 'authentic Appalachian talent.' What's that even mean? Gonna make us all famous?"

"He's got the money to do it," someone said. "Saw the man myself at the Farmacy, loading a basket with top-shelf bourbon and groceries that didn't even come from a can. Drove up in a Caddy, all polished and black. Didn't look at nobody, like we were the ones that crawled out of the dirt."

"Heard his hands are all scarred up from some accident," another said. "Not music hands anymore. That's why he listens, doesn't play."

Danny tuned them out as the laughter grew mean. He tipped his glass, felt the warmth run the seams of his chest, and remembered the last time he'd heard Randy Cobb's name: several years ago, the back room of a dive on Lower Broadway, Cobb sitting with a notebook and a stare that could strip you to bone. Danny had played two songs, maybe three, and Cobb hadn't said a word. Just left after the set. His was a good hand to shake, but Danny doubted he'd remember shaking his.

The memory caught in his teeth, bitter as old coffee.

Earl McKinney slid onto the stool beside him, moving slow from a lifetime underground. His fingers were black at the nail. He nodded at Danny's glass, then at Percy, who poured him a draft without being asked.

Earl spoke low, just for them. "Heard you used to know that Cobb fella. From your Nashville days."

Danny snorted. "Knew of him. Didn't take to him much."

Earl considered this, scratching at a scab on his jaw. "Man's got ears, though. Knows what a hit sounds like, if you believe the stories."

"I don't," Danny said.

Earl let it hang, the pause as heavy as a loaded coal cart. "You ever think about trying again?" he said. "Music, I mean. Now that he's in town."

Danny laughed, but it didn't reach his eyes. "Not much demand for sad sacks with busted hands and worse reputations."

Earl shrugged. "Every sad sack I ever met secretly wanted a second chance. You got a voice, boy. I'd hate to see it rot down here."

Danny rolled the glass between his palms, felt the old ache pulse in his thumb. "You saying I should go kiss

Cobb's ring? Join the parade?"

"I'm saying he might listen, if you let him." Earl's eyes glinted in the barlight, the blue of them clear even through the cataracts. "Beats dying in the dark."

Across the room, the jukebox kicked up, somebody feeding it quarters to play "Coal Miner's Daughter" at a volume meant to piss off Percy. The men at the table howled along, their voices raucous and off-key, but there was a joy in it that made Danny's chest squeeze tight.

He thought of Shelby, the way she'd pressed his hand to her chest last night, the steady drum of her heart saying more than any word ever could. He thought of the hollow, and how it tried to keep you, how it trained you to want nothing but survival. He thought of the guitar in his room, with strings changing tune in the weather.

Percy poured him another, and Danny let the amber sit, watched the way the light bent through it. "You ever get tired of this?" he asked Percy, not really expecting an answer.

Percy wiped the counter, his face unreadable. "Every night," he said. "But I show up, just the same."

Earl clinked his glass against Danny's, the sound small but stubborn. "You think on it," he said. "Maybe Cobb is the south end of a north-bound donkey, but he's the only one looking for what you got."

Danny watched as Earl eased off the stool, slow and steady, then made his way back to the far table, where the other old-timers waited with their own ghosts and beers.

The music faded, replaced by the hum of the cooler and the scratch of boots on tile. Outside, the night pressed against the windows, but the buzz in the room still warmed the place.

He tapped his fingers on the bar, the rhythm automatic, the same three beats he'd played since he was a boy. For a moment, the sound filled the room, every ear tuned to the pattern, every silence leaning toward it. Then the talk started again, and the spell broke.

He finished his drink, left a bill on the counter, and walked out into the dark. The hollow felt different tonight, alive, maybe, or just restless. Danny didn't know which. He shoved his hands in his pockets; shoulders hunched against the cold and started the walk home.

Behind him, the lights of Percy's stayed bright, a stubborn star in a sky that refused to forget.

Next morning, the sky put on its best imitation of blue, but the color never made it past the slag piles or the scrim of powder-gray haze that floated down the valley. The whole hollow was awake, every soul turned out to Main Street and the spectacle at the center: Anchor Music, windows scraped clean for the first time in twelve years, sign painted a brave white with block letters crisp as a church bulletin.

They'd put out bunting for the occasion, red and blue streamers hung between streetlights, flapping weakly against the damp. Nobody dressed up, not really, but the air carried the smell of men in clean shirts and the sharp tang of the good perfume women saved for funerals. The crowd was thicker than anything since the Bicentennial, even thicker than the last union vote. Folks packed the cracked sidewalks, whispering in little knots, all eyes turned to the makeshift stage at the curb.

At the front stood Randy Cobb. In person he was smaller than Danny remembered, the years having whittled him to rough angles. His hair was still thick, streaked silver, and his suit, black, thin-lapelled, the kind you only saw on TV. Looked both out of place and somehow exactly right. His hands, tucked in his pockets, moved now and then, fingers wriggling as if he wanted to hold something but couldn't remember what.

Next to him stood three women from the County Chamber of Commerce, all done up and rehearsed, plus a couple of school board types and the mayor, whose jacket didn't quite fit over his belly. Percy had a spot in the front row, flanked by two day-drunk retirees who'd bet a carton of Marlboros on whether the event would end with a speech or a fistfight.

At ten sharp, the mayor tapped the mic stand until the whine of feedback cut the buzz of the crowd. "Ladies and gentlemen, neighbors, friends…" he started, and the crowd groaned as one, but he was mercifully brief. He welcomed Randy Cobb, made a joke about how the only thing "more out of tune than this old town was the music store before Mr. Cobb came and rescued it," and then handed over the stage.

Randy stepped up, straightened his tie, and let the silence stretch, eyes scanning the crowd with a hunger that made Danny's skin prickle. When he spoke, the voice was pure gravel and corn syrup, slow but sharp.

"Most of y'all don't know me. That's fine. Never been one for introductions," Randy said, thumb flicking at the mic cord. "But I know towns like this. My daddy mined coal in Whitley City, my mama scrubbed motels from there to Knoxville. I was supposed to work the seam, same as you. Instead, I got out, hit Nashville, tried to make sense of things there." He looked down, eyes going soft at the edge. "Turns out, the seam runs deep even if you leave it behind."

Somebody up front coughed, but nobody dared laugh.

"I came back because I wanted to. Not for money, not for fame. Truth is, I got both, and it didn't fix the hole. So here's what I think: this town's been bleeding out its best for too damn long. I want to stop that. I want to give you all something worth singing about."

He gestured at the music store. "This place, it's more than guitars and banjos and busted amps. It's a lifeline. You think I'm joking, but music's the only thing that keeps the soul from burning up and floating out your mouth when the world takes everything else."

The crowd was listening now, even the old-timers who'd come just to heckle.

Randy cleared his throat, voice climbing. "So, here's what I'm doing. Starting today, Anchor Music will run open jams every Saturday, for anybody who wants to play. Kids, drunks, church ladies, old men who can't keep time, don't matter. We're also hosting the first ever 'Mountain Mine to Shine' concert at the end of the month, right here on Main. A little competition where the winner gets a slot on an EP, cut in Nashville, all expenses paid."

A ripple ran through the crowd, part laughter, part real excitement.

"And for those who think this is a joke, I'll say this: Coal ain't the only thing worth mining in these hills. I've heard better voices in a church basement here than I ever did on Music Row. And I want them heard by all."

He paused, letting the words thump around. "Time to let this hollow be known for what we give, not just what it takes."

There was no applause, at first. It was as if the crowd needed time to chew on the idea, maybe spit it out. But then a handclap, then another, and soon a ragged burst of clapping, genuine if a little off-rhythm. The mayor beamed like a man who just remembered his own name. Randy Cobb stepped back from the mic, nodded, and the women from the Chamber took over, cutting the ribbon with the world's dullest pair of scissors.

Danny watched, arms folded, as the crowd began to drift. Percy caught his eye from the front, gave a sharp little nod. Danny nodded back, but his head felt loose on his neck, as if he was coming down with something.

He hung back as the others surged forward, lining up to see the inside of Anchor Music, still smelling of fresh paint and lemon oil. The window was open, and he could hear the first strum of a cheap guitar inside, the tentative picking of a kid learning "Cripple Creek." The sound hit him like a rock in the chest.

He started to turn away, but a hand clamped his shoulder from behind. Earl McKinney, grinning through a day's worth of stubble.

"Knew you'd come," Earl said. "Man like you, you gotta see it for yourself."

Danny tried to smile, failed. "Just wanted to watch the car crash," he said.

Earl shook his head, the look in his eyes making the lie transparent. "Nah. You're here because you want it. Even if you're too scared to admit it."

"I'm here because there's nothing else," Danny muttered, but even he didn't buy it.

They stood side by side, watching the line snake into the shop. Earl spoke low, meant for Danny alone. "You thinking of signing up for the thing?"

Danny laughed, but the sound came out more like a cough. "I don't do contests. Haven't played for a crowd since..."

"Since the last time you tried to matter?" Earl finished. The words landed, heavy and sharp.

Danny let it sting. "Yeah. Something like that."

They watched a minute longer. On the sidewalk, kids danced in circles, kicking up dust and old candy wrappers, arms locked as if the world wasn't set to break them any time soon. Inside the shop, Randy Cobb moved from person to person, shaking hands, looking them dead in the eye, like he was sizing up what each soul was worth.

Danny saw Shelby, hair caught up in a messy bun, holding a soda and laughing with a girl from high school. She glanced his way, blew him a kiss and just for a second, her smile faltered, then brightened, as if she'd decided to believe in him whether he liked it or not.

Earl clapped him on the back, gentle but firm. "You got time to think on it. Just don't wait too long. World's full of men who waited too long."

Danny didn't answer. He walked away slow, the crowd thinning around him, the echoes of Randy's speech still burning in his ears.

He found himself at the far edge of town, past the earthy store that once carried feed, the road turning to gravel and the houses getting smaller. He sat on a bench by the river, the sound of water louder here, blocking out everything else. He pulled the flyer from his pocket. "Mountain Mine to Shine. Open Call. All Welcome" and stared at it until the words blurred.

He ran his thumb over the paper, feeling the indent where the letters pressed, as if that alone could prove it was real.

Danny closed his eyes, let the air fill his lungs, and wondered if maybe, just maybe, he could still be something more than what the hollow had made of him.

That night the hollow pressed in on Danny, four walls crowding close and the ceiling a trap of water stains he'd learned to ignore. The air in the house was old sweat and new worry, every window shut tight against the fine black grit that blew up from the pit at dusk and crawled through every crack in the world. He sat at the kitchen table, guitar braced on his thigh, thumb running slow over the strings, testing their bite.

Each finger ached, but the pain was a comfort, a steadying thing. He played the first chord soft, then harder, letting the vibration rumble the wood under his elbow.

He'd been at it for hours. The song was close, so close he could almost taste it, but the bridge kept twisting away. He'd written three versions, torn them out, started again. Now the floor around the table was littered with crumpled notebook pages, some already going yellow at the corners from the humidity.

He tried the new bridge, mouthing the words as he played:

You and I like a lullaby

I'll love you till the day I die

One day when we're old and gray

And the world has changed

The words hung in the space, then collapsed, brittle

and wrong. He stopped playing, gritted his teeth, and swore under his breath.

On the counter, the old cuckoo clock ticked what might have been hours into shrapnel. The only other sound was the creak of the house, every beam settling just a little lower than before.

He set the guitar down, rubbed at his eyes, then went to the sink and let the cold tap run until it cleared the rust. He drank from his palm, wiped his mouth with the back of his wrist, and tried to remember what it felt like to be clean, to wake up not already behind on the day.

The kitchen window looked out onto nothing much, just the side of the next building over and the same moon that had always watched him, too distant to care. He caught his reflection in the glass: hair wild, eyes rimmed dark, mouth set hard.

He thought about Shelby. About the way her laugh used to cut through everything, clean and bright, and how it had sounded at the opening this morning, a lifeline tossed across a crowd. He thought about her engagement, about the time in between, about the way she'd looked at him today, like he might still be the boy who played for her under the willow tree. He thought about how badly he wanted to matter, just once, to her or to anyone.

He picked up the guitar, ran the first verse again, slower this time. The melody came easy, sweet and pensive, the way he liked it. He let the chords ring, let the song tell him what it needed.

He closed his eyes and imagined tomorrow: the crowd at Anchor Music, the cheap folding chairs, Randy Cobb sitting at a table with a legal pad and a pen. He could already hear the noise, the polite clapping, the way his own voice would sound small and broken when it hit the air. He wanted to run, to crawl under the house and never come out.

But something held him there, kept him strumming.

He played the chorus one more time, the words falling into place, the bridge still a mess but maybe that was fine. Maybe every song had a part that refused to be tamed.

He set the guitar down, careful, and poured a glass of bourbon from the bottle under the sink. He let the liquor burn down the sadness, then poured another.

He raised the glass, nodded to his ghost in the window, and drank it empty.

"Tomorrow," he said, to no one. "Tomorrow."

A song could be both a farewell and a beginning,
and like a puzzle, its vessel was never carved
by borders but filled by the pieces within,
gathering like water in search of its level.

SUFFER FOR THE MUSIC

Danny arrived early, hands in his jacket pockets and guitar in its battered case, the sharp air peeling at his cheeks. He circled Anchor Music twice before entering, the second time just to prove he still had the option of running. The store was quieter than he expected: the jam session posters still up but no kids inside, no old men arguing over bluegrass trivia, just the hollow knock of his own boots on the fresh-finished floor. He followed the scent of new paint past the racks of beginner Yamahas, through the room where two teenage girls picked at a mandolin and didn't look up.

The back office wasn't marked, but the door was half open, the light inside mean. Randy Cobb sat behind a desk that looked rented, his back to a pegboard wall where one lonely Telecaster hung like a threat. On the desk: a laptop, a coffee that might have been reheated six times, and a microphone the size of a baby's fist, pointed at the empty chair across from him. Two folding chairs, no décor, no pictures. Not even a trash can. The room didn't look like it belonged to anyone, just a place set up to get through.

Randy didn't rise when Danny entered. He just eyed

him through the blue smoke of a vape, his expression the color of old steel. He'd aged since Danny saw him last: the hair at the temples gone fully silver, the lines around the eyes deeper, more deliberate. He still wore a suit, but the tie was slack, the top button undone like a signature. He gestured to the chair with a nod, then set both elbows on the desk, fingers steepled together.

Danny sat, guitar case upright at his shin, hands clasped hard in his lap so the tremor wouldn't show. He tried to find a place to rest his eyes, but there wasn't one. Every surface was bare or hostile. The silence was measured, built to see who'd crack first.

Randy leaned forward. The way he did it, you could almost believe he cared.

"Name," he said, though he already knew.

"Danny Wallace."

"Good." Randy tapped the laptop. "Label wants video of every prospect. I'll stream them the show, but for now, I need a clean cut. You cool with that?"

Danny shrugged, but it wasn't a real answer. He could see his own hands trembling in shadow on the floor, the nail beds chewed raw from a week of not sleeping. He wished for a drink, but only a little.

"Relax," Randy said, but the word meant nothing. "You ever do this before?"

Danny looked at the microphone, imagined what it would take to swallow it. "You mean play, or audition?"

Randy almost smiled. "Either."

"I played in Nashville. And before that, here. Never was much for auditions."

Randy nodded, as if ticking boxes. "You'll get used to it, if you get past today." He reached for the vape, took a slow draw, and let it out over the desk in a haze. "What's the song?"

Danny uncased the guitar, the action a comfort more than a ritual, and set it across his thigh. "I wrote it last week," he said. "It's not done."

Randy's eyes flicked up. "That's the best kind. Finished songs are like finished people, only good for funerals. Give me the mess."

Danny felt the room shrink, the chair growing angrier under his ass. He tuned the G string down half a step, the pegs whining under his touch. He'd rehearsed what he wanted to play, but now the words fell out of order in his head, and the chords bled into each other.

Randy put the vape aside, steepled his hands, and leaned in with the gravity of a priest about to hear the last confession. "The music ain't good unless the artist suffers in making it. Did you suffer for this, Danny?"

Danny stared at the wall behind him. The Telecaster gleamed, a relic from a better place, and for a second he saw himself at sixteen, hands unscarred, voice clean, before the shaft and the hollow and the string of losses that followed. He thought about Daisy, about Shelby, about the long stretch of nights where he'd wondered if there was a path that would set him free.

"Humph," he said, just under his breath.

Randy heard it, eyes narrowing, but he didn't comment.

Danny closed his eyes. He let his thumb drag over the strings, not for show, just to remember the feeling. Then he started. The first notes came out softer than he wanted, and the verse hung up at the end, but he didn't stop. He let the song roll, let it gather speed and weight, let it trip when it wanted. It wasn't "Sweet Shelby" yet, not even close. It was raw, all bone and bruise, the words tumbling after each other like they were afraid of being left behind.

Sweeter than a honeysuckle, soft as summer breeze

Stronger than a shot of moonshine,
my Kentucky dream

My sweet Shelby

The song didn't end; it just ran out. Danny opened his eyes and stared at the patch of desk where the mic glared up, waiting for judgment.

Randy didn't move for a long beat. His face was still, no tell in the eyes, the only sign of life the tic at the corner of his jaw.

"Not bad," he said, after the silence felt like it might split Danny's ribs. "Play the last verse again, but don't try to fix it."

Danny did, the fingers stiffer now, but he let the line wobble, let the words fall where they wanted. It hurt, but he let them.

Randy nodded, once, then killed the mic.

"You're in," he said. "Three weeks from today, you're the anchor set. Don't polish it too much before then. I want it more real than pretty."

Danny set the guitar down, his hands numb at the tips. The relief he expected didn't come. It felt more like shock, or the aftermath of a punch you saw coming but couldn't dodge.

"That's it?" he said.

"That's it," Randy said, and for the first time, he smiled for real, a slow crook of the mouth. "Label wants dirt under the nails. You got plenty."

He turned to the laptop, typed something, then looked up again. "You got a way home?"

"Yeah," Danny nodded.

"Good. Get some rest. Don't overthink it. You show up drunk or broken, that's fine, but don't show up empty."

Danny stood, case in hand. At the door, he paused, not sure why.

Randy spoke without looking up. "You got a voice, Wallace. Don't let it rot down here."

Outside, the wind was colder. The girls were gone from the front room, and the street beyond was empty. Danny walked slow, the guitar biting into his palm, the words from the audition looping back in his head, each line heavier than before.

* * *

Three weeks ran out fast. The weather held, but only just, and by the time the day of the show arrived, the lot beside Hollow Hardware looked like the whole hollow had poured itself out and gathered there. The old man who ran the store had retired some time before, but the family still kept the place locked and upright, the sign sun-bleached but defiant. They'd swept the lot clean for the first time in years, hosed down the slab, and strung up cables to run lights from a rented generator. Two-by-fours had been hammered into a stage barely three feet high, the plywood still tacky underfoot from the last-minute paint job. At dusk, the place glowed, brighter than Christmas, the crowd pressed tight around the cheap folding chairs borrowed from the church.

Danny spent the hour before his set hiding behind

the tarp they'd thumbtacked to the fence. "Backstage," someone had called it, but it was just the dark side of the lot where the band gear and amps stacked in shadows and the smokers hid out. He paced, back and forth, thumb working a groove into the edge of his guitar, the wood soft from years of sweat and tuning. Every few minutes he peeked through a tear in the tarp, counting faces, looking for Shelby, trying not to count the number of eyes that would be on him.

They said it might be the biggest crowd White Oak had seen outside of a funeral. Danny believed it. The faces stretched all the way to the end of the block, a tangle of miners and their wives, teenagers in ball caps, drunkards from Main Street, and near the front row, Percy in his one good shirt, arms folded tight against his chest. Randy Cobb stood to the side of the stage, not in a suit this time but in a pressed flannel, sleeves rolled to the elbows, his hair combed neat. He worked the crowd, handshakes and nods, but never once broke a smile.

The closer it got to set time, the less Danny could feel his fingers. His heart hammered, the skin under his shirt hot and slick with sweat, but his hands might as well have belonged to someone else. He ran through the song twice, then three times, the same chord snagging every time. The voice in his head whispered what he already knew: they wanted him to be great because he left for Nashville, but they'd prefer him to fail because he came back. This was the hollow's way.

They called his name. Not Wallace, not the funny nickname he got stuck with in school, just "Danny," like everyone knew it and always would.

He hesitated. For a moment, the world tunneled down to the blue tarp, the cold air behind it, the sound of his own breathing. He could leave, just step out the back, slide between the cars and down the alley, and be gone before anyone noticed. He could never show up again, and they'd say he cracked under the weight, or that the city ruined him, or that he was never any good in the first place.

He stood frozen. The noise from the lot surged, then stilled. In the sudden hush, he heard a voice, not outside, but in his own head: "Know the season. Know when it's time to move." The words came in his father's voice, same as in the dream, but sharper now, edged with warning.

He saw the raven then, the one from his sleep, perched on the crossbeam above the stage. Its feathers singed at the edges, black gone to red, and it stared at him. There was no judgment, just a hard kind of recognition.

He remembered the wolf too, gray and lean, standing at the tree line, watching the hollow with a patience that could outlast anything.

Danny pulled the guitar tight against his chest, the strap biting through his jacket, and walked out.

The lights caught him in the eyes, blinding and white, and for a second, he couldn't see past the first row of faces. It didn't matter. The crowd was silent, even the children hushed, waiting for him to fill the gap. He took a seat on the old stool they'd pulled from the thrift store, adjusted the mic with hands that shook, and cleared his throat.

He didn't start right away. He just looked down, tuning, letting the silence draw out. It was the first time he'd ever heard the hollow shut up for anyone.

He looked up, just once, and saw Shelby moving to

side stage, her hands lifted in a warming wave, but her face unreadable in the shadow.

"This is for Shelby," he said, voice cracking on the name, but he didn't care. He rolled into the song before anyone could react.

The first notes were soft, the hush made them carry. He played slow, the way he'd practiced, but the words came raw, not the polished version he'd rehearsed for Randy, but the one that lived in his head, full of mistakes and second thoughts.

The chorus hit, and his voice came out stronger, lifting over the crowd, over the houses and the strip of river behind them.

He played on, the chords rough at the edges, his picking hand cramping halfway through. He didn't stop. The sweat ran down his jaw, his chest burned, but he kept singing, kept digging, pulling up every bit of truth he could find.

The bridge went off the rails, but he let it, and the crowd didn't care. He looked out and saw faces he'd known his whole life; Percy, Billy, Earl, even the mayor, every one of them held in the same blue-white glow, all waiting for the next word.

From the side of the stage, Shelby watched the whole town lean forward at once, every neck bent toward the boy on the stool, every mouth holding back a breath. The noise of the crowd had been thick before, all teeth and tobacco spit, but now even Billy and his drunk friends stood silent, arms slung over each other's shoulders, heads cocked in perfect, off-key harmony.

Her father stood with arms crossed, a mountain of a man who'd never said a kind word about music or art. His eyes were locked on Danny, the line of his jaw working slow, like he was chewing over something he didn't want to swallow. Shelby could feel his tension in the way his boot tapped, the way his hands formed fists and then forgot themselves, falling open.

Randy Cobb was just to her left, holding his phone in one hand, the other tracing a slow spiral on his cuff. He watched Danny with the same look he gave to a new piece of kitchen equipment: clinical, hungry, a predator's patience just barely in check.

The song ended, and the world stopped. Three beats, maybe four, with nothing but the hum of the generator and the echo of Danny's last chord hanging in the air.

Then it started. The clapping. The kind of applause that didn't sound like this town, louder, wilder, almost desperate. Shelby felt it go through her chest like a punch. She wanted to run up and grab him, but instead she just stood there, hands pressed to her face, breath stuck somewhere between a sob and a laugh.

Randy leaned toward her, his words barely more than a whisper. "There's a diamond in there. Let's cut it right and get it polished."

Her father, who never liked anything, nodded once. It was the highest compliment he'd ever given.

When Danny came offstage, he barely made it behind the tarp before Randy snagged him by the sleeve. "Come with me," he said, voice full of urgency. They walked fast, around the side of the lot, where the shadows ate the edge of the street and the noise of the crowd was just a dull, happy roar.

Randy stopped, punched a number into his phone, and waited. The cold was sharp on Danny's face, but he barely felt it. His heart was still beating time to the crowd's applause.

The call connected, and Randy's voice shifted, slick and professional. "Yeah, it's Cobb. I got something for you. No, not that country kid, this is the hollow one. Real pain, real voice. Think '70s bluegrass, but with the edge left razor sharp. Yeah. I'll send the video tonight. Give it a listen. If you don't like it, I'll eat the file." He paused, looked Danny up and down, then added, "Think the industry hasn't heard anything like this in a few decades. Could be worth your time."

He ended the call, looked Danny dead in the eye, and said, "They'll want to talk to you. Not tomorrow, but soon. You're on the roster. Just don't get dead before then."

Danny blinked, not quite believing it. "On the roster?"

"That's what I said," Randy nodded, and for a second, he let himself smile, small and sideways. "You did good, kid."

He clapped Danny on the shoulder and said, "Let's get drunk. You earned it."

Inside Percy's, the night had turned to party. Every table was full, and the neon "Open" sign bled red and green over the laughter, over the knock of cue balls and the slap of hands on backs. Percy himself was behind the bar, pouring bourbon with a smile that never broke, not even when the glass slipped and shattered on the counter.

Randy bought a round for everyone, then two more for just Danny and Shelby. They claimed the high table near the jukebox, and for the first time in forever, it played a song nobody had picked—a slow, yearning, bluegrass ballad, the kind that sounded like a love letter to the end of the world.

Shelby leaned in, eyes shining. "You killed it," she said. "I didn't know you could do that."

"Neither did I," Danny admitted.

She grinned, teeth bright in the blue-green light. "Guess we're both learning."

Randy raised his glass, waited until both of them followed. "To the hollow," he said, "and to the people who still make it sing."

Danny clinked glasses, the sound sharp and clean. For a second, he let the music and the laughter fill his head, let it push out the memories, the worry, even the ache in his body.

RIBBONS OF PINK

Recommended Listening: Sweet Shelby by Raleigh Keegan. This song is the marrow of Danny's journey, the sound of every hollow scraped raw, every stage played for ghosts, every wrong turn endured, until all that suffering bent itself back toward the only truth he ever carried: Shelby. Sweet Shelby isn't just music; it's his confession, his prayer, and the proof that love was the only stage worth standing on.

The next afternoon let up just enough for them to slip out of the house, past the drunks and the echoes of boots clapping in the vacant lot the night before. Shelby nudged Danny with her shoulder on the way down the front step, the touch so small it could've been an accident, but wasn't. The town was fresh from rain, streets shining with the memory of it, and the air carried a bite that made every breath feel like it could stick to your ribs.

They didn't talk at first, just walked, side by side, letting their shadows drift ahead of them on the wet blacktop. The hoot of an owl followed them, then faded out. Past the third streetlight, it was just the two of them and the hush, so thick it could've cushioned a fall.

Danny tried to get his hands to quit shaking. He stuffed them in his jacket, thumbs hooked through the holes where the pockets had split. He glanced at Shelby, waiting for her to say the first word, to offer a thread he could follow out of the tangle in his head. She didn't.

The hollow felt different today. Less haunted, changed. The wind in the poplars carried the same voices, but the pitch had shifted, less a warning, more a reminder. Shelby walked with her chin up, eyes locked on the line where the sidewalk buckled, like she'd trained herself to count every step, every crack.

At the corner, he finally broke. "You don't have to talk my ear off tonight," he said. "I'm not liable to say anything stupid if given the chance."

Shelby grinned, teeth catching the orange of the streetlamp. "I know. I just like the quiet."

He let that answer settle, heavy but easy. They moved on, past the pawnshop, past the row of empty storefronts with their windows covered in butcher paper or plywood. Shelby stopped, just a beat, and peered at a window.

Danny stared at her looking at herself in the glass, saw the way her mouth shaped the words before they came out. "Sometimes I liked what the hollow made us to the rest of the world," she said. "Invisible."

She leaned close, eyes bright in the glass. "But you never were, Danny. Not here."

He felt the way that pulled against every story he'd told himself about why he ran, why he stayed gone. He wanted to argue, but the words stuck. Instead, he turned his face to the window and watched her watch herself.

"Still scared me, a little," he said. "How easy it was to disappear outside the hollow. Like it wanted it that way."

Shelby drew a line in the evening dew on the window with her finger, a slow, thoughtful arc that didn't connect at the ends. "Some places swallow people," she said.

"Other places just chew on them, waiting for them to re-member who they are."

He thought about the mine and the way his hands still curled as if gripping a pick, even in sleep. He won-dered if Shelby's ghosts were anything like his, if they ever let up or just waited in the dark, patient as winter.

They kept walking, neither willing to say where they were going, but the creek was ahead, and they both knew it. The hollow always pulled you downhill. He watched the street, the shimmer of light on puddles, the way each step made less noise than the last.

Shelby stopped first, at the old bridge. She leaned on the rail, fingers spread, tapping a slow rhythm. Danny joined her, close enough to feel the heat radiate off her skin, close enough to hear the click of her nail against metal.

They stared at the water, black and moving slow, carrying bits of leaf and stick and the memory of the swimming hole upstream. The creek was higher than usual, the banks muddy and raw. Somewhere down-stream, a frog croaked, then another, until the whole hill vibrated with their chorus.

Danny let out a long breath. "You remember when we used to skip rocks here?" he asked.

Shelby smiled, soft at the corners. "You cheated. Al-ways palmed two at a time."

"Did not."

"Did too. That's why you always beat me."

He shrugged, the old pride surfacing. "I had an arm. Still do, some days."

They fell quiet, the easy silence of old habit. Danny fished a rock from the edge of the rail, turned it in his hand, then flicked it out over the creek. It skipped twice, then sank.

"See? Lost my touch."

Shelby bent down, picked a stone, and threw it underhand. It hopped three times before vanishing. She raised her arms in victory, then set them back on the rail.

Danny looked at her in the blue wash of the afternoon sky. "You ever wish it was still like then?" he said, voice softer now.

She thought about it, head tilted. "Sometimes. But only because we didn't know how bad it could get."

He nodded. "But we know now."

She turned to him, eyes dark as the creek. "I think that's better. Means we can handle it next time."

He wanted to believe it. He wanted to be that man. "I don't know if I can," he said, honest for once.

Shelby reached out and laid her hand over his. Her fingers were cold but steady. "You don't have to. We'll handle it together."

The word 'we' landed hard. He felt his chest tighten, then let go. He squeezed her hand, gentle, and let the silence swallow what was left.

Behind them, the world waited. Ahead, the water moved, slow and relentless, always looking for a way forward.

They watched the creek a long time, neither speaking, both holding tight.

When the hush finally broke, it was the creek that did it, water slapping rock in the same restless way it always had. They'd come here as kids to fish or just to watch the light catch minnows, and later as teenagers to drink warm beer and float dreams that never made it more than a mile past the bend. Now the banks were bare, the old garbage gone, firepit filled in with river stones. Someone had hung a tire swing from the same limb notched with scars from when they'd tried to cut it down years back.

Shelby walked ahead, boots skidding through mud, then dropped onto the mossy log at the edge. Danny followed, slower. He stood behind her, hands deep in his jacket, shoulders hunched against the wet.

"You see they cleaned it up?" Shelby said, toeing the edge where water churned black.

"Didn't know anyone cared enough," he said.

She picked up a rock, flicked it into the current, and watched the ripples eat low sunbeams. "I think the new mayor started it. Or maybe it was just some kids wanting a place to party. Either way, it's better now."

Danny looked at the log, then at her, then sat. There was enough room for both, but only if they leaned close. He watched the fireflies hover in the weeds, a slow pulse of yellow that reminded him of porch lights left on for lost dogs.

"Better than when I was here last," he said.

She nodded. "Your soul was bleeding then, alone."

They let the sounds fill the space between, the frog calls and the rush of water. It felt like the world could hold together, at least for a minute.

"I used to come here after shifts," he said, "when I couldn't stand the mine or the house or any of it. Just sat, listened to the creek, tried to feel something."

Shelby looked at him then, eyes soft in the encroaching twilight. "Did it work?"

He shrugged. "Sometimes. Mostly, I just got cold and went home."

She nudged him with her elbow. "Maybe you didn't

wait long enough."

He laughed, a dry, hollow sound, but it loosened something in his chest.

The log creaked as she shifted, turning to face him better. "What if this music with Randy pays off? What if you don't have to work the mine?" she asked.

He shook his head. "That's like asking a fish what it'd do if the river ran dry."

"Flop around, probably," she said, then grinned.

He snorted. "Yeah. Until it figured out how to breathe air, or just died."

Shelby twined her fingers together, a nervous habit he recognized. "I always thought you'd get out for real. Nashville, or even farther."

He looked away, the old guilt rising. "Didn't stick. Couldn't make myself belong."

She hesitated, then said, "I think you belong more than you know."

He didn't answer, just watched the water slide past, dragging all the old stories with it.

A firefly landed on her knee, blinked twice, then vanished into the dark. Shelby followed it with her gaze.

"I applied for a job in Sumerset," she said, sudden. "Special ed classroom, just a couple days a week. They want someone who can play music, help the kids with rhythm. I told them I wasn't much of a player, but I could teach if they wanted."

Danny tried to picture it: Shelby in a bright classroom, kids lined up with plastic drums or recorders, her laugh filling up the whole building. "That's good," he said. "You'd be good at it."

She shrugged, but her cheeks went pink in the light. "I don't know. I'm scared I'll screw it up. I've cleaned up at the diner for years now."

He tapped his foot, thinking. "You couldn't possibly screw it up when you care so much."

Shelby leaned back, hands braced on the log. "What about you?"

He frowned. "What about me?"

"If you didn't have to work the mine, what would you do?"

He thought about it. For a second, he almost said nothing. Then, "If this label thing doesn't pan out, maybe I'll manage the music shop. Teach guitar, fix amps, sell picks to the kids who want to be rock stars."

She turned toward him, close enough he could see the flecks in her eyes. "That sounds nice."

He shrugged. "Could be worse."

They sat with it a while, letting the possible future settle in. The creek kept moving, always downhill, but tonight it seemed less in a hurry.

"Do you think we could really do it?" she said, voice small. "Make something that's not just surviving?"

Danny felt the old ache in his hands, the tremor that came from too many years of working and not working things out. He reached for her hand, this time on purpose. She let him take it.

"Maybe we already are," he said.

Shelby squeezed his fingers, then relaxed. "We're not broken, you know. Just really bent."

He smiled, first at her, then at the idea. "Bent's better than busted."

She laughed, "There's a song for you," a bright crackle in the damp, and it drew an echo from the woods. For a second, the whole hollow sounded alive again.

A bat swooped low over the water, chasing a firefly.

Shelby pointed, grinning. "Look. Nature's own disaster."

Danny watched the bat dart and dive, graceful in its ugly way. "It'll never catch it," he said. "Fireflies and bats don't fly straight."

Shelby leaned into his shoulder. "Neither do we."

They stayed like that, side by side, letting the night close in, letting the idea of tomorrow inch closer. When the first chill touched the air, he draped his arm around her.

"I'm glad we came tonight," he said.

"Me too," she whispered.

The sky waited until they'd almost given up, then let loose the pink.

It came first as colorful strings, bleeding out over the hills. The kind of dusk that looked like it might change its mind, if only for spite. But it held, and the color deepened, a band of it sliding up through the bare tree limbs, catching on every scrap of nighttime cloud.

Danny squinted at it, felt the urge to laugh or cry, wasn't sure which. "You see that?" he said, voice caught between two gears.

Shelby straightened, eyes wide. "Looks like a pink ribbon."

He grinned. "Daisy would've liked it."

Shelby nodded, and for a moment, they both looked, letting the world be bigger than themselves. The ribbon stretched higher, alive and glowing. The cosmic lights wavered every time the wind caught a branch, like a flag refusing to lay flat.

Shelby reached across Danny's chest, fingers brushing the chain around his neck. "You still wear it," she said, voice barely above the creek's murmur.

She lifted the key that hung there, warm from his

skin.

"Never took it off," Danny said, watching her face. "Not even when I should have."

She closed her palm around it. "I wasn't sure if you remembered what it was for."

"Your grandmother's front door. The first safe place you ever found." His voice caught. "But that wasn't really what you meant when you gave it to me, was it?"

Danny stared until his vision blurred, then wiped his eyes on his sleeve. He thought of Earl, what he'd said the last time they'd sat on the old man's porch, the air thick with pipe smoke and regret.

You can't fill every hollow, Wallace. But you can learn to live with what don't ever leave.

Shelby rested her head on his shoulder, breath warming his neck. "You think we'll make it?" she said.

He watched the pink grow thin, watched the day give up its last piece of ground. "If we don't, it won't be for lack of trying."

She laughed, and it was real this time, not forced. "I think that's enough."

The creek ran on, oblivious. The fireflies thinned, retreating to their hiding places, but one lingered, a stubborn ember. It danced above their hands, then settled on Shelby's wrist, its light steady and unafraid.

Danny lifted her hand, palm up, so they could both see. The firefly glowed with a soft insistence, not a flash but a burn, like it had decided to outlive the rest of its kind.

Shelby touched it with her free finger, careful. "Never seen one do that."

"Maybe it knows something we don't."

Shelby turned her head, pressed her lips to his cheek,

and for once he didn't flinch.

They watched the creek a little longer, the firefly still perched, its tail a stubborn lamp in the evening breeze.

When they finally stood, Danny reached for Shelby's hand. She took it, no hesitation, and together they walked the muddy path back toward town, the pink ribbon just a rumor above the tree line.

AFTERWORD

The Music that Carried the Story

Music has always been more than background. It's been the heartbeat of these pages. Many of the chapters were written with Raleigh Keegan's songs in mind, and my hope is that you'll carry the story further by pressing play and letting those notes breathe new life into the words.

You can find the music featured in this novel, along with so much more, on nearly every streaming service available. Choose the one that fits your rhythm:

Spotify – https://www.spotify.com
Apple Music – https://music.apple.com
Amazon Music – https://music.amazon.com
YouTube Music – https://music.youtube.com
Pandora – https://www.pandora.com

Wherever you choose to listen, let the songs walk with you a little longer. They've been the companions of this journey, and maybe now, they'll become part of yours.

BOOKS IN THIS SERIES

3 Chords and a Lie
3 Chords and a Lie is a trilogy about music, memory, and the stories we tell ourselves to survive the ones we cannot outrun.

Set against the back roads and coal shadows of Appalachia, the series follows a dreamer who believes songs can still save them, even as time, debt, and silence conspire to prove otherwise. These are stories of a small town that remembers everything, relationships that fray under the weight of leaving, and the quiet cost of chasing something louder than the life you were handed.

Each book stands on its own, but together they trace the long echo of a single truth: some promises are written in melody, some in blood, and some are lies we carry because the truth would break us sooner.

This is not a story about fame.
It is a story about what it costs to want it.

Appalachian High - A Dreamer's Tale

Where the mine meets the melody. Danny Wallace steps out of the dust and onto a stage that might finally carry his voice. The story begins here.

The Broken Compass

When desire takes the heart, fame devours the lost.

The coal dust has settled, but Danny Wallace is still chasing a song he cannot quite name. The first book pulled him out of the mines for a taste of his dream. The Broken Compass asks what happens when the road, the bottle, and the memories become pervasive, the antithesis of stability.

Set against the same Appalachian ridgelines and small town ghosts as Appalachian High - A Dreamer's Tale, this second book pushes Danny to decide what he is willing to lose to keep his music, and what he must finally face to keep his soul.

Devil To Pay

Every demon keeps a ledger that must be balanced.

Caleb is now a star, carrying Appalachian New Grass on bigger stages. Shelby serves as mayor of White Oak Hollow. Danny keeps showing up where he can, fighting himself more than the world. The cost of dreams is settled up.

ACKNOWLEDGEMENT

To my wife, Shelly. Your love has been the steady tide and your sharp edits the guiding stars that kept this book on course. To Kim Wood, thank you for friendship that never drifts, for the kind of honesty that steadies the keel when the waters turn rough. And to Shelby Keegan, who shared Raleigh with the world. Your selfless gift of his music and storytelling lit the lantern that made this journey possible.

And then, Raleigh Keegan. Without your trust and your music, I'd never have thought to set pen to paper. Your songs gave breath to Danny, Shelby, Daisy, and to the town of White Oak Hollow, carrying the rhythm of Appalachia in every line. What shines so brightly in your roots became the spark that lit these pages. Thank you for your gracious permission to shape this derivative work. I look forward to every song still to come, and to carrying your music with me for years ahead.

And to the musicians who find themselves standing at the crossroads, caught between the pull of home, the call of love, and the fire of the stage, I offer my deepest thanks and my deepest understanding. I know what it is to stand in that place of decision, when both roads seem to cost more than they promise to give You live in the tension between dreams and familiarity, between what your heart refuses to let go and what the world expects of you.

But here's the truth I've come to know. The fouled anchor is not a broken one. It still has its strength, its purpose, its place. The struggle doesn't mean you're lost; it means you're alive, fighting, searching, still anchored to something worth holding on to. And when the day comes that the fouling clears, and it always does, you'll find that the anchor holds strong. It sets deep, keeps you steady, and reminds you that the struggle wasn't wasted. It was shaping you for the moment you would stand firm again.

ABOUT THE AUTHOR

Edward Collins

Ed is a storyteller forged by the sea. During his twenty years as a Sailor in the U.S. Navy, he filled endless nights with poetry, verses carried by the tide, shaped by solitude, discipline, and longing. Those words became the foundation of a voice that now rises fully in his debut novel, Appalachian High – A Dreamer's Tale. In this work, the characters live as an amalgamation of the life-breathed creations from Raleigh Keegan's double-album project and the struggles that Ed himself has faced. They embody the push and pull between dreams and reality, love and loss, home and the open road. With this novel, Ed does not arrive as a newcomer, but as a writer who has been steady with his pen all along, whether keeping watch at sea or giving shape to lives and places that echo the American story. Appalachian High – A Dreamer's Tale marks the beginning of his voice in literature, built on lived experience, literary roots, and a deep respect for the music that helped bring the characters to life.